DESTINY FULFILLED

MARJORIE JOSEPH

Higher Ground Books & Media
P.O. Box 2914
Springfield, OH 45501-2914
www.highergroundbooksandmedia.com
1-937-970-0554

ISBN (Paperback): 978-1-955368-32-2

Printed in the United States of America 2023

DESTINY FULFILLED

MARJORIE JOSEPH

FOREWORD

The wedding gown was classic white, and embroidered with crystals from neckline to train. The sun streaming through the expansive dressing room highlighted facets of the glittering stones as Melody spun around in it. Her special day was finally here! She was finally going to marry the great love of her life, Luke Bryant! Melody couldn't stop thanking God for all he'd brought them through in the past year.

She'd only been out in sunny California for a few months, but Melody loved it. In fact, she was amazed by how much she *didn't* miss Sands Port, Maryland-at least not as much as she'd imagined. She'd been tricked into coming out to Burbank to interview for a job. Melody was still mystified over the turn of events. Luke had pranked her, so that she'd come out there to interview for a designing position through Portals Unlimited. Portals Unlimited was Luke's quickly growing corporation. Luke had sent Melody a letter of invitation, and had introduced himself as *The Portal Master*. At the time, Melody had no idea that Luke and the *Portal Master* were one and the same. Tempted by the offer, she'd flown out to California a few weeks later.

Remembering how Luke had risked his life to save hers, still brought tears to Melody's eyes. He'd brought her out of an underground complex constructed by pharmaceutical mogul and covert mafia lord Clarke Vale. As a measure to evade the law, Clarke Vale had gone into hiding. However, Luke had exposed his operation. Thus, Clarke was discovered, and taken in by the authorities.

Soon after, Luke had told Melody he had to leave the town of Sands Port for a while. Heartbroken, Melody thought he was leaving town as a result of their failed relationship. However, Luke had totally different plans. Melody had no idea that he was flying out to California to spearhead his new business venture. It was an undertaking that was quickly growing into a conglomerate. Furthermore, Melody couldn't have imagined that this business would become a multibillion-dollar enterprise.

In just a matter of months, Portals Unlimited and Luke's invention of biometric portal transference had revolutionized the world. Portals transport was quickly becoming the new way of travel, and the most used mode of transportation and communication in the 21st Century. Also, the Power Portal, a feature of *Dimension Four*, was on the rise, and overtaking the competition in as far as software innovation.

Dimension Four was the latest and greatest way to vacation, and surpassed other technology, which served to connect the masses across the globe. The *Dimension Four* gateway facilitated and mobilized transport. The invention had the power to transmit the human body from one place to another-even if it was halfway around the world. Through the use of cell engulfment and indentation, a person in New York City wanting to travel to Cyberia, could do so effectively. Through the Power Portal and the Vortex to Vanish field of *Dimension Find Me*, one could be channeled to Russia in a matter of minutes. Cosmonauts were looking into eliminating light years of travel once *Dimension Four* was perfected. Space navigators were hopeful of finally getting close enough to discover intelligent life in galaxies beyond our own.

Because of the complexities and classified nature of *Dimension Four*, there were stringent government restrictions. Only intelligence, the military, and those in space aeronautics were allowed to explore the telecommunication in depth. The Vortex to Vanish feature was especially regulated because of its potential to be abused by criminals. The vortex was perfect for covert operations. Therefore, it held the capability to enable those who abused the law.

Only high officials, and the very wealthy could access the technology. Hence, a thorough background check was necessitated for anyone curious about utilizing the program. Incidentally, anyone with a parking violation on their record risked disqualification for this radical high-tech loop.

Melody couldn't believe Luke was worth over 30 billion dollars. Luke had literally gone from pauper to prince. It was something Melody still had difficulty wrapping her head around. All the same, she was fiercely proud of her husband-to-be. Luke had shared some of his pearls of wisdom with her a while back, and Melody knew his words were from the Lord.

Luke had explained how there were masses out in the world sacrificing their eternity, and endangering the lives of their loved ones in order to obtain fame and fortune. These individuals stood to lose their eternal souls for what they considered to be *hidden knowledge*. Often, these hapless folks dabbled in Eastern Mysticism and the occult just to be made privy to life's mysteries. Luke testified that his discoveries were boosted, and had finally gotten off the ground, after he received Jesus Christ as Lord. Luke also assented to the fact that *hidden knowledge* and true wisdom could only derived from the One who created the universe. All secrets and all power belonged to God!

Tears shimmered in Melody's eyes, as she stared at her reflection in the mirror in a wedding dress. She remembered meeting Luke on Mooney Beach out in Sands Port, Maryland. He'd just moved out to the area. His dog Cupid had literally tried to run her off the beach, and had chased her to the boardwalk. The dog had knocked her down, then had covered her in sloppy-dripped kisses. It was hard to believe that was over a year ago. So much had changed in her life-so much Melody could not have imagined.

All roses had their thorns, and the experiences that threatened her relationship with Luke last year still felt surreal. A month after meeting Luke and falling in love, Clarke Vale, billionaire and CEO of Vale Pharmaceuticals, made Luke an offer he couldn't refuse. At the time, Luke's dad had been deathly ill. He'd succumbed to a massive stroke on Rhode Island. Notwithstanding, Luke's family was under tremendous financial strain. So, when Luke returned to Rhode Island to be with his ailing father, he was forced to face the bitter reality that his father's CVA was only one setback of many.

He'd found that his parent's home was in squalor, and impending foreclosure. Apart from that, his older brother Branden had just been laid off from his job. At the time, Luke was working for Sands Port Elementary School as a janitor. So, the finances just weren't there to bail out his loved ones. During that incredibly tenuous time, Clarke Vale offered to step in and alleviate Luke's family burdens. However, Clarke had delineated the terms. He'd promised to perform those good deeds on one condition. Luke had to end the relationship with Melody, and never look back. Backed into a corner, Luke agreed to take Clarke's illicit offer. He decided to leave Sands Port and Melody behind.

Melody's world was shattered by Luke's sudden departure. However, Clarke was there to offer a shoulder to cry on, and tried to extend all kinds of *comfort*. With Luke gone and with a wound too profound for remedy, Melody allowed Clarke to step in. She had no idea how dangerous and controlling he truly was. The business tycoon was skilled at the art of deception. Later, Melody would learn that he was also a notorious murderer, who was waist-deep in international underground criminal activities.

Even if that was all in the past, Melody still struggled with feelings of guilt and shame. Her affiliation with Clarke Vale, Darien Stiles and their lackeys, had endangered the lives of her loved ones. Consorting with those murderers, had also cost her and Luke an entire year apart. Sean Winters, Luke's best friend, had suffered the most. He'd been shot in the chest, and had almost died at the hand of Clarke's minion. Sean was alive only by the grace of God. Because both were infamously treacherous, Clarke Vale and Darien Stiles were currently sitting in jail. They were pending trial with no bail set. Even if they were both behind bars, men like Clarke and Darien irrefutably still had ties to the outside world.

There were times Melody was tempted to give in to fear. And, there were moments of unrest, where she dreaded Clarke finding his way back into their lives, and continuing his ministry of terror. Melody was even more concerned for Luke. Luke had made fools of both Clarke and Darien by exposing their underground safe house months ago. There was no doubt in Melody's mind the two were chomping at the bit to enact revenge for having been outsmarted. Through Luke's groundbreaking invention, he'd been able to infiltrate the subterranean asylum, where Clarke was keeping Melody hostage. The Vortex to Vanish feature, part of Luke's unique brainchild, **Dimension Four**, was instrumental in bringing them out of that horrible situation alive.

Luke had told Melody how outraged Clarke was when the authorities had dragged him, and all of his men out of their holes one by one. When he was brought out in handcuffs, Clarke's acid stare had burned through Luke. Luke had been outside of the complex having word with the authorities when it happened. So, both Clarke and Darien knew he definitely had a part in the downfall of their evil empire.

"You should have seen his face, Mel..." Luke had celebrated. *"If looks could kill, I wouldn't be here with you today. I had to capture that moment on my phone,"* Luke had raved, when Melody had first come out to California. He'd shown her the video of the authorities dragging Clarke Vale out of seclusion.

"I'm just glad you're safe, honey bear. It would have killed me if anything happened to you. I never want to think about Clarke and that awful experience." Melody had hugged him. She prayed Clarke Vale never crossed their paths again.

Still, Luke wasn't the *only* man Clarke had propositioned to walk away from her. Melody had been a bargaining chip between Clarke Vale and Darien Stiles. Clarke had offered Darien millions to stop dating her.

Melody had been dating Darien only for a short while, before she found out he was a married man. Melody was actually only *one* of the *many* women Darien juggled at the time. All the same, when Clarke saw Melody on Darien's arm, he'd decided she was the woman he wanted. And, because Melody was only one of Darien's conquests, it wasn't difficult for him to accept Clarke's offer.

But now, Melody's life was at a pretty good place, and she had absolutely no interest in revisiting the past. She still had those moments where she felt as if she'd failed God and her loved ones. Melody couldn't help feeling directly responsible for exposing them to the likes of Clarke Vale, Darien Stiles and their dangerous henchmen. However, she resolved to live moment by moment in faith trusting God. She chose to believe God would protect her and her loved ones from ever going back to that place of danger. And, they would evade the retribution of a sinister crime lord. Melody refused to live in fear. God was in control, and they were all safe in his hands. More importantly, "No weapon formed against them would prosper..." (Isaiah 54:17).

Chapter One

"Have you made any progress in respect to what we talked about?" Clarke spoke on the phone in a lethal whisper of insidious urgency.

"Of course... I'm working on it. Still, I need to know you *can* get your hands on that money," Simon Winds appealed. Simon was an associate of Clarke Vale's. He and Clarke had had dealings in the past, and Clarke had recently resolicited his services.

"Do you *really* think that I would waste your time, if I couldn't deliver what I promised? Don't waste *mine*, if you can't keep your end of the bargain."

"With all due respect, CV, all you have is *time*," Simon derided.

Simon was in some way satiated, and honestly relieved that Clarke Vale was now behind bars. There seemed to be no possible way out, as there was no bail set. The sad part was that Vale's empire had been brought down by a smart kid, who was now worth more money than the world even owned. It was kind of poetic to see how low the mighty had fallen. In spite of all of this, Simon perceived Clarke Vale probably still had a few tricks up his sleeve. So, even if the man was currently behind bars, he was not to be trifled with.

"I'm glad your humor's intact, Simon, but this is no laughing matter. Can you do what you said or not?" Clarke growled.

"What about Stiles? Do you want him in on the plan?"

"If you can work it out so that we *both* benefit from this deal, that's great but I'm *really* not concerned about Darien at this point."

"I'll pull some strings, and try to get some more

information about Dr. Felix's lab and his work. Then, I will get back to you."

"You *need* to work this out as soon as possible, because…" Clarke sized up the grimy and dingy cage, which he'd been forced to call home for close to three months, and got a whiff of the rancid odor of the yellowing toilet bowl in his cell. "I can't see myself staying in this hole for one more day."

"You know if we *do* pull this off, there might be complications. It's not going to be a cakewalk."

"I am well of the risks, Simon, but I don't care. I'm willing to do whatever it takes to get my life back. Listen, I'm not paying you for *psychotherapy*. If I'm shelling out that kind of money, you need to make this happen as soon as yesterday. Are we clear?"

"We're crystal clear."

"And by the way, if *I* were you, I would lay off of those jokes. Sometimes, you ride on the wrong person and…"

A chill rippled through Simon's body. It struck a chord that Clarke Vale wasn't good at taking jokes. Simon had heard of Vale's tendencies to hold a grudge, because the man seldom found potshots humorous. "Message received. Sorry, Sir…" He gulped.

"*Don't* even bother calling me again, until you find a way to infiltrate that lab, and you know for sure what we talked about can be done."

"Of course, Sir. I understand," Simon said, more reverently. It occurred to him that making jokes at Clarke Vale's expense while the man was down and out, could potentially backfire. So, Simon made a mental note to tread a bit more cautiously-as Clarke Vale was notoriously dangerous.

"You've had enough time on the phone, Vale. I'm afraid I have to take it away. Someone else needs it," one of the corrections officers opened up Clarke's jail cell.

Clarke issued a clement smile, and gladly handed the device over to the officer. He was determined to be the model prisoner and play by the rules. Still, the entire experience was totally mortifying. He was aghast over the fact that he needed to *ask* for permission in order to use a public phone. Clarke thought about his former lifestyle, and gritted his teeth in frustration. He was now living in some rat-infested hole he could not have conjured up in his worst nightmare. *How had he gone from the Ritz to the rats?*

How had he gone from having everything to having absolutely nothing? Vale Pharmaceuticals had been acquisitioned. The company he'd sacrificed blood, sweat and tears for was being run by total strangers, who were totally unaware of the history and the struggle. Clarke traced the course of his life in the past year, and realized the *one* defining factor.

Falling in love with Melody Maxwell was a total game-changer. First, Clarke had contended with Darien in order to have Melody. But, that was a walk in the park compared to what followed. Darien had honored their deal, and had stopped seeing Melody. However, Melody meeting with Luke Bryant was happenstance. It was now Clarke realized that Melody loved *Luke*. And, despite his best efforts, there wasn't enough money to purchase Melody's heart or her love. Clarke had earnestly hoped Melody would fall for him.

Making Luke Bryant an offer he couldn't refuse seemed like a stellar move on the chessboard at the time. Everything was lined up in Clarke's favor, because the chips were down for Luke and his family. His father had suffered a stroke, and the family was abjectly poor. Desperate, Luke had taken his offer to rescue his family, thereby breaking Melody's heart. He'd walked away from their relationship, and agreed to leave Sands Port, Maryland.

Clarke laughed with a sense of irony, as he considered that same poor kid, was now the richest man in the world. Through Luke's groundbreaking invention, and the use of biometric transport and communication, he had the world virtually eating out of his hand.

*Ironic, isn't it? You propositioned young Luke Bryant, a poor kid working as a janitor at an elementary school at the time. You promised to help **him** solve his family's financial troubles, if he walked away from Melody for good...*

Clarke recounted the events. For a while, he'd been the one on top. He'd made billions through Vale Corp, and through several extra, classified financial activities. He'd finally gotten Melody exactly where he'd wanted her. In Luke's absence, she *was* falling for him. *I loved you so much, Melody! I don't think you even realize the sacrifices I made to have you...* Now, Clarke perceived that things had gone wrong because of his feelings for Melody. He was so enamored and bedazzled, he'd lost his objectivity. Loving Melody had made him weak. He hated even having to admit that to himself. Another knife to Clarke's heart was realizing that as much as he'd tried to hate her, he was still very much in love.

Veins hammered at Clarke's temples, and his face reddened in outrage, as he slammed his fist into his palm. "You were *supposed* to be mine, Melody. We were *supposed* to get married that day. You were *supposed* to be living abroad with me-starting a brand-new life." He stewed in rage, revenge and regret. "Luke Bryant, *you* took all of that away from me. Do you think for one minute you've won the war, because of your newfound wealth and fame?

"You think you can discard me so easily and steal Melody away? Not so fast, boy. You're about to find out why they call me Invincible Vale (Invalable). You might have won this battle. But, there's a whole new arsenal of weapons headed in your direction, and for your Portals conglomerate you know absolutely nothing about." Clarke's eyes now matched the wine color of his flushed face. "You want a war, Luke, you got it. But when it's all said and done, *I'm* not taking any prisoners."

***

Portals Unlimited out in Burbank California, hummed with as much vitality and spirit as Grand Central Station in New York City. Everyone had a role to play. And, each person played their roles instrumentally and adeptly. Like an attuned orchestra, they promoted and negotiated the **Dimensions Four** brand, and made billions of dollars for their boss, the *Portal Master*. To everyone around, Luke was the *Portal Master*, but all of his employees called him *PM*.

Yet, to Melody, he was just *her* Luke. He was still the sweet, charming, goofy and funny guy she'd fallen in love with on a chance encounter on Mooney Beach out in Sands Port, Maryland. Still, Melody couldn't gloss over how impressive it was to watch Luke and his motivated employees run Portals with such ingenuity and grit. She was so proud of Luke it was difficult to define.

Nevertheless, on *that* particular afternoon, she was a bit put out. It was the third time she'd stepped out of Luke's eclectic, but lavish office looking for him. But, he was nowhere to be found. Nowadays, it seemed she had to make an appointment just to see her own fiancé. Melody had come by the office with a picnic lunch. Then, she and Luke had made plans to head over to the beach. However, she'd been there for close to an hour, and wondered if they had to cancel. Arianna Ward, who was Luke's top public relations person, had reassured Melody she would usher Luke right over to the office the moment she saw him.

"I guess, those interviews are taking a lot longer than Luke anticipated." Melody sighed in disappointment. She crossed back over into Luke's office, and shut the set of doors. She was always taken aback whenever she took in the cutting-edge model of Luke's private office. When Luke had described some of the insane props he'd wanted to include in the layout, Melody honestly thought he was joking about a lot of it. And, for the most part, he was-that was in respect to some of the more unconventional details. However, Luke wasn't joking around about erecting a gateway, or something resembling a portal at the very center of the spacious room. Undoubtedly, a huge portal was exactly what Melody had helped design and commission.

The rectangular shaped portico stood at about 15 feet. It shimmered more radiantly than the sun. Inside the vortex field were prism-like lights that whirled like the beams of an Aurora Borealis, only at warped speed. The laser sharp lights whizzed and shimmered like meteor showers. Although beautiful, they had the capability to absorb matter. The portal contained the power to transport the human body from one place to another.

Melody had never seen Luke using the gateway in his office. However, she was certain he could activate it if he needed to. She had every confidence in Luke's technology. After all, he'd allowed her to experience the consuming waves of the Power Portal firsthand in the trial stages. And yet, even with all of his latest accomplishments, Melody perceived Luke was only getting started. He'd only just scratched the surface insofar as the fullness of **Dimension Four** and its components.

Melody traipsed back over to Luke's desk. It was where she'd set the picnic basket. She'd already thrown an off-white linen blanket on the cobalt blue carpeting, and had set placemats on it. There were also containers of Thai Food from their favorite restaurant. To the side, Melody had set a small silver cooler with a variety of beverage options.

Luke had promised to spend the afternoon together. It was their last day as a single couple, because they were getting married in the morning. So, they'd made plans to have lunch, then sneak off to the beach with Cupid. Spending time out on the beach with Cupid was an ideal last date as a single couple. The beach held special meaning for both Melody and Luke. *Mooney Beach* out in Maryland was where God had used Luke's silly dog Cupid to bring them together.

Melody searched the picnic basket, and noticed she'd forgotten to take out the container of chocolate covered strawberries. They were Luke's favorites. So, she gingerly removed the frosted container out from the basket. However, she clumsily dropped it back into the basket, when she felt the firm grasp of arms about her waist from behind.

"Hey there, honey baby," Luke whispered into Melody's ear, as she instinctively veered towards him. Melody's face was white as a sheet, as Luke pulled her securely into his arms. "Did I scare you?" He smiled puckishly. Mischief danced in his eyes, because he was certain he had.

"Luke…," Melody whined. Clutching her heart, she gave him an exasperated look. "I don't think I'll *ever* get used your blinking in and out." Her face wrinkled in feigned annoyance. "It *would* have been nice if you'd given a girl the head's up about using the vortex to pop back into your office." Melody gave him a reproachful look, but softened. She couldn't stay mad at him, and grudgingly slipped her arms affectionately around his neck.

"I'm *so* sorry, honey baby. I was just a little anxious to see you." Luke stared yearningly at her. "Ari told me you've been in here waiting on me for a while. So, I just couldn't get here fast enough."

Melody gave him a wistful look. "Luke, you promised it would only be an hour or two. Then, Cupid and I would have you for the rest of the day. That crazy dog of yours is back at home, and he's even more anxious than *I* am to hang out with you." Melody's fingers plowed through is curls, as she straddled his head in her hands.

Luke hunched down, and tenderly coaxed Melody's lips. It was like taking sips from an intoxicating drink. "I'm so sorry, honey. We had a few more people interviewing for programming slots than anticipated." Luke's face rumpled apologetically. "Do you forgive me?" he asked in between soft kisses.

"I'll think about it." Melody pulled back, and stared dreamily into Luke's eyes. Her resolve was quickly dissipating, because Luke had his arms protectively around her waist. It also didn't help that he was delicately fondling the contours of her waist with his strong, yet gentle hands.

"Mel, the last time you said you'd *think* about forgiving me was…"

"For that texting incident at the church last year…" Melody snickered.

Luke shook his head humorously. "It was our *second* legitimate date." His face wrinkled curiously. "Are you *still* holding a grudge for that?" He gently massaged her waist, as his eyes avariciously brushed over every inch of her.

Melody looked away elusively. "I *might* still be just a little bit upset…"

"No, you can't be serious…" Luke's face creased in feigned dread.

"That texting incident really threw me for a loop." Melody tried to keep a straight face.

Luke hunched down, and softly bridged his lips to Melody's. Taking a moment, he explored the regions of her mouth. He kissed her as if she were his lifeline, and he was incapable of surviving without her. "Are you *still* angry at me?" he asked again. "Please, forgive me, okay?" His face bridged intimately with hers. "Do you have any idea how much I love you?"

"Uh-huh," Melody whispered, entranced. "I *might* forgive you after all." She pressed a kiss to the tip of Luke's nose.

"Yay!" Luke cheered, and covered Melody's lips with sugarcoated kisses. "I'm so glad you're going to forgive me, because you know what discovered a while back?"

"*What* have you discovered, Mr. Bryant?" Melody

stared lovingly at him, and secured her clasp about his neck.

"I realize I can't live without you," he said croakily.

"Is *that* all?" Melody flirted. "Well, in that case, I *might* love you too," she said with a wavering voice, in spite of the teasing.

"So, you're *not* sure?" Luke tested.

"I'm ninety-nine percent sure."

"Well, how can I make that a solid one hundred percent?" Luke swept over Melody's face with loving kisses.

"Just keep doing exactly what you're doing now."

"Your wish is my command, honey baby."

"There's only one thing wrong…"

"What's the matter, babe?" Luke pulled away, and searched Melody's eyes uncertainly.

"I've got to find a way to get my heart to stop racing." Melody covered Luke's face with kisses.

"Is your heart racing because I scared you just now?" Luke found himself lost in Melody's embrace. There was very little he could do to resist her hugs and kisses.

"No, I'm over that." Melody tenderly plowed her fingers through Luke's butterscotch curls. "Honestly, my heart *always* races whenever you're around."

"Well then, it's just as well that we're getting married in the morning." Luke gave her a roguish wink and smile.

"You think that'll alleviate the symptoms?" Melody gave him a quirky look.

"It might help us both to feel better. Having you close to me *every* day will *definitely* make *me* all better." Luke pulled Melody affectionately into his arm, and crushed her in them. "Do you have any idea how happy I am, Melody Christine honey baby-soon to be *Bryant*?" Luke rocked her delicately in his arms.

"I might have *some* idea." Melody cradled Luke's face in her hands, and caressed it fondly. "You've made me happier than I can even express." She stared into his eyes admiringly. "I still can't believe how good God has been to us. For a while there, I was so scared I'd lost you. I honestly lost hope that you would ever come back to me," she admitted.

"Even if I had to crawl back on my hands and knees, I would have found my way back to you. You're my whole world! And we *never* have to think about that awful time." Luke's eyes delved intently into hers. "I'm never going to let *anyone* hurt you that way again." He stared reassuringly into her eyes.

Totally stirred, Melody's eyes misted. "I *know* I'm safe with you. I've known that from the day we met."

"You *are* safe with me, and my *job* is to take care of you forever." Luke nodded in affirmation.

Melody laughed through the tears. "Funny…, I don't remember hiring you." She chuckled.

"Well, I sort of run the company…so I *kind of* hired myself." Luke's face crinkled in waggishness.

"So, you're a bigshot now?" Melody shook her head inanely, unable to stop smiling.

"I'm only a bigshot around here." Luke stared all about at his state-of-the-art man-cave office. His eyes then reconnected to Melody's, and he stated in earnest, "But, I'm just Luke, your honey bear and humble husband-to-be, who will gladly worship at your feet forever."

Melody nodded in agreement. "I can work with that whole feet-worshipping thing." Her cheeks turned rosy with joy, and her heart melted over Luke's clear love for her. "In fact, I *did* bring a fan, and we have grapes somewhere around here. So, you can start fanning and peeling, thank you very much!"

Luke laughed. "Okay. Just give me a chance to get out of this jacket, and then I will gladly start fanning and peeling grapes, my queen!" His arms tightened around Melody's waist, and he caressed the outline of her curves.

"Sounds like a plan," Melody said softly.

Luke had a way of making her go all mushy on the inside. Melody knew she couldn't resist him if she tried. However, she could feign cheekiness, because he'd scared her before. "I still can't believe you popped up in here using the vortex." She rolled her eyes facetiously. "And, I'm still upset that you kept me waiting in here for over an hour."

"You have any idea how difficult it was to focus on interviewing potential employees, when I knew you were in here all by your lonesome?" Luke pulled back, and gave melody a playful grin. He then redirected. "Honey baby, I *know* these past few months have been an adjustment for both of us. You've been amazing at putting up with my crazy schedule. But, once we cut through all of the red tape, you'll be seeing so much of me you'll probably be shoving me out the door every morning."

Luke stared at Melody like a man about to embark on a faraway journey. Such was his need to have every part of her burned into his memory. Sometimes, the fact that they were together felt like a dream. They'd endured so much in the past year. Luke perceived that Melody had no idea his intention was to keep her forever. In fact, he imagined that if she understood how deeply he loved her, she would be overwhelmed.

"*Me*, push *you* out the door? I don't think so. I'm definitely going to be one of those wives who will do *anything* to get you to call in sick, and keep you hostage for the day."

Luke laughed and winked mischievously at her.

"Being held hostage by my beautiful wife...? Well, we can definitely arrange for that at least twice a week." His eyebrows furrowed roguishly.

"Really...?"

"Uh-huh...whatever you want."

"I really don't like being away from you, honey bear. However, I'm willing to put up with *anything* in order to support your work. I'm so proud of you, Luke Bryant!" Tears shimmered in Melody eyes. "I love you!" She reached up, and pressed her lips meaningfully to his.

"That means more to me than anything! All I want is to make you proud of me. I want to give you the world, baby!" Luke's voice broke. "I can't believe I get to make you all mine in the morning. I can't wait to hold you in my arms all through the night. I love you more than I've found a way to express."

Luke pulled Melody back into his arms, and gave her an affectionate squeeze. Melody crushed him lovingly to herself, and held on for dear life. Neither spoke, as they held each other in silent contemplation of their future together.

——

"So, what do you think, Mel? We can have Galaxies Inc. create alien effigies and flying saucers in every corner of this room?" Luke stood to the side of the huge portal in his office. He held his right pointer finger up as a philosopher would, in order to drive his point home. "Then, when the building's empty at night, security can walk patrons through for a grand tour. Since everyone's buzzing about Portals... I think it's a great idea! What do *you* think, Mel?" Luke enticed.

He honestly tried not to laugh, but his flushed face gave him away. He loved messing around with Melody by coming up with the most outlandish ideas. He enjoyed seeing the look on her face whenever he pulled bizarre concepts from his bag of tricks.

"I think you've had one too many…chocolate covered strawberries." Melody shook her head in skepticism. "You're *so* crazy, but I love you so much!" She stood to her feet, and walked across the room closer to her weird fiancé.

"Are you saying you *don't* like my idea?" Luke frowned, feigning hurt feelings.

Melody tenderly draped her arms about his neck. "I *love* your idea, honey bear. I love it *almost* as much as the one you had last week to launch all your employees to a neighboring galaxy for the holidays. That would definitely be an *extended* holiday," Melody teased.

"Very funny, Melody… Yeah, I *get* it. We probably wouldn't return in this century." He nodded in agreement.

Melody shook her head comically. "We definitely have to get you out of the office. You need to get a little air, because you've been cooped up in here for far too long. Besides, we've got to go rescue Cupid from boredom."

Luke smiled mischievously. "When you think about it, *fuel* would be murder on a trip like that." His cheeks were ruddy with banter.

"All right then…" Melody stared at him as if he had two heads. "By the way, you *also* owe Cupid an apology for keeping him waiting so long."

"Lucky for *me*, Cupid doesn't hold a grudge…like some other people who will remain nameless (Luke playfully coughed out Melody's name)."

"Whatever, Luke." Melody rolled her eyes. "Oh, by the way, you might want to rethink that whole alien and flying saucer tour during Portals' off hours."

"You are wrong on *so* many levels, honey baby." Luke shook his head contrarily.

"I *know*." Melody reached up, and pressed a kiss to his mouth.

Luke sighed. "I can't believe you don't like that idea. That *really* hurts."

"You'll get over it." Melody playfully adjusted his tie.

Luke shook his head incredulous. He then crossed back over near his desk, and began gathering up the picnic effects. He and Melody were in the process of cleaning up after their lunch date, when the knock came to Luke's office door. Both Melody and Luke exchanged knowing looks of angst.

Melody frowned in defeat. "Uh-oh…" Her face strained in uncertainty. "I guess, you'd better go get that." She sighed. "Here we go again…"

"Don't worry, Mel. It'll be fine." Luke winked, as he coasted backward over towards the set of doors. However, he kept his eyes fastened to Melody's. "I promise, we'll be out of here in no time."

Luke set the folded linen blanket on his desk, and crossed over to the doors. He dreaded even seeing the person on the other side, because he knew they would make demands of him. Still, without hesitation he opened them up. An instant smile broke across his face, when he saw that it was Arianna.

"Hey, Ari! *Please*, tell me you have good news. Tell me, it's all right to escape with Melody for the rest of the day." Luke's face rumpled in playfulness, as he awaited an answer.

Arianna smiled at him, but guffawed. All the same, she felt totally misled standing there staring into Luke's perfect face and amazing teal eyes. She loved it when Luke horsed around, because his entire face usually lit up like the moon. Her heart skipped a beat, and it was difficult to think clearly whenever he was near.

"What I *can* tell you is that I'll see to it that all loose ends are tied. I promise you won't have to deal with any of it. Besides, I've already sent the memo to our contractors, contributors and personnel that you'll be unavailable for the next couple of weeks." She gave him an earnest smile.

Luke impulsively pulled Arianna into his arms. "Thank you. You are the *most* awesome, you know that?" He pressed a loving kiss to her cheek.

Arianna shrugged back uneasily, forced to pull away from Luke's immuring arms. "It's the least I could do, seeing *you* had absolutely zero time to yourself in the past few months."

"You're a gem, Ari. I *have* to say, *forcing* you to come out here is one of the best decisions I've ever made!" Luke gave her a playful wink. He genuinely loved Arianna as a person. She was a great friend, and an awesome employee.

"You hardly *forced* me to come out here. You just made me an offer I couldn't refuse… There's something I…"

"Ari, you've been my eyes and ears around here from the very beginning. I'm so grateful you're here! Did I tell you how much I appreciate having you around *these them here* parts?" Luke razzed.

Arianna snickered, and her cheeks turned florid. "Luke, no more gifts, and no more special perks. Everyone around here's beginning to think… Well, you've not only *told* me, but *shown* your appreciation a gazillion times."

Luke smiled quietly, and realized how he might have embarrassed Arianna with his grandiose gestures. "Sorry… I'll *try* to keep my appreciation under wraps."

Arianna was still a little bit winded, because Luke had hugged her so robustly. Heat radiated through her pores like fire, because of his touch. Notwithstanding, the musky scent of his cologne lingered on her clothes, and on her skin. She only imagined how flushed her cheeks were from embarrassment. Smiling awkwardly, her eyes momentarily wandered away from Luke's.

Arianna had doubted it was even possible to feel any stronger for Luke than when they'd worked together at Body Electric Era out in Virginia. However, she now grasped just how wrong she'd been, because she was more in love than ever. In fact, she was totally in awe of Luke. He was the best person in the world! Not only was he insanely good-looking and *hot*, he was a genius. His gifts and talents had made him a multibillionaire.

It felt surreal that she'd known Luke when he worked for BEE. She was in awe watching him effortlessly run a billion-dollar industry as *The Portal Master*. Arianna wasn't sure why she'd thought Luke's wealth and fame would have changed him. That was also something she was wrong about. Luke had changed. Undeniably humble, he was even kinder and more compassionate than ever.

Because Arianna couldn't stop loving Luke, it was a knife to her heart whenever she saw him with Melody. Hence, as much as she loved Melody, it was gut-wrenching to watch her be close to Luke. Out of respect for the couple, when Melody had asked her to be a bridesmaid, Arianna had agreed.

In the morning, Luke and Melody would become man and wife. So, on that very afternoon, Arianna wanted to put in her two-week notice. She'd already made up her mind to leave Portals Unlimited soon after the wedding. There was no way she'd survive watching Luke and Melody be a married couple.

As a person of faith, she had prayed extensively on the matter. Things being what they were, Luke was obviously outside the will of God for her life. And yet, Arianna didn't know how to stop wanting him. And lately, her desire for the man had been bordering sinful. So, she'd decided that it was in everyone's best interest if she went away. She had to find a safe space for her tenuously bleeding heart to heal.

For a moment, Arianna stood there dazed but smiling, as she stared at her boss. Luke's mouth was moving, and he was speaking. However, it was difficult to decipher anything

he said, because she couldn't stop gaping at his well-formed
mouth. Wistfully, Arianna sized up just how awesome Luke
looked in his black designer dress suit. With every move he
made, his muscles rippled through his pristine gray shirt.
Arianna tried arduously not to ogle. However, it was a real
challenge, because Luke was so desirable, and she yearned to
feel his arms around her again.

"Hey there, are you all right, Ari?" Luke's face
creased in concern. "You should take the rest of the day off. I
can't believe I let you talk *me* into *letting* you come in today.
You and Mel shopped your little hearts out the other day. I
know how exhausting that must have been. Also, you've
helped her so much with last-minute details for the wedding.
You *should* go home."

"I'm a lot stronger than I look. I'll be okay, Luke.
Yes, Mel and I shopped till we dropped, but I promise to be
bright-eyed and bushy tailed for the wedding."

"Okay…no pressure. But, in the event you get tired of
looking at these for walls, let Brenda take over for a while."

"I will think about it. That's *really* kind of you."
Arianna stalled momentarily, and held her head down in
deliberation. "Luke, there's something I wanted to talk to you
about…"

"Of course, Ari. Honestly, I'd want to give you my
undivided attention. Right now, Mel and I are seriously trying
to put some distance between us and this building." Luke
frowned, conflicted.

Arianna shook her head humorously over Luke's
comment. "I get that, Luke. I promise it won't take very
long. I just thought…"

"Everything all right, Ari?" Luke searched her
eyes ponderously.

"Everything's fine. It's just that…"

"Ari, I *thought* I heard your voice out here!" Melody sauntered over to the set of doors. She brushed past Luke, took hold of Arianna's hand, and ushered her into the office. "Did you get my text, and the link I sent?" Melody asked, excited. She loved Arianna to death, and she was overjoyed Arianna was one of her bridesmaids.

"You mean from Pinterest?" Arianna asked distractedly. Her eyes kept wandering back over to Luke. She couldn't help noticing the way Luke stared at Melody. For all intents and purposes, she was an oasis out in the hot dry desert, and he was parched. Luke's smile was painted on as he listened to Melody go on about some of the pins she'd found on Pinterest. It occurred to her that Luke *always* stared at Melody that way.

"I *did* get your text and the link. I texted you back a little while ago," Arianna said absently. She handled Melody's phone to show her the text, and some of the similar pins she'd found on Pinterest.

"Sorry, I didn't see it until now." Melody realized she'd had a lot on her mind. "Aren't those quotes amazing? I thought they were perfect."

"I think *this* one'll be perfect for when you and Luke exchange vows tomorrow." Arianna pointed to one of the memes Melody had texted to her phone.

"That's the one I like too," Melody said in a hushed tone.

While the ladies chatted, Luke took a moment. He crossed back over to his desk, and accessed the computer. He just remembered he had a few emails to respond to.

"You're so lucky, Melody!" Arianna stared admiringly over at Luke.

Melody eyes misted and she smiled. "He's the greatest blessing of my life!" Melody couldn't help noticing the way Arianna stared at Luke. Melody grasped just how difficult it was for Arianna, but she had no idea how to mitigate the circumstances. "Ari, you *do* know *you're* next right?" Melody heartened. "I know you're next, because you've got every single guy in this building in love with you!"

Arianna's eyes connected pleasantly to Melody's. "Yeah right... I wish..."

"Ari, are you kidding me? I guess, you haven't noticed how they all gawk at you around here. You're like this celebrity they want to get close to. But, they're all so intimidated, because they think they're out of your league." Melody wrapped her arms affectionately around Arianna. "Believe me when I say you're wowing them all...especially *Mr. Hot shot blue eyes* himself," Melody introduced, and gave Arianna a knowing wink.

"You mean *Peter*?" Arianna shook her head skeptically.

"Who *else* would I be talking about? Those girls out there follow him around like lost puppies, and hang on his every word."

Arianna frowned. "Don't I know it? It's *so* ridiculous. Peter just eats it all up, because he's *so* full of himself, Mel. Not to mention how arrogant and vain he is." Arianna's face knotted in disapproval.

Melody seemed confused. "Peter's the *first* person I met when I came out here. He met me at the airport. We hung out that entire afternoon. He was polite, efficient, responsible and-"

"He's also a player, Mel. He must be juggling at least half a dozen of those girls in accounting alone." Her face flushed red, and she shook her head contrarily. "It doesn't really matter anyway. I trust God. *He* has to lead me to the right person." Arianna smiled sadly.

"Well, I'm sure it won't be long before God *does* bring that special someone into your life. You really shouldn't close yourself off, Ari. You never know what God wants to do." Melody smiled encouragingly. "Who knows? You might meet *Mister Right* at the wedding tomorrow. By the way, I can't wait to see you in that sequined cranberry-colored gown! They'll probably have to rush all the guys over to the ER for chest pain," she teased.

Arianna laughed. "Oh, Mel, you're too much! I seriously doubt that will happen, but I *am* crazy about the dress. I'm also happy for you and Luke. The two of you deserve so much happiness!"

"And so do you, Ari! God's going to shine on you in such an awesome way." Melody gave her an encouraging smile.

"You *still* wanted to talk, before Melody and I make our great escape?" Luke rejoined the ladies. He slipped his arms around Melody, and stood protectively behind her.

Arianna's heart sank to see how happy they were. In spite of the awkwardness and the pain, she earnestly loved them both. So, the last thing she *wanted* was to make their special time all about herself. So, she rethought telling Luke and Melody that she wanted to quit her job through Portals Unlimited.

"I guess, it can wait. Now, go on. You and Melody should get out of here before everything blows up."

"Luke and I are definitely going to take you up on that offer, Ari." Melody threw her arms affectionately around Arianna. "Love you. Come by the house at about nine. If I'm not there, Serena definitely will be."

"Love you too, Mel, and I'll be there. Now, go on. Get out of here," Arianna goaded. Her eyes connected furtively to Luke's. He smiled, and mouthed the words *thank you*. She gave him a compliant nod, and smiled back.

"Thanks, Ari," Luke emphasized, just before he and Melody slipped through the office doors. Melody had already rushed ahead of him. "Are you sure you've got this?"

Arianna nodded. "Are you doubting me, *PM*?" She gave him a cheeky look.

"Not at all, because I *know* how awesome you are! Thanks again for everything." Luke then rushed out of the office, and darted away.

"You're welcome…," Arianna's voice drifted out into the hallway. And, just like *that*, Luke was gone! Arianna stared all about his amazing office. *I'm going to miss you so much, Luke. Even if you're gone for only one day, Portals just isn't the same without you.* She took a moment to properly shut things down. Luke's office would be closed off for the next two weeks or so.

Moments later, Arianna stepped outside of the office. She took a moment to lock the set of doors. Making a sudden turn from completing the task, her heart jumped into her throat to see Peter Lawton standing feet away. Arianna clutched her chest in order to still her pounding heart.

"You scared me, Peter," she said annoyed. Just then, it occurred to her that the man she loved was going to marry someone else, and there was nothing she could do about it.

Arianna's eyes glimmered with tears, but she blinked them back. It also didn't help matters that Peter was the *last* person she wanted seeing her so emotional.

With his dramatic dark hair, piercing blue eyes and ripped body, Peter Lawton had the women who worked through Portals Unlimited and beyond it, virtually swooning. Impassively, Arianna assessed how *perfect* he looked in his dark gray business suit, with gray and burgundy accents. Everything about Peter screamed flawlessness-right down to his strong hands, and freakishly clean fingernails. Arianna resented the fact that he used his looks to get pretty much anything he wanted from his adoring fans at the company.

Peter had left his office just to find Arianna. Truth be told, he was worried about her. She seemed pretty upset that morning. Not only was Arianna beautiful and intelligent, but there was something totally different about her. She had a depth that was difficult to find in women nowadays. Rationally, Peter knew there was absolutely no reason for him to be standing outside his boss's office, especially since Luke had obviously left for the day. However, Peter had to come up with a good reason why he was following behind Arianna like a lost puppy…again.

He tried to keep his voice from wavering and to establish eye contact. Whenever Arianna was around, in spite of how confident he seemed, he *was* just a little boy. "I'm sorry. I *really* didn't mean to scare you." Peter found himself involuntarily closing in on Arianna, even if he felt shaky on the inside. Every time he tried to talk to her, he always wound up putting his foot in his mouth.

"Is *PM* Around?" Peter asked, trying not to come off as a total office stalker.

"*PM* and Melody just left for the day," Arianna told him, shortly, still fighting back the tears.

"Oh, okay…" Peter frowned in uncertainty. "I just

was looking to touch base in as far as the applicants we interviewed today. I guess, it'll just have to wait, since PM *is* getting married tomorrow." Peter's eyes wandered awkwardly away from Arianna's angelic face. There it was, another insert-foot-in-mouth moment.

"I'm pretty sure that can wait," Arianna said wryly. "Was there something else you wanted?" Arianna was oblivious to the fact that she was coming off as impolite and downright rude.

"Nope. I was just hoping to catch *PM* before he left for the day." Peter's heart twisted in knots, as he inched in even closer to her. Concern wrinkled his comely face. "Are *you* all right, Arianna?" Peter recoiled from reaching out and touching her.

"I'm fine." Arianna's eyes wandered away from Peter's probing stare. "You can try PM on his cell later, but I really don't think that's a good idea for the obvious reason." She gave him an admonishing look. *Why was Peter still standing there? Why wouldn't he get out of her face? Could you please go away now? You might have all the ladies in the office swooning, but you're* **so** *on my nerves right now, dude.*

Peter had his own fan club at Portals *and* beyond it. However, Arianna didn't care very much for him, even if she *would* be on *his* arm at the wedding together. They were paired off as bridesmaid and groomsman for Melody and Luke's wedding.

"Did something happen here…?" Peter reached out to touch her arm. However, the acid look on her face made him pull back again.

"No, Peter, *nothing* happened. I'm fine. Thank you for asking." Arianna's crystal blue eyes skimmed tensely over Peter's exploratory stare. "You *do* realize Luke only swung by the office this morning to handle those interviews? He had absolutely no intention of working on the day before his wedding." Arianna rolled her eyes.

She wasn't sure why she'd gone over the rhetoric, because she certainly wasn't telling Peter anything he didn't already know. Nevertheless, it behooved her to hold it together in the presence of such a conceited jerk. In as far as running Portals Unlimited, Peter's title was just a cut below hers, but Arianna evaluated their differences. They were like night and day.

Peter nodded understandingly. "Thanks, but I'm *well* aware of *PM's* schedule. I'm the one who writes it out remember?" His eyes intimately searched Arianna's. "I was just *hoping* to catch him before he left the building."

Arianna's eyes wandered away again from Peter's intent gaze. She didn't want him seeing the tears in her eyes that threatened to snake down her cheeks. Furthermore, she didn't want to rush away like some unstable little girl. So, she shifted nervously on her heels, and propped her head up. She tried to exude a bit of confidence as she reestablished eyes contact. "That's right." She guffawed. "I'm not sure why I told you all of that. I guess, I'm just a little tired today."

Peter found himself drifting over magnetically towards Arianna again. He wanted to be close to her so bad it caused physical pain. It was gut-wrenching to feel so strongly about someone who obviously couldn't stand him. He'd dreamed of touching Arianna a thousand times. And yet, he had absolutely no idea how to make that dream a reality. She seemed locked away in some fortress beyond his reach.

With a thrumming heart and quavering limbs, he tried to be brave. However, he found himself breathing spasmodically as he faced her. "Arianna, if you're not feeling well…" He gulped, but took a deep breath in order to finish his train of thought. "If you wanted to go home, Brenda and I can handle things around here." He gave her a reassuring but awkward smile.

Surprised, Arianna shrank back, realizing how close Peter was to her. He was standing so close she could hear the thudding of his heart. Taken aback and stirred by his offer, she forced a smile. "That's very kind of you, Peter but I'm *really* all right." Arianna tried to offer a more optimistic smile.

Peter nodded amenably, and flinched, as if he'd been electrically shocked. "All right, but if you change your mind…"

"I won't-but thank you anyway. Now, if you'll excuse me, I've got to return to my desk," Arianna said hurriedly. "By the way, if *PM* calls me before *you* reach out to him, I'll ask him to give you a call."

Arianna shifted edgily on her heels. The last thing she'd expected was to have a semi-intimate moment with her archenemy Peter Lawton. It creeped her out.

"Thanks. I would *really* appreciate that, but no worries. Talking to *PM* today isn't urgent." Peter momentarily made himself look away. He didn't want to make Arianna any more uncomfortable than he sensed he already had.

Realizing it made no sense to remain there, Peter began pulling away from the angelic blonde. He would have inched back a hundred feet, if the wall wasn't a barrier. Bumping backward into the wall, he gauchely pressed up against it, and tucked his hands in his pockets. However, he found himself gawking at Arianna with a lost expression on his face, while she fiddled with her phone.

"Me, Kevin and Brenda were about to order from *Japanese Plaza*. Is there anything on their menu *you* might want?" Peter hesitantly asked.

"You say something, Peter?" Arianna looked up at him pretending to text someone. She was completely aware of his presence, but confused about why he was still there. If Peter wasn't going away, she had to find a way to politely get away from *him* without falling apart.

"We're ordering from Japanese Plaza. Did you want anything?" Peter's eyes were ravenous, and he couldn't get his heart to stop hammering, as he skimmed over every inch of her. Her scent was intoxicating. And, with the sun filtering through the hallway, there seemed to be a halo encircling her golden tresses.

"No. I'm good," Arianna's voice cracked. Tears pushed through her eyelids, and she felt emotionally overwrought at that point. Her head was spinning, and she had to get out of that building as soon as humanly possible. "On second thought, Peter, I think I *will* take you up on that offer. I *just* remembered that I had to take care of something…for the wedding," she fibbed.

Peter gave her a questioning look, but nodded understandingly. "Absolutely. You should go and take care of whatever it is you need to. Brenda and I will handle things around here."

"Thanks." Arianna turned her face in the opposite direction, as tears rolled down her cheeks. "I guess, I will see *you* in the morning." She didn't even bother looking back at Peter.

"Sure. I look forward to-"

"Bye, Peter," she said abruptly.

Arianna turned her on heels, and scampered in the opposite direction. She couldn't let Peter see her coming apart at the seams. She then rushed back out to the work area. As she zipped through the spacious office, she avoided eye contact with all of her coworkers. All the same, the smile plastered to her face, couldn't hamper the tears in her eyes. Arianna rushed over to her desk, grabbed her pocketbook, her sweater and car keys. She dashed over to the elevator like someone being chased.

Confused, Peter had hurried back out to the main office area after her. He watched Arianna agitatedly gather up her things. He stood a distance away behind the hallway barrier. So, she didn't notice him shamelessly ogling, like a deer caught in the headlights. His leer followed her every move, until she slipped into the elevator and disappeared.

Peter thrust his clenched fist against the wall in frustration. "She'll *never* be into you, man. You've just got to find a way to deal with it. There are a lot of women here who want to go out with you, all except for the one you *really* want. Ari won't give you the time of day. I'll never be as good as *he* is…at least not to her. I'm Luke's sidekick, but *he*'s the *Portal Master*. Apparently, he's also the one who holds the key to her heart. Just deal with it, Pete…"

Chapter Two

The Quartz Castle Inn sparkled like obsidian stones, as the wedding party gathered to celebrate Melody and Luke's wedding. The picturesque backdrop was the fairytale venue Melody had always dreamed about. The guests were already seated in the magnificent floral garden, overlooking the water. The glass front castle with stretches of lush greenery, and breathtaking flowers covering acres of the property, was a glimpse of utopia. The three bridesmaids were already poised out on the terrace. Once the wedding processional began, they'd be ushered away by the groomsmen.

Now, Melody, her mom, Tonya Braithwaite and Serena, lingered inside the luxurious and expansive bridal suite. Tonya and Serena were almost done preening, and Melody anticipated seeing the finished product. She was an emotional wreck, as she stared at herself in the full-length mirror in her winter-white lace wedding gown with crystal beading and accents. The beads shone with the fire and intensity of millions of diamonds. The new morning sun filtering through the picture glass windows, made them shimmer all the more.

Suddenly, memories of all she and Luke had endured in the past year overwhelmed. The recollections washed over her more forcefully than ocean breakers. She recalled falling head-over-heels in love with Luke from the beginning, even if she arduously tried to fight it. After their first kiss, Melody realized she was fighting a losing battle. Their kiss had ignited a special fire on the inside. That special moment had meant so much, and had left her heart forever altered. Luke's love was branded into her heart.

Nevertheless, Melody readily gave all the glory to God. God had been so faithful in answering her prayers. After the horror show she and Luke endured in the past year, they'd been gifted with such a special blessing. Everything had come full circle. Exhilarated, Melody frolicked in front of the mirror. She couldn't wait to exchange vows with the man who'd altered her life forever.

Melody was more in love with Luke than ever, and their love grew stronger every day. In fact, Melody couldn't wait to see him. Not a stickler for tradition, she and Luke had spent a few hours apart after their lunch date yesterday. However, at that point, she yearned to be in his arms again, and to feel the tenderness of his touch.

"I still can't believe my baby's getting married today!" Tonya Braithwaite stormed excitedly back into the dressing room to join her daughter.

Jarred from reverie, Melody made a sudden turn. Her smile was brighter than a hundred-watt bulb when she saw her mom making her way over to the full-length mirror. Melody turned away from the mirror in order to give her mom undivided attention. Her mom looked positively exquisite in her sequined, crimson, formfitting gown. The gown accentuated all the right curves. Melody felt like a child admiring her mother's glamor. Tonya looked both radiant and youthful with her cinnamon and auburn-streaked short-styled hair. The coloring enhanced her coffee skin.

"Having *you* here has made my day, Mom! I'm so glad you're here! It means so much to me…and to Luke." Sentimental tears shone in Melody's eyes.

"Where else would I be, baby girl? I'm *over the moon* God has given me the opportunity to see my *Melody Girl* get married today!" Tonya stated with dignity. She took a moment to admire how resplendent her only daughter looked on her special day. For Tonya, it was a blessing she had prayed for exhaustively. Now that the time was right, she had the honor of seeing her baby girl exchange vows with a man-who not only loved her, but loved the Lord Jesus Christ.

Tonya was pleased by the choices Melody had made along the way. The most essential decision was that she'd surrendered her life to Jesus Christ in her teen years. That life-altering choice had kept Melody from making egregious mistakes. Tonya's only regret was that Melody's dad wasn't there. She imagined how overjoyed he would have been to walk her down the aisle, and give her away to a wonderful man. Tonya's eyes glimmered with tears remembering her late husband.

Seeing her mom so emotional, Melody's face warped in sentimentality. "Mom, please don't start again. If I start crying, I'll ruin my makeup, and Serena will kill me." Melody smiled nostalgically. The excitement and *gravity* of what was about to occur overpowered her. In a matter of minutes, she would be meeting Luke at the altar. They would exchange vows, and become man and wife.

Melody had been out in California for a few months. However, her life had changed drastically since the move. She and Luke now owned a house near the ocean out in Beverly Glen. All the same, they'd made a unilateral decision to live separately until they were married. That determination had centered on their respect for God and for each other. Not succumbing to sex outside of marriage was indeed a challenge, but Melody and Luke were both grateful they'd waited. Quite soon, they would no longer have to say goodbye, and retreat to separate living quarters. They would only say goodnight.

"Melody Christine, are you crying again?" Serena marched into the dressing room looking positively divine in a dark cranberry-red sequined gown. Her upswept, light brown highlighted hair made her look like a queen! Serena turned towards the side of the expansive full-length mirror, and saw Melody's mom standing close by, and her face flushed in embarrassment. "Oh, I'm sorry, Mrs. Braithwaite," she said quietly.

"That's all right, Serena. You can *blame* it all on *me*. *I'm* the one getting all sappy only minutes before my baby walks down the aisle." Tonya gave Serena a reassuring look. "*You* look positively radiant!"

Serena gave her an earnest smile. "Thank you! But, you don't have to apologize for being sentimental today."

Melody set her hand on her heart mawkishly. "Reena,

you look like a dream!"

"Mel, stop... You're going to get *me* crying up in here." Serena stared wistfully over at her bestie, and tried not to gush.

"And yes, you *can* blame my mom for being so emotional today, because it's *all* her fault." Melody gazed lovingly over at her mom.

Tonya shook her head humorously, as she cautiously caught the tears under her eyelids with tissues. "I can't *even* apologize. It's what moms do at their children's weddings." Her eyes shimmered again, as she continued to fuss over her daughter.

"How can you blame her when she loves you so much, Mel?" Serena defended. "Let's take a look at that face." Serena cradled Melody's face in her hands, and examined her makeup. "Please, don't mess up Kyla's work before you walk down that aisle." Serena feigned a stern demeanor.

Melody's makeup artist, Kyla Morgan, had spent hours getting them all ready for the big event. Serena grabbed a few tissues from out of the box, and patted Melody's face here and there. "Now, that's more like it." She stood back, and examined her work. Serena assessed how perfect her bestie looked. Melody's Victorian upswept hair was embellished by shimmering pearl beads, and her gingerbread skin emitted a healthy glow. Serena was overjoyed for her best friends. God had been gracious enough to grant Melody and Luke the desire of their hearts. Serena acknowledged how much the two had suffered. So, the love they now shared was a sweet reward.

Tonya floated over, and stood next to Serena in order to get a better look at her daughter. The only thing she could do was to admire. "I only wish your father was here," her voice wavered. "He would have been so proud."

"I wish he were here too, mom. Today more than any other I miss him..." Melody's face twisted in sadness, and she breathed spasmodically. "But, daddy won't be underrepresented today. His chair is all decked out with fresh flowers. It'll be the one to your right-hand side."

Melody had left an empty seat in memory of her late father. "So, it'll be just as if he was here with us today," her voice broke. "It *would* have been so nice if daddy had gotten to meet Luke. He would have *loved* Luke." Tears filled Melody's eyes again, but Serena quickly caught the loops with tissues, before they rolled down her cheeks.

Serena tried not to get too emotional herself. "*Everyone* loves Luke!" She cautiously wiped stray tears from beneath her own eyelids. She and Tonya took turns hugging each other in support, as they talked about Alistair Langford Maxwell-Melody's late father.

"Your father would have been so proud to see his baby girl so successful and happy." Tonya wrapped her arms around Melody, and crushed her in them. Pulling back, she cradled Melody's face in her hands. "You *are* beautiful! Honestly, God could *not* have chosen a *better* man for you to share the rest of your life with!" She caringly stroked her daughter's cheeks.

"*Even* if Luke *is* a little on the light side…?" Melody chuckled through the tears. Her mom and brother Calvin were just starting to get used to the fact that Luke was white.

"For a guy who is a little on the *light* side, he's all right." Tonya shook her head humorously, and got both Melody and Serena laughing.

Serena nodded and wiped tears from her eyes. "Yeah, Mel, I have to say I agree with your mom. Luke *is all right*." She gave Melody a playful wink.

"So, I'm gonna get going, baby. I need to check in on Max. Then, I'll go out, and take my place with everyone else." Tonya gave Melody one last loving squeeze.

Maxwell Braithwaite was Melody's stepdad. Along

with Sean, Melody's brother Calvin was already waiting in the wings to walk Melody down the aisle. Melody loved and respected Sean as an older brother. So, it was fitting for both Calvin and Sean to walk her down the aisle, and give her away properly. It was also an honor she wanted to bestow upon Luke's *best man* and *best friend*.

"Okay, mom," Melody said. "I'll be out in just a little while." Wistfulness shaded her sweet face, as she air-blew a kiss at her mom.

"Bye, baby, I love you!" Tonya stared sappily over at her daughter before she turned away.

Melody smiled quietly over at Serena, as they watched Tonya walk out of the expansive dressing room.

Serena took Melody's hands in hers. "Mel, I'm so excited. You've waited so long, and I can't believe this is finally happening!" Her eyes searched Melody's in awe and wonder. "I have to admit there were times…" Serena's eyes shimmered with tears again.

"Reena, if you want *me* to stop crying, *you* have to tuck away the sappy." Melody's face warped in wistfulness. "There were times where it all seemed so impossible. I didn't think it would *ever* happen. Luke and I have come so far."

"Hate to say I told you so…." Serena pointed a playful finger of accusation at Melody.

"But you *did* tell me so." Melody shook her head inanely. "You kept telling me everything was going to turn out all right. You had faith even when I lost mine." Melody's face creased in guilt. "You told me God had a plan for me and Luke and…"

"God *does* have a plan for you and Luke. And, *what* a plan it's been so far! I still can't believe Luke Bryant is the *Portal Master* you were vilifying when you first came out here."

"I was so embarrassed when he stepped into the house,

and announced that he and the *Portal Master* were one and the same." Melody laughed. "I can't believe how he tricked me."

"I'm *so* proud of Luke. He executed that plan without a single hitch." Serena laughed mischievously.

"Gee, thanks, Reena." Melody smiled uncertainly.

"Come on, Mel. Even *you've* got to admit he got you good."

"I'm so glad you're such a fan." Melody laughed, incredulous. "So *you're* never going to let me live that down?"

"Nope." Serenity propped Melody's face affectionately.

"And, Luke definitely won't let me forget that day." Melody had a reflective expression on her face.

"How *can* he forget any of it, Mel? He loves you so much!" Serena brushed over Melody's cheek fondly.

"I love *him*! It's so hard to define how I feel about Luke. Saying I love him doesn't even come close to expressing how I *really* feel about him." Melody grimaced mawkishly.

"God has *truly* given you the desire of your heart. Still, Mel, I think God wanted you to fall in love with the *poor* man first." Serena gave Melody a knowing look.

Melody nodded. "I've thought about that too. But, I realize that it wouldn't have mattered one way or another. Once I fell in love with Luke, any dream I had of marrying into wealth faded into oblivion."

"I think that's the way God wanted it. And, guess what?" Serena laughed in irony. "After you fell in love with Luke's heart, he gave you a billionaire anyway." Serena cheered.

"God sure did." Melody looked wistful again.

She suddenly wrapped her arms around Serena. "You have no idea how blessed I am that you and Dane walked me through all of the ups and downs. I'm ecstatic that you're here to share this special day with me." Melody crushed Serena in her arms.

"Where else would we be, Mel? You and Luke are family."

"We *are* family, Reena. So, family stays together. Please, think about moving out here... Please, Reena. It's so strange being out here, and not having you around. What am I going to do, Reena?" Concern wrinkled Melody's face.

"You'll probably wither away under the California sun, and turn into a raisin." Serena took more tissues from the box, and made a few adjustments to Melody's makeup. "Whatever *will* you do?" She set the back of her right hand dramatically on her forehead, and spoofed her best southern accent.

"Reena, I'm serious." Melody pouted, and gave Serena a pining look. "What *am* I going to do without you?"

"Mel, please don't make me feel any worse about this. Dane's family still lives out in Sands Port, and you *know* how close they all are. So for now, we'll just have to make the most of calling, texting and Facetime."

Everything was finally falling into place. Even so, Melody realized she couldn't have it all. Serena and Dane would be flying back out to Sands Port, Maryland in the morning, while she and Luke would be on a flight headed for Fiji, then later Australia.

"I *know* you and Dane have strong family ties out in Sands Port. Still, you can't blame a girl for trying." Sadness veiled Melody's face.

"No, I can't blame a girl at all, because *this girl* feels the same way. But, Mel, I'll *never* be too far away. I'm always here if you need me." Serena blinked back tears. "*You* better call me every day." She pointed a liable finger at Melody.

"Are you kidding me? I'll be calling you at least three times a day. Our phone bills are going to be insane." Melody smiled. "I love you!"

"I love you too!" Serena hugged Melody again, then abruptly pulled away. "Now, let's go get you *good and married* to Mrs. Lucas William *Portal Master* Bryant." She winked at her bestie.

Melody laughed. "Luke said he would wear his old green janitorial jumpsuit today," Melody brought up humorously.

"You mean the one he used to wear when he worked for Sands Port Elementary?"

"*That's* the one." Melody snickered. "Knowing my baby, I wouldn't put it past him. He's full of surprises." Her face radiated with joy and hopefulness.

"Well, let's go see if Luke makes good on that promise. Are you all set?" Serena hugged Melody in a sustaining manner.

Melody nodded. "I'm all set."

Melody and Serena walked out of the dressing room. It was time to go and join the rest of the bridal party. Melody had very few friends out in California. So, her bridesmaids were the three young ladies she'd recently befriended; Arianna Ward, Lauren Rhodes and Talia Grayson. All three worked through Portals Unlimited. Melody knew a lot less about Lauren and Talia than she did about Arianna. Lauren and Talia were great! Lauren worked for the accounting department, while Talia had recently been hired to work through sales and promotions.

Arianna, on the other hand, was Melody's buddy. The fact that Arianna was in love with Luke hadn't eluded Melody, even if Arianna tried to mask her feelings. It was a very fragile situation. However, Melody avowed to be sensitive to Arianna's feelings. On a number of occasions, Melody had tried to set Arianna up on a few dates. More often than not, Arianna always respectfully declined. She often alluded to being extremely busy, or to already having plans.

Melody realized there was no remedy for the way Arianna felt. She perceived that Arianna needed someone else to fill that void in her life, someone who'd make her insanely happy. Arianna already had the most important factor covered. She had a relationship with Jesus Christ. So, Melody was encouraged that God would honor her, and give her his very best. It was only a matter of time before God blessed Arianna with someone special.

Regardless, Melody couldn't even pretend to be angry about Arianna's clear love for Luke. She judged that if the circumstances were reversed, she'd probably love Luke as well. Arianna was the complete package, and Melody adored her. Ari was one of the few people who'd shown her immense kindness on her first day out in California, and their friendship had only blossomed since then.

However, growing friendships were one thing. But, Portals Unlimited was also expanding. Luke already had subsidiaries out in NYC, Dallas, Texas and Atlanta, Georgia. Ironically, success hadn't changed Luke one bit. He was still the same sweet, funny, thoughtful, kind and irresistible guy Melody had fallen in love with. Melody knew that her feelings for him would never change. She would champion all of his talents and ventures. It followed that whether Luke was scarcely getting by, or owned a multibillion-dollar empire, he was still *her* Luke and always would be.

***

"I need you to cover every inch of these grounds one

more time. I *have* to know all bases are covered from the
courtyard to the reception hall. I can't afford to take any
chances today," Luke spoke over the phone with the head of
his security staff. He and Melody would be meeting at the
altar in less than an hour, and they had enemies. Luke was in
the groomsmen dressing suite all decked out in his deep navy,
satin edged notched lapel tux.

To say he was nervous was an understatement. In his
heart and mind, he kept counting down the minutes and
seconds until event time. Yet, there were a few more loose
ends that needed tightening in order to ensure his and
Melody's special day went off without a hitch. Logically,
Luke understood that Clarke Vale and Darien Stiles were
behind bars. However, he wasn't taking any chances. No
doubt, Clarke Vale's power was still far-reaching on the
outside world.

So, security at the wedding venue was extremely tight.
Aside from the threat of Clarke and his lackeys finding a way
to infiltrate the premises, there was also the press and media.
Luke's new status made it so that he *had* to contend with the
press at all times. Already, a handful of helicopters had been
sighted buzzing overhead just waiting for the opportunity to
pounce. So, for a number of reasons, Luke had to guarantee
that this long-awaited day was perfect for Melody.

"My men and I just combed through the grounds for
the third time, *PM*. I assure you security is as tight an eighties
popstar's spandex pants," Eugene Morrow told Luke. He was
head of security detail.

Luke tried to remain lighthearted and upbeat. He was
honestly content watching his groomsmen, his best man Sean,
and Melody's older brother, Calvin Maxwell, frolicking
around in good spirits. Luke smiled, and nodded a lot
passively observing their interactions.

Sean perceived Luke's security concerns. So, he was
doing his part in keeping the guys entertained. Sean wasn't
only Luke's best man. He, along with Melody's brother
Calvin, would have the honor of walking Melody down the

aisle, and giving her away. Luke only had three groomsmen, Peter Lawton VP of public relations and administration for Portals Unlimited, Derek Thorpe, who was a software developer, and Keith Grand, head of advertising.

"Just to be on the safe side, have them comb through the area one last time," Luke ordered. "I apologize if I'm stressing you out, Gene-"

"No worries, *PM*. We *know* what we're dealing with here, so I get it."

"Check every entryway, exit, lobby, and every inch of those back balcony doors within the reception area," Luke emphasized. His face wrinkled in angst, as he brushed his fingers nervously through his curly hair. That was his nervous habit. However, he caught himself and stopped short. He didn't want his nerves to get the better of him.

"You got it, boss," Eugene assented.

"Call me back in a few."

"Sure will, *PM*."

Luke sighed after getting off of the phone. It suddenly occurred to him just how quiet the room was. Skimming over the dressing room, he noticed all the guys were gone. Just then, he realized just how late it was, if the groomsmen had already gone out to the terrace to take their places. Luke honestly thought he was alone. However, he suddenly felt a hand on his right shoulder.

"You all right, buddy?" Sean's face wrinkled in uncertainty. "I'm sure Eugene has everything under control. You *don't* have to worry about that maniac, or about any of his lackeys crashing your party today."

Luke turned to face his best friend, and frowned in uncertainty. "Sean, I know that in my *head*, but I can't help feeling as if I've got to do everything in my power not to risk it. We've all been through too much." He shook his head in irony.

Sean nodded in agreement. "I get that, buddy, but we also can't live in fear. *God* has given you and Mel this special day. So, he will see to it that you make that girl your wife today." Sean's eyes gunned into Luke's in conviction.

Luke took deep breaths in order to remain calm. "Things *have* to go the way they're supposed to today." He stared earnestly into Sean's eyes. "I couldn't stand it if…"

"Things *will* go the way they're supposed to, Luke. So, let go, and enjoy this awesome blessing. It's a gift from God! Melody is so special!" Sean smiled.

Luke beamed like the morning sun. "She means *everything* to me. I can't live without my Mel." Love radiated through him. "I can't believe I get to see her every day and every night. I get to hold her in my arms, and never have to let go." His eyes shone in sentimentality.

"Now, *that's* what I'm talking about. You can't let Clarke Vale, Darien Stiles or their sleazebag minions ruin your wedding day, Luke. They've already taken away so much from all of us. So, today, we've got to behave as if they were never a part of our lives." Sean patted Luke's arm.

Luke chortled, and shook his head humorously. "You're absolutely right, Sean. I refuse to let those dirt bags take anything else from any of us."

"It's going to be all right. You *will* marry Melody today, and those deviants will be convicted, and spend the rest of their lives in prison. You do believe that, don't you?" Sean lowered critically into Luke's eyes.

"Of course I do, Sean. God has been so faithful. He helped us through that dark time. I just…"

"You *just* can't afford to leave things to chance…?" Sean filled in. "Guess what, buddy? We're never in control of anything anyway. God is. So, give God the reigns of control today."

Luke nodded again and exhaled. "It scares me

sometimes to hear *you* make sense," he razzed on his friend.

"Well, it doesn't happen often. So, you'd better listen up." Sean smiled quirkily.

"Yeah, I'm listening. Honestly, Sean, it happens a lot more than you think." Luke shook his head inanely.

"Gee, thanks." Sean chuckled, and followed Luke into the dressing area. "Only you...," Sean teased. He reached over, and fiddled with Luke's tie. For one reason or another, he thought it needed straightening.

"So, what do you think is next for *you*, big guy?" Luke asked Sean. He glanced down at his digital watch, and realized time was slipping away. Soon, Sean would have to go out there, and take his place on the promenade in order to walk Melody down the aisle.

"What do you mean?" Sean frowned, befuddled.

"You and Nicole are welcome to stay out here. You can help me run this insane company. It's actually a conglomerate now." Luke's face rumpled in puzzlement, as the reality of the matter internalized.

He was very much the anxious groom with his dark, stylish designer suit. Luke's hair had been lightened by the California sun. It was shades lighter than it used to be when he lived out on the East Coast. Slowly but surely, he was beginning to look more like his old self. He'd gained back some of the weight he'd lost in the past year. Having Melody back in his arms, had mended the wounds he'd sustained while they were apart. And, Luke couldn't wait to start their journey together as a man and wife.

"Luke, Portals is *your* baby, and you're doing a bang-up job running it yourself." Sean shook his head in skepticism. "I always knew you'd be successful one day, but no one could have prepared me for all of this." Sean sized up the lavish backdrop. "This is just insane." He shook his head, incredulous.

"It *is* insane, Sean, but I'm smart enough to know that it's only by God's grace." Luke smiled pensively.

"You got that right." Sean looked around again, amazed.

"Don't get me wrong. I *am* thankful to God for the awesome people he's sent to help me run Portals. That said, Sean, *you're* my right hand. We've done *everything* together since middle school. I could sure use my best buddy out here." Luke gave Sean a suppliant stare.

No doubt, he *did* need Sean around. Now more than ever, Luke understood just how fragile life was. Last year, Clarke and Darien almost killed his buddy. The fact that Sean survived made Luke realize just how much he needed to keep his brother and friend close by.

Luke's head slumped momentarily, and he grew pensive. "I know I probably sound totally selfish right now, and Nicole would probably *kill* me if she heard me trying to convince the two of you to move out here." Tears gleamed in Luke's eyes. "But, we're family…," his voice broke.

Sean's eyes glimmered as well. "I would love nothing more, but you've got to give me and Nikki the chance to work it out. I don't think it's *impossible*, but we just can't up, and relocate at the drop of a hat." Sean gave Luke a knowing look. "You *know* I'm your right-hand man, and I got your back whatever you need." Sean fraternally patted Luke's shoulder.

Luke threw his arms around Sean, and gave him a rough hug. "You know I won't stop asking. Who knows? If things continue to go well, maybe Mel and I can vacation out in Sands Port sooner than we planned." Luke smiled elusively.

"That would be great! Sands Port definitely hasn't been the same without you, Melody or Cupid," Sean joked.

"*Cupid* definitely put Sands Port on the map." Luke chortled.

"He's the head dog of all of Sands Port!" Sean shook

his head humorously. "Seriously, I'm so happy for you, man! You have no idea…"

Luke beamed. "You couldn't be happier than I am. I'm so in love with Melody!" he stated emphatically. "If I'd known God would have given me a second chance with her, I wouldn't have fallen apart the way I did a year ago. I would have trusted God to guide us through the danger, the pain and the misery of being apart." Luke had an elusive expression on his face.

"Things *had* to play out that way, Luke. All in God's time and according to his plan," Sean wisely assessed.

Sean's awareness of God's control over every detail was growing every day. He was also discovering just how real Jesus Christ was, and how important it was to trust Him to lead and guide throughout one's life. Sean took nothing for granted, since his brush with death a few months ago. God had spared him, and had given him a second chance at life.

"Listen to you, *preacher man*." Luke gave Sean an impish grin. "I agree with everything you said, buddy. Things *had* to play out in the way they did, so that Melody and I could cherish our God-given love all the more. Facing that kind of danger made us all stronger."

"*Now*, it's time to put that entire nightmare behind us. I know *I* have. We *all* need to move forward. No more Clarke Vale or Darien Stiles in Melody's face-thank God," Sean assented.

Luke laughed. "Clarke who, Darien who…? As far as I'm concerned, they don't even exist. And, in light of the charges they're facing, they'll spend the rest of their natural lives in prison." Luke smiled with a sense of satisfaction. "The trial's in a few months. Still, the last thing I want to focus on is Clarke Vale and his band of thugs. I'm going to put my time and energy on being the best husband I know how to be to my new wife." Luke's eyes shimmered in affect.

Sean grabbed him playfully by the neck, and squeezed

it amicably. "Sounds like a great plan! No one deserves to be happy more than you do. You've paid your dues, buddy." Sean nodded affirmatively.

"I didn't think it was possible to love someone so much!"

"Lucky for *you* Melody loves you back."

"Am I not the luckiest…?" Luke cheered.

Just then, Peter Lawton charged back into the dressing room. Peter was all decked out in his designer tux. His dark hair and intense blue eyes played against the royal blue of his notched lapel. As one of the groomsmen, in as far as perfection, Peter looked more like a painting.

"*PM*, it's time," he announced. "*Everyone's* taken their places except for you and Sean," he huffed.

Luke nodded in compliance. He was trying hard not to laugh, because Peter was always so straitlaced. Everything was *over the top* serious. "I'll be out there before you can blink. Thanks, Pete."

"Is he always that serious?" Sean susurrated, snickering.

"For the most part. But, Pete's good people, and he's an even better worker." Luke chuckled, hoping Peter hadn't heard anything he and Sean had just said.

"So, just as soon as the processional begins…" Peter smiled at his boss, who was more like a buddy. There wasn't a better boss or person out there. So, in spite of the fact that Luke held Arianna's heart, Peter admired him immensely. Peter couldn't help noticing how enigmatic Luke looked in his wedding attire.

Peter assessed Luke was no cookie-cutter groom on top of cake model. As mysterious and esoteric as his breakthrough inventions, Luke looked just as arcane and inscrutable only moments away from getting married.

"You got it," Luke assured.

"Good luck, boss."

"Thanks, Pete."

That said, Peter turned, and coasted out of the room, leaving Luke and Sean to themselves.

"I guess, that's *my* cue to join the others out on the promenade," Sean submitted. "Can't afford to be late, and can't have *you* being all late for your own wedding," he razzed.

"Late, to marry Melody...?" Luke set his hand on his chin introspectively. "I think I'm going to have to use the Power Portal to transport us out there. That's the quickest way. It'll only take seconds," he suggested.

Shock and bewilderment covered Sean's sharp features. "You *are* kidding right?"

Luke tried to keep a straight face. "Does it *look* like I'm kidding, Sean?" he tested.

Sean's face creased in befuddlement, as he stared into the waggish eyes and expression on his buddy's face. "You are...?"

Luke smiled dismissively. "Okay, so I *am* kidding about using the Power Portal to make it to the altar but..." Mischief played on his face and in his eyes.

Sean shook his head in skepticism. "I wouldn't put anything past *you* at this point. You're just full of surprises."

Luke brows arched fiendishly, and he lowered his voice. "Just call me 'Mr. Surprise' all the way! I love the shock factor." He chuckled. "But in *this* case, I *am* actually kidding. *Today*, I will gladly take that walk over to the garden, and take my place at the altar to meet my Melody. Let's get out of here, Sean. All of a sudden, this can't happen fast enough."

"That's what *I'm* talking about, buddy. Melody's waiting for you, and we can't keep Lady Melody waiting."

"No...never."

***

In spite of the distraction of hovering helicopters, and entertainment media clambering to catch a glimpse of the highly anticipated wedding of the wealthiest man in the world, it was a perfect sunny California morning. The sun glinted potently in the velvet blue sky, and the temperature was a seasonable 80 degrees, which was a lot warmer than usual for October.

The instrumental processional music ebbed, as the groomsmen and bridesmaids took their places. They were all set to welcome the bride. And, right on cue, the wedding march began to play. There were over two hundred guests. Melody and Luke's families, and their closest friends stood to their feet in acknowledgment and honor of the bride's arrival.

The smile on Luke's face was iridescent, and tears shone in his eyes, as he waited for a glimpse of his wife-to-be. He couldn't stop thanking and praising God for such a blessing! There was so much to be thankful for. Things were finally taking shape for him and for his family. His parents, and his brother Branden were there to support him. Even his baby sister Rachel had flown in from Chicago to support him on the most important day of his life.

William Bryant was also recovering nicely from the stroke he'd suffered a year ago. Luke's brother Branden kept a tight grasp on Cupid's leash. The dog was excited and agitated to be surrounded by such a large group of people. Luckily, he wasn't barking. However, Cupid wagged his tail frenziedly and panted. Because Cupid was family, Luke couldn't leave him home on this special occasion. Furthermore, Luke recognized that Cupid's silly antics had brought Melody into his life. So, he would forever be grateful to and indebted to his fun-loving dog.

Melody finally came into plain sight for Luke. Seeing her melted his heart, and inundated his heart with joy. Sean and Calvin walked proudly on either sides of her. Tears were in Luke's eyes, because of all he felt for Melody. Remembering the obstacles and challenges they'd face leading up to this precious moment, made Luke all the more grateful to God.

There were quite a few guests gathered there, but the only person Luke saw was Melody. His eyes were fastened to hers. She smiled nostalgically at him. Her eyes were all aglow, full of affect and expectation. Luke took deep breaths in order to still his hammering heart. He quietly, yet timorously anticipated finally having her close at the altar.

Melody felt anchored and loved, as both her brother Calvin and Sean escorted her down the aisle to give her away to the man of her dreams. Her heart whisked in excitement and expectation of marrying Luke. Melody was awestruck seeing how flawless Luke looked up at the altar. He was her perfect prince charming. She could honestly say she'd never seen him look more dashing, and that was saying lot. Luke's light features were a contrast to his midnight blue tux, and made him look completely mystical.

"Chrissy, you got this. You're doing just fine," Calvin told his sister, and squeezed her hand in loving support.

"You're almost there, Melody," Sean encouraged. Melody was trembling, so he sensed her nervousness.

Melody breathed deeply as she neared the altar, oblivious to anything else. Her eyes were full of Luke, as they smiled furtively at each other. All of a sudden words were unnecessary. It was as if she and Luke's minds were attuned. Melody knew what he was thinking, and he could also read her mind.

"Who gives this woman to be joined to this man?" Pastor Theodore Porter asked, when Calvin and Sean escorted Melody up to the altar. Pastor Porter was Melody and Luke's new pastor. He pastored Overcomers Tabernacle in Burbank, and had been gracious enough to agree to officiate their wedding.

"We do," Calvin and Sean said in unison.

At that moment, Melody and Luke were finally united at the altar. Everything else faded into obscurity for the pair at that point.

"You're stunning, honey baby!" Luke said in quiet contemplation, as his eyes explored Melody's. She was a vision! Her gown flowed over her beautiful body like liquid jewels, and her upswept hair glimmered like sunlight knifing through streams of water. Luke found himself utterly spellbound, and he wondered if he'd have the strength to speak when the time came.

"I don't think I've ever seen you more handsome!" Melody said reservedly. She was totally captivated by Luke's perfection. He was a mystery in his dark navy tux. The colors on his tux were a dramatic contrast to his bronze curls and intense teal eyes.

The pastor took a moment to welcome family and friends, and expounded on the blessings of marriage. He stated it was God's gift, and not to be entered into lightly.

Soon after, he introduced his daughter Lilah Porter. Lilah was there to sing a special selection for the couple.

Lilah stood in front of the floral arch, decked out with the most ornate and fragrant arrangements. Her mist-gray gown sparkled intensely in the sunlight, as she began to sing a song entitled, *"Lonely No More."* Pastor Porter's lovely daughter was a true songstress, and sang from the heart, stirring the hearts of everyone there.

Soon after, Pastor Porter took time to expound on the true meaning of marriage. He drew reference from the book of Ecclesiastes. Ecclesiastes 4:9-16 from the King James Version of the Bible. 9. "Two are better than one because they have a good reward for their labor. 10. For if they fall, the one will lift up his fellow: but woe to him that is alone when he falleth; for he hath not another to help him up. 11. Again if two lie together, then they have heat: but how can one be warm alone? 12 And if one prevail against him, two shall withstand him; and a threefold cord is not quickly broken."

Pastor Porter emphasized how a man should love and cherish his wife according to the word of God. He reminded everyone there that a man should love his wife as Christ loved the church and gave His life for her (Ephesians 5:25-33). He then expounded on how love isn't a feeling. To the contrary, it's a choice made from day to day to honor, and love your God-given spouse in good times as well as bad.

Then, given a moment to express his heart, Luke held Melody's hands devotedly in his. Laughing with a sense of irony, he tried to express himself. "I really don't know how we got here, Mel." He shook his head in total skepticism. "It was just a walk out on the beach with Cupid. That's all it was supposed to be."

Melody stared fondly into Luke's eyes, and laughed as

well.

"How on earth could I have imagined…? How could I have fathomed that taking a walk out on the beach with my dog when we first moved to Sands Port, Maryland, would alter the course of my life forever…?

"There just aren't enough words in the English language to express how much you mean to me. I didn't think it was even possible to love someone as completely and unconditionally as *I* love you. Loving you is the easiest thing in the world, Mel. I *want* to be your best friend, your safe place to fall, your haven and your soulmate for the rest of our lives…" Tears twinkled in Luke's eyes, as he shared from the profound store of his love for her.

Melody tried not to surrender to tears, but she found herself getting emotional. "I love you so much!" she whispered, breathing spasmodically.

Luke tried to keep the tears at bay. "Love is such a small word to define, and encompass the *big* feelings I have for you, Melody Christine. Promise me that you'll stay by my side forever, because I honestly don't know how to live without you." Luke brought Melody's hands up to his lips and kissed them repeatedly. "I love you!"

"I love you, Luke!" Melody blinked back tears.

She worked through tangled emotions, because Luke's words had left her floored. Melody strove to quiet her breathing, and kept a firm grasp on Luke's hands. "You are my best friend, my safe place to fall, my anchor and my soulmate forever. I didn't think I'd ever find someone so totally perfect for me. God heard the cry of my heart all those years. He honored my prayers, and sent *you*.

"You came along, and redefined everything I thought I

needed. And, you are exactly all I'll ever want and need for the rest of my life. I finally met your parents a while back." Melody stared over at Luke's parents. They were sitting in the front row listening attentively to every word she and Luke exchanged. Luke's mom was in tears, and air-blew a kiss over at Melody.

"I love you, Mom!" Melody emphasized. "This week, I thanked your mom and dad for raising such an upstanding and wonderful man! I thanked them for teaching you how to love from your heart. Not everyone knows how to do that. So, I *know* you're something special, Luke. You mean everything to me!" Melody's voice wavered.

Luke's eyes shone in affect, and his face flushed red with love and wistfulness. "*You* mean everything to *me*, baby!" His hands brushed sensitively on hers, and he smiled into her eyes. Luke stared longingly and admiringly at Melody.

Pastor Porter shared a few more words of encouragement. He inspired faith in the hearts of everyone there before he had the couple share the sacred covenant vows of marriage.

"I Lucas William Bryant, promise to take you, Melody Christine Maxwell as my wife…" Luke slipped the gold band around Melody's finger.

Melody repeated the vows just as fervently, and slipped the gold wedding band on Luke's finger. She felt immensely proud, because their love was now sealed by God.

Silence hummed in the locale, as they finalized their solemn promises. Even the whir of helicopter blades hovering above in the clear sky above, quieted down just before Pastor Porter pronounced the couple as husband and wife.

Thunderous applause crashed, as Luke gently drew Melody into his arms. With great love and tenderness, his lips bridged hers, and he slowly yet meaningfully drank from the sweet nectar of her mouth. Videographers and the press descended like locusts in order to capture this rare moment. As the newlyweds kissed, Luke activated the Vortex to Vanish field, and encircled Melody and himself in a mesh of effervescent lights which blinked in and out. The temporary disappearance act created even more of a stir for the guests.

"Are we invisible?" Melody questioned, completely transported by their kiss. She was incredulous and surprised to see how many tricks Luke had up his sleeve.

"Yeah... We're kinda, sorta blinking in and out. So, one moment they see us, and the next..."

"You're *so* bad, Lucas William Bryant. I guess, nothing's ever status quo with you." Melody laughed in between hungry kisses from her new husband. She shook her head humorously, as they were enveloped by the luminescent rings of rainbow colors. "But, I guess that's the way I like it." She held on to him graspingly.

Luke took his time to reacquaint himself with the outline of Melody's lips. "I'm so glad I can still surprise you, Mrs. Bryant. I can't believe you're all mine." He celebrated, and crushed her lovingly in his arms. "You've made me the happiest man alive!"

"Honey bear, I think we need to stop blinking in and out. We need to sign the marriage certificates. Besides, *your* parents and *my* mom are going to kill us when we're not invisible anymore," Melody joked.

"Come back, buddy," Sean called out through the mesh of Luke and Melody's cosmic disappearing bubble.

"I can hear you just fine, Sean. It's rude to raise your voice you know," Luke teased. "Besides, Melody and I need a moment."

"Okay… I can respect that. Just wanted to congratulate the two of you!" Sean shook his head humorously.

"Thanks, Sean."

"You're welcome, buddy! I'll give you and Mel your moment, and not say another word." Sean chuckled. The one thing he *could* say about his best friend was that he was totally unpredictable. Luke didn't even tell *him* he planned a light show after he and Melody finalized their vows.

"Luke," Melody argued, "we *can't* make our great escape now. We've got to join everyone for the reception, and properly thank our family and friends for…" Luke silenced her with yet another kiss.

"Okay… Mrs. Melody Bryant. Let's blink back in, and thank our guests for all of their love, support and well wishes. But first…" Luke took a moment to steal a few more kisses, before they blinked back in to see their excited *and* bewildered guests, who weren't yet familiar with Luke's technology.

Melody and Luke were barraged by their loved ones. Family and friends took turns congratulating and loving on them. They also had to contend with the press, and virtually fought their way over to the limo. The limo would transport them over to the other side of the Quartz Castle Inn. There, they would take pictures along with the rest of the bridal party.

Regardless of the celebration and fanfare, Luke managed to stay on top of security at every turn. There was no denying or pretending. Not everyone was happy for them, and the world could often be a cruel place. So, even as they reveled in such joy, Luke resolved to keep them safe. Not only did he have to contend with old enemies like Clarke Vale and Darien Stiles, but his new status had probably ushered in a crop of new ones.

"I'm almost one hundred percent sure that the televised version doesn't do the wedding justice," Clarke told Simon Winds over the phone. As a *model* prisoner, he was finally given use of the phone. Even so, every move he made was under intense scrutiny from prison officials.

"They don't call it the Quartz Castle Inn *paradise* for nothing, Clarke. The happy couple just exchanged vows. That kid, Luke, used one of his featured inventions, and gave the guests a serious lightshow, as he kissed his new bride," Simon informed.

Clarke's blood boiled in his veins, and threatened to submerge him. Jealousy erupted on the inside like fomenting lava. And yet, he tried to uphold his composure. "What are they doing now?" he asked through gritted teeth.

"They'll eventually head over to the reception area. But first, they're going to take pictures with the wedding party on the other side of the grounds."

"Keep me posted as to every move they make. Let me say again how pleased I am that you found a way to attend the auspicious event!"

"Eugene Morrow, the head of security, is an old friend. When I told him that my family and I need a few bucks to make ends meet, he asked me to be a part of the security detail."

"I guess, your good friend-who just happens to be a fed, has absolutely no idea how much you've benefited from moonlighting and doing odd jobs. It's literally made you a millionaire," Clarke said in a snarky manner.

"Nah, he has no clue what I do on the side, and I want to keep it that way. Why is all of this so important to you, Clarke?" Simon asked boldly.

Clarke laughed in incredulity over Simon's brashness. "Ordinarily, I would tell you to back off, and stick to your job. However, I *will* answer your question. I'm in love with the girl, and I have every intention of winning her back."

"But, she just married Bryant, and she's in love with him."

"Well, all new brides are happy and in love. *Widows* not so much," Clarke said icily.

"*Widows*…?" Simon examined.

"That's the *one* mistake I made last year. I decided to *bargain* with Luke Bryant. But, not this time around. My plan isn't only to comfort his *grieving* young wife, but to take over Portals Unlimited in the same way Vale Corp was stripped away from me."

Simon shrank back hearing Clarke's words. It was the first time Clarke had divulged his plans. Simon followed every move Melody and Luke made. Melody and Luke were two extremely good-looking kids, who seemed to love each other immensely. They were so happy, and obviously couldn't keep their hands off of each other, even if they *were* surrounded by family and friends.

Simon stood all the way towards the back end of the expansive garden setting, and examined everything around him. It suddenly occurred to him that his loyalty wasn't to Luke and Melody. As nice as they seemed, Vale was the one paying him an obscene amount of money to plot against them. At that point, the voice of cash resonated louder than the voice of reason.

"Whatever you want to do is fine by me, boss," Simon emphasized. He worked past the warm and fuzzy feelings he had in respect to how loving and kind Melody and Luke seemed.

"You know *what*? I think I'm actually beginning to *like* you. I might not have you *killed* after all," Clarke said cryptically.

"What…?" Simon asked, rattled. Perspiration beaded his forehead, and he loosened his tie, as the early morning sun shimmied above.

"Ha, ha, ha… Laugh, Simon. It's a joke," Clarke derided. "Aren't you always telling me that I need to lighten up? Ha, ha, ha…," Clarke's laughter sounded as if it was coming from a deep dark tunnel.

"Oh yeah… Ha, ha, ha." Simon coughed nervously, and chuckled. "Yeah… You really got me. That's hysterical, Clarke."

***

"Pete, you're drunk. You need to go home and sleep it off. You're so lucky *PM's* on a flight headed for Fiji right now," Bryan Kent, Peter's coworker warned.

Peter waved a dismissive hand, and staggered back over to the bar. Slurring, he asked the bartender for another drink, as he clumsily hopped up on a stool set around the bar, and almost toppled off of it. He was at the wedding reception inside the Quartz Castle Inn reception hall.

"Thanks again," Peter said, when the bartender handed him the drink. Holding the glass above his head, he garbled, "This one's for every guy out there with a broken heart..."

Sean and Calvin, along with Derek and Keith, the other groomsmen followed behind Peter to make sure he was okay. Sean and Calvin didn't know Peter very well. However, they'd initially been introduced to his straitlaced, responsible and organized twin. Needless to say, they were more than shocked to see what a difference a few drinks had made. Peter's workmates were even more astounded to see their boss's right-hand man behaving so recklessly-at his boss's wedding reception no less.

"Come on, Pete. My wife and I are headed back out to Beverly Glen, along with Cupid. So, we can give you a ride over to your place." Sean set a firm hand on Peter's shoulder.

"I'm not ready to go home yet, Sean, but thanks. By the way, I had a blast hanging out with you this week! Your friendship with *PM*'s pretty cool."

Sean nodded with a sense of understanding. "Thanks. *PM's* been my buddy since middle school."

"He's the best! I guess, that's why every woman who works for Portals are crying today. He's off the market, and they'll never get to..." Peter dropped a string of expletives, and started singing a very suggestive song.

"Whoa, dude... You *really* need to go home, and sleep it off," Derek said sternly. "Pete, this isn't a good look for you right now. This is *PM's* reception." Derek cautiously removed the glass from Peter's hand, and set his hands forcefully on Peter's shoulders. "Let's get you home."

"I'll go home when I'm ready to, Derek. Now back off..."

Peter yanked away from Derek's iron-clad grip on his shoulders, while dropping a barrage of profanities, and cogently reclaiming his shot glass. Instinctively, Peter turned and looked away from the bar. His heart plunged to the floor when he saw Arianna standing feet away. She'd undeniably been watching every move he made. Peter's expression changed from self-pity to instant remorse. Surprised, he dropped the glass, and it shattered against the wooden edge of the bar.

Arianna's face was mired in disgust, condemnation and shame. Her expression relayed how sorry she felt for him, and how pathetic she thought he was. Even from a distance, her eyes gunned into his as if he were transparent. Arianna lingered on the busy dance floor for a moment. She then took a long hard look at him, turned and rushed away..

"Ari, Ari... Arianna, wait," Peter called out, and staggered after her. He stumbled, weaved and bobbed awkwardly dodging couples out on the glistening hardwood flooring. In fact, he almost knocked down a guy holding a drink, and ineptly offered an apology for splashing the bronze-colored libation on the man's pristine dark suit and white shirt.

Sean stood at a distance observing Peter's behavior. Peter was desperately following after Arianna. *"Poor guy,"* Sean judged. It then occurred to Sean that Peter had it pretty bad for the beautiful blonde. Just then, Sean made a quick decision to play damage control.

He gathered everyone, and had a stern talk with them. "*I* will tell Luke what happened this afternoon. I don't want any of you spreading any rumors, or going behind Peter's back to tell *PM*." Sean's expression was critical.

Peter's friends, and his coworkers in the wedding party, all agreed not to tell their boss that one of his top employees and good friend, got wasted at the wedding reception. *PM* was a pretty cool boss, but Peter's behavior that early afternoon was just downright disrespectful.

"Calvin, do me a favor. Please, don't tell your sister about this," Sean spoke privately to Melody's brother.

"Tell my sister about *what*?" Calvin winked at Sean to relay that he understood.

"Thanks, man."

"No worries… My sister's definitely not going to hear anything from me. Peter's just having a rough time right now."

"Tell me about it." Sean shook his head solemnly, as he skimmed over the room looking for Peter. However, Peter was nowhere to be found.

Arianna, wait. Please, don't leave…" Peter followed Arianna out to the parking area of the exclusive club. "Please, don't go home…"

At that point, he was doing all he could to counter the effects of the poor choices he'd made that afternoon. It wasn't even four in the afternoon, and he was completely *drunk*. Peter felt weak and totally incompetent. He honestly believed he would have been strong enough to handle the look on

Arianna's face during the wedding ceremony. The pain on her face and in her eyes was evident when Melody and Luke had exchanged vows. It had killed Peter, but he'd felt completely helpless to do anything about it.

Peter knew that he would have done *anything* to take Arianna's pain away. However, no matter what he did, he always wound up messing up in one way or another, and leaving a bad taste in her mouth. Peter readily acknowledged that Arianna wasn't a part of his fan club. However, after his little display over at the bar moments earlier, she'd probably lost all respect for him.

Having spent most of the wedding reception crying in the ladies room, Arianna tried to conceal her crimson eyes. She was irked to hear someone calling her name. Making a sharp turn, Arianna saw that it was Peter. There he was following her again… "What *is* it that you want, Peter?" Her face warped in misery.

Peter kept shaking his head contrarily. "I'm really sorry. What you saw in there… That's *not* really who I am." Peter zigzagged over to Arianna, and gently took hold of her right arm.

"Look, Peter, you don't owe me any explanations. It's a wedding reception, and there's a bar. Sometimes, that's too much temptation for-"

"No, no. You don't understand," Peter argued. His eyes explored Arianna's sweet face, and her crystal blue eyes. Her eyes made the sunny California skies pale in comparison. "I'm ashamed to have you see me this way, because I have a great deal of respect for you."

The stench of alcohol on Peter's breath made Arianna

shrink back in disgust. She firmly reclaimed her arm from his gentle grasp. A leery and mistrustful expression covered her face. "Okay… I'm happy to hear how much you respect me. I respect you too, and I think you're great at your job." She tried not to flinch.

Peter forced a smile. "You *really* think I'm great at my job, and you respect me?" Peter stammered.

Arianna nodded, and suppressed the deep sorrow bubbling just underneath the surface. Luke was married to Melody. Her hopes and dreams of ever having him were shattered. *Where's the car they said would be out here waiting for me? They said prompt service. Come on, can you get here already. I just want to find a safe place to cry. Can't you see that I just want to be alone right now, Peter? Why is it that you always have these epiphanies whenever I need to be alone?*

In spite of her frustration, Arianna remembered how understanding Peter was on the day before. He'd allowed her to leave the office early. So, she tried to tolerate him for a few more minutes, as she waited on her ride. "Yes, of *course* I respect you. You do a bang-up job running the department, and *PM* also thinks the world of you!" she heartened.

Arianna caught a glimpse of Peter's dramatic dark blue eyes, which shimmered like pools of water against the backdrop of the sunny afternoon. It suddenly occurred to her just how *sad* he was.

"Yeah, *PM's* a great boss and friend, but… He really *doesn't* deserve you know," Peter said deliberately, as fresh tears surfaced in his eyes.

"*What* did you just say?" Arianna's face warped in bewilderment and exasperation. "What are you talking about?" She tensed up defensively.

"I *know* you're in love with him, Ari-"

"You have no idea what you're talking about, and I'm *not* having this conversation. You know absolutely nothing about my relationship with Luke. He's my *boss* for crying out loud!" Arianna shouted, incensed. She stared nervously and agitatedly around for any indication that the car they'd promised to send was nearby.

Peter held his hand out in a halting manner, and tried to explain. "I'm sorry. I really didn't mean to upset you." He sighed. "Ari, it's obvious you love him, but he honestly doesn't deserve you. He married Melody today. I don't know how *anyone* could walk away from *you*. You're so special!" Peter's face strained in melancholy.

Arianna's heart fell in misery, and the tears she'd fought so hard to conceal ambled down her cheeks. Her chest rose and fell dramatically, and her breathing was labored.

"You don't know anything, Peter Lawton. Please, leave me alone, and mind your own business. Yes, I *know PM* married Melody today. We're at their wedding reception. But, of course, you're probably too drunk to realize it," she said, shaming him. Arianna darted away, because the black luxury car had finally pulled up to the front gate. The driver had word with security.

Arianna's words impaled Peter's heart like a merciless spear. He stood outside of the Quartz Castle Inn reception hall feeling totally useless. His entire world seemed to be tottering out of control. No matter how hard he tried he always messed up. Furthermore, he realized that he'd probably overstepped in respect to what he'd just told Arianna. He felt both ashamed and remorseful that he'd rushed out to talk to her while intoxicated.

No doubt, he'd just added insult to injury. Not only did Arianna hate his guts, but at that point, she probably perceived he was an alcoholic. Peter watched Arianna rush away in order to confirm her ride. He couldn't escape how surreally beautiful she looked in her flowing sangria-colored gown. The dress dripped with gleaming blood red stones in the blazing afternoon sunlight. And yet, in spite of all of his blunders, he couldn't help thinking she was the most perfect creature he'd ever laid eyes on. Peter knew that nothing and no one, not even Arianna herself, could ever make him feel any differently.

***

The picturesque scenery of their private cottage out in Fiji was postcard perfect. Melody stood out on the deck, and watched the sun dip into the aqua waters for a much needed swim. Dusk also waved goodbye, as the balmy night air caressed her skin, and the rush of ocean waves reeled to and fro on the shoreline. It was a sense of serenity she'd never experienced before.

Melody felt an unmistakable sense of tranquility, because she was finally married to Luke. It took a minute to wrap her head around being Luke's wife. For a long time, it seemed as if this day would never come. So, Melody worshiped God for making her dream come true. Being married, and having someone to share a honeymoon night with had been a lifelong dream. Melody was also grateful that she and Luke had waited for marriage in order to share intimacy. So, that night out in Fiji was all the more special and sacred.

The robe of her champagne rose-colored negligee fluttered in the wind, and Melody cradled her shoulders, in an effort to shy away from the cool ocean breezes. Uncertain as to why, she was just a little nervous.

This was a totally different chapter in her story. She and Luke were about to cross over a new threshold. It was the very first time they'd been alone in this way. Although they'd always been madly in love, they were finally free to express that love on a deeper level. Melody trembled with intensity over the prospect. Yet and still, in spite the uncertainties, she loved Luke so much, she yearned to demonstrate her feelings for him in depth.

"Hey, honey baby! What are you doing out here all by yourself?" Luke's voice was throaty. His hand on Melody's waist was firm, yet gentle, as he shifted her body towards himself.

Melody was overpowered by how enticing Luke looked bare-chested. He had on a pair of smoke-gray silk pajama bottoms. Judging just how naturally toned her husband was, Melody set her hands on his chest, and massaged its stalwart contours. For so long she had desired to be closer to him, and it felt heavenly.

"I was waiting for *you*, honey bear," Melody said softly, and surrendered to the arms of her husband. "It was so well worth the wait." Melody lost herself in Luke's mystical blue eyes.

"I couldn't wait to come out to *you*, honey baby. I'm sorry that I kept you waiting, my love," Luke whispered in her ear. "I just wanted to smell nice for you. Did I succeed?" Luke covered the contours of Melody's face with honey kisses, and buried his head in her fragrant bed of hair.

"Uh-huh…," Melody susurrated with her head propped up to Luke's chest. "You smell wonderful! I missed you so much!"

"I missed you too, baby, but I don't think I was gone *that* long," Luke teased, cradling Melody in his arms, and holding her acquisitively. He issued a deep sigh. "I can't believe you're *really* mine. I've prayed, hoped and dreamed…"

Luke pulled away just enough to stare into Melody's eyes. However, his arms still acquisitively encircled her waist. Tears gleamed in his eyes, as he evaluated how dreamy Melody looked against the backdrop of the cobalt blue sky, and the off-white pearl pasted on it.

"I've wanted to be with you for such a long time. I'm so glad God answers prayer." Melody cradled Luke's head in her hands, and plowed her fingers through his frosted golden curls. She reached up, and pressed her lips softly on his. "I love you so much!" Tears sparkled in her eyes, as she trembled.

"Oh, honey, I love you more!" Luke gently took hold of her hands, and slipped them about his waist. Staring devotedly into her eyes, he cradled her face. "Are you scared? You *know* you never have to be afraid with me. Mel, I would never do anything that wasn't right for you, or that would in any way hurt you." Luke tenderly kissed the contours of her face.

"I know that, honey bear. I'm *not* scared. I guess, I *am* a little anxious," Melody admitted, as she stared intuitively up into his eyes.

"You don't have to be, baby. We've got our entire lives to be together. Honestly, all I want is to keep you close forever. I love you so much!"

The two held each other potently but silently for a moment.

Luke then gingerly pulled away. His eyes intently explored Melody's. "Come here..." He swallowed the chunk lodged in his throat, as he took Melody's hand in his.

Melody silently and compliantly allowed Luke to lead them back into their bedroom within the cottage. Luke then conveyed her over to their bed, and had her sit down for a moment. Shutting the picture glass windows, he dimmed the lights.

Luke then coasted back over to Melody. She sat quietly on the bed as he'd asked. There was so much he wanted to say, but he suddenly found himself at a loss for words. Melody looked breathtaking in her champagne rose negligee. Her hair cascaded down her shoulders, and the lips he could never get enough of beckoned to him like a furtive song.

"I've wanted this night for so long. I've wanted *you* for so long, Melody Bryant!" Luke celebrated. "I *really* like the sound of...Melody Bryant."

Melody laughed, but her eyes shimmered sentimentally. She gently took Luke's face in her hands. "I *love* the sound of Melody Bryant too. I'm so in love with you!"

"I adore you, Mel!" Luke basked in the warmth of Melody's caress. He explored her eyes in awe and wonder. "I have something for you."

Melody respired in surprise. "You have something for *me*?" She marveled.

"Uh-huh."

Luke stood to his feet, and walked across the room. He accessed one of the dresser drawers. Opening it up, he pulled out a fancy gold, engraved deep, brown-colored music box. Luke smiled delightfully, as he appraised how royal the music box looked. He turned, and walked back over to Melody.

Melody was already in tears, and couldn't believe Luke had a gift for her on their wedding night. He'd already given her so many presents since she'd joined him out in California. "Luke, what is this?" She clutched her chest, gasping in utter incredulity.

Luke took her hand, and helped her off the bed. "Please, just open it." He shook his head contrarily, relaying she not object.

"Okay," Melody acceded. She took the box Luke tendered, and cautiously opened it up. On the inside was the most breathtaking garnet bracelet. The stones were a deep blood red, and the heart designed garnets outlined by diamonds left her absolutely breathless. However, that's not what brought tears to Melody's eyes. The music box was playing a certain tune. It was one Melody was all too familiar with from Michael Jackson's *"Off the Wall" album; "She's out of My Life."*

The song was reminiscent of the night they shared their first kiss out in Sands Port. She and Luke had taken turns singing the Karaoke version of that song. Tears snaked down Melody's cheeks, and she clutched her heart sentimentally. "Luke, it's so beautiful! You're so wonderful! I can't believe you remembered."

"How *could* I ever forget our first kiss? I can't forget

anything about you, Melody…about us." Luke caressed Melody's face sweetly.

"Will you help me put on the bracelet?"

"Of course, I will."

Luke delicately took the music box out of Melody's hand, and removed the bracelet from it. The tune was still in progress, so Luke decided to let it play. However, in a tractable manner he adjusted the bracelet on her left wrist.

"I love it!" Melody's heart rose and fell dramatically, as she studied the exquisite piece of jewelry on her wrist.

"I love you!" Luke manipulated her back into his arms, and swayed her body in a quiet rhythm. Pressing in close, he softly sang the tune of *"She's out of my Life"* in her ear; *"I made her my wife. I made her my wife, and I am the happiest man in the world, because I found my precious pearl. So, for the rest of my life… I made her…my…wife… Hmm, Hmm…,"* Luke's harmonious voice pealed in Melody's ear, and got her laughing.

"Is it any wonder why I fall more in love with you ever day, you silly nut!" Melody threw her arms around her husband, and held on possessively.

"Is that *so*? Well, *I* fall more in love with you every second! It's true you know," Luke's voice broke. "I *am* the happiest man in the world since I found you!" He stared lovingly into her eyes.

"*I'm* the luckiest…" Melody didn't get to finish her train of thought, because Luke's mouth bridged compellingly to hers. Exigently drinking from the source of her mouth, Luke kissed her in abandon.

Delicately taking Melody up into his arms, he quiescently laid her on the bed. Tenderly and with immense love, he kissed every inch of her, and cradled her in his arms. Before taking a journey into the arcane regions of their newly found *love realm*, he had to know that she was okay. "Are you scared, honey?"

"Not with you. I'm *never* scared with you," Melody whispered into his ear. "I just can't get close enough to you right now," she said between explosive embraces.

"I've wanted this so long... I've wanted *you*, Melody. I'm never going to let you go."

"Promise you never will." Melody surrendered to Luke's devoted and caring hands.

"Nothing and no one *will* or *can* pull me away from you." Luke activated the Power Portal, and enclosed Melody and himself in the private secure world of **Dimension Four.** They were blanketed like two children by vivid lights and the power of the field. "Tonight is just you and me, honey baby. I literally want the world to go away for a while."

"That's what I want too. I just want to be with you," Melody susurrated, and lost herself in the secure grasp of her husband. They hovered over the material world-firmly held by the power of the portal. Melody was too overwhelmed to speak, because she was consumed by the flames of her husband's desire. The resonating vortex, which ignited more fervently than the maelstrom lights swirling around them blazed. Now that she was able to express her feelings for Luke in this whole new way, Melody knew she'd never want to be with anyone else.

Chapter Three

"Notorious pharmaceutical mogul, and mafia lord Clarke Vale, was found dead in his jail cell early this morning from an apparent suicide. The former pharmaceutical tycoon was found hung in in his jail cell. There are still speculations as to how he was able to access a power cord. So far, there hasn't been any evidence to suggest foul play.

"The billionaire/mafia lord was scheduled to stand trial in a matter of months for a string of charges, ranging from second degree murder to blackmail and extortion. It is alleged that the infamous crime lord wanted to evade trial, as he was staring at consecutive life sentences. So, he probably took what he considered to be the easy way out.

"Vale's body was removed from his jail cell a few hours ago. An autopsy will be performed to assess if drugs played a role at the time of his death. We will keep you posted in the days ahead in as far as the toxicology report. Again, Clarke Vale was found dead in his jail cell early this morning. We will bring you more on this story as it develops…," CNN reporters detailed what had the entire world up in arms in October of that year.

"That reporter did a fantastic job! It actually sounds authentic," Clarke told Simon, as he listened to CNN News. They were both relaxing out on the veranda of Dr. Anselm Felix's medical complex on an island on the Adriatic Coast on the outskirts of Croatia. Dr. Felix was an expert in the field of Bioengineering. Clarke had managed to escape jail, cleverly disguised by prison officials. Moreover, he'd been given carte blanche to travel under another identity.

"I've *got* to say, you made a believer out of me, CV!"

Clarke laughed dissolutely. "Even if *I* guided you every step of the way, you *still* doubted me, Simon. That's truly insulting." Clarke gave him a reproachful look.

"Sorry about that, Clarke. The plan seemed so outlandish, you know. All the same, I've got to say you covered all your bases."

"Don't I *always*?"

"What about Stiles?"

"What about *him*?" Clarke hissed.

"Well, aren't you going to help him out of jail?"

"I guess, I *could* throw him a bone, once I make my comeback in America."

"That's downright decent, Clarke."

"Well, Darien and I go way back. You can say he's the Bonnie to my Clyde, so of speak." Booming laughter issued from the hollow of Clarke's throat, like forceful waters gushing through a pipe.

Simon laughed as well. "Yeah... I guess, Darien would have to be *Bonnie*. Ha, ha, ha..." He shook his head in total incredulity, and amazement over Clarke's maneuvers.

Simon still couldn't believe Clarke was out of prison. The disreputable mogul had bribed the warden and other prison officials with millions, in order to fake his own death-suicide by hanging in his jail cell. As it went, he was far too depressed to go on after losing Vale Corp. Notwithstanding, he'd refused to stand trial, because he was facing multiple life sentences. It was brilliant!   Notwithstanding, Arnold Willis and Seth Nugent, heads of the prison had to substantiate a body. So, they'd called in a few favors from Sands Port

Correctional, and won their bingo game. A recent stabbing had claimed the life of an inmate, and the victim fit Clarke's description in as far as hair coloring, height and build.

So, for the sake of the press, a fake picture had been doctored with the man's body hanging in the jail cell with Clarke's photo-shopped face on it. Now more than ever, Simon realized Clarke Vale was notorious for a number of reasons. Furthermore, he realized that he had to tread a bit more cautiously now that the man was out of jail.

"How are you doing underneath those bandages?" Simon evaded the subject. The last thing he wanted to talk about was how he'd underestimated, and had doubted Clarke Vale.

"It's uncomfortable. The skin is still a little irritated, but Dr. Felix said they come off tonight, so I am both hopeful and grateful."

"I can't believe you're going to have a whole new look. Aren't you a little freaked out by that?" Simon asked thoughtlessly, realizing instantly how stupid his question sounded.

Clarke worked past his annoyance, and didn't even bother answering Simon's inane question. Simon Winds was a fool, and Clarke planned to shake the man off just as soon as he could. When he no longer needed Simon, it was his plan to sever ties…*permanently.*

Clarke's face, upper torso, including his arms and hands, were wrapped in bandages as a result of Dr. Felix's procedure. He'd submitted to the biochemical genetic transformational procedure that only Dr. Felix could perform. Clarke had paid the good doctor millions in order to secure a permanent change of identity. Granted, it *was* prickly having bandages covering his face and other parts of his body, but Clarke *could* tolerate it for a little while longer. That very night, Dr. Felix would remove the bandages, and Clarke would get to see his new face. He'd requested that Dr. Felix, an expert in facial reconstruction and cloning, make him unrecognizable to the world.

Dr. Felix was the *go-to* person for anyone who had enough money to pull a disappearing act from the world. He had cloned a number of subjects, who had successfully maintained their existence below the mainstream radar. So, when Clarke had heard about Dr. Felix, he had to find a way to connect to him. However, cloning wasn't something Clarke had wanted to submit to. However, he now had a brand-new identity. Moreover, thanks to a number of friends on the outside world, he was now resuming the identity of a man named Emery Lloyd. The *real* Emery Lloyd had dropped off the face of the earth years ago. Lucky for Clarke, the young eccentric had no family and no heirs.

As a result of his disappearance, there were a number of bank accounts containing billions of dollars left untouched. Even if most of Clarke's trust funds had been seized, and his assets frozen, he had a number of other accounts in Europe that he still had access to. So, amassing some of his *old* wealth, and also Emery Lloyd's *new* wealth, would keep him in nice things for a while so to speak.

"You're free to take a look in the mirror now, Clarke," Dr. Felix said with a sense of pride. He set the bandages to the side, after removing them from Clarke's face, and from parts of his body. "I don't think I've ever done better work!" he assessed in a heavy South Slavic accent.

Clarke smiled clemently, as he walked over to the full-length mirror within the grand hall of Dr. Felix's secluded mansion. At first, Clarke flinched, shocked from seeing his reflection in the mirror for the first time. However, it was a *good* shock to see his new face. He looked at least ten years younger. In fact, his face was as smooth and wrinkleless as a baby's bottom. Moreover, as if that were even possible, he was even better looking than ever before.

Clarke touched the contours of his face in total amazement. He was enthralled by how good-looking he was. His eyes hadn't changed. They were still the deep blue cups of water they'd always been. However, the contours of his face, his cheekbone structure, his nose, jawline and lips were more pronounced and astonishingly more appealing.

Clarke kept nodding in approval. "Yes... Yes... I believe this *just might* be your best work, Dr. Felix!" Clarke was unable to stop staring at his reflection. "I think I'm in love with the new me!" he delighted.

Dr. Felix stared at his subject in quiet contemplation. He was utterly pleased with himself. Clarke Vale was a good-looking man before, but now he was a complete masterpiece. Dr. Felix felt a tremendous sense of dignity knowing that he'd created such an intriguing work of art.

"You look like a brand-new man, Clarke Vale, a man at least ten years younger!"

"Yes, I know." Clarke smiled deliriously. Rushing over to Dr. Felix, he grasped a hold of the man's right hand, and shook it in utter euphoria. "I can't thank you enough for this. I *will* pay you an extra twenty percent than what we originally agreed on."

Dr. Felix laughed, and shook Clarke's hand fervidly. "So, I'm guessing you're pleased...," he said facetiously.

"*Pleased* doesn't even begin to cover how revitalized I feel. That's exactly what this is. This *is* a revival...a *resurrection*!" Clarke rushed back over to the mirror literally skipping in delight.

"Would you like to call Mr. Winds in, so that he can see the new you?" Dr. Felix asked discreetly.

Clarke made a sharp turn towards Dr. Felix. "No. Mr. Winds will get to see the new me in the morning. If it's all the same to you, I'd like to have tonight all to myself. I'd like a chance to acclimate to all of the changes-that is if you know what I *mean*?"

"Of course... I will leave you to yourself."

"I appreciate that, Dr. Felix," Clarke said, never once turning away from the mirror.

"With you being so young and handsome, I can only imagine that the women will be all over you." Dr. Felix gave him a knowing wink through the mirror.

Clarke turned to face the man. "No...no...the ladies...Well, there's actually only *one* woman I am interested in."

"Well, no doubt you're finally going to win her heart," Dr. Felix inspired, with a smile brighter than a harvest moon.

Clarke nodded in concurrence. "From your lips to God's ears... That's exactly what I'm counting on." His face stretched into a contemplative smile. His head was spinning in respect to a hundred different ways he could reconnect to Melody, and to pull her away from Luke Bryant. With his new damning good looks, the art of seduction would be so much easier.

Clarke was up with the sun, and essentially felt like a new man. How different he looked was empowering. And quite soon, he would have the world as his oyster. Dr. Felix had been up with the sun working in his lab, but Simon Winds was still asleep. There was a breakfast table set out on the colonnade which overlooked the ocean. The greyish-white foamy waves fizzled onto the shoreline in cadences, and the balmy winds made the palm trees sway against the rhapsody of the rushing waters.

Velda, Dr. Felix's live-in help, ventured out onto the colonnade, and came close to dropping the tray of breakfast Danishes, when she saw Clarke sitting out there alone. From the look on her face, Clarke ascertained the woman had absolutely no idea who he was.

"I apologize, Sir. I didn't know the doctor had a *new* guest. Is there anything special I can get for you?" she asked politely.

Clarke was pleased as punch. "The garnishes on the table will do just fine thank you," he said cordially. Watching the older woman walk away clutching her chest, Clarke assumed she was both shocked and bewildered.

Clarke shook his head, tickled and amused, because he'd passed the test. No one would *ever* recognize him. Moreover, by the time he left the medical complex out in Croatia, even his voice would be *different*. Nevertheless, he had to get the ball rolling right away for *phase two* of his plan. Clarke pulled out a cellphone, and put in a phone call to America.

"You've reached Portals Unlimited. This is Peter Lawton-director and head of public relations. I'm away from

my desk right now, but if you leave me a brief message…

"No messages for now, *Peter*. However, I *do* look forward to speaking with you in person quite soon." Clarke smiled artfully in anticipation of seeing Melody again. He could honestly say at that juncture that the goal was almost within reach.

***

Luke held Melody comfortingly on the plane headed back for the United States from Australia. Since they'd heard about Clarke Vale's suicide, Melody had been eerily silent. Clarke Vale was the embodiment of evil. However, neither Luke nor Melody could have ever imagined things playing out in this way.

Melody buried her head in Luke's chest and sobbed.

"It's all right, baby… I promise. It's going to be okay," Luke placated. Tears shone in his eyes as well, because he grasped why Melody was so broken up about the matter. Luke understood that in spite of all Clarke had put them through that year, he was someone Melody was close to for a while.

Melody pulled away, and her tears-filled eyes connected melancholically to Luke's. "Clarke was a total monster. All the same, I'd hoped and prayed that he would turn his life around-even open up his heart to a relationship with Jesus." Melody kept shaking her head inanely. "Why do some people *choose* evil, when they're given a choice between right and wrong?"

Luke rubbed Melody's shoulders in pacification. "I don't know, Mel. I know you'd hoped and prayed for Clarke to become a better person." Luke shook his head in the negative. "The truth is that we may never know why people make certain choices. But, Jesus talked about that in the gospels. He talked about good fruit and evil fruit. He said that there are those who are just evil. They can't relate to, or do good-even if they want to." (Matthew 7:15-20)

Luke shrugged mindlessly. "It's tragic Clarke Vale decided to end his life that way. Honestly, I can't say that I feel sorry for him, Mel. Clarke made his choice a long time ago." Luke's head bridged lovingly to Melody's.

"Please, don't let this break your heart, honey baby. We've been sad for far too long. It's time to put the past behind us and enjoy God's blessings." Luke sighed. "We need to look at it from a different perspective. With Clarke out of the way, we have one less monster who has to face trial for hurting so many innocent people. At this point, we have to focus on ensuring that Darien and the others are put away for good. Okay…?" Luke supported Melody's head in his hands, and pressed kisses to her face.

"It's just sad." Melody shook her head in denial. "Such a waste of life"

"Sad it *is*, my love. We only get this *one* life-this *one* chance to get it right. It *is* sad how so many people make such poor choices. I am grateful to God that we were some of Clarke's last casualties. We have to look at it this way, honey baby. Clarke's reign of terror in the lives of countless victims has ended."

Melody nodded. "I wish that I'd never gotten close to

him." Remorse and regret creased on her face. Melody still tussled with feelings of shame, because she'd given Clarke a foothold in her life, when Luke had left Sands Port last year. Turning her head in the opposite direction, more tears rolled down her cheek.

Luke gently pulled her to himself, and clasped her face in his hands. "That's all over and done with, baby." He propped his face to hers. "Things played out in the way God wanted them to. Remember Romans 8:28. 'All things *do* work together for good to those who love God.' We don't have to revisit that place, Mel. It was a terrible time for both of us. So, please let it go. I *never* want to hear you condemn yourself for what happened. You forgave *me* for leaving Sands Port last year. So, you need to forgive yourself. Clarke would have stopped at nothing to have you. You *do* get that don't you?" he questioned.

Melody nodded. "I love you so much! I just wish I knew then how things were going to play out. I would have never..." She shook her head contrarily.

"Neither of us knew what was going to happen, and so we both did things we aren't proud of. But, baby, it's time to put it all behind us." Luke guffawed with a sense of skepticism. "It's all over now, honey baby. So, we move on from *that* chapter of our lives, and embrace this new one." He covered her face in tender kisses.

Melody threw her arms around him, and held on for dear life. "How did I ever get this lucky?" She pelted Luke's lips, his face and head with loving kisses.

Luke laughed. "I ask *myself* that question every single day. I asked myself that question for the past couple of weeks, waking up beside you. I love you more than life itself! And honey baby, no matter what we have to face, we will do it together."

"I never want to be apart from you again." Melody rested her head on Luke's strong shoulder. He was the only one who could help her sort through her tangled feelings in respect to her past relationship with Clarke Vale and his ostensible suicide.

Melody dozed off resting tranquilly on Luke's shoulder on their extended flight back to America. Luke whipped out his phone in deliberation. He thought about sending Sean a quick text, but desisted, realizing it would be a waste of time, because they were traveling across the Atlantic Ocean. There was something totally unsettling about Clarke Vale's *apparent* suicide. The entire matter was completely untenable.

Luke couldn't process how someone as narcissist and egomaniacal as Clarke Vale could ever commit suicide. He had read the news, and had seen the footage from the jail, but there was something totally off about all of it. The Clarke Vale he remembered loved himself far too much to even mess around with a hangnail. So, Luke couldn't even imagine the man wrapping a cord around his neck, and ending his life.

Since he couldn't use his cell on the plane, Luke made a mental note to contact Sean just as soon as he and Melody got back to California. He tried not to allow the matter to rattle him, as he stared down at Melody, who was sleeping peacefully in his arms. She meant the world to him, and for both their sakes, he had to ensure that Clarke Vale was indeed dead.

***

"With the development of *Dimension Shield Me,* we did run into a bit of red tape. It was just as complicated to obtain a Copyright for *Shield Me* as it was for *Dimension Find Me* and its components. It's taken quite a while, but *Shield Me* technology*'s* finally set in place, and should be viable in a matter of weeks. The failsafe security buffer will be used to cover individuals and objects for up to 30 feet in diameter, and extends unlimited protection in respect to altitude. Those were the findings of recent tests.

"However, as the program continues to develop, I am confident that it will hold the capacity to cover neighborhoods, cities and even countries. Its activated censor can potentially detect the negative intent of others. Just as a Polygraph picks up on physiological changes, *Shield Me* does the same. However, the censor is considerably more advanced. *Shield Me* deciphers human emotions, and locks them in for protection when evil intent is perceived. When the indicator senses harm from the outside world, it automatically creates an impenetrable shield to the user," Luke explicated at an early office meeting on the first day back from his two-week honeymoon. Only his top Portals employees were present, and made privy to the latest in technology.

Luke already had separation anxiety from Melody after a honeymoon of sheer paradise. That was the extent to which he missed his new wife. Luckily, Melody wasn't too far away. As the supervisor of the Graphics Designs Department, she was only a few floors down from his. Melody was still passionate about her work in as far as interior designs. However, she now generated business via the internet through her website *Melody's Masterpieces.*

Luke was inundated by memories of being away with Melody. Images of their sun-drenched days in Fiji, sightseeing out in Australia, and making love until they fell asleep in each other's arms, flooded his thoughts. It was an even greater challenge to focus on running Portals, because it was busier than ever. All the same, Luke understood that running a multibillion-dollar industry required multibillion dollar attention.

And, it was his intention to keep **Dimension Four** ahead of the game. So far, they were light years ahead of the competition. The only annoying factor was that most of their technology had to be vetted through the federal government. And even if they were all eager to launch their new brand, Luke had to keep reminding his team of how top secret their technological breakthroughs were.

"So, are you sure we'll be able to make *Dimension Shield Me* an official brand in a matter of weeks?" Peter's face strained in uncertainty.

"Give or take. We're hoping for sooner rather than later," Luke told him. "Still, I'm sure you're aware that government regulations are so stringent for fear of our technology falling into the wrong hands. You know the drill. Just as soon as the program is regulated, and extensively tested, we'll be given clearance to move forward."

Luke paused for a moment, and skimmed over the room. It dawned on him that his top rep was missing. "Has anyone seen or heard from Ari all morning?"

"Sorry, *PM*, I forgot to mention that Ari called earlier on. She said she was running behind schedule," Brenda Fields, one of Portals top managers told Luke.

Luke nodded and smiled faintly. He decided to move the meeting along, but he *was* a little worried about Arianna. It was totally unlike her to miss a meeting, or to come in late.

"I wish we had the authority to bypass all the government red tape, and move forward now. All of these guidelines are stifling. They make it so *hard*. Then, we have to decipher a bunch of jargon, before we can start marketing our brand." Peter shook his head inanely, and sighed in frustration.

"You're right, Peter. It's all very tedious, and costs millions, but we have to play it by their rules. I'm excited about *Shield Me* too," Luke explained. "I'm especially excited to see how law enforcement does away with the dated use of bulletproof vests and protective gear. If we're allowed to move forward, the military, the police, FBI and Secret Service, will have access to a shield capable of protecting themselves, and those feet away in the line of fire."

"No doubt, once they realize what *Shield Me* is, and what it's capable of doing, they'll be clambering over our gates to get their hands on Portals' latest groundbreaking telecommunication." Peter nodded in satisfaction. "This is huge, and stands to make billions!"

Luke smiled quietly, then addressed the group, "The latest in Portals' technology needs to be lucrative, because I want to keep you all in nice things." He gave a clever wink. A hum of laughter filled the room, and got him laughing as well.

"Let me just take a moment to thank all of you for the awesome work you've done in helping me develop our latest in technology. You make me proud every single day!" Luke pronounced. He was stirred to tears. "My only regret is that Arianna missed our meeting this morning. But, I'll fill her in later on how we've decided to tweak *Shield Me* in order to pass government guidelines."

Peter momentarily looked away from Luke after hearing him say Arianna's name. It felt like a knife to the heart. Flashes of his atrocious behavior at the wedding reception came rushing back to his thoughts. Since that horrible display, Arianna hadn't even looked at or spoken to him. Peter baulked in shame, because of the way he'd unscrupulously confronted her about her feelings for Luke. He regretted making such a poor decision. Peter now realized just how out of line he was.

Peter liked and respected his boss immensely. However, he hated how clueless Luke seemed to be in respect to the way he was hurting Arianna. Peter didn't know if he could successfully restrain from calling his boss out on the matter.

"So, I will keep you all posted in regards to *Shield Me.* You all know the drill and the preliminaries. Once it's all said and done, Portals will be free to equip the world with yet another groundbreaking tool that will launch us further out into the future," Luke addressed the group. They applauded in response. "Thank you for your time this morning," he said graciously, and simultaneously adjourned their conference.

Luke stepped out of the conference hall, and started back for his office. As he coasted through the hallway, he could no longer resist the urge to hear Melody's voice. So, he autodialed her number on his phone.

"Good morning! Portals Graphics and Designs, this is Melody speaking," Melody primly responded.

"Good morning, Mrs. Bryant!" Luke's cheeks flushed red, and he picked up the pace, as he passed through the general office area.

"Good morning, Mr. Bryant!" Melody sat down in the comfortable armchair in her private office.

"*Mr. Bryant*? I'm the *Portal Master* remember?" Luke teased.

"Good morning, *Luke*!" Melody badgered and laughed.

Luke shook his head amused. "I knew you would look at me differently after you saw me in my PJ's. You can't even bring yourself to call me the *Portal Master* anymore." He frowned facetiously.

Melody chuckled again. "I have a news flash for you, *PM*. Most of your employees have seen you in your PJ's on your fun Fridays. But what *I've* got on you is a little bit more incriminating."

"What is it that you *think* you have on me, Mrs. Bryant?" Luke rose playfully to the occasion.

"Well, I just may have pictures of the boss wearing *Iron Man* PJ's. And, it isn't outside the realm of possibility that those pictures *might* fall into the wrong hands. Don't be surprised if they're circulating around here within the next few days."

"You wouldn't?" Luke challenged.

"Oh, wouldn't I, now?"

"Man, I just *can't* win with you, can I?" Luke complained, standing only feet away from his office. "You're really cutthroat."

"I'm not as mean as you might think. I would *never* cut your throat. I love you way too much!"

Luke shook his head humorously. "I love you too, baby. But, please don't send those pictures to anyone," he said, only half joking."

Melody laughed. "Okay… I won't send the pictures to anyone…at least not today."

"You're *so* mean, Mel." Luke feigned hurt feelings.

"I *am* really mean, but I do miss you so much!" her voice pealed like bells.

"You miss me? Baby, I can't even describe how much I miss you. I want to just come down there…" Luke let himself into his office, and carefully shut the set of double doors.

"I want to see you too, honey bear…but duty calls," Melody quickly added. "Will you let me take you out for lunch a little later, *PM*?" she asked properly.

Luke's smile brightened. "Why Mrs. Bryant, are you making romantic advances towards your boss? Don't you know this kind of behavior is frowned upon in the workplace?"

"Not if the boss happens to be my husband…"

Luke took his place behind his desk, and immediately noticed a white envelope on his desk with Arianna's name on it.

"Luke, are you still there?" Melody asked, puzzled that he didn't have a quick and clever rejoinder.

Worry creased Luke's face, as he picked the envelope up and examined it. "I'm still here, baby. So, if the boss's your husband, *I* might not *frown* as much," Luke joshed, still studying the letter in his hand, befuddled.

"So, is that a yes? Will you let me take you out to lunch?"

"It would be an *honor* to have lunch with you today,

beautiful! Let me tie up a few loose ends up here, and then I will literally jump down to the fourth floor to see you."

"Or you can take the elevator like everyone else."

"I *could* do that," Luke joked. "But, it wouldn't be as much fun."

"Okay…," Melody said curiously. "So, I'm going to go ahead and take that as a yes." She cheered.

"I can't wait to see you...," Luke's voice was throaty.

"You're not behaving *professionally* right now, *PM.*"

"You're right. I'll try to keep my feelings for you, Mrs. Bryant, under wraps. And, I will do my best to behave like a conventional boss around here."

"Well, that's good to know, *PM,*" Melody said delightfully.

"Mel…?"

"Yes, *PM,*" she said primly.

"I love you!"

"I love you more!"

Luke's smile was irrepressible after speaking to Melody. He was overjoyed! Not only did she support all of his endeavors, but she'd gotten onboard herself. It made him immensely happy knowing Melody wasn't too far away. It took tremendous restraint for Luke *not* to take the elevator down to the fourth floor in order to spend time with her, but he was determined to remain strong-at least until lunchtime.

Luke stared at the envelope Arianna had left on his

desk. He was stumped, because he and Arianna were in the habit of *talking*. No longer deliberating, he opened it up, pulled a letter out from it, and read. When he got done, Luke pushed back into his comfortable armchair and sighed.

He then instinctively reached for the office phone, and dialed Arianna's extension.

"Portals, this is Arianna speaking," Arianna said professionally.

Luke was happy to hear her voice. "Good morning, Ari! Listen, when you get a moment, can you stop in to see me? No…everything's fine. I just wanted to talk. I'll be in here waiting."

Arianna froze up, because Luke asked to see her. She had stopped in his office while he was in conference, and had left her letter of resignation on his desk. Unable to stop thinking about the matter, she decided to go see him right away. Her heart pulsed, as she hiked over to Luke's office. Arianna wasn't only nervous because she was unsure of how to explain her decision, but she had no idea how she'd handle seeing Luke again. He and Melody had been on their honeymoon for a little over two weeks, and a lot had happened since then.

Luke had treated her like family from the start, and in many ways like the older brother she'd never had. Luke had also been kind enough to fly her out to California, and *created* a position for her in his multibillion-dollar empire. Notwithstanding, since she'd been there, he'd looked out for her in so many ways. Luke was such a good guy and an awesome friend!

How on earth could she tell him she wanted to leave Portals after only a few months of being there? Yet and still, in spite of the consternations, Arianna perceived that leaving Portals was the best recourse. Having such strong feelings for a married man had no place in the life of a Christian woman. And, for that very reason, she thought it wise to remove herself from the equation altogether.

Arianna paused at the set of doors, and took deep breaths before she knocked.

"Come on in, Ari," Luke called out. Pushing away from his desk, he crossed over to the set of doors in order to connect to her.

Arianna slowly opened up the set of doors, startled to see Luke standing so close by. She clutched her chest in order to still her lashing heart in surprise. "I didn't think you'd be standing so close by," she said winded.

All the same, an instant smile curved over her lips to see Luke again. He looked breathtaking in an olive-green colored dress suit. The color accentuated his bronze-kissed skin. Luke's eyes were aqua like the waters of the Caribbean, and his athletic build was highlighted.

"Ari…!" Luke celebrated, and instantly took her up into his arms.

"Welcome back, Luke!" Arianna heralded, gasping for air as a result of his affectionate hug.

"Thank you." Luke pulled away, still smiling. "I've missed you!" Luke ushered her into the office, and invited her to take a seat across from his desk. He veered, and walked around in order to take his place behind the desk.

"I've missed you too! Mel called me when you guys got back from Australia on Saturday night. She said you had the best time!" Arianna halfheartedly celebrated, as she slipped into the armchair across from her boss's.

Luke's face turned crimson, as memories of his honeymoon flashed in his thoughts. Bashfully, he disclosed, "It *was* the best time in the world!"

"I'm glad. I'm also glad you're back," Arianna said reticently. It was a challenge not to openly stare at her insanely desirable boss.

Once again, Luke took her breath away. His rugged and toned body had even greater definition, and his skin was hazelnut from having basked in the sun. Sadly, what Arianna found the most appealing was the very thing that was breaking her heart. Seeing the wedding band on Luke's finger was more alluring than she could interpret. Seeing the ring symbolic of endless love and fidelity on his finger only heightened his appeal. Arianna gulped nervously, as she sized him up. He was much too beautiful for words!

"I'm glad to be back, Ari." Luke frowned. "But, I have to say that I *am* a little thrown off by this." He held the letter up.

Arianna instantly snapped out of daydream mode, when Luke delineated the envelope she'd left on his desk earlier on. "Well, I honestly wanted to tell *you* before you and Melody left-"

"So, you no longer want to work for Portals?" Luke asked, confused. "Is there something *I'm* doing wrong?" Hurt, he set his hand on his chest in query.

"No, Luke... You've done everything *right*. You've been such a great boss, and the best friend. It's just that..."

"Is there someone giving you a hard time around here? If that's the case, you can tell me, and I will immediately address the matter." Luke's eyes lowered urgently into hers.

Arianna hung her head down in silence as her heart lacerated. She'd perceived Luke would take her letter of resignation hard, but he seemed honestly crushed. She forced herself to look up into his eyes. "No one's giving me a hard time. *Everyone's* been great! I guess, I just miss my family back out in Virginia."

Luke hung his head down for a moment and deliberated. He then looked up into Arianna's crystal blue eyes. "Okay. I can understand that. Still, are you *sure* that's all it is?" His face twisted in ambiguity. "Ari, if *I've* done something to offend you... I realize I've been a little bit too demonstrative with my gratitude. It's just that I truly love having you here. It's honestly such a privilege for all of us!

"Aside from Mel and Sean, *you're* the only one who knew me before all of this." Luke gestured to the trappings of his lavish office. "You're family to me," he extended genuinely. Tears shimmered in his eyes. "I'm going to be totally honest. The fact that I *don't* want you to leave is totally selfish. No one runs Portals more efficiently-not even me," he said modestly.

"We'd be so lost without you here. If you need a little time off to go visit with family, please take as long as you need but..."

Arianna was floored by Luke's reaction, and the affective tears shimmering in his eyes. She knew that he'd be sad, but she could not have fathomed to what extent. Tears brimmed over in her eyelids, and rolled down her cheeks. "Oh, Luke. That's very kind of you! It's so like you but-"

"Ari, you wouldn't only be breaking *our* hearts around here. Melody would be devastated, because she loves you so much. Don't even get me started on Cupid. That dog absolutely adores you," Luke pointed out.

Arianna laughed when she remembered how much fun she and Cupid had, when she'd kept him for Luke for a couple of months when they both lived out in Virginia. She hung her head down, and fiddled with her fingers. Inwardly, guilt rose up like helium in a balloon. She hated causing pain to those whom she loved most. At that point, she struggled to break free from it all. It was overwhelming to realize just how much Luke cared about her. Being kind and caring was just who Luke was. Knowing how deeply he cared about those closest to him, made Arianna feel even more envious of Melody.

"Maybe, I *do* need to go out to Virginia for a little while," Arianna said cautiously, as she sized up the melancholy on Luke's face and in his eyes.

Luke smiled, and issued a sigh of relief. Reaching across the desk, he covered her hand with his. "Take as much time as you need. You *are* our family, and I love you, Ari!" Luke said earnestly.

"I love you too, Luke!" Arianna said softly.

"Will a month be enough time?" he asked considerately-totally relieved that Arianna honestly wanted to reconsider her decision. Luke cared about her as much as any big brother cared for a baby sister. So, he felt intrinsically driven to look after her. Maybe, it was because his baby sister Rachel still lived so far away. Rachel *had* agreed to move out to California in the months ahead, but it was still difficult being separated.

Because Luke didn't get to see Rachel very often, having Ari around made him feel like a good big brother. Luke perceived that Arianna still had a bit of a crush on him.

So, for that very reason, he wanted her to meet the right person. Because she was so special, he was protective of her, and wanted to make sure she fell into good hands.

Arianna laughed in incredulity. She was overwhelmed by Luke's kindness and concern. "A *month*? Luke, I was thinking a couple of weeks. I just need a *little* time to myself. Is that all right?"

Luke chuckled. "That's more than alright, Ari. You take all the time you need. But, can I be completely honest with you?" Joy winnowed on his face and in his eyes again.

Arianna smiled thoughtfully, because it dawned on her that she didn't have the heart to hurt Luke or Melody by suddenly bailing on them. Regardless, Arianna deemed she would need to find a way to pull away without being hurtful. "Of course, you can," she encouraged.

"I'm so glad you said *two weeks*." Luke breathed a sigh of relief. "I can't imagine what we'd do if you were gone for an entire month."

"Oh, is *that* all?" Arianna joked.

Luke nodded. "Yeah, pretty much. If you'd like, feel free to take the rest of the day off?"

Arianna considered the circumstances. Witnessing Luke and Melody's wedding was difficult enough. And now, the couple was fresh from their honeymoon. So, Arianna knew that seeing them married and happy would only make matters worse. What she needed was a little time to brace herself for the inevitable. "Thank you for offering. Maybe, I *should* take the rest of the day off. It will give me a chance to take care of some last-minute things."

Luke nodded and smiled openly at her. "You do

whatever you think is best," he offered generously but solemnly. "So, I guess, we won't see you in these them here parts for the next couple of weeks."

Arianna smiled stirringly and nodded. She couldn't believe how deeply affected Luke seemed over the thought of not having her around. She reached across, and set her hand on Luke's from across the desk. "You'll do just fine without me. I'm *really* going to miss you."

Luke nodded in concurrence. "*Both* Melody and I are going to miss *you*... But, I get what it's like to feel homesick and missing family. So, you go ahead, and give your parents and your sisters my love." He smiled into her eyes.

Arianna smiled back at Luke sentimentally. "I definitely will." She pushed out of the armchair, and stood to her feet.

Luke shoved away from his desk. He stood to his feet in acknowledgement of Arianna's impending departure. The two walked quietly over to the set of double doors. "Listen, Ari, I will be texting and emailing you information on the progress we're making with *Shield Me.*"

Arianna had almost forgotten how imposing Luke was, as he towered easily over her at the doors. She did her best not to stare dreamily and flatteringly at her newly married boss. She *had* to take a time out in order to process and pray through her feelings. She *had* to find a way to stop loving him. He was so wonderful! All the same, she needed to accept and respect the fact that he wasn't *her* guy and never would be.

"You mean the new layout?"

"You've seen it?" Luke asked surprised. She always managed to amaze him.

"I *have*. Brenda sent me the graphics, and she also shared the minutes of the conference this morning. I know how important that conference was. I was running late, but I wanted to be in the know. *Shield Me's* definitely blowing up!" she uplifted.

Luke gave her a knowing wink. "Is it any wonder why we *can't* do without you around here? You're always one step ahead of everyone else. I'm glad you approve. I can't wait until Portals makes *Shield Me* the latest and greatest thing out there."

"Everything you touch turns to gold, Luke Bryant! Don't ever forget that." Arianna set her hands on Luke's shoulder. In a deliberate way, she draped her arms around his neck, and pressed into him for a loving hug.

Luke wrapped his arms affectionately around Arianna's waist. "Thank you for saying that, Ari. It means more than you know."

Arianna considered how nice it felt to be in Luke's arms, even if it was for an ephemeral moment. She had to let him go. She internalized how much Luke *did* care about her. However, she would never have him to call her own. Even so, Arianna vowed to have faith. She would dare believe that God had a *Luke* out there for her. There had to be someone out there who would love her with the same intensity in which Luke loved Melody. Arianna deemed that a love of that magnitude was worth the pain and heartache she'd known of late.

"Now, if you need anything at all just call me." Luke gently pulled away, but stared devotedly at her.

Arianna nodded. "Thank you so much for everything! You've been so amazing to me! You are truly my..."

"*Family*," Luke filled in. Hunching down, he pressed a kiss to her cheek. "Oh, by the way, Ari, I *insist* you use the company's account for this much needed break."

"Luke…," Arianna whined in protest. "I can't…" She shook her head contrarily.

Luke nodded affirmatively. "*Yes*, you can." His eyes delved urgently into hers. "And, I'm not going to argue about it."

Arianna nodded, as tears brimmed over in her eyes. "Okay," she granted. "Thank you."

"You're welcome! Now, go on… Get out of here." He smiled.

"Will you please tell Melody that I'll call her later, and that she should expect a call from me every day while I'm back home?" Arianna's face rumpled in angst, before she opened up the set the doors.

"I'm sure Melody wouldn't want it any other way. She'll probably be blowing up your phone as well. Be safe, Ari and keep in touch with us."

"I will."

Arianna slipped through the doors, and Luke watched her bounce away excitedly.   Not that he'd ever taken it for granted, it occurred to him just how much Arianna did for Portals on a regular basis. She had a way of filling in all the gaps-often without even being told to do so. It seemed she loved the business as much as he did. And, if having her go away for two weeks would keep her from leaving Portals Unlimited, *it* was a sacrifice he was willing to make.

Chapter Four

On Tuesday afternoon of his first week back at work, Luke made a number of important phone calls in his office. Minutes ago, he was on the phone with a prospective investor for **Dimension** *Shield Me.* Of course, Luke couldn't go into very many details, because the program was still in the trial stages, and in process of being vetted out by the federal government. All the same, Luke wanted to generate excitement, and wanted everyone buzzing over this revolutionary security feature.

Luke checked his phone, and couldn't help smiling when he saw the hearts and love emojis Melody had texted him. He'd promised to meet his wife down on the fourth floor to spend a little time together as soon as things wound down for the day. Luke took a moment to text his wife back a little love note with a gazillion love Emojis.

While anticipating a loving response from Melody, Sean called him.

"What are *you* up to?" Sean's voice resonated.

"What's up, buddy? I was just about to head out of the office to meet with a prospective investor. Got anything for me?" Luke was curious. Luke had expressed his suspicions to Sean about Clarke's Vale's *purported* suicide. Sean had told Luke he was *just* as skeptical about the reports of Clarke's mysterious death. So, they were both eager to find the loopholes.

"I'm not sure, Luke. Everything seems copasetic. I visited the jail myself, and spoke to a number of officials, and there's nothing inherently off about what happened. They all share the same story. Vale decided he wasn't going to stand trial after all."

Luke shook his head contrarily. "I'm sorry, but I'm *not* buying it, Sean. Something's up. We're talking about Clarke Vale here-the biggest narcissist on the planet. We both know he *wasn't*-or that he *isn't* the kind of man who would even pull up the hood of his own car if he had car trouble. He'd never do it, because he'd risk potentially hurting himself. How much *less* is he the type to wrap a power cord around his neck, and end his own life?" Speculation and doubt shaded Luke's features.

"I agree with you, buddy, but unless we can prove he's still out there. I guess, we're just going to have to go deeper-"

"You mean going undercover in that jail?"

"You might have a point there, buddy. That may be the only way we'll find out just how deep Vale's pockets are."

"My guess is that they're pretty deep. You're *right*, someone going undercover in that jail is probably the only way. How much currency does it take for someone to *buy* their way out of several counts of murder one, attempted murder, extortion, blackmailing, underground drug dealing etc...?"

"Well, whatever *Clarke* paid, *we* can put in an offer of our own to find out," Sean said shrewdly.

"Now, *that's* what I'm talking about. So, theoretically, if Vale can *fake* his own death by buying off prison officials to help him concoct this asinine suicide plot, *we* can definitely pay them off to expose it. We'll just have to see who'll bite." Luke's thoughts raced.

"Money talks, man, and I'm all in. I'm all in for hammering nails into Vale's coffin *personally*." Sean entertained a number of different possibilities.

"First off, we need to find out if any of those prison officials recently quit their jobs, or opened up any overseas accounts. I seriously doubt that they'd be stupid enough to raise suspicion by dropping a wad of cash into a personal checking or savings out in Sands Port."

"Irregular banking transactions is a great place to start," Sean agreed.

"Then, we need an inside person in that jailhouse. He'll play nice with everybody there, and make them feel comfortable enough to *talk*. The only image we were shown was of Clarke hanging from a jail cell. We never saw a body in a coffin. And, there was no funeral service or family gathering. Even a sleaze like Vale *must* have family," Luke analyzed.

"We're about to expose a total fake. Luke, this time, *we're* throwing the first set of punches. Vale has no clue who he's dealing with."

"Sean, before, we didn't have the resources to handle Vale. That's no longer the case." Luke remembered finding Sean bleeding to death in the town of Royale Valley out in Sands Port. Chills rippled through him. Sean was his brother, and it overwhelmed him to relive just how close he came to losing his buddy. "Sean, *you've* done more than enough."

"Luke, I *know* what you're thinking. Please, don't shut me out, and label me *retired* because of what happened. This vendetta with Clarke is just as personal for me," Sean affirmed.

"Just saying… You and I *can* afford to be hands off this time around. As we both know, money *does* talk. And, I'm not trying to lose my brother," Luke stated emphatically.

"I get that, Luke, but I'm not about to do anything stupid. However, you better believe that I'll be pulling the strings behind the scenes."

"Absolutely. *We* will be pulling them together. And, this time, Clarke isn't coming back," Luke avowed.

"Dead or alive," Sean added. "By the way, Luke, Nicole and I *have* been talking about moving out to the West Coast," Sean said on a lighter note.

"Whoa! Seriously…?" Luke nearly fell out of his armchair. Ecstatic, Luke brushed his fingers through his curls, as was his habit whenever he felt anxious, nervous or emotionally charged up.

"Yeah, I think you and I won her over. Hanging out with you and Mel out in Beverly Glen a few weeks ago, made her a believer."

"Sean, this is insane! When…?"

"We're still talking about it. Of course, Nikki would have to give her notice to the hospital. But in as far as Chimera Inc., they can send *me* anywhere. Chimera Inc. was the software company Sean worked for out in Sands Port. "So, Nikki and I were thinking…maybe in a couple of months."

Tears of joy shone in Luke's eyes. "Sean, you have no idea! You just made my day. I can't wait. Chimera's cool and all, but I *really* want you to give serious thought to working for Portals alongside me," Luke said, trying not to get way too ahead of himself.

"All right, Luke. One step at a time, buddy. Honestly, I *have* been thinking about joining the Portals family."

"Sean, stop thinking about it. You and Nicole should

just get on the next flight out to Burbank. Melody's going to freak out when I tell her." Luke shifted about in his rolling armchair with nervous energy.

Sean laughed. "I'll keep you posted about Vale, and about mine and Nicole's impending move," Sean affirmed.

"Thanks, man. Wow! I can't wait to have you here!" Luke was over-the-top happy over the prospect of having Sean working alongside him.

"You're welcome! If I find out anything else, I'll text you a little later."

"Sure. If there's anything on my end, I'll keep you posted as well. Tell Nicole I said hey, and tell her how totally pumped I am that you're considering moving out here."

Sean chuckled. "That's a mouthful, but I will definitely tell her. Talk to you later, buddy."

"Bye, Sean."

Luke had mixed feelings after getting off the phone with Sean. On the one hand, he was overjoyed that Sean and Nicole were considering the move, but the conversation they had about Clarke Vale gnawed away at him. Now more than ever, Luke questioned Clarke's suicide. He couldn't help thinking that Clarke had masterminded the stunt. Perhaps, he'd pulled off this caper to evade the law, so that he'd be free to continue his evil and ruthless ministry.

Luke sighed, and sent a prayer upward. He asked God to keep them all out of danger. Psalms 34 was quickly becoming one of his favorites, and he quoted that the angel of the Lord is always around God's children, and keeps them from harm (Psalms 34:7). The very thought of anything coming between him and Melody again sickened him. He and his wife had suffered immensely for the kind of joy and happiness God had brought into their lives.

Their love was something Luke was more than ready to defend. Spending an entire year apart from Melody had left him a shattered man. So, Luke vowed to protect what they had even to the death. All the same, before allowing his thoughts to lead him to a dark place, he whispered a prayer, and committed the circumstances to God.

Luke was assured that the enemy's schemes would not prevail. Hence, no matter how many *lives* Clarke *thought* he had, the truth of it was that he only had *one*. Luke acquiesced to the fact that if Clarke refused to stop his onslaught of terror, things wouldn't end well for the man. God didn't take lightly to anyone trying to hurt, or take advantage of his children.

Luke checked the time censor within the sizable portal in his office, and realized he needed to leave ASAP. He had that investment meeting for **Dimension Shield Me**. Once that was out of the way, he'd be free to go bug Melody on the fourth floor. He was literally counting down the minutes until he could have her in his arms again.

Luke pushed back in his comfortable armchair, grabbed his jacket, and walked over to the set of doors in order to leave. Trevor, his top limo guy, was waiting downstairs to take him over to the Belle Chateau Bistro, an upscale French restaurant about 20 minutes away. There, he would be meeting with Bryce Baron, the CEO of Super Giant Technologies.

Running minutes behind schedule, Luke opened up one of the doors, all set to dart out into the hallway. However, he was stopped dead in his tracks by Peter. Peter was standing right outside of the office. In fact, the door came only inches from hitting him on the face. Peter seemed to be in a total huff. His scarlet face made Luke stop and take notice. The kid seemed both irritated and agitated.

"You all right, Pete?" Luke's face wrinkled in perplexity. More than mystified, he was a bit grated that Peter would come by his office at that time. More than anyone else, Peter knew he was running late for his scheduled meeting with Bryce Baron.

Peter stared cagily about the hallway, before establishing eye contact with his boss. "I'm fine, *PM*. Can I have a word with you?" he asked shortly.

"I was just about to leave to meet with that investor, but all right…" Luke stared at Peter warily. "Is there something, wrong, Pete?" Luke stepped back inside the office, and invited Peter in. Peter's crimson face and his scowl, relayed he was obviously miffed. So, Luke was genuinely concerned.

Still breathing unevenly, Peter plodded over to Luke's desk. He was so out of sorts he could no longer keep quiet. Arianna was gone, and he didn't get a chance to say goodbye. Word had it she'd handed in her letter of resignation the day before. However, Peter had been left out of the loop. Still, for all intents and purposes, it wasn't difficult to figure out why Arianna had gone away. Peter felt slighted, because he hadn't properly apologized for his behavior at the wedding reception. Now, she was gone, and he'd never get to show her just how different he could be…how much better. Sadder still, Peter realized that he'd never get to tell her how much he cared about her.

Luke found Peter's sudden intrusion totally bewildering. However, Luke compliantly took his place behind the desk, but didn't sit down. Setting both hands out in front of him, he placated, "Peter, please talk to me. What's going on? Did something happen? Is there something wrong with the program we talked about earlier? Whatever it is you *can't* freak out. This is just a business okay…" Luke was growing increasingly more rattled by Peter's incensed demeanor.

"You *do* know *she* left Portals because of you right?" Peter refused to sit down. Rather, he hovered over Luke's expansive, gleaming dark wood desk.

Luke abandoned the idea of taking a seat after hearing Peter's accusation. He was surprised, but decided not to react. Rather, he would hear Peter out. Peter was a good kid, always respectful and hardworking. "Pete, what are you talking about? *Who* left because of me?"

"Don't you understand she's in love with you?"

Luke shook his head contrarily, and a crazed expression covered his face. He was rendered momentarily speechless after hearing Peter's rant.

"*Ari's* in love with you. Don't you get how painful it's been for her to watch you and Melody together, when she has such strong feelings for you? She handed in her resignation, because it's gut-wrenching to watch you with your new wife. *I* saw the pain in her eyes on the day of the wedding. She spent the entire wedding reception crying her eyes out in the ladies room. She decided to leave just as soon as you and Melody did," Peter explained defenselessly.

Luke was shocked and totally stumped. He swallowed hard, and tried to weigh his words before speaking. In light of Peter's accusations, Luke ascertained the strong feelings *he* had for Arianna. "Pete, listen to me. Ari *isn't* leaving Portals.

She's going back out to Virginia for a couple of weeks to spend time with her family," he said quietly.

Peter gasped in shock. Remorse immediately rumpled his straight features, as his eyes fastened to his boss's. "She's coming back?"

Luke nodded. "In two weeks…," he said temperately, gesturing for Peter to calm down.

Peter sighed, and brushed his fingers through his thick, dark mane. His face shaded in embarrassment, as he stared at Luke. "I'm sorry. I didn't know."

"Since you haven't told me why you're *truly* upset, is there anything else you'd like to tell me?" Luke's face strained in understanding. "You've said a whole lot about how you think Arianna *feels* about me. Did *she* ever say anything to you?" Luke asked thickly. All of a sudden, he was consumed by guilt and concern for Arianna.

"No. We never talked about it, but everyone knows she's in love with you. She's so beautiful! All the guys around here have their eyes on her, but she can't see anyone but you," Peter admitted, exasperated. Mortified, he forced himself to reconnect to his boss's unwavering expression.

Luke sighed, and had a moment of pause before he said anything. It affected him greatly knowing that he'd hurt Arianna. Everything now made sense. He closed his eyes with a sense of remorse and compunction.

"I think you might be right, Pete. I *have* been a first-class heel. I've been completely clueless about Ari. When we worked together back at the company in Virginia, at my farewell party, we kissed…at least she kissed me," he confessed. Luke had never mentioned the incident to anyone before until now. It lacerated his heart to even bring it up. "I sensed she had a bit of a crush, but I made it clear that my heart belonged to someone else."

"What Ari feels for you is a lot more than just a crush, PM," Peter said solemnly. It was difficult to keep his jealous feelings in check, but he had to, because he'd already crossed a line with his boss.

"Arianna and I have been *friends* for a while now, and I just assumed we were okay." Luke shook his head in the negative, as he struggled with guilt. "I didn't know she felt that way."

"She's in love with you, *PM*, even if she'd never admit to it."

"And in light of your behavior today, *you're* in love with her, aren't you, Peter?" Luke redirected. His eyes gunned intently into Peter's. Luke couldn't even wrap his head around the pain he'd probably caused Arianna. Yet and still, he found himself utterly fascinated by how rapt Peter seemed to be by her.

"I think she's great! She's smart, classy, beautiful, kind and…"

"And *you're* in love with her," Luke emphasized again. This time his expression daunted Peter to say it differently.

"*So* in love it hurts," Peter disclosed, with florid cheeks.

Luke smiled. "I'm glad to hear you admit to that. So, I guess I *don't* have to fire you for losing it completely at the wedding reception." He gave Peter a knowing wink.

Shock colored Peter's already cardinal face. "You...

You know about that?"

Luke nodded. "Of course, I know all about it."

"But why haven't you addressed the matter with *me*? *PM*, let me just take a moment to apologize for what happened. I'm truly sorry for my behavior at the wedding reception. I really-"

"Pete, you're my right-hand man, and one of the very best here at Portals. You're cool…most of the time anyway. You're knowledgeable, passionate and driven in this industry. There's nothing to address. Besides, I know how it feels to be in love with a girl you can't be with. Believe me, I know taking a drink or two to numb the pain seems like the way to go. But, it never really is."

"I can't believe you knew about what happened at the reception, and didn't say anything. So sorry, *PM*, and I'm so sorry for barging into your office, and accusing you of making Ari leave."

Luke gave Peter a sympathetic look. "I guess, love makes us act irrationally. We'll have to address that whole barging in *thing*, once I get back from the investment meeting."

Peter's expression was that of angst and uncertainty. "Well, that's only fair."

"But in the meantime, I do need a rep to fly out to Virginia later in the week. Someone's got to spread the word about *Shield Me*. Think you can handle that, Pete?" Luke's face and eyes were imbued with mischief. It still broke his heart to internalize the fact that he'd hurt someone he valued a great deal. Nevertheless, he was over-the-moon happy that an upstanding guy like Peter was in love with Arianna. Luke determined to do everything he could to get that ball rolling.

"What...?" Peter asked confused. "You want me to fly out to Virginia while Ari's there?"

Luke smiled impishly. "Peter, I *didn't* say that. I said I need a rep to go out to Body Electric Era to meet with Stephen Sanderson. He and his administration were first in cutting me a break. So, I definitely want them in on it when *Shield Me* hits the market. What *you* do in your *personal* time while you're out in Virginia for the next few days, is totally up to you." Luke's expression was roguish.

Peter stared at his boss in utter skepticism. How sorry he was for jumping to conclusions, and falsely accusing Luke was an understatement. However, he was much too intrigued by the offer to pull back. "*PM*, I can't believe you'd ask me to be your rep with Mr. Sanderson. I *know* how much you respect him."

"I owe him everything, and *yes* I respect him a great deal. That's why I'm sending him one of our very best!" Luke uplifted.

"I guess, I can look Ari up while I'm out there," Peter thought out loud.

"That sounds *personal*, Pete. All I care about is the *business* aspect of your little excursion."

"*PM*, I *really* appreciate this opportunity. Thank you. I will *try*, even if I know Arianna can't stand me." Peter's head slumped in despondency. "I can't seem to get it right with her. I'm awkward, and I always say the wrong thing."

A quiet but understanding smile spread over Luke's face. He wanted to do all he could to put Peter's mind at ease. Peter was only a few years his junior, and Luke could definitely relate to how it felt to fall short of the expectation of someone you admire.

"I guess, you have your work cut out for you. It's up to *you* to show her you're not the guy she saw at the wedding reception. It's also up to you to show her how much you care." Luke smiled and shook his head quizzically. "I don't know how I ever missed just how strongly you feel for Ari. Just be yourself, and stop trying so hard. Ari's a wonderful girl, and she would never judge or condemn you for your mistakes," Luke enlivened.

"You mean, you really *want* me to try with Ari?" Peter was stumped.

"Why wouldn't I?"

"Well, it's obvious to everyone around here just how protective you are of her," Peter said plainly. At that point, he felt a lot more at ease to speak his mind.

Luke shook his head again humorously. "I would imagine, everyone around here is watching *me* pretty closely." He chuckled. The truth was that everyone who worked through Portals kept *him* on a pretty tight leash.

Peter put both hands out in a halting manner. "That's not a bad thing. It's because everyone looks up to you. They think you're awesome!"

"Thanks...I think." Luke's face crinkled in uncertainty. "For the record, I *am* very protective of Arianna. She's a dear friend, and a very special person. You can just think of me as her big brother, who won't hesitate to dislocate a limb or two if you hurt her in any way," Luke said cryptically.

Peter gulped, loosened his tie, and tenseness overshadowed his sharp features. "Message received. All I want is a chance. You think she'll give me a chance?"

Luke walked from around his desk, and walked over to Peter. Setting his hands fraternally on Peter's shoulders, he searched his eyes. "Pete, I'm only kidding about the limb dislocation thing. I'm not in the mafia, and I promise that I won't break your legs if things fall apart with Ari.

"All the same, I need you to listen to me." Luke hesitated, and took a deep breath before he finished his train of thought. "When Melody and I first met, *I* didn't think I had a chance with *her*. I was all over the place insecure." Luke shook his head in irony.

"I was working as a janitor for the local elementary school, lived in a small apartment…when *she* seemed to have it all together. I was so ashamed of who I was, and what I did for a living. So, I doubted she'd ever let me get close to her. I even led her to believe that I was one of the teachers, instead of telling her the truth about my work status.

"All of that almost came between us at first. One of the most miserable days of my life was not knowing if Melody would ever speak to me again."

"Why…?" Peter's face rumpled in affect and concern.

"Well, she stopped by the school to surprise me for lunch, and found me wearing green janitor's overalls." Luke shook his head illogically, as he remembered that account.

"What happened later on? How did you fix it?" Peter seemed intrigued.

"Like I said, it *almost* pulled us apart, before we ever really got started. And yet, from the very beginning, what Melody and I shared was so strong that neither of really knew how to let go… Peter, I said all of that to say this. Just be yourself. Don't try to be anyone you're *not* around her. Never lie to her. I hated myself for deceiving Melody in the beginning. I got it in my head that she needed me to be someone else-someone capable of giving her the finer things in life," Luke shared openly.

"Well, aren't you, *PM*?" Peter issued a clever smile.

Luke smiled thoughtfully. "My wife and I can appreciate the way things are *now*, because things didn't start off that way." Luke gave Peter a perceptive look.

Peter assented to Luke's words. "I get it."

"All you can do is to be one hundred percent yourself, and show Ari how much she means to you."

"What if that's not enough?" Peter asked shakily.

"Then, you'll *know* you gave it your all, and you'll have absolutely no regrets. A bit of advice, Pete…"

Peter nodded, and gestured for Luke to go on.

"Try to figure out what Ari considers important. For starters, you need to know she's a Christian person, who follows the teachings of Jesus Christ. Does that intimidate you?"

Peter smiled earnestly. "Not in the least. I *want* to know everything about her-that is if she'll give me a chance. My family and I grew up in the church. However, when my brothers and I, and my sister moved away from home, things changed."

Luke smiled quietly. "You might want to start looking into a good church again. Nothing's more important. Life's not even worth living without faith in God through Jesus Christ."

Shock spread over Peter's face. "You're a Christian,

PM?"

"Locked, stocked and barreled," Luke declared.

"I think that's super cool! If you're a Christian, *PM*, you *certainly* make me want to be one too."

Luke laughed. "You become a Christian because Jesus Christ died a brutal death on a cross, and shed his blood to save all of humanity from eternal separation from God. You don't become a Christian, because you want to run a conglomerate," he joked.

"Nah, it's a lot more than that. I *really* admire you, *PM*. I get that all of *this*," Peter stared all about the room, "is just icing on a cake and God's blessings."

"You're even smarter than I thought, Pete. And, that's why I *know* you'll do great with BEE down in Virginia." Luke winked. He glanced at his watch and sighed. "Pete, I *really* have to go. I'm about fifteen minutes behind schedule for that investment meeting."

"Sorry, boss. I didn't mean to…"

"It's cool. I just need to get going." Luke moved away from his desk, and hiked over to the set of doors. Peter was hot on his heels.

"So, we'll talk about the business trip later this afternoon," Luke told Peter, as he rushed out of the office, and shut the set of doors behind him.

"Definitely…" Peter rushed ahead of Luke out in the hallway. Turning back once more, he emphasized, "I just wanted to say thanks for everything, *PM*! I will do my best not to let you down."

"No worries, Pete. You haven't let me down so far,

and I seriously doubt you will," Luke's voice trailed as he rushed away. He breezed through the busy main office area, and quickly slipped into the first available elevator. Once secure inside, he sighed, with his back pressed up against the elevator wall. His conversation with Peter still resonated. It broke his heart to consider how much he'd hurt Arianna, because he cared so much about her.

Luke prayed for God's wisdom, and the strength to make things right with his friend. Hurting her was the last thing he'd wanted. Once off the elevator, Luke plowed through the lobby like a machine. Coming through the revolving doors, he found Trevor waiting just feet away from the limo.

"Don't worry, *PM*. I took the liberty of contacting Mr. Baron. He knows you'll be there shortly. Baron said not to worry about it, because he'll be waiting on for you."

Luke closed his eyes and sighed in relief. "Thanks, Trev. I really appreciate that."

Luke slipped inside the limo, and tried to focus on business. He had to prep in order to pitch his new cutting-edge tool, ***Dimension*** *Shield Me.*

***

"I've gone over your resume, your cover letter and references. Mr. Lloyd, I must say how impressed I am by your vast experience in the field. You also come highly recommended." Brenda Fields perused Emery Lloyd's paperwork.

Since both Arianna and Peter were out of town, Brenda was one of the supervising managers conducting job interviews for Portals in their absence. She had to admit she was utterly captivated by this prospective Portals employee. It also didn't hurt that he was the embodiment of tall, dark and handsome. The man was take-your-breath-away dreamy with his dark hair and deep blue eyes. His eloquence and resonating voice were spellbinding! Brenda wanted to hire him on his looks alone. However, she didn't have the final say.

Clarke's back pressed into the comfortable armchair in Brenda Field's extensive and cool office. Brenda was one of Portals' top representatives. From what *Clarke* perceived, she was already under his spell. The pretty young brunette couldn't stop smiling, her cheeks were scarlet, and her hazel eyes had frequently wandered away from his keen stare.

"If you'd like for me to furnish a few more references, I can have them to you in a matter of days," *Clarke* told Brenda, exploring the contours of her body in a provocative manner.

"The paperwork you've brought in this afternoon is more than enough." Brenda set the paperwork aside, but frowned in uncertainty. "My boss has to look over everything you've brought in. There has to be a background check, but he makes all of the final decisions." Brenda smiled. Clearing her throat, she nervously brushed over her tan skirt suit with her hands. She was virtually melting like butter in the presence of this incredibly handsome potential employee. The interview had taken all of half an hour, but it seemed as if this man already had the power to talk her into doing *anything* he wanted. Aside from all of that, he also had a *killer* body.

"Your boss…?" *Clarke's* brows raised in inquiry. Unequivocally, he knew that Brenda Fields was referring to the *thorn in his side*, AKA Luke Bryant, whom they all referred to as the *Portal Master*. It sickened Clarke to the core over the very concept of having Luke as his boss, even for a short while. "Will I have the privilege of meeting your boss this afternoon?" *Clarke* feigned excitement.

Everyone calling him *Emery Lloyd* was something he was trying to get used to. For all intents and purposes, Clarke Vale was dead. He was now Emery Lloyd, a man who'd resurfaced out in Europe after going missing for quite a number of years. Clarke rather liked his new identity. And, if he played his cards right, Emery Lloyd was about to bring Melody back into his life.

"Yes. He's tied up in meetings right now, but if you can hang out for about an hour or so, you *will* get a chance to meet him. I'm *sure* he's going to be just as impressed by your credentials as I am." Brenda shifted tensely behind her desk. Her goal was to emancipate herself from slipping even deeper into Mr. Lloyd's deep blue eyes.

"I'm looking *forward* to meeting him. I've heard a lot of great things... It's impressive how such a young person has created such groundbreaking technological advancements. **Dimension** *Find Me*, *The Power Portal*, The *Vortex to Vanish* feature… just to name a few." Clarke pulled his chair in closer to Brenda's desk. No doubt, he had *her* sold. Now, all he had to do was to sell her boss, and that would be quite an achievement.

"We *don't* take any of it for granted. Luke Bryant is an absolute genius! Honestly, he keeps coming up with cutting-edge tools, which has launched Portals so far ahead of the game, and virtually eliminated the competition. What my boss has tapped into through his work are advancements which were depicted as Sci-fi a few decades ago. They are now *our* reality in the twenty-first century. It's a genuine privilege to work *for* and *alongside* him." Brenda smiled musingly, and her eyes finally stopped wandering. "Besides, he's just the nicest person on the planet!" she praised.

Clarke laughed ironically. "Well, in that case, I absolutely *have* to meet him today. Am I allowed to make an observation?" he asked shrewdly.

"Of course..." Brenda gestured for him to proceed.

"I doubt *anyone's* better suited to represent your boss, and this company than you are!"

Brenda's cheeks reddened. "Thank you so much for saying that! I love both my boss and this company!" she said proudly. "I'm actually surprised that you're interested in working through graphics designs." Brenda's face wrinkled in confusion. "With all of this experience..."

"Graphics and design work are my forte. Don't get me wrong, I *am* quite savvy in other areas. However, graphics in particular is my passion."

Brenda nodded understandingly. "We can definitely present your credentials to *PM* today. However, you will also have to talk to his wife," Brenda said matter-of-factly. She was tickled by the irony of it all. Here she was hyping up *her* boss, when this prospective employee would need to have a sit-down interview with her boss's wife.

"His *wife* you say?" Clarke's face lit up.

"Yes. *Melody* Bryant's the head of that department, and you'll probably need to interview with her."

Clarke could not contain his smile, or the joy bubbling up on the inside. This was the moment he'd been waiting for. After all the pain and humiliation, he'd endured in recent

months, and after losing Melody, he would finally see her
again. Clarke was suddenly paralyzed by desire, and heat
permeated through his body, as he considered being in the
same room with her again.

"Is it possible that I'll have a sit-down interview with
Melody Bryant this afternoon?" Enthused and anxious, Clarke
edged in closer to the edge of his chair.

Brenda nodded. "Anything's possible I suppose." She
glanced at the time indication on the computer monitor. "It's
about half past two, and Melody leaves at four. She probably
won't be able to schedule you in for a *formal* interview today,
but you can meet her and tentatively set one up. I'll give her a
call to see if she has a minute." Brenda's eagerness
diminished. The dream of Emery Lloyd working for the
Administrative Team near *her* was dwindling.

"What is Melody Bryant like?" Clarke asked
cunningly, curious to see how Brenda would respond.

Brenda smiled and nodded. "She's just as wonderful
as her husband. Of course, we're all insanely jealous of her,
because she's an absolute knock-out! She's like Michelle
Obama. She has her own sense of fashion, in and out of the
White House, so to speak. The Bryants are a very good-
looking couple! *PM's* not only a genius, but he's also
extremely good-looking," Brenda openly admitted. Her
cheeks reddened again, and she laughed nervously, because
she'd obviously overshared.

"I guess, that was a little bit too much information."
Brenda looked away from Emery's keen stare in
embarrassment.

Clarke gave Brenda a disarming smile. "Not at all.
I'm actually impressed. Do you have any idea how many

people represent companies and people they care absolutely nothing about? It's refreshing to see something a little different. Besides, it's good to know all I can about my new employers." He winked convincingly at Brenda.

"Oh…?" She gasped in surprise, as a soft smile curved over her lips. "You're already *convinced* that you're going to be working for Portals?"

"A little confidence never hurt anyone. And, you've absolutely *sold* me on this company. Now more than ever, I want to work for Portals." Clarke gave Brenda a cajoling smile. On the surface, he seemed perfectly composed, but inwardly he was consumed by thoughts of seeing Melody again.

"Well, in that case you *absolutely have* to meet the Bryants today."

"You mean *Mr. and Mrs. PM?*" Clarke asked tenaciously.

"Absolutely…" Brenda laughed.

She was determined to leave an impression on the mysterious and shockingly handsome Emery Lloyd, even if he wasn't interested in working through *her* department at Portals.

"How's your dad doing, Reena?" Melody asked Serena over the phone. She frowned in concern as she anticipated an answer. Melody felt guilty, because she couldn't be there for her best friend. Serena's dad had been diagnosed with Diverticulitis, and admitted to the hospital last night.

"He's doing a little better today, Mel. Truth be told, we were all freaked out last night, because he was in so much pain. They've put him on a pain killer and strong antibiotics."

"Reena, I feel so bad I can't be there. I really miss your entire family. Tell your dad I love him, and that I'm praying for him." Melody sighed. "Being away from you guys is a lot harder than I thought it was going to be." Tears shone in her eyes.

"Oh, honey, it's all right. I miss you too, but *it is* what *it is* for now. Maybe, one of these days when things settle down, Dane and I can come out there to spend time with you and Luke."

Melody's face lit up, and her eyes widened to the size of tennis balls. "That would mean so much to me…and to Luke."

"How are you and Luke doing? I don't even need to ask, because the two of you have taken *happy* to a whole other level!"

"We're *so* happy, Reena! I never thought it was possible to be so content. God has done exceedingly and abundantly more than I could have asked or imagined (Ephesians 3:20)."

"God is good all the time, and he's faithful. When you pray for a long time, and you wait on him you get the very best."

"You, of all people should know that. You and Dane are so blessed!"

"And now, *you've* got your happy ending," Serena

enlivened.

"Happy doesn't even begin to cover it. I thank God every minute of the day. And, I refuse to take anything for granted."

"We should never take any of it for granted. We should always be grateful to God for all he's given us! Look at me... I'm rambling and holding you up. Are you almost done for the day?"

"In about twenty minutes or so... Luke usually comes down to get me, and we go home together," Melody said with a sense of dignity.

"Aww... That's so sweet."

Just then, a light rap came to Melody's office door.

"Come in," she called out. Her face lit up instantly when Luke deliberately opened up the door. However, he continued to knock on it politely. Melody instinctively jumped out of her armchair. "Reena, Luke's here. I guess, he's a little early." Melody rushed over to the office door, and threw her arms affectionately around her husband in celebration.

"Hi, baby!" She covered Luke's face and lips with hungry kisses, as he hugged her affectionately.

"Honey baby, I've missed you so much!" Luke's back pressed up to the office door, as he simultaneously shut it closed. Scooping Melody up in his arms, he carried her across the spacious office.

"Melody snickered, as her husband carried over to the comfortable office sofa. "Luke, Serena wants to say hello." Melody put her phone on speaker mode.

"How are you, Serena?" Luke's half dimples deepened

whenever he was earnestly happy.

"I'm good! How are *you*?" Serena asked pertly.

"I'm doing great! We sure miss you and Dane around here!"

"Aww… We miss you guys too! I just wanted to say thank you for the flowers, the card and the gift you sent over for my dad. It means so much to all of us!" Serena's voice wavered.

"It's the very least we could do, Serena. Tell your dad we're praying for a complete turnaround."

"I will definitely tell him."

"By the way, when are you and Dane coming back out here to stay? Mel and I miss our extended families. We've got Sean and Nicole onboard," Luke coaxed.

"I *know*. Mel told me. Dane and I are *talking* about it. I guess, one of these days…"

"Okay, so no pressure here. Just as long as you and Dane are on the next flight out, okay?" Luke joked.

"That's no pressure at all." Serena chortled.

"Not at all. Seriously, you guys are welcome anytime."

"Thanks, Luke. One of these days, we'll definitely take you up on that offer, so don't be surprised."

"Surprised? Mel and I will throw you a party," Luke encouraged.

Melody examined Luke's face as he spoke on the

phone. She could tell it also bothered him that they couldn't be there for Serena and Dane. Melody knew how deeply Luke cared, and it affected her. She stroked affectionately on his face, and plowed her fingers through his curls, as she listened to his end of the conversation.

"Just keep us all in your prayers."

"We always do, Serena. Give my best to your dad, and please tell Dane I said hey."

"I will do that. Bye."

"Bye." Luke handed the phone over to Melody.

"I'll call you later okay, Reena?" Melody said resignedly.

"Sure, honey. Bye."

Melody shut down the phone, and tossed it to the side of the sofa. She draped her arms around Luke's neck, and gently cradled his head in her hands. She stared lovingly into his eyes. "How was your day, my love?" She loved being in his arms at the end of the day.

"Hectic as usual… I'm sorry I couldn't come down here until now." Luke sighed, pulling Melody in even closer. Propping his face up to hers, he planted kisses all over her face, until his mouth rested on hers.

"Things were kind of hectic down here as well. But, that's all right. Just because my husband *also* happens to be my boss, I *can't* expect any special treatment," Melody said in between honey kisses.

"What do you mean by *special* treatment?" Luke took his time to kiss the contours of her mouth.

"*Special treatment...* You know; I can't expect you to come in here, take me up in your arms, and carry me over to the couch, and to be held this close," Melody vamped.

Luke laughed, and pulled away just enough to look into Melody's eyes. "So, it's a *no* on coming in here, taking you up in my arms, bringing you over to the couch, and cuddling?" Luke had a roguish expression on his face.

"Luke, we're acting like your stereotypical bosses who abuse their authority." Melody feigned concern. "You *did* say this kind of behavior is *frowned* upon. Tsk...tsk...tsk..." She gestured with her pointer finger.

"I'm too tired to *frown*. Besides, it's quitting time," Luke bantered.

"Well, in that case you can plant one on me." Melody pulled Luke back possessively into her arms.

"I would love nothing more than to plant one on you." Luke crushed her to himself. His face bridged to hers, and he lovingly coaxed her mouth with tender kisses. "I love you!" he saith thickly.

"I love you more!" Melody surrendered to Luke's embrace. "I missed you so much today," she murmured.

"Staying away from you gets harder and harder all the time." Luke lost himself to Melody's sugar kisses.

"I'll tell you what. Why don't we wrap things up here, and take this little conversation home?" Melody pressed a few more kisses to Luke's mouth before she reluctantly pulled away. Standing to her feet, she extended her hand out to him, and helped him off the couch.

Luke took the hand Melody extended, but pulled her

acquisitively into his arms the moment he was up on his feet. "Yeah, we should *definitely* take this party home..."

Just then, a knock came to Melody's office door.

"Oh no." Melody's face changed. Her smile was replaced by a panicked expression. "I knew it was too good to be true." She pressed her right index finger and her thumb together. "We were *this* close to making a clean getaway."

Luke guffawed and nestled her. "That's all right, honey. Who knows? We still might be able to make a clean getaway in a minute or two." Luke ushered Melody over towards the office door, and encouraged her to go and answer it.

Melody grudgingly complied, and trudged over to the door. However, before she opened it up, she looked back at Luke, and gave him her best sad face.

Luke smiled, and shook his head humorously. "Go on..."

Melody sighed, then pulled open the office door. She was surprised to see Brenda Fields standing beyond it. However, Brenda wasn't alone. She was accompanied by a very handsome and well-dressed gentleman.

Melody wasn't sure why she was startled, and felt unsettled seeing the gentleman for the first time. He was classically handsome and clean cut. His dark wavy hair, fair skin and intense blue eyes were also striking. He had a stalwart build, and wore a musky yet sweet scented cologne.

"Melody, I apologize for coming down here so late. I know you and *PM* are just about to leave for the day. Still, you do remember that I told you that I wanted to introduce you to Mr. Emery Lloyd? Well, Mr. Lloyd hung out here for over an hour waiting to meet you." Brenda grimaced in uncertainty. Her expression conveyed she was pushing the envelope.

Melody found herself temporarily bemused, and she was sure Emery Lloyd's good looks had very little to do with it. His eyes fastened to, and delved informally into hers. There was an intimacy in the way he looked at her, and a sense of familiarity about his eyes.

Melody's thoughts whizzed, and she found herself somewhat distracted. Nevertheless, she tried not to drift too far away. "That's right." Melody offered an affable smile. "I'm so sorry, Brenda. I meant to get back to you, but things got a little crazy down here. Luke and I were just about to leave, but we *always* have time to meet a prospective employee."

Luke walked over towards the office door, and took his place beside his wife. With a cordial smile, he extended his hand out to the stranger. "I'm Luke Bryant, and it's nice to meet you, Mr. Lloyd!" Luke stared squarely into Emery Lloyd's eyes, and sized up the man interested in working through the Graphics Designs department. Brenda had mentioned the potential employee earlier on. However, other responsibilities had made it impossible for them to meet.

"It's nice to finally meet you!" *Clarke* exclaimed. He and Luke exchanged a firm handshake. Although he tried hard not to, Clarke couldn't keep his eyes off of Melody. This had been the case since he'd first laid eyes on her. And, there she was, taking his breath away yet again. It was unnerving not being able to decipher what Melody was thinking. This was a whole new level of misery for Clarke. He wanted to take her in his arms, and kiss her within an inch of her life. However, he was forced to pull back.

Luke stood back for a moment, and examined Mr.

Emery Lloyd. The man apparently wanted to work through the GDD with Melody. Even if Luke wasn't the openly jealous type, it was unsettling to have the embodiment of a *James Bond* applying to work through his wife's department at Portals. Emery Lloyd was indeed urbane, and had a hundred-watt lightbulb smile. He undeniably exuded confidence.

Nevertheless, Luke refused to allow his personal biases to hamper his professionalism. Brenda had raved about the man's credentials, and Luke was eager to look them over. "Mr. Lloyd, I apologize that my busy schedule kept me from meeting with you earlier on. Brenda was impressed by your experience and qualifications." Luke stared over at Brenda, and gave her an earnest smile. "Honestly, I value her opinion a great deal."

"I trust that my credentials will meet your criteria. I do well with this kind of work, because I have a vast amount of experience in the field." Clarke smiled tautly, while trying to sound self-effacing.

"I'm sure you're just being modest." Luke gave Emery a querying look.

Luke then directed his attention to Melody, who was eerily quiet by his side. It was difficult to escape how sullen she'd suddenly grown. Perhaps, she was tired after a long day, but Luke perceived that something was very wrong. "You okay, honey?" His face strained in concern.

"Huh…?" Melody said, startled. She urged herself to look away from Mr. Lloyd. Melody couldn't seem to escape the way the man stared at her. It was a gape that relayed he was somehow capable of reading all of her secrets. Emery Lloyd *seemed* nice, and she liked the way he interacted with Luke. However, Melody couldn't ignore those intrusive eyes. She smiled, and brushed nervously through her hair. "I'm all right, honey," she reassured Luke.

Working past her consternations, Melody found the courage to address the daunting stranger, "Please, allow me and my husband to make up for making you wait on us this afternoon." She smiled cordially, and tried to maintain eye contact.

"There's absolutely nothing to make up for. I can't even imagine the pressures of running such a tremendous enterprise.

Clarke forced himself to look away from Melody. "Although, Mr. Bryant, I must admit I've heard a great deal about *you*."

"All good things I hope." Luke smiled good-naturedly.

"Yes...of course. All *excellent* things," Clarke said amicably. "I told Ms. Fields how much it would mean to me to have an opportunity to work through Portals Unlimited. I'm honestly impressed by all of your breakthrough technology."

Luke nodded, pleased. "Well, in that case, Brenda can pencil you in for tomorrow afternoon. We'll sit down, and get a look at that resume. Will tomorrow afternoon work for you?" Luke stared unwaveringly into Emery's face.

For Luke, it was difficult to overlook what a *charmer* this Emery Lloyd guy seemed to be. *Why did he feel threatened over the prospect of having Emery work closely with Melody?* Nevertheless, Luke caught himself. He refused to be *that* guy. He wouldn't be the guy who was overtly jealous and insecure. He *only* had eyes for Melody, and he knew she felt the same.

"That works perfectly for me-that is if it's all right with *Mrs*. Bryant." Clarke's eyes drifted cautiously back over to Melody, and quickly skimmed over her beautiful body. It was a sting to his fragile heart to see the sizable wedding ring and band on her finger. Clarke's eyes knifed through hers "Would that be all right with *you*, Mrs. Bryant?" his voice resonated.

Melody's heart jumped, but she tried to meter her breathing. *What on earth was wrong with her? Why did she feel so flustered and disquieted around this man?* It was difficult to deny both the intrigue and the uneasiness she grappled with. Emery Lloyd's good looks and apparent charm were *not* what fascinated her. Call her biased, but no one was more devastatingly handsome than *her* husband, and Melody undoubtedly had all the man she needed in Luke. Still, there was something compelling and mysterious about Mr. Lloyd.

Trying not to perpetuate the weird vibes between herself and Emery Lloyd, Melody forced a smile in his direction. "That would be just fine by me. I'm excited to look over your credentials."

Clarke surrendered to a slow nod, and smiled openly at Melody. "That's very encouraging. Thank you for the opportunity. I am looking *forward* to meeting with you tomorrow afternoon." Clarke had to pull back from ogling at his potential boss's wife.

Brenda stood back, and curiously watched and listened to Emery's interactions with her bosses. She felt immensely proud to have discovered Emery Lloyd. She could tell Melody and Luke liked him a great deal. As far as *she* was concerned, he'd already sold her on working for Portals. Nevertheless, Brenda had to admit she was the slightest bit jealous, because Emery couldn't seem to keep his eyes off of Melody Bryant. Yet and still, Brenda refused to take that personally. Melody was incredible, and it wasn't unusual for men to stare. Brenda had already made up her mind to ask Emery out, even if he would probably be working in a different department. The man was totally hot, and there was no wedding band on his finger. That was all of the motivation Brenda needed.

"You're welcome, and *we* look forward to seeing you tomorrow!" Luke gave Emery an affable smile, even if he couldn't escape the way the man kept eyeing Melody. This was definitely a test of character for Luke. So, he avowed not to succumb to jealousy and possessiveness. *Melody was extremely beautiful! Men stared at her all the time. Emery Lloyd wasn't the first, and he certainly wouldn't be the last man to notice her.*

"Thanks for bringing Emery by this afternoon, Brenda. You obviously have a knack for discovering talent when it comes to Portals. Keep up the good work!" Luke enlivened, and gave Brenda a thumb's up. "Mr. Lloyd…," Luke acknowledged, and extended his hand out to the gentleman.

"*Emery*…please," Clarke insisted. "Mr. Bryant…? Or should I call you, *PM?*" Clarke asked cleverly.

"You can call me whatever you're comfortable with." Luke gave Emery's hand yet another firm handshake.

"Mrs. Bryant…," Clarke redirected towards Melody. His heart throbbed, and fire radiated through him like a furnace, because Melody was close by.

"It was nice meeting you today, Mr. Lloyd!" Melody said politely, as her eyes shied away from the intensity of the man's gawp.

"Please, call me *Emery*," Clarke reminded. He shook Melody's hand firmly, but resisted the urge to bring her hand up to his lips, and press a kiss to it.

"We will see you tomorrow, Emery," Luke affirmed.

"Thank you again for agreeing to see Emery this afternoon. Sorry for taking up so much of your time, *PM.*" Brenda frowned in angst.

"Not at all, Brenda. I'm glad you did." Luke gave her a reassuring smile.

"It was nice meeting you both!" Clarke turned towards Melody and Luke. If he played his cards right, they *would* hire him. Then, he would work on making both Melody Bryant, and Portals Unlimited his own. "Good night." Satisfaction radiated on his sharp features.

"Good night," Luke and Melody said uniformly, while Brenda directed Emery away from the office.

"Are you all right?" Luke pulled Melody into his arms the moment Brenda and Emery disappeared down the hallway. He searched her face and eyes in concern. "You seemed a little rattled."

"I'm okay. It's just that…"

"What's the matter, honey baby?" Luke brushed caringly on her cheeks.

"Well, do *you* like him?" Melody's face twisted in ambiguity.

Luke smiled cleverly. "Never mind about me. The question is do **you** like him?"

Melody shook her head nonsensically. "Luke Bryant, I can't believe you'd *ever* be jealous of anyone," she said softly.

"Jealous? Me? Never…." Luke guffawed and spoke

nonchalantly. "There's nothing for me to be jealous about."

Melody draped her arms about his neck, and squeezed him lovingly. "I hope you know that nothing and no one compares to you," she whispered into his ear. She then pulled back to look into his eyes, as she plowed her fingers through his bronze curls. "Nothing and no one ever…"

"Yeah… Is that so?" Luke hunched down, and teased the corners of Melody's mouth with tender kisses.

"Uh-huh…" Melody kissed her husband in cadences. "Besides, *you're* the *Portal Master*," she uplifted.

Luke searched Melody's eyes urgently for a moment. "I couldn't help noticing the way he was staring at you. Does it make you uncomfortable?" Shrouding his usual upbeat demeanor, Luke's face wrinkled in gravity. "The power's in *your* hands, Mel. If you don't like him, we don't have to hire him." Luke delved critically into her eyes.

"He *did* make me feel a little uncomfortable. He's very intense, and a bit invasive. It felt almost as if he was reading me like a book."

"What do you mean, baby?" Luke grimaced in confusion.

"It's difficult to explain." Melody sighed. "He looked into my eyes as if we know each other, like we've met before. It was *that* kind of familiarity."

"I sure *hope* you haven't met before," Luke said possessively. "Maybe, the weird factor has everything to do with the fact that he was probably nervous?" Luke's brows arched in introspection.

"*Maybe*," Melody assented. "I can only imagine. I

can *see* how meeting the *Portal Master* and his wife could be intimidating," Melody teased. "Believe me, I'm *all* for second impressions, but we're getting ahead of ourselves. We'll see what happens during the interview tomorrow."

Luke nodded in agreement. "Sounds fair, but I *definitely* have to be in on this interview," he emphasized. When Luke noticed the inquisitive look on Melody's face, he tried to lighten up.

"Luke, you *are* jealous. I can't believe you would *ever* be," hurt and disbelief resonated in Melody's tone, and her eyes widened in shock.

"I guess, I *do* tend to get a *little* jealous when it comes to you," Luke admitted, with scarlet-shaded cheeks.

"Luke Bryant, don't you know I *only* have eyes for you? If you knew how much I love you, you would *never* feel jealous or insecure a day of your life."

"I'm sorry, honey baby. It's kind of hard to have my heart beating outside of my chest for the world to see. There *are* moments I get scared that someone's going to steal you away from me." Luke's face bridged affectionately to hers.

"Nothing and no one will or can steal me away. I will *never* let you go," Melody said softly. "Promise *you'll* hold onto me for dear life."

"I will hold on until my dying day."

"I'm all for that," Melody echoed.

And yet, in a corner of Melody's mind, she could still see Emery Lloyd's penetrating eyes. She kept reliving how intimately his eyes had explored hers. For all intents and purposes, Emery Lloyd had undressed her with his eyes. It felt as if he knew her deepest, darkest secrets. That gnawing feeling as if she'd in some way been violated, persisted on their way back home that afternoon.

It dawned on Melody that Luke probably thought she was *fascinated* with Emery Lloyd, because of his good looks and charm. The truth was that the man had just freaked her out. She felt conflicted, and felt uneasy with the idea of Emery Lloyd working alongside her in the GDD. Still, Melody didn't want to be biased, and deny a clearly talented and qualified worker a great job. Perhaps, she needed to pray on the matter. She would ask God what *his* will was on the matter. Melody would also ask God why this stranger had had such a bizarre effect on her.

Chapter Five

Peter stalled in front of the Ward's family home out Amber Woods, Virginia. His heart flagellated mercilessly, so he had to take a moment to quiet it down. He'd done a bit of sightseeing on his first day out in Virginia. However, for the most part, his main activity was keeping tabs on Arianna. Peter realized he'd become a stalker since she'd come into his life. Later in the day, he was scheduled to meet with Stephen Sanderson, CEO of Body Electric Era. So, Peter was about to take a chance in the hopes that Arianna might want to come along.

Peter knew she was at home. Arianna and her sisters had just gotten back from the local strip mall, where they'd shopped at a convenience store. Then, they'd stopped in at the fruit smoothie place. So, Arianna and her sisters had been home for at least a half an hour. Peter had come by in order to ask if she wanted to attend the meeting with him.

Peter judged that Arianna knew Mr. Sanderson a lot better than he did. After all, she and Luke had worked for BEE for a while. So, in Peter's estimation, having Ari by his side when he met with Mr. Sanderson, would be icing on the cake. Truth be told, Peter would consider his visit a success if Arianna even spoke to him. All things considered, Peter took heart when he remembered Luke's advice right before Luke had suggested he fly out to Virginia.

"Here goes nothing," Peter susurrated before ringing the doorbell. As Peter waited for someone to answer, his heart whisked like turbulent waves of the ocean. He was just about to give himself a little pep talk when someone came to the door.

"May I help you?" the beautiful, blonde woman with light blue eyes asked Peter with a cordial smile.

Unequivocally, Peter knew the woman was Arianna's mom. Even if the woman was probably in her mid-forties, she looked considerably younger. Peter smiled musingly, as he evaluated how much Arianna favored her mom. It wasn't difficult to see why Arianna's family was so beautiful. "Um…" Peter hesitated, smiling bashfully. "My name's Peter Lawton, and I work for Portals Unlimited out in Burbank-"

"You *must* be a friend of Ari's," she deduced. "Are you here to *see* Arianna?" Her face radiated in excitement.

"Yes, I am. Our boss sent me here on business for a few days-"

"Lovely! Come on in, Peter! I'm Elizabeth Ward, Ari's mom!" She opened up the door, and invited Peter in.

"It's *really* nice to meet you, Mrs. Ward!" Peter shook her hand in greeting, as she ushered him into the house.

"Mom, I thought I heard someone at the door…," Arianna's voice trailed when she saw Peter standing in the living room. *What on earth?* She found herself temporarily stunned and speechless. She thought she'd heard Peter's voice, but had chalked it up to her imagination.

Her mom turned to address her. "Yes… Your friend Peter's here on business from California."

Arianna froze on the steps, and she couldn't seem to form any words. She couldn't believe Peter was actually there. She'd seen him only a few days ago a little before she'd left Portals. However, it was strange seeing him again so soon-in her family's home no less. Peter looked amazing in his casual dark jeans, navy blue shirt and stylish comfortable shoes. She'd almost forgotten how he looked in casual gear, because he wore business suits religiously at work. Peter's strapping upper body was highlighted all the more by his navy polo shirt. The color accentuated his dramatic deep blue eyes. For all intents and purposes, he was a life-sized Ken doll.

Arianna found herself utterly captivated, as she sized him up. However, remembering his atrocious behavior at the wedding reception, stirred her from the trance. She deliberately dismounted the stairs, and crossed over into the living room. "Peter, what are *you* doing here?" Arianna's face wrinkled in perplexity. Despite her misgivings, she couldn't escape how much better Peter looked up close. It also didn't help matters any that he smelled positively divine!

"Ari, I apologize for just showing up at your parent's in this way. I didn't mean to upset you. I *know* that you're technically still on vacation. But, I honestly needed your help with something." Peter's eyes explored hers reticently. His heart danced a jig, because she was within range again. Recalling how drunk and out of control he'd been the last time they'd talked, made him flinch in shame.

However, at that moment, he was completely sober and alert. Peter found himself getting lost in Arianna's angelic face. Her pretty hair was out and wavy, totally unlike the straight bangs she sported for work. Her frilly, pale yellow top, picked up the honey tints in her hair, and made her ice blue eyes pop.

"You need *my* help with something having to do with work?" Arianna set her hand on her heart. "Did Luke send you out here?" she asked, baffled.

"Yes, he sent me out here for a few days on business. *PM* wants to give your old boss the head's up about *Shield Me*, and an informal presentation. So, he sent me as a rep. I have a meeting with Mr. Sanderson later this afternoon. And, since you used to work for BEE, I was kinda hoping you'd come *with* me." Peter grimaced in uncertainty. His heart lashed all the more nervously in his chest. And yet, in spite the nervousness, he found himself drinking in everything Arianna, as if she were his oasis out in the hot, dry desert.

Arianna gave him a quizzical look. She had no idea what to say to Peter at that point. It was also difficult to interpret anything he was saying, because for the first time since they'd met, she realized just how perfect his mouth was. Peter had the perfect lips, and his voice was both throaty and edgy whenever he spoke. She pursed her lips to speak.

However, Peter spoke up again. "I know you came out here for a break from it all. I promise, I'm not here to pull you back into all the stress. But, it would *really* help if you were there with me at that meeting." Peter inched in closer to Arianna, and his face wrinkled in appeal. "Ari, I respect your business acumen a great deal! You have such a way with people and *me*... Well, sometimes I'm a little too reserved, so I come off as awkward," he admitted, offering her the hint of a smile.

Elizabeth Ward allowed her daughter a moment alone with Peter Lawton. She stood back, and examined their interactions with keen interest. She was tickled pink, because Peter obviously liked Arianna. However, she was bewildered by her daughter's elusiveness towards this incredibly handsome, and seemingly nice young man. Elizabeth hoped that Ari would warm up to Peter, because nice guys didn't come along every day. "Ari, I'm about to go into the kitchen. Can I get you and Peter some iced tea?" she asked politely.

"I'm fine, mom. Thanks."

"Thank you, Mrs. Ward, but I'm fine as well." Peter turned to address Mrs. Ward with an affable smile.

"Okay, let me know if you change your minds." That said, Elizabeth crossed over into the kitchen.

Arianna sighed and tuned back into Peter. "Peter, you should have called, and given me the head's up. You can't just show up here while I'm on vacation, and ask me to attend a meeting over at BEE." She sighed.

Peter nodded in concurrence, as his heart plummeted to the floor. "You're right. I'm sorry. I guess, I didn't think it through. When Luke said BEE, I said to myself, if I could get Ari to come along, Mr. Sanderson will be all the more excited to invest in *Shield Me* technology. I apologize, Ari." Peter sulked, but then forced a smile. "It's all right. I think I can handle this one on my own." He waved a dismissive hand. "I'll be fine."

Arianna examined Peter's face and his eyes, and realized just how uneasy he felt. It occurred to her what a huge risk he'd taken to come out there in order to ask for her help. And, there she was again... She found herself skimming over how perfect Peter was in every way. Hence, she could have stood there listening to him talk forever. She'd seen Peter a hundred times before. However, at that very moment, her eyes were opened as to why a ton of women who worked through Portals Unlimited, were so up in arms about him. Arianna tried to shake herself free from her daze. She tried to remember how Peter was in habit of *working* his popularity with their coworkers in order to get exactly what he wanted. That realization grounded her back to reality.

All the same, Arianna remembered how kindly Peter always treated her, even when she herself wasn't always receptive to his thoughtfulness. In spite of his lapses in judgment, he'd never done anything but to uplift her. She wanted him to see that *she* wasn't the monster he probably thought she was. Time spent away from Portals for the past few days-time away from Luke, had helped tremendously. Arianna had prayed extensively on the matter, and she was finally confident of overcoming her feelings for her boss. Above all else, Arianna perceived what Peter *really* needed was a relationship with Jesus Christ, and *she* wanted to show him that she had one herself.

So, in a carefree manner, she tilted her head back, and gave Peter a heartening smile. "What time did you say you were meeting with Mr. Sanderson again?"

Peter baulked in shock. "What…?"

"When do *we* have to meet with Mr. Sanderson?" Arianna clarified with an earnest smile.

"Two." Peter shook his head in skepticism. "Did you just say 'we'?" His entire face lit up. It took every bit of restraint he had not to throw his arms around Arianna, pick her up off the beautiful hardwood flooring, and spin her around like a little girl.

"That's right, Lawton. You *heard* me." Arianna's smile brightened. "So, you should pick me up at about one thirty," she emphasized. "If we leave early enough, traffic shouldn't be too bad."

"Thank you." Peter's deep blue eyes glistened in affect. The more Arianna spoke to him and smiled, the faster and harder Peter found himself falling for her.

"Well, just don't be late." She cheekily crossed her arms over her chest.

"I'll be here on time… I promise." Peter turned to

leave, and Arianna followed him to the front door.

Arianna held the door open for Peter. He crossed over to the doorway, but she kept the door slightly ajar. "So, I'll see you in a little while."

"Definitely…" Peter's smile was irrepressible. Joy bubbled up on the inside like a spring.

Arianna laughed lightly to see how happy Peter was. Even if he was definitely not her type, she acknowledged that Peter could be decent at times. She shut the front door after watching him get into a wine-colored BMW and pull away from the house.

"Arianna Brooke Ward, what on earth was that all about?" Elizabeth Ward demanded to know the moment Arianna shut the front door.

"Mom, you scared me." She clutched her heart in surprise, but smiled nonetheless. "Peter works alongside me at Portals, and Luke sent him out here on business."

Elizabeth grasped hold of her daughter's shoulders excitedly. "Honey, he's so handsome, and he seems super nice. Does he have a girlfriend?" Anticipation radiated on her beautiful face.

"Mom, Peter has hundreds of girlfriends at Portals alone."

"Oh…?" Elizabeth said a little disappointed. However, she had to point out, "Ari, Peter might have a gazillion girlfriends back at Portals, but he's definitely got his eye on you. You can't tell me you don't notice the way he looks at you?"

Arianna laughed. "Mom, Peter is the kind of guy who

likes to make women happy-and I mean *every* woman he meets. He's nice, polite and great at his job." She shook her head contrarily. "I hardly think he's ready for any type of serious relationship."

"I say you're wrong. The way he stares at my daughter is pretty *serious*. Anyway, are the two of you going out?"

"We have a business meeting with my old boss at two. That's all, mom." Arianna shook her head nonsensically over her mother's observations having to do with Peter.

"Well, that's a good place to start," Elizabeth muttered before walking away.

"Whatever, mom," Arianna answered, hearing what her mom had said. She kept shaking her head in denial over the entire matter. Arianna suddenly looked over at the antique grandfather clock at a corner of the living room, and saw that it was 11:45 a.m. "Oh my goodness! What are we doing, Ari? We have to find something decent to wear for this business meeting. Peter's coming back in just a little while…"

Arianna veered, and climbed back up the stairs. She had to get ready for when Peter came calling again. She heard her younger sisters Alexa and Raina scrambling to return to their rooms. They obviously didn't want her knowing that they were eavesdropping, and watching her interactions with Peter. Arianna knew for sure that her sisters would find her at some point, and she'd never hear the end of how *hot* and *nice* they thought Peter was.

***

"Mr. Sanderson was *so* happy to see you, Ari! It

really made his day that you came along. It was such an
unexpected surprise!" Peter was all smiles, as he led Arianna
into Scully's. It was an upscale restaurant, just a few miles
away from the Body Electric Era building. Peter was on cloud
nine, because Mr. Sanderson was completely onboard, and
more than ready to invest in Portals' latest technological
breakthrough, ***Dimension*** *Shield Me.*

　　Knowing that it was Luke's innovation, BEE was all
in. They were fiercely proud of anything associated with Luke
Bryant. However, the fact that the meeting over at BEE had
gone well, wasn't the only reason why Peter couldn't stop
smiling. For the first time in their history, he and Arianna had
worked on something as a team. Indisputably, the more time
Peter spent around Arianna, the more it solidified the fact that
he was in love.

　　"I was happy to see him too. Mr. Sanderson's the
best! I can't believe how much they all said they missed *me*."
Arianna shook her head, marveling. Peter kept his hand
pressed to the small of her back, as he led them over to a quiet
table towards the back of the restaurant. The setting was cool
and dim. Moreover, through the tinted picture glass window
was the most amazing skyline. Arianna was amazed by how
safe, and secure it felt to have Peter's hand on her. He'd kept
his hand on the small of her back, and had guided her along in
this way all that afternoon. And, honestly, it felt nice.

　　"Well, how could they *not* miss you when you're so
awesome?" Peter pulled out a chair for Arianna, and helped
her settle in. Smiling into her eyes, he evaluated just how
beautiful she looked in her deep red colored wrap dress.
Arianna had on matching accessories. Peter loved the blood-
red teardrop-dropped shaped earrings hanging on her dainty
earlobes. He loved anything red on her.

　　"Thank you for saying that." Arianna smiled at him,

but pointed a liable finger in his direction. "I didn't think I'd be saying this, but thank you for inviting me out to the old office today. It was nice seeing everyone again. Honestly, being at BEE today, only makes me appreciate Portals that much more." She laughed lightly.

"There's no way we're ever giving you back," Peter razzed, with twinkling eyes.

"Oh, don't worry. I'm *not* looking back." Arianna shook her head senselessly.

"Good, because we're never letting you go," Peter established.

Arianna smiled quietly, and her cheeks turned ruddy, as she stared diffidently into Peter's eyes.

Peter clasped his hands together, and his eyes fastened to Arianna's. "Thank you for coming along. It really means a lot to me...*really*." Peter stared at her wonderingly, almost like a child seeing snow fall for the very first time.

"You're welcome!" Arianna fiddled nervously with the table menu. The waiter had not yet brought over the full menu.

"So, you like Portals a lot more than working for BEE?" Peter's face and eyes were inquisitive.

"I do miss all of my old coworkers, but *everyone* at Portals is so great. And, I *love* working for Luke," Arianna admitted. Her heart perforated a little upon saying Luke's name, but she was determined to move past the hurt. God had someone out there for her, and that person wasn't Luke Bryant. So, she had to trust that God knew what was best.

Hearing Arianna say Luke's name was a stab wound

to Peter's heart. However, he forced a smile and went on to say, "*PM's* awesome! There isn't a better boss on this planet! I have to say that landing my job at Portals from the very beginning is literally a godsend." Peter nodded affirmatively.

Arianna was impressed, and offered a sincere smile. "I'm blessed that I got to know Luke before all of it, and I feel the same way. For the record, I'm also glad *you* landed the job. You're amazing at what you do!" she said reticently.

Peter's face was all aglow. "Thank you. For what it's worth, Ari, no one does a better job than you. Even *PM* knows it!"

"Aww... That's really sweet of you to say, Peter." There was a quiet lapse between them, but Arianna felt Peter's stare hot on her face, as she perused the menu. "Are you okay?" Arianna looked up and steadied her gaze into his eyes.

Peter sighed heavily, and his face rumpled in guilt and remorse. "I'm okay. I just wanted to apologize for how I behaved at the wedding reception-"

"No, no..." Arianna kept shaking her head contrarily. "It's all right, Peter. You don't have to explain-" Her face warped in sympathy.

"Please, Ari... Please, let me explain. I want you to know that the man you saw at the bar that day, the one who followed you out into the parking lot, and made all of those horrible accusations..." Peter kept shaking his head in contrition. "Ari, that's not who I am. I'm sorry for behaving like an out of control drunk." His eyes glinted in affect.

Arianna's face wrinkled in compassion and understanding. "It happens sometimes to the best of us. You don't have to keep punishing yourself for what happened. *I'm* sorry for the horrible things I said that day. I guess, it's true.

Hurting people truly *do* hurt others." Arianna sighed, and her head slumped. Tears sparkled in her eyes, when she looked up at Peter again.

"Ari…" Peter gasped in shock, and reached for her hand from across the table. "Please, don't cry…" He felt mislaid, as he stroked caringly on her dainty hand. He honestly wanted to rush to her side, and take her up in his arms.

"I understand what it's like, Pete. Sometimes, the pain screams so loudly on the inside that it takes all of the restraint you own *not* to take a few drinks… You're not the only one who struggles," she disclosed. All the while, the feel of Peter's strong, yet gentle hand brushing hers was enrapturing. The way in which he touched her was more comforting than she could define. The expression on Peter's face, and the depth in his eyes, relayed that he understood, and that she in some way mattered to him.

"Ari, is there something you want to tell me?" Peter asked thickly, as he explored her eyes stirringly and empathetically.

"*You* were right," Arianna admitted. Her sad eyes connected critically to Peter's. "You were right about everything you said out in that parking lot." Fresh tears glimmered in her eyes at that point. She'd never confessed her feelings for Luke to anyone-not to her mom, her dad or her sisters. Arianna had no idea why she felt compelled to come clean with Peter. Maybe, it was because she'd suffered for such a long time, and had kept everything bottled up.

"*I* was right…?" Peter looked puzzled.

"You were right when you said I have feelings for Luke." Arianna's face twisted in misery.

Arianna admitting her feelings for Luke was a bulldozer to Peter's heart. It felt nice being close to Ari, and even nicer that she'd confided in him. However, having his heart pulled apart was the worst feeling in the world. It also resonated that he was playing completely out of his league.

Peter swallowed hard and nodded. "I've known for a while. I'm so sorry, Ari. I honestly *wanted* to be wrong." He continued the pacifying motion of caressing her hand. "I can't imagine how difficult that's been for you." It killed Peter to discuss the matter, but he avowed to be there for Arianna no matter what. He loved her so much that even if they could only be *friends*, he was willing to accept that.

"It's been *so* hard," Arianna confessed. "I've felt like such a fool. Every morning that I've walked into that office, I've struggled to keep my feelings in check. I feel like such a hypocrite, Pete. Melody and I are friends…" Arianna's cheeks reddened in embarrassment and shame.

Peter tugged softly on her hand. "Ari, you're being way too hard on yourself. No one's judging you. *Luke* should be so lucky to have someone so amazing care about him. Besides, I'm certain Melody would never judge you. Arianna," he said quietly, "loving someone is nothing to be embarrassed about."

"I fell in love with Luke when we worked down here together last year. He and Melody weren't together at the time. Luke had just gotten hired by BEE. From the outset, I knew he was something special. Luke knew that I had feelings for him, but he was *always* in love with Melody. Luke also didn't take me too seriously, because he thought I was so young." Arianna had a pining expression on her face.

"On Luke's last day, the company threw him this huge party. *I* decided to keep him close that entire night." She laughed ironically to remember the account. "I refused to let him dance with anyone else. When we danced a slow number, I kissed him, but Luke pulled away..." She went on to explicate how Luke let her down gently, and how he'd never made her feel weird about what happened.

"You didn't deserve that. Ari, I hope you know just how special *you* are. You *deserve* to be with someone who knows that. You should be with someone who will move heaven and earth just to prove that to you," Peter emphasized. He brought her hand up to his lips, and pressed a kiss to it. "I meant what I said that afternoon, even if I was totally wasted. *PM's* great, but he isn't the guy for you. You do get that?" Peter sensitively searched her eyes. "I know you're a woman of faith, Ari. So, if Luke married someone else, he can't be God's will for you."

Arianna nodded, and allowed Peter to hold her hand for a little while longer. "Rationally, I understand that. I guess, my heart's having a hard time catching up."

"Matters of the heart take time. Give yourself some time, Ari. You are *so* beautiful! You know that?" Peter kissed her hand repeatedly, and never wanted to let it go.

"Thank you for saying that, and thank you for letting me rant." Arianna cautiously wiped tears away from her eyes with her free hand. "Sounds like *you* know what it's like to love somebody you can't have," she said insightfully.

Peter swallowed hard and forced a smile. Pressing one last kiss to the back of her hand, he didn't say anything more. Just then, the waiter sauntered over with the official menus, and asked if they were ready for appetizers. Peter finally let go of Arianna's hand, and stared quietly and contemplatively over at her, as she perused the menu.

Even with the sad expression and tears in her eyes, Arianna still took his breath away. So, Peter ascertained that if talking about her love for their boss was their only point of intersection, he was willing to endure it, even if it broke his own heart. What Peter unequivocally grasped was that he would *never* want anyone or anything more than he wanted Arianna.

***

The California diamond-studded night sky shimmered with vitality. Brenda was ecstatic, because she'd just had the best night out with Emery Lloyd. Asking him out was a risk which had panned out in the best way. Emery was smoking hot, and now that he was working through Portals Unlimited, he was definitely financially set. So, Brenda was committed to making this catch of a man all hers.

"Would you like to come in for a drink?" Brenda asked Emery, as he stood at her front door. They'd gone out to dinner, and had talked about everything under the sun. Mostly, they'd dallied, and had flirted all night long at the upscale restaurant on West Burbank Blvd. And now, Brenda wanted to find out if this man was ready to put his money where his mouth was.

Brenda was elated that her boss, and his wife had hired Emery for a key position in the Graphics Designs department. Furthermore, Brenda was even happier that she'd asked Emery Lloyd out first. Notwithstanding, there were a number of women who worked through the office, vying for his attention. He was the new eligible bachelor onboard, and had many of the ladies talking.

Clarke was totally pumped about the turn of events. He was now a supervisor for the GDD of Portals Unlimited. That meant working closely with Melody Bryant. Clarke had perceived Melody and Luke's initial reservations about hiring him. Perhaps, Clarke considered, Luke had picked up on his keen interest in Melody. Subsequently, Clarke wasn't hating the fact that a number of women who worked for the company, had shown romantic interest in him.

So, Clarke figured that his newfound popularity with all of the *other* women, helped put *Mr. Hot Shot Portal Master's* mind at ease. Even so, the only woman Clarke was interested in was Melody. Still, having the attention of many others was a welcome distraction. That distraction would only enhance his goal of making both Melody Bryant and Portals Unlimited his.

Clarke smiled seductively at the temping young woman. "Brenda, we had a nice time tonight, but I'm afraid I'm going to have to take a raincheck on that drink." His mien was mesmeric, and his mellifluous voice resonated.

"Are you *sure* about that?" Brenda coaxed, as she turned the key in the lock to her house.

Clarke grasped her hand firmly, and tugged her back to face himself. Setting his hand possessively on her waist, he pulled her into his arms. "I may not be staying for a drink tonight, but allow me to *show* you how much I enjoyed your company tonight," Clarke whispered into her ear.

"Oh…? By all means…" Transported, Brenda closed her eyes, as Emery closed in. With a great deal of finesse, he brushed his lips on hers.

Clarke thoroughly covered Brenda's lips, and kneaded

them hungrily. However, just as quickly as he'd initiated their kiss, he abruptly pulled back. "Next time, I promise to show you for just a little bit *longer*. Honestly, Brenda, if I kiss you again, I will *not* be able to leave your house tonight," he said gutturally, exploring her eyes.

"That's just fine by me. I don't *want* you to leave, Emery. We can finish what we started back at the restaurant." Brenda draped her arms about his neck, and smothered his face, hair and neck with kisses. "Stay the night?"

"As tempting as an offer as that is, it's our *first* date. So, please allow me to remain respectful." Clarke tried not to sound too short or rushed. And yet, all he wanted was to return to his private beach house on Newport Beach and unwind...*alone*-far away from Brenda Fields.

"All right... So, would you like to do this again tomorrow night?" Brenda's eyes danced in anticipation.

"I would definitely love to go out with you again. Maybe, we could do this again on Sunday night?" Clarke negotiated. He needed at least one day to himself, and refused to compromise his privacy by having this needy young woman up in his face all the time.

"Sunday night is great. I would love to make you a nice dinner." Brenda gave him a come-hither look.

"That sounds lovely, but I would *rather* take you out for a presentation, and then buy *you* a nice dinner...that is if that's all right with *you*. I wouldn't want you slaving over a hot stove for me." Clarke's face and eyes were drunk with manipulation, even if all he wanted was to run away as far as he could.

"That's so thoughtful of you, but I really don't mind-"

"Allow *me* show you the town, and to buy you a nice dinner," Clarke insisted.

Brenda nodded in agreement. "Okay... As long as we're together, I really don't care *what* we do, or where we go." She draped her arms about his neck again, straddled his head in her dainty hands, and pressed kisses to his lips. "I guess, I should say goodnight then. Good night, Emery. Thank you for dinner tonight."

Good night, Brenda. You're welcome!" Clarke said politely. He gently pulled away from Brenda's predatory grasp.

"Good night," Brenda said again, and lingered at the door.

"Good night, Brenda!"

Clarke was almost to his car when he turned, and waved at the eager young woman. He slipped into the automobile, and smiled with a sense of satisfaction. He had Brenda Fields exactly where he wanted her. She was completely wrapped around his finger. Befriending her was an added benefit. She was one of Luke's top employees. So, Clarke grasped that if he played his cards right, she would help him access some of Portals groundbreaking technology such as; the *Power Portal*, the *Vortex to Vanish* gateway, **Dimension** *Find Me*, and the latest... **Dimension** *Shield Me.*

Clarke's intention was to utilize these unique modes of transportation and telecommunication to bring Luke Bryant down, and to make Portals Unlimited *his* conglomerate. So far, things were going according to plan. He'd *wowed* Luke and Melody during their sit-down interview. He'd also managed to reign in the bizarre deer-caught-in-the-headlights expression on his face. It was the one he'd had on his face upon reconnecting to Melody.

Clarke resolved to maintain absolute aplomb, and not weird Melody out. His performance during the interview was impeccable. He'd convinced both husband and wife that he was all about the *business*. They'd hired him on the spot that afternoon. And, now, he had a job working down the hall from the object of his affection. Clarke determined to be circumspect in as far as his performance at Portals, because he couldn't yet afford to cause any ripples in the water.

The mission was already outlined; making Melody his again by any means necessary, rubbing Luke out by any means necessary, and taking over the Portals Unlimited conglomerate. So, until those plans were secure, he would exercise extreme restraint, and do everything in his power not to behave inappropriately towards his boss's wife. And yet, it was scrupulous to suppress the strong feelings he had for Melody whenever he saw her. Nevertheless, for the moment, Clarke grasped that just *seeing* her was going to have to be enough, even if he wanted so much more.

***

"This is outrageous!" Sean marveled. He and Nicole followed Luke and Melody, as they led the way for a walk-through a very expansive and upscale house. It was the sixth house they were all viewing on that day. This particular house located in Atherton, was worth over ten million dollars. It had eight bedrooms and bathrooms, its own villa, wine cellar, spa and an Olympic-sized pool. Only ten minutes away from the beach, there was a movie theatre, a private gym, and a gazillion other perks.

"Well, do you guys like this house? If you and Nicole

lived *here*, you'd only be ten minutes away from me and Mel," Luke told Sean and Nicole. Melody remained close to his side, as they all explored the lavish house.

"Honestly guys, what's *not* to like?" Nicole stared all about in incredulity, as she perused the property. "Still, Luke, Mel, what on earth would Sean and I do with all of this space?" Nicole shrugged inanely.

"Luke, this house and all its amenities is *sick*, but Nikki and I need something a little more reasonable. It's honestly out of our price range." Sean frowned, and shook his head in the negative. "There's no way we could ever afford to live here."

The four of them continued the tour, and took the set of stairs leading down to the wine cellar. The spacious, cool vault looked more like a library of fine wines.

Luke himself was totally impressed by the property, and he was completely stoked for Sean and Nicole. "Mel, do *you* want to tell them, or should *I*?" Luke and Melody exchanged knowing looks, and impish smiles.

"I think *you* should be the one to tell them, *PM*," Melody razzed on Luke, and poked him playfully on his side. She was so proud of him she could burst. She couldn't hold back the excitement she felt that Sean and Nicole were getting the grand tour of the house.

"So, I'm going out on a limb here. I'm guessing that out of all the houses we've seen today, *this* is the one you and Nicole are the most impressed with?" Luke's expression was roguish.

"Luke..., what are you up to?" Sean stopped short when he noticed the mischief on Luke's face. "What's going on in that crazy head of yours?" His brows furrowed in perplexity and suspicion.

"Oh, nothing…" Luke stared all about, feigning total cluelessness. "I *might* be just the slightest bit excited, because this house is kinda, sorta *yours*…" His face crinkled in playfulness.

"Shut up!" Nicole's eyes dilated, and she cupped her mouth in shock.

Melody eyes glimmered affectively to see the astonished and delighted looks Sean and Nicole shared.

"You can't be serious, Luke. *What…?*" Sean kept shaking his head, stunned. "You mean all this…?" He took in the upscale and extensive house.

Luke nodded, laughing over Sean and Nicole's reactions. "If you and Nicole want something else, we can keep looking." His eyes sparkled emotionally.

"Luke, I can't accept…," Sean said thickly.

"Yes you can, Sean. You and Nicole are family. Luke and I just *love* making family happy one *home* at a time out in California," Melody argued.

"That's right. Just ask *my* mom and dad," Luke pointed out. "They finally sold the old house out on Rhode Island. You should see my dad walking around in a house so big he keeps getting lost in it." Luke shook his head humorously. "I love it! I don't think my parents have been able to find the kitchen yet, but I plan on going by tomorrow afternoon to help them find it. They've been doing a lot of take-out for the past few weeks."

Sean kept shaking his head in denial over the matter. Tears rolled down his cheeks, as he grabbed Luke by the neck, and pulled him in for a rough hug. "You're something else, you know that? I don't even know what to say-and you know *I'm* never speechless."

"I *know*… That's actually a first for you," Luke teased. "You don't have to say anything, buddy. Mel and I are so happy that you and Nikki decided to live close by. Ah, and just in time for Thanksgiving!"

"Yeah, just in time for the holidays." Sean's head was still spinning.

"It's all right, Nik…" Melody wrapped her arms around Nicole in comfort. They swayed quietly in a loving grasp, because Nicole couldn't stop crying.

"How could you be so wonderful?" She hugged Melody, and pressed a kiss to her cheek. "I love you!"

Melody squeezed Nicole affectionately. "I love you too! Luke and I are so happy you guys came out here to join us!"

"Oh, Luke…" Nicole threw her arms around Luke, and hugged him meaningfully. "Thank you! Thank you so much! Sean and I don't know what to say."

Luke laughed, and crushed Nicole affectionately. "Just say you'll take it, and that you'll be happy here. Can you do that for me?"

"We're sure going to try. So, are we having Thanksgiving here, or over at *your* place?" she asked excitedly.

"We can do Thanksgiving here, then have Christmas over by us," Melody suggested, overjoyed.

"The holidays are definitely going to be hectic." Luke

chortled.

"You knew about this all along didn't you, Mel?" Sean feigned a suspicious look over at Melody. "I thought you were my buddy. You could have said *something*."

Melody wrapped her arms around Sean, and pressed a kiss to his cheek. "Don't be mad at me, Sean. Your buddy swore me to secrecy," Melody admitted. "He also made Cupid promise not to *bark* out any secrets." She snickered.

Sean kept shaking his head in utter shock and skepticism. "I can't believe this…"

Melody pulled away, and grasped Nicole's arm. "Come on, Nik, let me show you *my* favorite part of the house. It'll be perfect for your *Diva Den*," she enticed.

Nicole laughed. "Okay. Mel…?" Her eyes widened in surprise, when Melody tugged on her arm, and conveyed them back up the stairs.

Sean was stupefied, and still in denial. He couldn't wrap his head around what was happening. "This is *way* too much, Luke. Seriously, how are Nicole and I *ever* going be able to pay you back?"

Luke's face changed in doubt. "Pay me back? Sean, you and Nicole have just uprooted your entire lives to come live out here. *You're* going to be my right-hand man running a multibillion dollar enterprise. Not to mention the fact that you're my brother, my ride or die and partner in crime. Are you *seriously* asking how you and Nik are going to pay me back?" Luke's face rumpled in disbelief.

"Sean, I don't think you get it. Whatever happens to *me* happens to *you*. We're family. We've been family since we were those snot-nosed kids in middle school. *You're* the one who kept telling me that I'd get here someday. You never stopped believing that it would happen, even when I was cleaning toilets for a living." Tears glinted in Luke's eyes again.

Sean teared up, because he was completely stirred by Luke's words. "I *did* tell you that you would be using a golden mop and pail someday." He smiled in irony.

Luke pointed and gave him a knowing look. "I *did* go out there, and I purchased a gold-plated mop and pail for me and Mel. We keep them in our cleaning supply closet."

"There you go." Sean winked.

"Seriously, Sean, *I* should be asking what I owe *you*," Luke emphasized. He pulled Sean to himself and patted him on the back. "Don't ever ask me that again." There were tears rolling down Luke's cheeks when they broke free.

Sean nodded in agreement. "Okay, I get it. But this house...?" He sized up the splendor of the place in awe.

"If you and Nicole want to look for something else...?" Luke joked.

"No. I think we're good here." Sean smiled earnestly, and allowed Luke to take him on a full tour of the incredibly huge and lavish home.

"You and Sean can have them set up a Jacuzzi in this corner right here. If you want to turn this entire corner into your own personal spa, that shouldn't be a problem," Melody brainstormed. She and Nicole were standing inside one of the huge newly furnished rooms. It had the potential to be Nicole's little get away from it all. Luke already had a man-cave designed for Sean. So, Melody wanted to make sure Nicole was also getting what *she* wanted. "What do you think, Nikki?" Melody asked, excited.

Nicole laughed. "I think I need a moment to catch my breath." She held her hands out in a halting manner. "I'm out of breath. It literally took five minutes to get here."

Melody sighed. "I promise, you'll get used to it."

Nicole stared all about, amazed. "I suppose, I would have to get used to something like this."

Just then, Melody's cellphone went off. Her heart dipped to the floor, because the call was from Portals. It was early Saturday afternoon. And even if she wasn't working, some of the folks who worked through the GDD were busy weekend bees. She hoped and prayed there wasn't an emergency or a crisis of sorts. Melody looked over at Nicole, and excused herself in order to take the call. "Hello."

"Yes, good afternoon, Melody! It's Emery," the voice resonated over the line.

"*Emery...?* Is everything all right over there?" Melody scowled.

"Everything's going well. I was just calling to find out if it's all right to work through the entire evening. I'm not terribly busy this weekend, but I *do* have a lot to get caught up on down here."

Melody's heart raced in angst, but she was uncertain as to why. In spite of the reservations she and Luke had had about Emery Lloyd, hiring him seemed to be a stellar move on their part. The man was hardworking and respectful. He was extremely cooperative, and kept pretty much to himself. And yet, in spite of all of his notable qualities, there was something totally odd about him.

Emery reminded Melody of nobility, a count or viscount who'd lived centuries ago. However, due to circumstances beyond his control, he'd been forced to acclimate to the fast-pace and brashness of the twenty-first century. But, there was a lot more to it than that. As polished as Emery appeared to be, there was something quite daunting about his aura. In short, he wasn't the easiest person to comprehend.

"You want to work through the night? Are you sure? You could always work overtime next week if you want to catch up on work," Melody suggested. She didn't realize how her entire demeanor had changed, until Nicole stopped exploring the beautiful room, and zeroed in on her in concern.

"I could *also* work overtime next week, but I'm on the cusp of creating a fantastic new layout. So, I'm afraid if I don't strike while it's hot, I'm going to lose my motivation," Clarke cajoled.

Melody laughed uneasily. "Okay. If that's the case, we wouldn't want you to lose your motivation. I'm glad you're working so hard. I wish everyone in our department would follow suit."

"Ha, ha, ha… I'm not trying to show anyone out, but I do appreciate you're saying that. I won't let you down," Clarke said cunningly.

"No. You've been great! Keep up the good work, Emery!" Melody enlivened.

"Thank you. I definitely will. Thank you for giving me the overtime."

"You're welcome!"

Melody looked over at Nicole. She'd sat down on the extremely comfortable sectional towards the right-hand corner of the sizable room, staring oddly at her.

"Who was that?" Nicole's face wrinkled in puzzlement.

Melody crossed the room, and sat down next to Nicole on the sectional. "*That* was Mr. Emery Lloyd." She smiled vaguely. "He's new to the Portals family. Luke and I hired him to work through the GDD along with me."

"Why'd you look so frazzled while you were on the phone with him?" Nicole grimaced, nonplused. "Mel, you should have seen your face. You're *his* boss right? So, why should a regular employee intimidate you?"

"Did *I* look nervous while talking to him over the phone?" Melody set her hand on her heart in inquiry.

Nicole nodded. "You looked like someone who just discovered there's an intruder in the house. What's up with this Emery guy anyway?" Nicole prodded, worried for Melody.

Melody told Nicole how Emery Lloyd made her feel. She conveyed that Emery's references had all checked out, and that he was the model employee. However, there was something totally unsettling about him, in spite of the fact that he worked harder than anyone else.

"So, from what you're telling *me*, he's the good-looking, cosmopolitan type, who has all of the women at the office swooning?" Nicole clarified. "You have a picture of him?"

Melody thought for a moment. "No… I…wait I think I might from the office luncheon two weeks ago." Melody accessed pictures on her phone, and sure enough, there was one of Emery. He was standing near the serving station looking distinguished, yet aloof as usual. He had on a smoke-gray colored business suit, and held a drink in his right hand, as if *posing* for a picture. "That's him." Melody displayed the picture.

"Oh my…! He *is* gorgeous!" Nicole studied the photo a little more. "Mel, he is good-looking, but even from the picture I can tell he's a bit of a prude. So, I gather he's the kind of guy that makes others feel just the slightest bit inadequate." Nicole poured over the photograph. "But he *does* remind me of someone." She had a reflective expression.

"Really…? Who do *you* think he looks like?" Melody asked, curious.

Nicole's face changed completely, and urgency shimmered in her eyes. "I apologize first and foremost for bringing up bad blood, but he favors Clarke Vale," Nicole said plainly, as she examined the image on Melody's phone.

Melody's heart somersaulted. Swallowing hard, she stuttered, "Clarke…?" Melody inched in closer to Nicole in order to scrutinize the picture, but she couldn't see the resemblance.

"I know the *face* is different, and this guy's a lot better looking, but I guess around the eyes…" Nicole's eyes narrowed in introspection.

Melody guffawed in skepticism. "Maybe, that's why I've been so uncomfortable around him. It's his eyes. Emery's eyes *do* remind of Clarke's." Melody shook her head in remorse. "But Clarke's…"

"Gone… He decided to take his own life." Nicole's face twisted in sorrow, remembering how close she came to losing Sean, as a result of Clarke Vale's criminal activities.

"Yeah, well... He won't be able to hurt anyone else. *Now*, I get why I've been so indifferent to this man. On a subconscious level, he reminds me of Clarke. But that isn't very fair."

"No. The man can't help the way he looks. Is he nice?"

"He's polite and works very hard," Melody admitted. She sighed remorsefully. "I guess, I can *try* to be a little bit more cordial to him."

"Mel, we don't have to worry about Clarke anymore. That whole nightmare is behind us," Nicole reassured.

Melody nodded and forced a smile. She and Nicole hugged. "God brought us all through that horrible time, and we're not looking back."

"God always protects his children. I thank God every day, because Sean is still here with me," Nicole's voice wavered, but Melody squeezed her hand in support.

"And, God will *keep* Sean healthy and whole." She hugged Nicole again.

However, at that point, Melody grasped why Emery Lloyd made her feel so ill at ease. Something about him reminded her of Clarke Vale. But, Clarke Vale was dead. It wasn't Emery's fault that something about him, made them think of someone whom they'd all had a horrendous history with. Talking the matter over with Nicole, gave Melody fresh perspective. So, Melody resolved to stop penalizing Emery Lloyd for Clarke Vale's sins, even if they had the same eyes.

"So, you're all set-that is if you and Nik decide to spend the night. Mel and I set up a couple of the bedrooms. There's plenty of wood in the fireplace, if you want to get a fire going, because it *does* get a little nippy at night. Your fridge and pantries are stocked," Luke said, pulling cold drinks from the ginormous, brand new state-of-the-art fridge from the main kitchen.

"Wow, I can't believe you thought of everything." Sean drifted further out into the kitchen. Following Luke's lead, he gladly took one of the cold bottles of brew. Hopping up onto the glossy, cream-colored island counter, he popped open the bottle. "I could *definitely* get used to this." Sean sighed after chugging from the bottle.

Luke leaned up against the side of the island counter. "You should *definitely* get used to it. As a matter of fact, are you and Nik spending the night, or are you coming back to the house with me and Mel?"

"I guess, I'll have to ask Nikki what she wants to do-that is once she and Melody get back from Nikki's *Diva Den*." He chortled, and got Luke laughing as well.

"Melody probably has a gazillion ideas." Luke shook his head humorously.

"Oh, to be a fly on that wall…" Sean razzed.

Luke's cell phone rang just then. His expression changed when he saw the name on the lock screen. He and Sean exchanged nonplused stares before Luke answered.

Sean knew the call was urgent. So, he immediately snapped to attention, and tuned in to Luke's end of the conversation.

"You *are* using the phone I sent you right?" Luke

frowned in seriousness. "All right, that's fine. So, what do you have for me?" Luke asked Daryl Pearson. Daryl was his and Sean's undercover guy whom they'd sent to work through the jail out in Sands Port. Daryl was there to expose the discrepancies in and surrounding Clarke Vale's *ostensible* suicide.

"So, a few of the workers *did* hand in their resignation? How long did you say they were working there? A few of them were only a year or two away from retiring, and from collecting their pensions?" Luke's face crinkled in skepticism. "So, a total of four veteran workers quit in less than two months?

"Uh-huh… So, you made friends with this Gabe kid, who's only been working there for a couple of years?" Luke gave Sean a knowing smile. "You think Gabe would *talk* if an offer was made?" Luke asked artfully. "All right then. Work on *that*, and get back to me. Good work, Daryl. By the way, I put a little extra into your account earlier on. Keep me posted. Bye."

Luke nodded, and smiled in satisfaction after shutting down his cell. "Bingo!"

"Are you thinking what I'm thinking, buddy?" Sean fretted.

"What *are* you thinking?" Luke smiled in anticipation.

"Those employees who up and quit, were definitely rewarded for their trouble. Why else would any of them quit, only a year or two away from collecting their pensions?"

"I agree with you, buddy. I'm beginning to think their *pensions* were supplemented by Clarke Vale. In light of all Daryl's told me, there's no longer any doubt in my mind Clarke's out there somewhere." Worry creased Luke's usually easygoing demeanor. "Wherever he is and whatever he's up to, can't mean anything good for any of us."

"Maybe, his end game is to evade jail time. He *was* staring at consecutive life sentences," Sean theorized.

Luke stared urgently into Sean's sea blue eyes. "I *wish* that was the case. I just can't help thinking that if he went through all that trouble to fake his own death, at some point he's going to pop up. He definitely has an axe to grind with *me*...with all of us. The only thing Clarke is more obsessed about than Melody is revenge. We've already established that he's not the type to forgive and forget."

"No he isn't. Have you shared your suspicions with Melody?" Sean set his right hand on his chest. "*I* haven't said a word to Nicole."

"No, I haven't told Mel. The last thing I want is to freak her out, and have her living in fear." Luke's eyes gunned into Sean's in criticalness. "I don't think you should tell Nicole either. It might be better that way."

"I agree on that, Luke, but there's got to be something we can do. I mean, Daryl's working undercover out in Sands Port and all, but I think we'd definitely make a lot more progress if we..."

"I'm already on it, Sean." Luke moved in closer to his friend. "How would you like to take a portal ride with me tomorrow afternoon?"

Sean's expression was of both surprise and intrigue. "Are you serious?"

"I would *never* joke about something like that. Our use of the *Power Portal* is government regulated." Luke rolled his eyes in annoyance. "How *dare* the government try to regulate how many times a person can pop in and out of another country or a state?" His face and eyes were laced in mischief.

"Yeah, the nerve…" Sean rose impishly to the occasion.

"But that doesn't apply to *me* since I'm the *Portal Master*," Luke humored. "I think you and I should pay a little visit to the Sands Port jail. *We* would know exactly what to look for, and who to connect to. Being there would also expose the weakest links. We've got to find that *one* person or persons willing to sing like a canary for a few bucks here and there." Luke clasped his hand together, and looked like a movie villain.

Sean nodded in agreement. "I like that idea. It would only be for a few hours right? Nicole and Melody *won't* like it if we dropped off the face of the earth for hours at a time."

"I *know*. That's why we're going tomorrow afternoon. The girls have plans, remember? Mel wants to take Nicole sightseeing for a while."

"That's right." Sean was reflective again.

"So, we're going to use that little window of time to show *you* around Portals, Sean-at least for a few hours or so." Luke smiled insightfully.

"It's a great idea, buddy, but we can't just go visit the jail as ourselves. No one out in Sands Port can recognize us," Sean calculated.

"That's where *you* come in, my friend. It's up to *you* to ensure that two *different* men come out on the other side of the portal tomorrow afternoon."

Sean's thought raced with possibilities, as a clever smile curved over his lips. "I could definitely make sure we're unrecognizable. Going out to Sands Port jail's a great start. But, there's got to be something else we can do to protect ourselves if that lunatic is out there."

Luke nodded, but seemed a million miles away. His eyes suddenly reconnected to Sean's. "There *is* something we can do to protect ourselves, and I'm going to show you how to both access and utilize the program for you and Nicole. **Dimension** *Shield Me's* still in the trial stage, but I can personally attest to its effectiveness. I can give you access to the app. The censor's a virtual field-something like an impenetrable bubble. Much like a polygraph machine, it picks up on an outsider's mood, every intent, whether good or bad. When the shield detects potential danger from an aggressor, or predator, it automatically locks in, and creates an impenetrable, and impervious shield around the targeted individual.

"Won't that get in the way of day-to-day activities?" Sean's face wrinkled in doubt.

"That's the beauty of *Shield Me*. As long as the censor's activated through the app-which I'm about to download on your phone, you're connected to surrounding satellite signals wherever you go, whether or not the device is present. Very few things can interfere with the shield, not even a nuclear explosion," Luke detailed. "It's a powerful virtual and invisible buffer from anything you can possibly think of. Most importantly, it's as undetectable as the air we breathe."

"But, won't the girls notice they're surrounded by that kind of energy? When they realize they're being *shielded*, they're going to want to know why we're going to such lengths."

"They'll never know unless they're directly in harm's way. *Shield Me* allows for day-to-day activities, and normal interaction with others. You can hug, touch, kiss, etc.… The shield's protective field locks in *only* when a threat is detected, or when bodily harm is impendent."

"So, the field protects from outside threats like gunfire, fires, explosions, stabbings and the like?" Sean questioned. "What if someone tries to hit, grab or shove the one being shielded?"

"Again, *Shield Me* will repel the threat by automatically locking in for protection," Luke explained. "I plan on setting up the system on Melody's phone tonight. Setting up the system on the phone is an added measure. *We'll* control the program on our end. We can't tell the girls we're using our latest state-of-the-art homeland security system to keep them safe. You've got to promise not to tell Nicole, Sean." Luke's face and eyes relayed the criticalness of the matter.

Sean nodded in agreement. "All right, I'm all in. Let's get this thing going." Sean pulled his phone from the pocket of his jeans, and handed it over to Luke.

Luke removed what appeared to be a tiny silver pixel out from a miniscule silver box lodged inside of his wallet. The pin was smaller and lighter than a needle. Setting both his and Sean's phones side by side, Luke issued a command to his. Accessing the app, Luke fiddled with numbers and letters on Sean's keypad. Seconds later, there was a transfer from Luke's phone which contained the originated program, to Sean's.

Luke felt empowered using *Shield Me*. He was grateful to have developed it, because he could protect himself and his loved ones, in the event Clarke Vale was looking to enact revenge. In addition, using ***Dimension*** *Find Me*, he could flush Clarke out of wherever he was hiding. Since his inventions were government regulated, and using ***Dimension Four*** and its accessories always had to be accounted for, Luke would find a way around the restrictions.

He had the tools and the technology. So, he was going to employ the knowledge to keep his loved ones safe. He and Sean would start with a quick trip back out to the Sands Port jail using the *Power Portal*. Going out to Sands Port would hopefully give them some of the answers. Once there, they could possibly access a few of Clarke's personal effects. Retrieving his belonging would facilitate *Find Me* in pinpointing an exact location.

***

Later back at home, Luke had just gotten into bed. Melody had left her phone on their nightstand, and was in the adjourning bathroom getting ready for bed. Luke figured that it was the perfect time to link her phone to *Shield Me*. Luke stared down at Cupid, who clung to his side of the bed, and pointed a liable finger at the dog. "You'd better not bark out any secrets to Melody. I know you like her better than you like me." Luke chortled, reached down, and ruffled Cupid's golden mane. The dog looked up at Luke and moaned in fatigue.

"I know you're a good boy! Yeah, I know you're tired. Get some rest okay." Luke watched Cupid's head slump over his paws and close his eyes. Smiling quietly, Luke shook his head humorously, realizing Cupid always had the ability to make him laugh. However, their current set of circumstances was no laughing matter. Luke hated not being able to tell Melody what he and Sean suspected. Clarke Vale had faked his own death, and had purchased his freedom through a crooked system. The last thing Luke wanted was for his wife to live in fear.

"I'm *so* happy for Sean and Nicole!" Melody breezed back into their bedroom from the adjourning bathroom.

Luke radiated joy. His heart melted, taking in just how beautiful she looked in her pink satin negligee. "I still can't get over the looks on their faces when we told them about the house.

"You *really* did a great job keeping them in suspense until the very end." Melody laughed.

Luke chuckled. "Sean and Nicole have no idea that this is only the beginning."

Melody crossed over to Luke's bedside. "Does Sean have any idea what you have planned for him at Portals?" The tint from the pink negligee radiated on Melody's face, and gave it a mystical glow.

"Sean thinks he's going to be one of our supervisors. He has no clue that he'll be running the conglomerate alongside me," Luke contrived, overjoyed. He wanted Sean to have as much-if not even more authority than he had. The way Luke saw it, Sean was an extension of himself. So, if *he'd* stumbled upon billions of dollars through his innovation, Luke wanted to ensure Sean and his loved one had the same.

"Sean and Nikki are two of the best people I know, so I am so happy for them!" Melody's face twisted in sappiness, as she stared lovingly down at Luke.

Luke got off the bed, and gently pulled Melody into his arms. "*I'm* happy for them too, and I'm excited over the fact that they chose to spend the night over at their *new* home."

Luke's face bridged sweetly to Melody's.

"I think *you're* good people, Luke Bryant! You're so amazing and generous!" Melody pressed kisses to his face.

"You *think* I'm good people?" Luke basked in the moment.

"Yes... I'm *so* proud of you, honey bear!" Melody inched back to stare into his face, as she gently massaged his shoulders.

"That makes my day! And, you know what? I'm sure proud of *you*, honey baby!" Luke smiled into her eyes, and celebrated the rare gift God had given him in Melody. "You're doing such an amazing job running *your* department over at Portals."

"You *have* to say that because I'm your wife," Melody whispered, and pressed her lips fondly to his.

"You know, you're right... I've got to admit that I *am* just the slightest bit partial to you. Well, how can I not be when you're my entire world? I love you so much!" Luke crushed her in his arms, and held on as if for the very last time. "I promise never to let anything or anyone hurt you!" Luke's grasp grew even more acquisitive.

"I love you more! Everything okay, honey bear?" Melody murmured into his chest, confused by his sudden display of protectiveness.

Luke tenderly cradled Melody's head in his hands, and pressed kisses to her forehead. "You're always safe with me, Mel, and that's the way it's going to stay." Tears shone in his eyes.

"You make me feel safe every day." Melody pulled

away to look into his eyes. "Luke, you're crying..." Shock veiled her face.

Luke smiled, and tried to placate her fears. Crushing her in his arms once more, he reminded, "I always cry whenever it occurs to me that you're really mine." Holding her head delicately in his hands again, he stared meaningfully into her eyes. "I will protect this rare gift God has given us with everything in me."

Up until that very moment, Luke hadn't factored in what it meant that Clarke was possibly alive, and biding his time until he could strike again. However, this time around, Luke resolved not to take any prisoners. So, even if Clarke Vale was still out there, when Luke got through with him, the man would wish he was dead.

"We're okay, baby. Everything's okay. God brought us together, so he will keep us safe," Melody enlivened. It bemused and saddened her to see Luke in tears. However, she trusted her husband. Melody knew that if something was really wrong, Luke would have told her.

Luke was sensitive by nature, and he was often moved to tears while expressing his heart. "I promise to never let you go, Luke Bryant! You're my heart!" Melody uplifted. However, Luke didn't say a word. He just held her quietly, and refused to let go. So, in the stillness, Melody held on to him, and took refuge in the safe harbor of her husband's immuring arms.

Chapter Six

"I have to say, Ms. Brenda Fields, you make a man *want* to work overtime every weekend. Thank you for having dinner with me and for…" Clarke examined the backdrop of Brenda's quaint little bedroom. He was in her bed, and on the verge of getting everything he wanted from the gullible young woman.

Clarke had worked overtime in past weeks. It was a strategy to impress Melody, and to get closer to Brenda. Not only was Clarke putting in the time in order to date Brenda, but he wanted her to see how serious he was about working through Portals. It made him sound cosmopolitan whenever Brenda inquired about his weekend plans. For the past few weeks, Clarke had been quick to tell her he was working overtime through the GDD.

What Clarke *really* wanted was to join the software engineers and developers-who worked closely with Luke Bryant, Arianna Ward, Peter Lawton and Brenda Fields. An administrative position had recently opened up in software innovation. The position was a cut or two below Brenda Field's job. Clarke wanted the job so badly he could taste it. So, he figured if he kept Brenda happy, she'd be more inclined to help him out.

Even if leaving the GDD would mean seeing a lot less of Melody, Clarke was willing to make that sacrifice for the greater good. Melody was the *ultimate* motivation for being there. Every move he made would bring him one step closer to getting her back. So for the time being, he was willing to forfeit seeing and speaking with her every day. Clarke would do whatever was required in order to take her away from Luke Bryant for good. Nothing and no one would *ever* make him give up on the most important goal of his life.

The most important aspect of connecting to the very top feeders on the Portals Unlimited food chain, was gaining an access key to top secret applications, and mastering the esoteric nature of ***Dimension Four*** and its components. A change in status would also mean access to Luke Bryant's private office. Clarke had heard rumors of the portal Luke had designed solely for *his* office.

Clarke was utterly riveted. He was chomping at the bit to be in the *know* of the specialized advancements, masterminded by his enemy. Even if at the core, he despised Luke Bryant, Clarke was willing to admit that the kid was a total genius. For that very reason, Clarke resolved never to underestimate Luke again. Clarke's plan was to use Luke's own technology against him.

"You were absolutely amazing! It was so well worth the wait to be with you tonight," Brenda susurrated, and gently rested her head on Emery's chest. "Please, don't go home tonight. Stay over?" She graspingly wrapped her arms around his waist.

Clarke's laughter was both profound and provocative. "Don't worry, Dear Brenda. I'm not the kind of guy who comes to the party, and doesn't help clean up afterwards." A roguish expression covered his face. Brenda was a beautiful girl, and so *eager* to please him. So, for Clarke, seducing her was only icing on his cake.

Brenda's head inched up closer to Emery's face, and her eyes bridged to his. "You're so *weird*, but you're so *hot* it doesn't even matter." She shook her head absurdly.

Clarke laughed again. "You have absolutely no idea just how right you are." He then pulled her back into his arms, and mauled her affectionately, as a bear would romp around with her cubs. "I think you're rather *hot* yourself!" He gave her an alluring smile.

"You do...? Well then..." Brenda surrendered to his arms, and kissed him until she lost herself in the act.

Clarke was up with the sun, and saw Brenda sleeping

soundly beside him. He cautiously slunk out of the bed, and scrambled to find his clothes. He'd spent the night with the lonely, yet beautiful Brenda Fields. He'd put in the performance of a lifetime-if he did say so himself. Nevertheless, the sun was up, and he had to get going. During their *pillow talk*, he and Brenda discussed the new position over at Portals. Clarke had asked her opinion, in as far as him being a good fit for the job. Brenda was all smiles, but remained somewhat enigmatic.

She really didn't need to say very much, because she couldn't hide the fact that she was totally enamored. Things being what they were, Clarke could easily see Brenda doing *anything* he asked. No doubt, he had the young woman exactly where he wanted her.

Clarke rushed to get dressed without making too much noise. His goal was to leave without waking Brenda up. Brenda tossed and turned on the bed, but remained asleep. However, her constant shifting about made Clarke feel uneasy. Still, he was ready to play it cool if she *did* open up her eyes. Clarke's cunning smile blinked on and off in suspense. He had no idea whether or not he'd make his great escape, or if he had to-on impulse, resume playing the role of Brenda Field's doting lover.

He crept around the room in order to garner the rest of his things, but Brenda tossed and turned again. This time around, she began calling out for him, "Emery...Emery, where are you?"

Clarke speedily slipped out of his slacks and T-shirt, rushed over to her, and flashed his mechanical smile once again.

Brenda turned to face him with a relaxed and pleasant expression on her face, because Emery was hovering over her.

"I'm right here, beautiful!" Clarke took the hand Brenda extended to him, and covered it in kisses.

"I was worried you left," Brenda said sleepily.

"No. I'm *still* here." Clarke slipped back into bed.

Taking Brenda up in his arms once more, he pelted her with kisses.

"I'm so glad you stayed over." She wrapped her arms around him, stroked his face, and plowed her fingers through his hair.

"I'm glad I stayed over too, Brenda. You just made my morning!" Clarke crushed her in his arms. "Don't worry, my darling, you have me for the next few hours, and then I *really* have to go."

"Well then, I think we should make those hours *really* count." Brenda draped the comforter over their heads, covering Emery and herself from head to toe.

Clarke didn't mind putting in a little overtime in as far as his performance with Brenda. He was convinced she'd unequivocally endorse *him* as the prime candidate for the new position over at Portals. Now, he was free to consider which of the multifaceted components of **Dimension Four** would best serve in getting Melody back, while simultaneously destroying her husband. The possibilities were endless, because everything seemed to be working to his advantage.

***

Violet, gray and white lights whizzed like a cyclone, as Luke and Sean spiraled through the vortex of the *Power Portal*. The portal they were using was the huge one only Luke had access to in his office. Luke and Sean were dressed like two older, but well-off men, who could possibly pass for CIA agents. With their graying hair and wrinkles, they popped into the Sands Port jail out in Maryland.

The two breezed into the facility unconventionally, and chatted with a few of the guards and corrections officers.

For a while, everything seemed routine. However, in an unexpected turn of events, one of the corrections officers, named Valerie Strom, singled *them* out. From what Luke and Sean deciphered, Valerie seemed to be the eyes and ears of the place.

She had all kinds of theories. So, she voluntarily detailed her suspicions in respect to Clarke Vale's stint at the jail, and his ostensible suicide. She also shared her theories in respect to the deputy director who'd recently retired from the facility. His name was Phillip Lombard. Apparently, the middle-aged man had retired early a few months ago, and had moved down to the Cayman Islands.

Luke and Sean made no verbal agreement to offer Valerie any monetary reward for her cooperation. However, that they *would* seemed the unspoken protocol. Luke and Sean asked Valerie if Phillip Lombard had left behind any personal effects. Without hesitation, she brought them over to the man's old locker. There, she retrieved an old pair of work gloves. She gladly handed them over to Luke and Sean without even asking why they needed it.

When they asked if any of Clarke's personal effect had been left behind, Valerie led them over to another part of the facility. It was an expansive room with hundreds of small metal lockers. "I don't know what we'll find in there, but I'm hopeful we can pull something up." Valerie led the way down a long stretch of hallway.

"We *really* appreciate you're going out of your way to help us out," Luke said, throwing his voice. He sounded more baritone than usual, as he and Sean exchanged knowing looks.

Valerie turned towards them and smiled. "It's no problem. That entire sudden suicide seemed fishy to me too. It's hard to imagine that stuck up prude ending his life." She meandered down the winding passageway.

Luke and Sean eagerly followed behind her. Valerie kept looking cagily about, as if someone would pounce on them at any given moment.

Valerie's head whipped back to look at Luke and Sean. "Here we are! If anything *was* recovered from his jail cell that morning, it should be in here!"

Luke and Sean didn't say a word. Rather, they watched the young woman fidget with a number combination. Their hearts thudded in apprehension. They were anxious to see if anything had been left behind, which could be filtered through **Dimension** *Find Me.* So, if Clarke, who was the sorriest excuse for a human being, was still out there, they'd be able to locate him.

Slipping gloves on her hands, Valerie cautiously removed what appeared to be a Zip-locked bag from the small, square, metal locker. "What do we have here!" she said to no one in particular, as she unzipped the bag. Her face twisted in disgust when she pulled out a toothbrush, a shaving kit and a small hair comb.

Luke and Sean exchanged knowing nods, and grins, because they'd just hit pay dirt.

"Those were the only items recovered from his jail cell that morning?" Sean tested.

"Yep, nothing of any real value." Valerie turned to face them. "I can't let you take anything with you. His belongings are considered official jail property, and you're not allowed to touch any of it," she emphasized.

"Trust me, we're not interested in touching *any* of his personal effects," Luke ensured. "There is one thing we're going to need. Is there a table nearby? We have to lay out all of his things." Luke cautiously perused the winding halls. .

"Sure." Valerie guardedly looked from left to right, before gesturing for them to follow her.

Luke and Sean trailed behind Valerie. She led them feet away from the never-ending hallway, and made a sharp right in the direction of what appeared to be a private room. Valerie fiddled with a large key ring, which held hundreds of keys, until she found the one for that particular room.

Luke and Sean were conveyed into a small, cramped

dark gray room. The room was virtually empty, with the exception of more lockers, and a small table, with two chairs on opposite ends. With gloved hands, Valerie gingerly removed the contents within the zipped-locked bag found in Clarke's former locker, and spread them out onto the table. Valerie suddenly flinched.

Neither Luke nor Sean had to ask why she was startled, because they'd heard the footsteps drawing closer to that area.

"You two wait here. I'll handle this." Valerie set her index finger over her lips, indicating they not make a sound. That said, she scurried out of the room.

"This won't take long at all," Luke said. He pulled out his phone, and accessed the *Find Me* feature. "If Clarke's DNA's on any of these items, *Find Me* will track his location."

Sean also accessed *Find Me* on *his* phone. He figured two trackers would work better than one. Sean flinched, hearing the footsteps again. "Luke, I think she's coming back." He instinctively tucked his phone in the inner pocket of his dress suit.

"No worries. We have more than enough through the scan. However, I do think we need to pay Mr. Phillip Lombard a visit. We need to hint that we're on to him," Luke conspired. "Once we get him to tell us the truth about Clarke and the fake suicide, we can use *Find Me* to get to Clarke himself."

"Luke, I doubt that man will readily confess to helping a known criminal to fake his own death, and flee the country."

"Oh, we're going to get him to confess. We're going to come at him as if we already know he's guilty. And, if *that* doesn't work, we're going to offer him an even more obscene amount of money than Clarke did."

Sean nodded and smiled cunningly. "Then, we put in a call to the cops, and tip them off that this Phillip Lombard guy's hiding out on the Cayman Islands."

"No, Sean. If we get the authorities involved, *Clarke*

will know we're on to *him*. That will only make him dig an even deeper hole than the one he's hiding out in. So, we'll let *Phillip what's-his-face* think he's safe, and that he got away with taking a bribe from Vale. Make no mistake about it, once we take Clarke down for good, we'll find Lombard and his cohorts, and make them pay for releasing a known murderer and mafia lord out into the free world...," Luke's word trailed, because the footsteps were drawing closer.

Luke and Sean exchanged agreeing nods, simultaneously accessed the *Vortex to Vanish* feature on their phones, and blinked out of sight. They remained quieter and more tranquil than stifled air on a torrid day, as they watched Valerie storm back into the stale and depressing room.

"Hey, where'd they go?" she asked silently, and scoured every corner of that room. "Where are you guys? You can come out now. It's safe. It was just one of the officers. He needed to access a locker as well. Man! I can't believe this." Valerie shook her head incredulous. Suddenly, shock sprinkled over her face. "I could get into *real* trouble if those guys..." She took deep breaths in order to quiet her drubbing heart.

Luke and Sean remained perfectly still, silently watching Valerie frenziedly search the room. They waited for Valerie to leave the room again. When she did, Luke pulled an envelope out from the inner pocket of his suit jacket. Through the invisible vortex, he reached into the material world, and set it on the solid wood table for Valerie. It contained ten thousand dollars. Luke smiled satisfyingly in anticipation of Valerie seeing the envelope. He knew all her doubts and fears would evaporate the moment she saw the envelope. "She deserves this and a lot more," he told Sean.

"She *sure* does. I'm so glad I got to travel *Portal First Class* with you this afternoon, my friend!" Sean winked.

"We just have *one* more stop to make. There's someone else we really need to see." Luke's smirked.

Luke and Sean waited for Valerie to return to the room

in order to claim her reward. Moments later, she returned, and shut the door warily behind her. Her eyes widened in shock when she noticed the envelope on the table. Suspiciously, she walked across the room and picked it up. Valerie opened it, and immediately thumbed through the bills. A smile wider than the ocean spread across her cute face. "Thanks fellas," she whispered, and tucked the envelope into her uniform shirt. "I guess, it *pays* to help out the *right* people." Once again, she looked from left to right before shutting the door, and drifting away from the room.

"Are you ready for the Cayman Islands?" Sean asked Luke, still on a high from their adventure.

"You wouldn't believe how ready I am!" Luke reveled, and toyed with his phone. It didn't take long for them to be consumed by the zipping lights of the *Power Portal*. Luke and Sean reeled and whirred in a world of overpowering illumination, which would transport them to another part of the globe. If asked, they would both attest to the fact that **Dimension Four's** *Power Portal*, was the only way to travel.

***

Phillip cast his line out onto the waters. Inhaling deeply, he basked in the sun-toasted air, and the perfect blue skies near his villa out on the Cayman Islands. This was indeed the life! He no longer had to answer to anyone, or deal with the depressing backdrop of working through the Sands Port jail out in Maryland. He'd seen enough in that jail over the years to write a book. And, maybe, he *would* write a book, because he finally had the time.

The *best* decision he'd ever made was partnering with Clarke Vale to pull off the greatest cover up of the twenty-first century. He, along with a few former coworkers, who'd worked through the jail, had all benefited greatly. They'd all helped the known mafia mogul fake his own death. Phillip was ten million dollars richer for having played his role in the unique caper.

Unlike his former colleagues, he had no wife or kids. So, he'd already started enjoying early retirement out in paradise. Life was just one big party. There was literally a party every night in the locale. Notwithstanding, there were no shortage of women for a *confirmed* bachelor. Notwithstanding, being financially set, had upped his game with the ladies.

Phillip stretched out on his boat, brought his linked hands to the base of his head, and waited for the fish to bite. Loops of sunlight shimmering through the clear waters, created a balance of light and shadow. Also, the swaying motion of the rocking boat made his eyelids heavy.

Uncertain as to whether or not he'd surrendered to the lure of sleep, Phillip was awakened by what seemed like an explosion of some sort. Only, the detonation was noiseless. Blinding lights radiated all around and encapsulated his boat. The beams swirled, and there was a low whirring noise that sounded like the swinging of a thousand blades.

"What the…?" Phillip instinctively jumped to his feet. His heart flailed, and felt as if it would pop right out of his chest. Two men, who looked like the *Men in Black*, had materialized out of nowhere on his boat. His eyes widened to the size of saucers, his knees knocked like maracas, and he peed his pants. "What's going on here? Who are you?"

Luke and Sean tried to keep straight faces, and not chuckle. Their expressions were urgent, as they waited for the portal's brightness to ebb. They were on Phillip Lombard's boat out on the Cayman Islands. Luke was impressed by how **Dimension** *Find Me's* tracker had brought them directly to the man. At other times, the tracker would come scarily close. However, this time around, they were staring Phillip Lombard in the face.

"We're *visitors*," Sean said cryptically, closing in on the man. All the while, Sean estimated how perfect the weather was this time of year in this tropical paradise. Sean was honestly blown away by the effectiveness and precision of *Find Me*. It was the first time he'd utilized the technology with Luke.

"*Visitors*-like from another planet?" Phillip asked, crippled by fear.

"That's *exactly* what we mean," Luke roared, using the special voice modifier of *Find Me*. His voice boomed like the voices of a hundred men.

"What…do…you…want…with…me?" Phillip clasped his hands together, as if he were about to say his prayers. "What…?" He sized up the two men. They were still glowing like aliens who'd just stepped out of a spaceship. Their dress suits were terrestrial, but the sound of their voices, and the luminosity surrounding them was extraterrestrial.

"We're known peacekeepers from the planet Glaxo. We've come from lightyears away to help the people of earth eliminate many undesirables-or those you might call *criminals*."

Sean chortled, but kept the noise level quiet. This was *way* too much fun to have in one day.

"Glaxo…?" Phillip stuttered. "Peacekeepers?"

"We need to know where Clarke Vale is," Sean minced no words. He crossed his arms valiantly over his chest. "We already know you're responsible in helping him fake his own death."

"We're fully aware that you-and a few others who worked through the Sands Port jail, helped Vale in carrying out this scam. Now, tell us where we can find Clarke Vale," Luke demanded.

"I dunno… *They* didn't tell me," Phillip admitted, mislaid and adrift. He wasn't even sure how his legs were supporting him at that point, but he was beginning to falter.

"*Who* didn't tell you?" Sean's voice echoed throughout the entire island.

"There was this guy-this guy was working for him on

the outside."

"Name please?" Sean obliged.

"His name is Simon... something...Simon *Air*...*Blow*...no, I think it might be *Winds*." Anyway, this Simon guy took care of everything, and helped Vale travel outside the country."

"Where outside of the country are we talking about?" Luke antagonized.

"Someplace strange...like you might see in them old vampire movies. Croa..."

"Croatia," Sean established.

"Vale's out in Croatia?" Luke's face creased in bewilderment.

"Yeah, but please don't tell him, and please don't take me up to your planet." Phillip smiled awkwardly and timorously. His lips quivered, and his face was redder than a crab's. "Don't *beam* me up or nothing like that. I helped you today. I'm begging you not to tell Vale or that Simon guy I told you nothing." Fear seemed to paralyze the man.

"*Why* did Vale go out to Croatia? Is there something special out there?" Luke tested.

"They never told us. They just gave us the money to make it look like he hung himself in that jail cell. Vale and Simon planned it all out while Vale was still in jail," Phillip sang like a Canary. He was shaking so much, anyone could have easily concluded there was an earthquake.

Luke and Sean gave each other satisfied smiles, and simultaneously blinked out. The moment they disappeared, Phillip's legs gave way, and he passed out on the boat.

Luke then reactivated the *Power Portal*. "I can't believe we were right all along, Sean. This is insane! *Thinking* that Vale faked his own death is one thing. But, *hearing* that loon admit to helping him do it is another." Luke wasn't only miffed, he was stunned. If Clarke Vale *was* a free man, no doubt the man would resurface in order to make trouble for them.

"Vale bribed his way to freedom…. but *Croatia*?" Sean was stupefied.

"Well, it's certainly remote. No one would *ever* think to look for him in that region. But, *we're* going to find him. Sean, *we've* got to get to Vale first, before *he* launches a surprise attack," Luke reasoned.

"That's a given. I can't imagine what he has planned, but we've got to hit first. This time we have to hit hard enough to make sure he *stays* down. There's way too much at stake." Sean shook his head in disbelief over the matter.

"As soon as we deal with Clarke, I'm going to see to it that everyone responsible for putting a *known* murderer back out into the free world, are put away for good. Let them enjoy their millions in bribe money now, and let that idiot Phillip Lombard think he was visited by aliens. He has no idea we're about to take him on a spaceship ride he'll never forget." Luke was incensed. He would do everything in his power to assure his loved ones remained safe. And, if that meant finding a way to make Clarke Vale disappear for good, that's exactly what had to happen.

Luke assessed just how production his and Sean's little excursion had been on that afternoon. Prior to *confirming* their suspicions, it had been all fun and games. Now that he knew for sure Clarke Vale was indeed alive and free, Luke would leave no stone unturned until the man was found. Once he did find Vale, Luke would make him wish he'd stayed in the jail out in Sands Port.

***

It was early Sunday evening when Luke and Sean popped out of the *Power Portal* in Luke's office in Burbank. Luke deactivated the device, and went over all security measures in order to shut it down completely.

"Melody just text me back. She's home now. Says

she and Nicole had the best time! Have you spoken to Nicole?" Luke frowned, as he fiddled with his phone.

Sean was still checking *his* phone, but he looked up and smiled. "Nikki's fine. She's excited about having dinner for the first time over at the new house."

A fleeing smile broke across Luke's face. "Congratulations!" he told his friend.

"Thanks," Sean said plainly. However, similar to Luke, his thoughts whizzed. Sean clenched his fists skittishly as he brooded. "So, *Shield Me's* still in effect for all of us?" He double-checked the app on his phone.

Luke nodded. "Yep, and it's pretty much on all the time-that is unless we decide to deactivate it. But, we can't afford to do that, because we know that monster's still out there."

"But what's out in Croatia?" Sean obsessed.

"I don't know, Sean but we're about to use *Find Me* to figure it out." Luke fiddled on his phone. "We've got enough of Vale's DNA to establish a location."

"What are we waiting for?" Sean seemed puzzled.

Luke pulled up Clarke's DNA through the samples he and Sean had garnered out in Sands Port. He quickly issued a command to the program. "*Find Me*, generate an image of the person with this unique DNA structure."

The deep violet, white, gray meteoric lights fluttered at a phenomenal speed. Usually, whenever Luke issued that command, an image would generate within seconds. However, this time around the lights just kept zipping.

"Master Luke, there seems to be a problem."

"What is the problem, *Find Me*?" Luke's face creased in jeopardy.

"The DNA belonging to that individual doesn't seem to be in one set location."

"What...? What do you mean by that, *Find Me*?" Luke was all the more perplexed.

"I realize that an individual cannot be in two places at one time, but that's how the DNA's coming up," Find Me informed.

"Two places at the same time… *Find Me*, please key me in on the two locations where this DNA is present."

"Two locations, Master Luke; one on the outskirts of Croatia and…

"Can you produce an image from either of these places?" Luke emphasized.

"No, Master Luke, I cannot. In order to generate an image, the DNA would have to hold to one location. This is the first time I've encountered such a conundrum," Find Me detailed. The blinking lights whirred with even more intensity than usual, because the program was working overtime-all to no avail.

"Find Me, please tell me what the second location is, even if we both know that it's impossible for an individual to be in two places at the same time."

"We've established Croatia as a possible location and the other…" There was a pause. However, the zooming light show blazed even more intently, and heat radiated throughout.

"Find Me, come on," Luke pressed. His face reddened in frustration, because he feared that he'd in some way damaged the technology. All the same, he was desperate to know exactly where Clarke Vale was.

Sean was riveted as he watched the process. It was strange to watch his buddy issuing commands to the state-of-the-art tool he'd designed. Seeing Luke in his element on that day, and being a part of the mix, made Sean radically proud to be Luke's best friend.

"Come on, *Find Me*," Luke goaded, and awaited a definitive answer.

"Master Luke, I've examined the DNA several times, and the second location keeps coming up as right out here in California."

Luke's heart dipped to the floor, and his befuddled

expression immediately connected to Sean's.

Sean's expression paralleled Luke's. "Luke, what on earth does that mean? It's confusing," Sean thought out loud, and kept shaking his head in irony.

"Hold up, Sean, let me try to get to the bottom of this for myself. I'm *just* as confused as you are. *Find Me* has never *snagged*, so I've got to believe it knows what it's talking about."

Luke spoke into the app again. *"Where out in California, Find Me?*

"Currently Palo Alto, the DNA has traveled in different parts of the state."

"What about a permanent residence?"

"Newport Beach seems to be where the individual spends most of their time, Master Luke."

"Has this person *ever* been out here in Burbank?" Luke posed the ultimate question. His heart thudded in anticipation of an answer, as he and Sean exchanged foreboding looks.

"That individual commutes to Burbank for work every morning."

Sean gestured for Luke to hand over the phone for a minute. *He* had a question for *Find Me*, but wasn't certain if the feature would take a command from him.

Luke was surprised Sean wanted to issue a command, and didn't hesitate to allow him to do just that. He watched Sean curiously.

"Find Me...?" Sean said in uncertainty.

"Yes, Sean Winters-best friend of Master Luke?" Find Me was all too accurate. Sean was surprised that *Find Me* recognized him, and Luke chuckled. "Has the individual with this DNA been inside of the Portals building?" Sean delineated.

"From what I gather-if my calculations hold correct-the individual's DNA is present at the Portal's building Mon-Fri." Sean's bemusement and dismay mirrored that of his best

friend's.

However, there was something they both needed to know.

"*Find Me,* can you give us a name or generate an image?" Luke cut to the chase.

"*Master Luke, the details are still too sketchy to procreate an image. The DNA is still coming up for an Island on the outskirts of Croatia* **and** *for various places here in California. An image can only be generated if the DNA holds to only one location. Sorry, Master Luke.*"

"*Can we make a positive identification? Can we get a name?*" Luke pressed.

"*The two locations are throwing me off, Master. Perhaps, when we're able to zero in on one, I could possibly pull up an image, and come up with a name.*"

"You've been more than helpful, *Find Me.* Thank you," Luke spoke into his phone.

"*Your wish is my command always!*"

Luke shut down the program.

"Sean, what the hell does that mean? *Find Me* has *never* been wrong. The technology has never failed to produce an image, or come up with a name. It's *always* effective. That's why the authorities swear by it in their searches for missing persons." Luke brushed his fingers nervously through his hair.

Sean kept shaking his head in total skepticism. "I don't know, man. *Find Me's your* baby, and I hate to say it, but *Find Me didn't* sound off."

"Yeah, but how can Vale's DNA still be out in Croatia *and* out here? Have I unwittingly *hired* Clarke Vale?" Luke asked facetiously.

Sean laughed. "No, I think you'd *definitely* know if you had."

"This makes absolutely no sense. For the first time *Find Me's* coming up inconclusive. This is the worst possible time, and with the worst possible identification." Luke sighed, utterly miffed over the matter. "Why did *Find Me* specify Vale's DNA is here at the Portals building Mon-Fri?"

Sean shook his head baffled. "I don't get that either. I *know* Clarke Vale isn't working for you. If he were under our noses, I think we'd know it. Maybe, *Find Me's* got it wrong on that one."

"*Would* we know it, Sean?" Luke speculated.

"Yeah, we would know if Clarke was working here, even if he went by a different name, and wore a wig, a scraggly beard and moustache. This is *your* industry. You're the one calling the shots, and there's definitely a way to resolve this. Do you know *everyone* who works for Portals *personally*?" Sean asked.

"Because of the nature of what we do, everyone who works through Portals has had to submit to extensive background and criminal checks. Even those who were hired to work through the housekeeping department, have been thoroughly vetted.

"Allow *me* go over that list again with a fine tooth comb." Sean crossed his arms over his chest.

"You want a list of everyone who works for Portals, including our magnet sites in other states?"

"Not necessarily those hired to work through Portals out in Atlanta or Denver per se. *Find Me* specified that Clarke- or someone closely related to him-"

"Stop right there." Luke pointed at Sean as if he were under arrest. "You might be on to something. You just said 'someone closely related' to him." Luke brainstormed.

"Like a family member? But we both know that no two individuals-no matter how closely related, share the same DNA. It makes no sense. We gathered DNA for Clarke Vale, not for a member of his family. *Vale's* DNA went through the tracker," Sean explained.

"I know, Sean. I know none of it makes sense. It's driving me completely crazy. I don't do loose ends, and *Find Me* has never been inconclusive. I've got to get to the bottom of this." Luke's eyes shone with tears of frustration. "Vale's *not* coming back into our lives. If it's the last thing I do, I *will* stop him in his tracks." Luke scowled. "*I* can only conclude that *Find Me* has some kind of technical glitch. All the same, we can't afford to sleep on this. For all intents and purposes, *Find Me*'s usually about 99.9 percent accurate."

"Maybe that .1 percent is the defining factor right now." Sean argued.

Luke kept shaking his head in denial. "I don't know, Sean. I guess, that's something I'll have to look into. No program or device is infallible."

"Let's look into it *together*, Luke. In fact, this week, I plan on making it my priority to conduct a mass screening of all Portals Unlimited workers. We're going to run thorough background and criminal checks on everyone who works for you-"

"For *us*, Sean…everyone who works for *us*," Luke filled in. He had to break it down to Sean what his new status entailed at Portals.

Sean's face winkled in confusion. "For *us*…?" He shook his head contrarily. "I'm a product manager and software advisor. *That's* what we agreed on."

"No, Sean, you're going to be co-chief-executive, running Portals right alongside of me. So, you can pretty much do whatever you like." An earnest smile broke across Luke's face.

"Luke..?" Sean shook his head nonplused. "What…? I don't…"

"We've been partnering up all our lives, and I honestly don't think that should change now. You'll have access to all of the names, the files, and all classified material having to do with **Dimension Four**. So, you have every right to screen and vet out everyone who receives a regular paycheck from us."

"You're something else, you know that?" Sean was floored. "You want *me* to run Portals alongside you?"

Luke laughed. "What…? Did you *really* think I asked

you to come all the way out here to be a product manager and software consult?"

"That's *exactly* what I thought. I guess, it *really* pays to have friends in high places. I won't let you down, buddy," Sean's voice wavered. "We're going to figure this thing out, and we're going to hit Vale first."

"*I* should be worried about not letting *you* down," Luke reversed. "And, I *know*... We'll get it all sorted out before Vale can even *think* about launching an attack. So, I think you're on the right track. A do-over on criminal and background checks should be interesting. However, first and foremost, my old friend... We're taking a first-class trip out to Croatia- 'Vampire Land' as our *brilliant* Phillip Lombard put it earlier."

"Can *Find Me* clue us in as to when we're interacting with the individual in question?" Sean queried.

"*Find Me* does have a range indicator. However, it might be a little tricky, because we're still dealing with a mystery man who can be out in Croatia, and simultaneously out here on the West Coast. Let's zero in on one location for now,' Luke wisely suggested.

"Then one location *it is*. Croatia first," Sean settled.

"Yeah, I think it makes a lot more sense. If you faked your own death, and you were trying to evade the law, the last place I image you'd want to hang out would be at a government-regulated operation like Portals."

"I totally agree. Newport Beach is lovely, but it's in no way a safe hiding place for a notorious criminal like Vale."

"So, we'll meet here at five a.m. tomorrow morning, and use the *Power Portal* again. This time, next stop...Croatia. Maybe, we'll have a lot more luck out there. I can't imagine Vale faking his own death, just to come out to California and live in Newport Beach." Luke checked his phone again.

"He probably started a whole new life out in Croatia," Sean speculated.

"Not for long," Luke said. "We're about to create a few ripples on his quiet lake."

"Swing by for me tomorrow morning?" Sean requested.

"Are we carpooling now?" Luke humored with a clever smile.

Sean guffawed and chuckled. "We're really beginning to turn into our parents, Luke."

"I knew it had to happen sometime," Luke joshed.

Luke was willing to admit that **Dimension** *Find Me* was probably a little off. There was no way Clarke could be simultaneously out in Croatia and California. All the same, he couldn't let it go, and refused to sleep on the matter. This time around, Luke resolved to strike first, and this defining blow would be the last. So, he had to make sure he hit Clarke hard enough to eradicate him from their lives for good.

***

Eerie, was the only way to describe the large, isolated mansion on the hilltop. It was hemmed in by mossy greenery and nestled by the ocean. Luke and Sean were skeptical, and felt as if they'd somehow stumbled upon the set of a gothic Sci-fi movie. Even if someone might have seen a similar backdrop in a horror flick, it was nothing compared to being only feet away from the deserted mansion out in Nepa, Croatia.

"Are you sure this is where *Find Me* indicated?" Sean flinched, totally creeped out.

Luke kept checking the tracker. The zipping lights emitted an even greater intensity, as they neared the antiquated residence. "I'm one hundred percent sure this is the place." Luke had heard that the weather was usually mild this time of year. However, he stared up at the lead gray skies, still shivering from the early evening chill. It was barely six a.m. out in California. However, it seemed as if the day was quickly closing its curtains out on that island.

"Luke this is weird. Why would Clarke Vale *ever* be tied into a place like this?"

"We're about to find out, Sean. This is where *Find Me* led us, so we just have to go with it." Luke kept checking the whooshing lights on the tracker.

He and Sean climbed the winding steps, and rushed up to the heavy wooden door. Luke lifted the primeval heavy metal latch in order to knock on it. He shifted about with nervous energy for a number of reasons. He was anxious to learn how, and why Clarke Vale's DNA was tied into the *Munster's* house. Secondly, it was freezing. He hadn't double-checked the weather patterns, and had failed to factor in that he and Sean might need a coat.

Sean stood next to Luke quaking from the cutting winds. He couldn't help thinking they'd made a mistake by coming out there. Perhaps, they were taking steps towards something darker and considerably more dangerous than anticipated. And yet, Sean was all in, if it meant making Clarke Vale disappear for good.

The heavy door deliberately swung open, and Luke looked sidelong at Sean with a bewildered expression on his face.

"May I help you?" an older silver-haired woman asked in a welcoming voice. However, her demeanor appeared just as bleak as the gloomy backdrop. She had on a prim black dress with a white ruffled apron.

"Yes…," Luke said, with a convivial smile. "We're law officials from America. We're conducting an investigation on a man who is a known criminal out in the states. We have reason to believe he's been *here*," Luke detailed straightforwardly.

"*Criminal*-here at Dr. Felix's home?" the woman

questioned, scowling. "There must be some kind of mistake. This is the private Island and residence of Dr. Anselm Felix. There has never been-neither will there ever be any criminal activity at this address," she refuted.

"*Dr. Anselm Felix*?" Luke's brows furrowed in query, as he glanced over at Sean.

Both seemed confused at that point. "What is Dr. Felix's field of expertise, if I might ask?" Luke addressed the woman again.

"Dr. Felix is world-known for his work in Biogenetic Engineering," the woman answered plainly.

"*Biogenetics* you say?" Sean queried. "Doesn't that mean he's a glorified plastic surgeon?" Sean prodded, hoping to prompt the woman to share even more information.

"Velda, who's there?" Dr. Felix dashed over to the front door.

"These men are from America, Sir. They say they're conducting some form of an investigation concerning a *criminal*, who might have wandered over to these parts." Velda turned towards the middle-aged man. Dr. Felix was tall and lanky. He had salt and pepper hair, but an oddly youthful face. No doubt, his presence troubled the older woman.

"Let *me* handle this, Velda. You've been most helpful, but *I* will take it from here."

"Yes, Sir," Velda said, compliant. She rushed away, and disappeared into the house.

"Are *you* Dr. Felix?" Luke ignored the man's lack of propriety, and the grimace on his face.

"I *am*...and who wants to know? Why are you on my island?" He glowered angrily from Luke to Sean.

"We're with the authorities in America. We have reason to believe that a known criminal has come through these parts," Luke reiterated. The lights on the tracker whizzed out of control at that point on both his and Sean's devices. So, Luke knew they were unequivocally on the right track.

"You're looking for a criminal here in *my* home? Do you have any idea who I am?" Dr. Felix impugned. "How dare you come on my private property, and make such a bizarre accusation?"

"We're looking for a man who has evaded arrest in the states. This isn't personal, Dr. Felix," Sean said meekly. "We're only trying to protect you, and your household from potential danger."

"I will have you know that I've *never* associated with criminals. I am highly selective of my clientele, and work only with the crème de la crème of society. I have no affiliations with lowlifes," he disparaged.

Impatient, Luke pulled out a picture of Clarke Vale, and held it up to Dr. Felix's face. "If *this* man came to your island, you might not have known you were entertaining a felon. He's very urbane and refined, but also extremely dangerous."

Dr. Felix's face rumpled in horror, and his eyes widened to the size of pool balls, when he saw the picture. Fear rippled through him like electric currents. *How was it possible for these men to know that Clarke Vale had stayed at his home during the recovery process of his physical transformation? Every precaution had been taken to ensure their affiliation was totally covert. Had they come all the way from America to arrest **him**?*

Dr. Felix realized he needed to find a way to cover up his involvement in helping Vale change his identity altogether. He had taken millions from the man. *Would they be able to trace the money to his private accounts?* He was terrified.

"I've never seen, neither have I ever had a connection to this man," Dr. Felix said offhandedly, trying to remain calm.

"Are you *sure*?" Luke held the picture up, and posted it closer to the doctor's face. He sensed the picture made Dr. Felix uncomfortable, so he knew the man was lying through his teeth. Dr. Felix was a world-known and reputable doctor. He was obviously rich-if a bit eccentric.

"Yes, I *am* sure. Now, if you gentlemen will excuse me, I have a great deal of work to do."

"We just have a few more questions-" Luke flinched when draft from the heavy wooden door struck their faces.

"He's lying, Luke. I know that much."

"Yeah I *know* he is. *Find Me's* indicator's flashing out of control."

"I keep thinking *Find Me's* going to short-circuit. You *really* think Clarke's here?" Sean stared all around at the macabre and godforsaken island.

"It's possible that Clarke *was* here. *He* may not physically be inside there, but according to *Find Me,* his DNA's all over this place. Sh..." Luke set his finger over his lips. "I think he's coming back. We need to blink out of here before the *mad scientist* really calls the authorities."

Luke and Sean were about to reactivate the *Power Portal.* They were just about to issue the command, when the heavy wooden door swung open again.

Luke sighed, relieved. It wasn't Dr. Felix, but Velda had returned.

Velda stared from Luke to Sean, and set her right pointer finger over her lips, indicating they keep their voices down.

Startled by her sudden reappearance, Luke dared not say a word, and he knew Sean felt the same way.

"I couldn't help overhearing your conversation with Dr. Felix. I also caught a glimpse of the picture you held up," Velda said in a hushed tone.

"So, the man in the picture *was* here?" Luke affirmed, still a bit skeptical.

"He was here a couple of months ago. He stayed at the mansion with Dr. Felix for a little over a week." Velda nodded in affirmation.

"But, what happened to him?" Sean susurrated.

"He and Dr. Felix conducted *business* for a short time. Dr. Felix always has his clients come and stay on the property for a while. In any event, the stranger was the perfect gentleman-"

"When did he leave? It's imperative for us to know exactly what happened," Luke emphasized. "He might have *seemed* like the perfect gentleman, but he's actually quite dangerous."

Velda's face veiled in dread. "I had no idea, but thank God he's no longer here. I can only surmise once he and Dr. Felix concluded their business dealings, he left the island. Honestly, I can't say that I even recall seeing him leave. All I know is that he was here for a short while, and then he was gone."

"Did Dr. Felix ever talk about the man, or discuss the nature of their business?" Sean prodded.

"The doctor never discusses his professional affairs with me. Because the gentleman stayed on for a little over a week, I have to conclude he *must* have submitted to one of Dr. Felix's procedures. One morning, I stepped out onto the colonnade looking for him. I wanted to ask if he needed anything else from the kitchen, but he was gone. Dr. Felix had already brought in another client that morning." Velda was undeniably anxious. She kept shifting to look behind her. She was scared Dr. Felix would return, and find her there. "I'm afraid that's all I know."

"Did Dr. Felix perform some form of facial or physical reconstructive surgery on the gentleman?" Luke asked plainly.

Velda nodded. "I'm not sure about a complete reconstructive procedure. Dr. Felix *could have* worked on rectifying a terrible burn, a deformation or a scar. I only saw glimpses of him when Dr. Felix brought him into the mansion. Before long, there were bandages on his face, and on parts of his upper body… I guess, the gentleman must have left the mansion once Dr. Felix removed them."

Luke and Sean shared knowing looks.

"You never got to see the finished product?" Sean asked, perplexed.

"No. The gentleman left very abruptly." Velda frowned.

"We understand. Was there anyone else staying on the mansion while Clarke was here?" Luke prodded.

"There *was* another gentleman associated with him. I believe his name was *Simon*," Velda disclosed.

Luke and Sean exchanged furtive looks again. Just yesterday, Phillip Lombard had divulged Clarke's association with a *Simon Winds*. So, the pieces of the puzzle were coming together nicely.

"Simon and Clarke were together?" Luke tested.

"Yes. Both men vanished in and around the same time." Velda kept looking behind her in angst. She feared Dr. Felix would overhear her discussing his personal affairs with the strangers from America.

Luke perceived Velda's agitation. He estimated how helpful she'd been, and didn't want to create trouble for her with the doctor.

"Thank you so much for all you've told us. You really didn't have to come back out here, so we *really* appreciate it." Luke took the woman's hand in his, and pressed a business card into her palm. Something about her reminded him of his late grandmother. "If you should ever want to get away from all of this, and you're ever out in California…" Luke skimmed over the miserable backdrop. "Feel free to give me a call."

Velda smiled earnestly for the first time in a while. It was refreshing to have two of the most handsome men she'd ever seen standing at the front door of that dreadful mansion. It was indeed a rare occasion, and a little pocket of sunshine in her overcast skies. "I *might* just do that."

"If you ever need anything at all…," Sean added. He grasped that Velda had risked her neck in order to help them out. So, he wanted her to know they were aware of her sacrifice.

"You're both very gracious, but I suggest you leave *right* away." Velda's expression was stern.

Luke nodded in agreement. "We're leaving." His eyes connected critically to Sean's. "Thank you, Ms. Velda!" Luke hunched down, and pressed a kiss to her cheek. "Be safe."

"Thank you for all your help." Sean planted a kiss on her cheek as well.

That said, Luke and Sean moved quickly away from the unpleasant mansion. They dismounted the winding steps, rushed all the way down to the shoreline of the ocean, and waited for Velda to shut the mansion's front door.

"So, Sean...?" Luke speculated before he issued the command to the *Power Portal* to take them home.

"You don't even have to say it, Luke. Clarke Vale underwent some form of facial reconstruction. He's taken on a brand-new identity, and he's out in Burbank working for *us*."

"Dr. Felix specializes in facial reconstruction, cloning and varying forms of Biochemical engineering miracles. Maybe, Clarke's old *face*, and a few of his fingers are still up there." Luke pointed up to the creepy old mansion.

"I'm not sure which parts of him remained in the doctor's lab, but his DNA's definitely linked to this place. However, his *body's* a totally different story. It's like you said, Luke. He's probably working through Portals Unlimited Mon-Fri, just like *Find Me* indicated. Sean kept shaking his head in irony.

"I'm honestly beginning to believe that too, Sean. We've got to find out *who* and *what* he is before it's too late. For all we know, Dr. Felix could have transformed him into a robot."

Sean laughed. "In as far as background checks, I'm going to start with the GDD. Mel's in charge of that department. I'm guessing, if he *is* working through Portals, it's most likely near her."

"Absolutely... Clarke in his reincarnated state, would make every effort to get close to Mel." Luke was still processing all they'd learned.

"Where there's smoke, there's definitely a fire. We'll

find him, Luke, even if *Find Me* hasn't generated an image of who he's parading around as. We just have to keep our eyes open."

"At least, we know Clarke was definitely on this island, and he paid Dr. Felix for a whole new identity. Thanks to Velda, we also know that he and Dr. Felix concluded their business dealings. So, we go home, and sniff out a rat." Luke was incredulous. "You're pretty clever, Clarke. I will give you that, but you'll always be just a few steps behind."

Chapter Seven

"Congratulations, Emery!" Brenda threw her arms around Clarke in celebration. She, along with Arianna and Peter, had just offered him the job as one of Portals Unlimited new software developers. All the same, they had to run the decision through their bosses. Nevertheless, Brenda was convinced that Emery was a shoe-in. Thus, she was *determined* to help him move up the Portals ladder.

Clarke's smile was irrepressible. "Thank you for your vote of confidence in me, my dear. However, from what I understand, the administrators-that's including Sean Winters, have to be in agreement. Clarke celebrated only superficially. Inwardly, he seethed in resentment, because Luke had recently brought Sean Winters into the Portals Unlimited family, and had made him Co-CEO.

The way Clarke saw it, Luke Bryant was trouble enough without his trusty sidekick. Clarke was disconcerted, and felt a bit intimidated, because both Luke and Sean were experts in the field of software innovation. So, if Luke had designed **Dimension Four** and its tools, there was no telling what the two would accomplish together. Even so, Clarke would power through the obstacles. He had only one goal in mind, and that was to make Melody his in the end.

"I'm sure the *Portal Masters* will offer you the job. You've been such an asset to the Graphics and Designs department. So, I'm certain that Melody Bryant herself will give you a glowing recommendation. You've done such a great job, Emery!" Brenda praised. She winked at Clarke, and gave him a come-hither look. They were sitting in her office, trying to uphold professional decorum. However, Brenda was chomping at the bit for Clarke to come by her place later.

"Thank you for all your help and support, Brenda. It really means a lot to me." Clarke's expression was inviting, as he took a moment to scrutinize every inch of Brenda's body.

Brenda's demeanor relayed how utterly fascinated she was. "Are you *still* coming over tonight?" she asked fetchingly.

"Seven thirty on the dot." Clarke's voice was throaty, as he stared tantalizingly at her. "I'll bring the champagne."

"Please do, because I would love to *personally* congratulate you on your promotion." Brenda gave him an enticing wink.

"I can't wait." Clarke leaned in closer to Brenda's desk, and virtually undressed her with his eyes. She was indeed desirable, but Brenda Fields was just a means to an end.

"So, Mr. Lloyd...," Brenda cleared her throat, feigning total composure. "If you wouldn't mind signing off on these documents, and getting them back to me at the end of the day...?"

"I will sign, seal and deliver them to you *myself* by the end of this business day," Clarke philandered.

Brenda pushed away from her desk, and walked around in order to interact with Emery. She extended her hand in order to shake on their deal. "I guess, that concludes our meeting for now. I will most likely have an answer for you by lunchtime." Her avid eyes inspected every border of the man.

Clarke took the hand Brenda offered, and fondled it in a beckoning manner. "I look *forward* to hearing from you later, Ms. Fields," Clarke said properly, as his fingers brushed tantalizingly on her skin.

Brenda gulped, and gently reclaimed her hand from Emery's irresistible touch. If they lost their cool, the potential to get into trouble was all too real. "Yes, you will definitely be hear from me later." She smiled, and took steps in order to distance herself from the good-looking tempter in her office.

"Thank you for your time." Clarke lingered in front of Brenda's desk for a moment, mercilessly gaping at her. An impish smile stretched across his face just before he turned, and headed for the office door. Before slipping through it, he waved at Brenda. Brenda clutched her trouncing heart, and continued staring at him. Entranced, she nimbly waved back. Clarke smiled and discreetly shut the office door.

There was a tremendous sense of gratification to know he still had the magic touch with the ladies. Brenda was totally spellbound. So, Clarke was convinced that Brenda would do all she could to secure his new job. When that happened, he would have access to *Dimension Four*. And once he did, he would be one step closer to having Melody in his arms again.

***

"Come on in. My hands are a little full right now," Melody called out from her office. She couldn't cross over to get the office door, because she was balancing three sizable swatch books full of new ideas for an upcoming promotion.

"Good morning, Mrs. Bryant!" Clarke popped his head through the door, reticent to come in.

"Emery…? Good morning!" Melody said, somewhat startled. Suddenly, she was holding her breath. "You needed to see me?" Melody was unable to budge from the center of her spacious office. Hunching down, she set the books on the floor.

"I promise not to take up too much of your time," Clarke said sheepishly. On the surface, one could have easily concluded he was composed and even a little bashful. However, inwardly, he burned. For all intents and purposes, he was a teenage boy, and Melody was his crush. Such was his openness and vulnerability around her.

Clarke was captivated by how appealing Melody looked in her coffee-colored business suit-with matching heels and accessories. In that color, she looked good enough to eat, and Clarke was growing hungrier by the minute. It was just as well that he was leaving the Graphics Designs department. There was no way he would have been able to continue to abstain from touching her in some way, if he'd stuck around.

"That's fine… Come on in, Emery," Melody said perfunctorily. Her chest tightened, and her stomach plummeted in dread, because Emery was there. She was uncertain as to why his presence was still such a tremendous source of controversy. She and Nicole had established that there were characteristics about Emery Lloyd which reminded her of Clarke Vale. However, logically, she and Nicole knew that Clarke had recently committed suicide in his jail cell back out in Sands Port. So, Melody realized how unfair it was to repudiate an individual, because they reminded her of someone else.

"I'm sorry to interrupt your busy morning," Clarke said apologetically, as he diffidently traipsed the plush carpeting in Melody's office. Stealthily, he shuffled towards the center of the room, and came to stand in front of her. Seeing her up close and personal, made his heart skip a beat.

Startled because Emery was so close, Melody flinched in incertitude. *Why was she spooked out whenever he came anywhere near her?* That was something she hadn't yet figured out. Emery was handsome, a sharp dresser, a hard worker and extremely cosmopolitan. In short, Portals Unlimited needed people like him around. "You're not interrupting at all. That's why I'm here." Melody's smile felt cemented.

"I just wanted to take a moment to say a proper thank you. You've been so kind to me while I've worked through this department. You've been a delight to work for and with," Clarke's uplifted, as his eyes delved magnetically into Melody's. For all intents and purposes, she was a cold bottle of water, and he'd just completed a 10K run.

"Oh…" Melody guffawed, trying to move past feelings of skittishness. "That's awfully kind of you to say. *You've* been great! You've worked so hard. I'm excited for your new position over at software developing. From the start, I said you're much too qualified to settle for what we do down here," Melody praised, with eyes wandering from Emery Lloyd's anesthetic gaze.

"You're much too self-effacing, Mrs. Bryant."

"You're always so formal, Emery. Please, call me Melody." Now that Emery was moving on to another department, Melody felt a little bit more at ease.

Clarke smiled openly into her eyes, and instinctively took hold of Melody's hand. "Thank you for all you've done, *Melody*!" His eyes invaded hers, and he stroked fondly on her hand.

Melody gasped, and baulked from Emery's sudden touch. His probing eyes seemed to be peeling back all of her layers-and not in a good way. "You're welcome!" she stammered, and respectfully reclaimed her hand. "I hope you're happy with the staff upstairs. I wish you every success!"

"So, you're *not* put out that I've decided to move on so soon?" Clarke's eyes lowered in query into hers.

"Not at all. I *know* you'll probably enjoy working with *PM* and his team even more than you liked it down here." Melody's face twisted in humor, as she feigned total nonchalance. "I happen to *know* for a fact they have a lot more fun than we do. Besides, they're the *real* power players. Everyone's rooting for you, Emery!" Melody rambled edgily.

"Thank you so much...really. Thank you for giving me this opportunity. Between you and me," Clarke's gape was hypnotic, "you're the best boss on the planet!" He gave her a pleasant smile. The smell of lilacs emanated through the pores of Melody's skin, and made Clarke all the more ravenous to close in.

A hesitant chuckle resonated from the hollow of Melody's throat. "You're much too kind. I'm going to miss seeing you around here." She had a generic expression on her face, and hinted at a smile.

"Well, it'll be nice to be missed by *you*, Melody," Clarke said straightforwardly.

"Are you all packed up for the big move?" Melody evaded. Her chest was taut, and her stomach felt queasy.

"I'm just about done. I just wanted to take a moment to acknowledge my boss!"

"You really didn't have to, Emery. I'll be around, and I'm sure we'll see each other from time to time." Melody's rubbery smile remained intact.

"I sure hope so." Clarke gawped mercilessly at her.

Melody laughed reticently. "Good luck, Emery!" She couldn't escape how intense he was. If she didn't know better, she would have surmised the man was coming on to her.

"Take care of yourself, Melody," Clarke said plainly, respectfully pulling back. There were times he was unaware of how strongly he came off. The last thing he wanted was to scare or to alienate Melody.

"Thank you, Emery. All the best," Melody faltered.

"Take care now." Clarke took Melody's hand in his again. However, this time around, he brought it up to his lips, and pressed a kiss to it. "Such a *pretty lady*!" he said before turning away.

Melody cringed the moment Emery kissed her hand. The instant his lips made contact with her skin it felt familiar. *Clarke* used to take her hand in the same way, and press kisses to it. Melody felt both violated and conflicted, as she watched Emery make his way over to the office door. Before opening up the door, he turned and waved goodbye.

Melody forced a smile, and waved back. Then, she watched him slip through and shut the door behind him. The hand kiss was upsetting enough, but what Melody found even more disturbing was when Emery had called her *pretty lady*. *Clarke* used to call her that as if it was her name. Melody felt iced cold and totally unsettled. Shakily, she ambled back over to her desk, and set on the armchair.

She felt a headache coming on, so she cradled her head in her hands. The incident with Emery had so upset her that tears shone in her eyes. "Lord, help me," Melody prayed. "I've got to pull it together. What's wrong with me? Am I *always* going to live in fear of this man, even if he's dead?"

She surrendered to tears.

Just then, a light rap came to her office door again. Melody quickly pulled tissues out from the box on her desk. She wiped tears from off her face, and blew her nose. Abruptly, she pushed out of the armchair, and shifted over to the door. "Come in," her voice undulated.

"Hey, honey baby!" Luke opened up the office door grinning waggishly at his wife. "I had a few minutes before meeting with that investor out in Cumberland Heights. So, I decided to come down here to steal a few kisses from my beautiful wife!" Luke's face was laced in mischief.

Melody closed her eyes meditatively, and sighed in relief to see Luke. Without hesitation, she rushed straight into his arms. She was still trembling when she buried her head in his chest. "Oh, Luke," she muttered, striving to catch her breath.

"Baby, what's the matter?" Luke's face immediately changed, as he cradled her head in his hands. "What's wrong?" He frowned in jeopardy and concern. "Are you all right?"

"I don't know what's wrong with me," Melody said thickly, shaking her head in dismay.

"Come here." Luke guided her over to the office couch. Pressing in close, he supported her head in his hands again, and tenderly brushed her tears away. His intent eyes searched her tear-filled ones. "Did something happen?" his voice broke, and tears instinctively glimmered in *his* eyes. "Did someone upset you?" he exacted. Luke was ready to take on, and destroy the guilty party or parties.

"No. Nothing's happened. I just overreacted to something."

"What do you *think* you're overreacting to, honey? Please, tell me." Luke pulled her into his arms, and held her acquisitively.

"I'm too embarrassed to even know where to start. You'll probably think it's ridiculous."

"Why don't you try me, honey? If it's upsetting you this much, *we* need to talk about it, okay?" Luke pelted her face with loving kisses. He held her securely in his arms, as he listened attentively to what she had to say.

Melody detailed the exchange she'd just had with Emery Lloyd. She explained how spooked out she was, because the man had kissed her hand, and had called her *pretty lady*. Upon hearing Melody say those words, Luke's heart crashed to the floor.

"So, you don't think I'm overreacting, or that I'm losing my mind?" Melody inched away in order to look into Luke's eyes.

Tears pushed through Luke's eyes, because he wasn't quite sure how to handle the situation. "I *don't* think you're overreacting *or* losing your mind," he reassured.

"I mean, Clarke *is* gone, and he can't bother us anymore. I just don't understand why I can't stop obsessing about him. It isn't Emery's fault he reminds me of Clarke Vale."

All kinds of warning signals and bells went off in Luke's head. "So, Emery *reminds* of you Clarke?" His eyes delved urgently into Melody's.

"He *does* remind of Clarke. I guess, that's why I've been so on edge since the day we met him."

"Honey, why didn't you tell me you felt that way? If keeping Emery around makes you uncomfortable, we can resolve the matter," Luke settled.

Melody's eyes searched Luke's. "How fair would that be, Luke? Emery's a hard worker, and has done his best for this company. We *can't* discriminate against him, because he favors someone who made our lives a living hell not too long ago."

"So, what do *you* want to do, baby?" Luke gently prodded. "I don't want anything or anyone upsetting you, or making you feel ill at ease around here. We could always have Emery transferred to another office." Luke's expression was critical.

Melody pulled away, and propped against the plush sofa. Shaking her head in the negative, she argued, "It's all right. I'm actually relieved that he's joining your team. That means, I'll be seeing a lot less of him. It isn't fair to have the man uproot his entire life…again, just because he creeps me out," she reasoned sagaciously.

"What do you mean uproot his entire life, Mel?" Luke asked, puzzled.

"Emery *recently* moved out here. He came out to California just to apply for work at Portals," Melody informed.

Luke's thoughts were whizzing, and he had a faraway expression on his face. "He told you that?" He tried not to seem too perturbed by Melody's disclosure.

"Yes, he said he'd heard a lot about Portals, and he moved out here just to apply for a job." Melody's face veiled in confusion. "You didn't know that?"

"No," Luke said, moving in closer to her again. He

pulled Melody protectively into his arms. "I guess, I didn't know. Did he say where he uprooted from?" Luke rubbed caringly on Melody's back, and brushed his fingers through her hair. Melody was propped up to his chest, and her head nestled just underneath his chin.

"He didn't say exactly where he uprooted from. What he *did* say was that he came a long way to have this opportunity," Melody explicated.

"Mel, my love…." Luke was reflective. "Are you *sure* you don't want me to have him transferred?" he tested.

"No, there's no need for that. I'll get over it. I guess, everything that happened with Clarke is still so fresh."

"Honey baby, would it help if you talked to someone about everything that happened with Clarke?" Luke frowned in concern.

Melody shook her head in the negative. "No. I'll be all right. Honestly, talking to *you* is the best medicine. I can't blame Emery for Clarke's reign of terror over our lives. I *am* however thankful for answered prayer. I won't be as uncomfortable, if he's no longer working down here." Melody reached up, and pressed a soft kiss to Luke's mouth.

Luke reflexively pressed a dozen kisses to her mouth. Regardless of his collected veneer, his thoughts were all over the place. What Melody didn't realize was that hearing her allude to Emery Lloyd reminding her of Clarke Vale, had left *him* feeling unsettled. No doubt, God was answering Luke's prayers as well.

He and Sean had had no luck in tracking Clarke Vale. *Find Me* had a glitch of some sort. The program maintained Clarke's DNA was indeed in two places. Therefore, the tracker had been unable to generate an image. However, this conversation with Melody had zeroed in on Emery Lloyd. For one reason or another, he reminded her of Clarke Vale. *Perhaps*, Emery Lloyd reminded Melody of Clarke Vale, because he *was* Clarke Vale. Luke's head was spinning.

Once he worked out the details, Luke knew he would have to tell Melody the truth. She had to know that Clarke Vale had faked his own death, and was in all likeliness working through Portals Unlimited. Luke's powwow with his wife that afternoon was elucidating.

He had no idea that Emery Lloyd had uprooted his entire life just to come out to Portals. Perchance, he'd uprooted from Croatia, after submitting to facial and physical reconstructive surgery. And, he'd returned to the states just to make trouble for them. At that point, Luke had a solid *lead* as to where Clarke Vale might be hiding. Plausibly, he was hiding inside of Mr. Emery Lloyd.

As soon as he put the puzzle pieces together, he would tell Melody. She had to know what they were dealing with, and that Clarke Vale was still very much alive. As much as Luke wanted to protect her, he had to give her the head's up. However, seeing just how shaken Melody was that afternoon, Luke concluded that it just wasn't the right time.

***

"Did you find anything yet?" Luke popped into Sean's office on a Tuesday morning in November. Since their trip out to Croatia-and more recently, being made privy to his wife's suspicions, Luke was anxious to move forward with the criminal, and background checks for all Portals employees.

Things being what they were, they hadn't had very much luck in pinpointing the person parading around as someone *other* than Clarke Vale. They'd had their suspicions about Emery Lloyd. However, so far, they'd failed to substantiate any real evidence that they were on the right track.

"Nothing yet, buddy. Everyone seems to be on the level so far. We've run extensive background checks on a hundred employees. Luke, with the exception of traffic violations and a DUI here and there, everyone's all right." Sean sighed in frustration. "What about you?"

"*Find Me* maintains Clarke's DNA *is* tied into Portals. I've even put some of my top reps under scrutiny, and there's nothing life-altering on my end either," Luke explicated. Stepping fully into Sean's office, Luke shut the door. Mistrust wrinkled his features, as he inched in closer to Sean's desk. "You *did* interview again with Emery Lloyd right?"

"You mean, that straitlaced dude who just started working in software?" Sean asked.

"Yeah, what do you think about him?" Luke said in a hushed tone. "He's a great worker. Mel says nobody works harder, and that's why he got the job. But, between you and me, Sean, the other day I stopped in to see Mel before going off to a meeting, and she was totally freaked."

Sean's face wrinkled in jeopardy. "Why? Is she all right?"

"She was shaken up and in tears. *Emery* stopped by to officially say goodbye to her, and to thank her for being a great boss." Luke had a cynical expression on his face.

"That's not a big deal. Why would that leave Mel shaken up?"

"Sean, Mel said *Emery* reminds of her Clarke Vale. He kissed her hand, and called her *a pretty lady*. That brought back all of those horrible memories." Luke hopped up to the side of Sean's desk.

"Seriously...?" Sean questioned, disconcerted. "That sounds a tad bit unprofessional. Still, I haven't been around him very much. I guess, I'll have to keep my eye on him. Mel told you that he reminds her of Clarke Vale?" Sean was perplexed.

"Honestly, *I* was even more creeped out than she was. When Brenda brought the guy over to Mel's office for an informal interview that first time, I was there, Sean. The guy was so intense, and he literally couldn't take his eyes off of Mel. I tried not to think too much about it, and gave him the benefit of the doubt. In fact, both Mel and I decided to give him a fair shot."

"You had your suspicions that something was off?" Sean seemed even more bewildered.

"More so Melody than me."

"Then, why did you guys hire him?"

"He was perfect for the job. His qualifications and references were a dream. His references checked out by the way. So, being the equal opportunity employers that we are..." Luke sighed, bemused over the entire matter. "Sean, to be perfectly honest, I sense something totally off about him."

"He's a little prudish and straitlaced, but he hasn't been disrespectful to Mel, has he?" Sean shifted in his armchair in order to look into Luke's eyes.

"That's just it, Sean. He's been absolutely perfect. He's here bright and early. He's helpful, knowledgeable, and he's always smiling. Melody says he goes above and beyond, and he's worked like every weekend when he worked through the GDD. How on earth could we *not* hire someone like that? We couldn't turn down a qualified applicant, because he just happens to freak us out."

Jeopardy riddled Sean's usually calm demeanor. He stood to his feet, and walked around the desk to face his best friend. He kept shaking his head in skepticism. "If this guy *is* really Vale in disguise, *man* do we ever have a problem on our hands!"

"You should have seen the way he stared at Mel the first time we met him. He reminded me of one of those doctors trying to work his hypnotic powers on her. I've caught him staring at her in the same way on a few occasions. However, he's never disrespectful about it," Luke added, still muddled in respect to the circumstances.

"Melody *is* beautiful! Maybe, he just finds her fascinating, but he hasn't acted on his obvious attraction to her?"

"No. He's absolutely perfect-too perfect. He just has one truly bad habit of staring at my wife, as if she were his last meal. The guy rubs me the wrong way, Sean," Luke admitted.

"If this guy's *really* who we think...," Sean theorized.

"Think about it, Sean. Emery Lloyd applied for a position about a month after Clarke Vale was ostensibly found hung in his jail cell. Melody told me that Emery uprooted his entire life to come out to California to interview for Portals. I'm still trying to figure out where he uprooted from. Maybe, it was from Sands Port, Maryland, or maybe even from Croatia. He has the most impressive qualifications, and he *had* his pick of departments here. But, which department did he choose to apply for?" Luke asked rhetorically.

"Graphics Designs," Sean filled in naturally. "But he *just* started in software developing," Sean countered. "I guess, he's over working through the GDD."

Luke held his finger up in conjecture as a philosopher would. "I've thought about that. If we're on the right track, then Clarke is even more calculating than we're giving him credit for. What could potentially be more important than getting close to Melody?" His brows furrowed in intrigue.

"Learning all there is to know about **Dimension Four,** using it against *you*, and *then* moving in on Melody," Sean collated. Curiosity and keenness covered his set features, as he assessed the case in point.

"I love the way you think, Sean." Luke nodded in affirmation. "This is all guesswork, but I say we keep a very close eye on Emery Lloyd. That'll be a lot easier to accomplish now that he'll be working up here closer to us."

Sean nodded. "Absolutely… Keep your enemies closer. Still, Luke, what about *Find Me*? The indicator showed no variation when I talked with Emery. What about you?"

"Not a thing. In fact, the lights hardly blinked, and showed very little DNA activity. Not too long ago, *Find Me* detected Vale's DNA was both out here and out in Croatia. Now, the tracker's coming up completely inconclusive. No location is indicated." Luke plowed his finger nervously through his hair. "I feel as if I'm grasping at straws here, Sean. *Find Me's never* let me down before." He sighed in frustration.

"Maybe, we need to tweak it a little. We work on *Find Me*, and figure things out. But, in the meantime…"

Luke gave Sean an indistinct look. "I wish there was a way to validate my suspicions about Lloyd."

"Luke, if you suspect Emery Lloyd is parading around here trying to find a chink in your armor, and trying to get to Mel, maybe we need to let him go," Sean suggested.

"Not a good idea, my friend. You just hit the nail on the head by saying we need to keep our enemies closer. We stay on him, and monitor his every move around here."

"Luke, he now has access to top level information." Sean's face warped in concern.

"Yes, he does. So, we're going to be watching what he does with that information," Luke said evenly. "I *am* a little bit worried about Brenda, though. I might have to have a talk with her about her *relationship* with Lloyd. I think they might be sleeping together," Luke disclosed.

"Yeah, I kind of figured that out." Sean shook his head in the negative. "What are you going to tell her?"

"Brenda's a good girl, and an awesome employee. I really don't want to see her hurt. Something tells me *Emery Lloyd* has been using her to make his way up the *corporate ladder*, so to speak. Brenda and I have to have a serious talk about intra-office romances."

"That's a heavy one, Luke."

Both sternness and remorse covered Luke's face, as he reflexively clasped his hands together. "Someone's got to lookout for her. I'd rather have her nursing a broken heart, than to have her come up missing or dead."

"We've already run background and criminal checks on Emery Lloyd. All of his information checks out. So, what if there's more than *one* Emery Lloyd we need to run background and criminal checks on?" Luke introduced.

"All right then, we'll conduct background checks on all of the Emery Lloyds who live out in here."

"And also abroad. Something tells me we're looking into the background of the wrong man." Luke gave an affirming nod, as his eyes gunned into Sean's.

"Maybe, Emery Lloyd's a former patient of Dr. Felix's. I *did* a bit of research on him by the way. Dr. Anselm Felix is an expert in biogenetics, cloning, facial and physical reconstruction. He also does a bit of cosmetics. I can't believe Clarke *really* went that far, cloning and facial reconstruction…?" Sean shook his head, incredulous.

"What could be more perfect? Bear with me here, as I try to piece together this theory. If I were rich enough to bribe corrections officers to help make me disappear, the first thing I'd do is to leave the US.

"Secondly, if I knew of a doctor out in Croatia who had the capability to give me a brand-new face, burn away my fingerprints, and give me a totally new identity, I'd do whatever I had to." Luke paced back and forth as he hypothesized.

"And, with this brand-new identity, I'd find a way to reconnect to the woman I'm absolutely obsessed with, while simultaneously plotting behind the scenes to destroy her husband. And, in order for me to do that, I would need to apply for a job through the company her husband owns. I would make my way to the top, and learn all top government-regulated secrets. Then, I would use them all against my boss," Sean added.

Luke stood still for a moment, and stared at Sean in

awe. "Not bad, buddy. That's a total possibility. That's why we need to find out who Emery Lloyd is-and that's all of the Emery Lloyds out here and abroad. I'm *not* buying into the model employee act. I'm convinced there's a lot more than meets the eye with that man."

Sean shook his head in denial and skepticism. "Emery Lloyd *is* Clarke Vale?" His heart dipped down to the floor just to enunciate those words.

"That's what I'm feeling in my gut, Sean. We have to watch him like a hawk around here."

"Are you going to tell Melody about this?"

Luke's demeanor expressed his inner conflict. "At this point, I probably have to tell her. She'll never forgive me if something happens."

"That's why we have *Shield Me* set in place, Luke. I don't want to have to tell Nicole either."

"Sean, we'll *have* to tell them in a rational way. We just have to remain calm and level-headed. If they discover our suspicions on their own..." Luke shook his in the negative. "That will be disastrous."

There was a defeated expression on Sean's face, as he considered the implications of *not* telling his wife they were quite possibly entertaining Clarke Vale on a regular basis.

"Luke," Sean's face winkled in dread, "we know for sure that Clarke was out in Nepa, Croatia, and that he in all likeliness submitted to reconstructive surgery. Velda was kind enough to share that bit of information with us," Sean examined.

Luke nodded. "*Find Me* also concluded that the

person with Clarke's DNA shows up to Portals on a daily basis."

"Can we be sure this Emery guy is Clarke Vale?" Sean's face wrinkled in turmoil.

"It's all very outlandish, but he's our number one suspect, and definitely a person of interest. Still, I get that it might be just a little bit too obvious," Luke brought up. "*Find Me* hasn't established anything else, aside from the results that Clarke's DNA can be found both in the US and out in Croatia."

"There *might* be one way to settle this DNA mix up once and for all. We need to isolate Emery's DNA, and have the tracker compare the two. Maybe, that will eliminate this one person being in two different places at the same time."

"Sounds like a plan. It's mindboggling, because *Find Me's* detector has shown little to no variation whenever Emery's around. The tracker blinked out of control when we made that trip out to Croatia."

Sean nodded in agreement. "I don't get that either, but *Find Me's* accurate for the most part. So, we're just going to have to get to the bottom of things."

Luke's face strained in uncertainty, and he sent a prayer heavenward. "I pray we do, Sean. Something tells me we're quickly running out of time."

Brenda was just about to knock on Sean's office door, when she overheard her bosses discussing Emery Lloyd. She couldn't make out everything they were saying, but the word *suspect* had grated her ear. *Why was Emery a suspect? What had he done to rouse suspicion from her bosses? Were they planning on firing him?* All kinds of warning signals went off in her head. Emery was the perfect employee. He was also quickly becoming a model boyfriend and lover. Brenda was in love with him. So, she resolved to do everything in her power to ensure he stuck around.

She hadn't heard her bosses' entire conversation, but was aware that they were planning to run Emery's DNA through *Find Me*. Brenda had an idea. She would change the data on file for Emery. So, when they ran his DNA through *Find Me*, it would come up inconclusive. Then, she'd find and use someone else's DNA, and store it on file for Emery Lloyd. Moreover, she would implant a microchip from **Dimension Four's** latest technology, *Shield Me* into Emery's access card. This would create a protective field around him, and make him invulnerable to *Find Me's* tracker. That was a secret only an elite few from Portals Unlimited knew.

Find Me's tracker could be temporarily disabled, or rendered inept by *Shield Me's* protective field. Brenda was grateful to be on the inside track. The esoteric knowledge was intact to protect her *boyfriend*. She'd finally found someone who understood her, and who seemed to want to stick around. She was falling in love. So, there wasn't anything she wouldn't do to protect the growing love in her heart for Emery Lloyd.

Nonetheless, she had no idea how long she could stifle her boss's suspicions, and keep them in the dark. Luke and Sean were brilliant! Moreover, she realized there were aspects to **Dimension Four** that the *Portal Masters* kept to themselves. All the same, Brenda resolved to use the arcane knowledge she'd acquired so far to protect her boyfriend. Emery was the man she loved. Nothing else mattered, neither would anything get in the way.

Chapter Eight

Swarovski Crystal Christmas trees ornamented strategic areas of the party hall. The spacious venue sparkled like diamonds, and decorative Christmas-themed paraphernalia had been dispersed to various corners. There were bigger than life gift boxes set tactically in certain areas of the extensive party hall. The gifts came in every conceivable color; from red, to gold, to green, to silver, blue and bronze.

It was Portals Unlimited first Christmas party, and the actual event far exceeded all of the hype. Arianna, who did much of the coordinating, had to admit it was even more grand-scale than she'd envisioned. She stepped into the party hall wearing a stylish wintergreen-colored dress, with matching accessories. Her upswept, freshly highlighted hair, shone like gold in the array of lights. There was an irrepressible smile on her pretty face, because things were definitely looking up.

Taking a moment to skim over the spacious venue, she noticed the couples out on the dance floor. She couldn't escape seeing Luke and Melody dancing. They looked picture perfect, almost as if they were poised for a red-carpet event. Seeing Luke with Melody didn't hurt as much. Arianna was ready to admit that her blossoming friendship with Peter had a lot to do with why. The turning point in their relationship, occurred while on her minibreak out in Virginia with her family.

Peter also came down to Virginia on business. And even if he only stayed a few days, they'd hung out quite a bit. On Peter's last night out in Virginia, they went out for dinner and a movie. So, for the time being, in as far as a friendship, Arianna felt as if she and Peter were on terra firma.

Though, lately Arianna's heart had been singing a different tune. She now grasped why so many of the girls who worked through Portals were literally throwing themselves at Peter. Arianna couldn't say *she* was ready to *throw* herself at Peter Lawton. But, she found herself growing more attached to him with time.

Peter knew about her feelings for Luke, but had never judged her. In fact, Peter had tried to understand, and had remained totally respectful. Arianna was honestly getting to know the *real* Peter Lawton. He was extremely kind, thoughtful, sensitive, caring and highly intelligent. There was so much more she *wanted* to know. However, she worried she'd kept him in the friend zone far too long.

That night, Arianna wanted to show Peter she was ready to take their friendship to the next level. Of course, she had absolutely no idea how to express her heart. However, she'd prayed for wisdom. First on the agenda was to *find* Peter. He'd asked to pick her up, so that they could attend the party together. But, Arianna had agreed on meeting him there instead.

It would have looked too much like a date, if they'd come out to the party together. She didn't want Peter getting the wrong idea. And yet, Arianna felt like kicking herself for making such a ridiculous decision. She honestly no longer cared what anyone at Portals thought. She really liked Peter, and she was ready to let her guard down. After almost two years of holding a torch for Luke, there was finally someone else on the horizon. Arianna praised God for giving her a brand new start, and she was excited to risk her heart again with Peter.

"Hey, Pete," Raya Hodges said spiritedly, standing in the doorway of Peter's office. Up until that very moment, Peter was on cloud nine, because Arianna had promised to meet him at the party. He was also excited, because he'd just finished wrapping up her Christmas present. Furthermore, he'd taken time to express his feelings in a personal letter and Christmas card. To say he was in love with Arianna was an understatement!

Spending time with Ari and her family a couple of months ago, was a total game-changer. Their relationship had taken a favorable turn during an impromptu lunch date. They'd decided to go out after a productive meeting with Stephen Sanderson, CEO of Body Electric Era. Peter and Arianna had shared a great deal that afternoon. Arianna finally admitted her feelings for Luke. Discussing the matter wasn't easy for Peter. However, he did appreciate that she'd confided in him. That afternoon, Peter avowed to wait it out until she was ready to give him a chance.

So, as a result of their new level of closeness, Peter was confident of moving forward. He was finally ready to ask her out. It was the first time he'd had to wait it out for *any* girl. Nevertheless, Peter deemed Arianna was so worth it. All the same, Peter's face soured seeing Raya standing at his office door. He took a moment to set Arianna's gift, the card and letter in his desk drawer. "Hey, Raya!" Peter gave Raya a cordial smile. "Merry Christmas!"

"Merry Christmas, Pete!" Raya gave him captivating smile. "Can I come in for a minute?" She brushed past him, and sauntered in, before Peter could say a word.

Raya had on a formfitting, black and silver dress with matching heels and accessories. She was totally crazy about Peter Lawton, and had tried to get his attention for months. She now realized how difficult it was to get the attention of one of Portals' most eligible bachelors. All the same, she refused to give up. It was, after all, Christmas, a season of miracles. She had something special for Peter, and kept it concealed behind her.

"What are *you* doing in here all by yourself? The party's out there." Raya pointed towards the office door. They could hear the music and bustle from a distance.

Peter smiled bashfully. "I'm actually waiting on someone. I just stopped in here for a minute to take care of something." His face and eyes were imbued with joy and expectation. Peter gravitated towards the center of the room. "Were you looking for me?" Confusion rumpled his clean-cut features.

"Well, since I didn't see you out there with everyone else, I kinda figured you *might* be in here. I just took a chance," Raya explained.

"Did you need my help with something?" he asked politely, puzzled as to why Raya had been looking for him. This was after all a Christmas party, and he *wasn't* on the clock.

"You could say that."

"What can I help you with, Raya?" Peter asked straightforwardly.

"This…" Raya set her right hand up, revealing the mistletoe branch she'd kept hidden.

Peter tried pulling away, and shook his head contrarily. "Raya…no," he protested.

"You wouldn't turn down a kiss from a girl holding mistletoe over your head at Christmas, now would you, Peter Lawton?" she said enticingly. "Merry Christmas…" She leaned into Peter, bridged her lips magnetically to his, and fondled them with hers.

"Come out, come out wherever you are…," Arianna teased, and pushed open Peter's office door. "Are you hiding out from everyone at the party….?" her voice trailed when she saw Peter locked into a kiss with Raya Hodges. She didn't know the girl very well. What Arianna knew was that Raya worked through the Accounting Department.

Peter abruptly pulled away from Raya's tight grasp. "Ari, hey. I'm so glad you stopped by. Come on in." Peter's heart had already crashed to the floor.

"I'm sorry that I barged in. I didn't know you were

busy. I guess, we'll talk later," Arianna's voice wavered. Her throat felt scratchy, and tears pooled in her eyes.

"Ari, please, stay… I've been anticipating seeing you all night."

"I think I'll go back to the party now." Raya rolled her eyes in annoyance. She hated Arianna Ward with a passion. Arianna was the *only* girl Peter seemed to care anything about. Nevertheless, all was fair in love and war, and she resolved to keep trying. She wanted Peter Lawton more than anything else!

Arianna stood in the office doorway feeling totally defeated. It suddenly occurred to her why she'd been so hesitant to open up her heart to Peter to begin with. Peter loved the ladies, and some habits truly died hard. Her head had momentarily slumped, but she forced herself to look up. Her sad eyes connected acutely to Peter's. "Suddenly, I'm not feeling very well."

Peter ambled over, and softly took hold of her hand. "Ari, please don't go. I've been looking forward to this night forever," he confessed, as tears glimmered in his eyes.

Arianna kept shaking her head contrarily. "I'm sorry, Pete. I'm sure there are plenty of other girls, all lined up to spend time with you at this party, but *I'm* going home." Her face warped in melancholy, as she veered and rushed away, leaving Peter standing in the office doorway.

Peter darted out after her. "Ari, please don't go. Come back." Frustrated and disillusioned, he stopped midway down the hall. "Great…," he susurrated cynically. "What are the odds that Arianna would come looking for me, while Raya was kissing me underneath mistletoe?

"Why is this happening? Every time I take one step towards having the girl of my dreams, we take a dozen steps backward. God, help me." Tears of frustration filled Peter's eyes. His heart was broken, as a result of this unexpected setback. Peter prayed for a way to make things right with Arianna. She had to understand definitively that he wasn't interested in anyone else. He had to make her realize she was everything he'd ever want or need.

"Portals sure knows how to throw a Christmas party, Luke!" Sean caught up with Luke in Luke's office during the party.

Luke temporarily hung back from the festivities, so that he could monitor the activities taking place in the party hall from his office. That way, he was free to watch everyone's interactions-especially those of Emery Lloyd's and Brenda Fields'. "Thanks, Sean." Luke smiled. "It's a pretty nice turnout for Portals' First Christmas bash-if I do say so myself." Luke kept his eyes on the sizable monitoring system.

"You're watching everyone out there, aren't you?" Sean coasted over to see what had Luke so fascinated.

Luke nodded absently. "I don't understand it, Sean. How did *Find Me* go from detecting Clarke's DNA out in Croatia, and then out here, only to recant it all?" Luke was frustrated. He was confused as to why *Find Me* had recently specified that the person with that DNA was dead.

Sean sighed. "I don't get that either. Weeks ago, we were convinced this Emery Lloyd guy *was* the reincarnation of Clarke Vale. However, since running his DNA through *Find Me* that initial time, we haven't gotten any closer to proving it. Maybe, we've got the wrong guy," Sean assented.

Luke kept shaking his head in the negative. "*Find Me* doesn't make those kinds of egregious errors. That's why I'm so baffled. I've been keeping my eye on Lloyd's every move. So far, everything he's done *seems* to be on the level."

"I'll even admit that the guy's doing a great job working through software developing. He's the *model* employee, but something's got to give. Nobody's *that* perfect."

Luke watched Emery dancing out in the party hall. He'd danced with a number of his work colleagues throughout the night. Emery's eyes veered towards Brenda. From what

Luke and Sean could decipher, Brenda was standing on the sidelines drinking. Her face was taut with jealousy and disillusionment. Using special features, Luke zeroed in on Brenda's face, and she was clearly upset. Emery hadn't danced with her all that night. "I wonder what that's about," Luke said quietly. "It's sad, but I think she's in love with the guy."

"You *did* speak to Brenda about her relationship with Lloyd right?" Sean asked.

"I didn't warn her about Lloyd per se. What I *did* say was that it was brought to my attention that there were inappropriate intra-office relations. So, I advised her to be cautious about romantic entanglements in the workplace. She was receptive, respectful and seemingly compliant. But, from the look on her face right now, she's definitely in love with Lloyd."

"Yeah, I have to agree with you there, buddy." Sean scrutinized the sour expression on Brenda's face.

"Sadder still is that whenever someone's *in love*, rationality goes right out the window." Luke shook his head sympathetically.

"They're also obviously still romantically linked, even if they're going to great lengths to prove otherwise."

"Oh, I *know* Brenda's in love with this guy. My greatest concern is that she has access to many of *Dimension Four's* classified components." Luke eyes suddenly connected to Sean's.

"You think she would ever...?" Sean gave Luke a bewildering look.

"Breach knowledge of *Dimension Four* and use it against us," Luke filled in. "Brenda's a good girl, but there's always that one percent chance..." Luke rethought the matter. "Brenda's well aware of the consequences. She could even be imprisoned if top secret government information is leaked. If she decides to share classified information with the general public, she's asking for a heap of trouble. So, I doubt she'd risk it. All the same, I'm keeping my eye on one of my top employees, who's romantically linked to Emery Lloyd."

"We're *both* keeping our eye on this bizarre match. She seems so vested in him, but Emery obviously doesn't feel the same way," Sean deduced.

"Yeah, this situation is sad for a number of reasons. That's why we need to remain objective. I sure hope Brenda's not planning to put it all on the line for someone like that."

"We'd better get back to the party." Sean smiled, as he caught sight of Melody and Nicole looking for them on the monitor. The two were standing at a corner of the party hall chatting, and munching on appetizers.

"You're right. We'd better get back out there. I told Mel I'd only be a few minutes. Sean, by some miracle, let's hope the tracker's on point in indicating Vale's dead, even if that's highly unlikely."

"Are we still sharing our suspicions with the girls?" Sean asked, with a taut expression on his face.

"We should definitely tell them, even if *seems* as if the danger is past." Luke seemed skeptical. "Melody and Nicole should know our theories about Clarke Vale. They should definitely know he's quite possibly alive, and out there somewhere... We *know* he's alive. Whether or not he's hanging around here is a totally different story."

"That's the mother of all questions. If *Find Me's* no longer detecting his DNA out here at Portals, maybe he's moved on." Sean couldn't even convince himself of that statement.

Luke's brows furrowed as his thoughts raced. "Even if 'moving on' was a possibility for Clarke, it doesn't mean that he isn't biding his time to launch an attack."

"Now more than ever we have to tighten security around our families. And, you're right. We definitely need to tell the girls." Sean frowned, irritated.

"We *owe* it to our wives to cite our suspicions. I won't rest until I figure out *who* Vale is, and where he's hiding," Luke stated critically.

"Yeah, I'm with you. I don't get what's happening with *Find Me*, but we can definitely work on decrypting it." Sean deliberated.

Luke nodded. "We'd be foolish if we thought for one minute that Vale was hanging around here, but then suddenly changed his mind about exacting revenge."

"We both know that isn't who Vale is. So, no doubt, he's lurking somewhere nearby, and we've got to find out where. There's way too much at stake."

"I will find that man if it's the last thing I do," Luke avowed. "*Now*, I think we should go back out there, and find our lovely wives, before they come in here looking for us," Luke said on a lighter note.

Luke and Sean cautiously deactivated the equipment inside Luke's office. Before they left, they secured the set of double doors. Soon after, they returned to the party hall, and rejoined their wives for the biggest Christmas bash of the year!

Arianna was crushed after seeing Peter with Raya in his office. She had drifted away as far as she could. And now, she found herself standing in front of Portals' main lab. Using her access key, she let herself inside. It was a restricted area only very few Portals employees had access to. Aside from herself, only Luke, Sean, Peter and Brenda had access keys. Arianna figured no one would come looking for her in there. All she needed was a moment to pull it together. She'd spent the last hour in tears after walking in on Peter's kiss with another girl.

Everything had blown up in her face. She'd been all set to show Peter just how much she liked him. However, seeing him kissing Raya, only solidified the reasons why she'd been hesitant to trust him in the first place. The sad part was that she still yearned to connect to Peter. She longed to hear his voice, and to feel the tenderness of his touch. Peter's touch made it impossible to resist him. So, Arianna was clueless in far as how she'd train her heart to stop wanting him.

Burying her face in her hands, she sobbed. She cried out to God as her heart rent in half. Why was love always so complicated? For the first time since Luke, she was falling for someone. Nevertheless, she'd just found out in the worst way she couldn't trust her heart to him. Arianna opened up her mouth to speak, but couldn't verbalize the words. Something had shut down on the inside.

However, just then, there was another matter to contend with. The sensor for the lab's doors had just gone off. Startled, Arianna's heart lashed, because someone was obviously coming into the lab. Why would *anyone* come into the lab during the Christmas party? Arianna took off her heels, and scurried under one of the lab tables. Her heart pounded into her eardrum, as she anticipated the intruder.

Arianna's jaw dropped in utter shock when she saw Brenda Fields and Emery Lloyd brazenly step into the restricted area. Arianna was flabbergasted. She wasn't only stunned because the lab was top secret, but the pair engaged in deep kissing and fondling. "What have I stumbled upon?" Arianna said quietly, incredulous and aghast.

"I couldn't wait to get you alone tonight." Brenda wrapped her arms possessively around Emery's waist. She pressed in close, and lavished every corner of his mouth with kisses.

"I was anxious to have you all to myself as well, my love," Clarke said generically. Life was good, because he had Brenda Fields virtually eating out of the palm of his hand. It was obvious there wasn't anything she wouldn't do for him. "You look tantalizing in this dress!" he trifled. "Did I tell you how ravishing you look tonight?"

"No, you didn't. We haven't talked very much at all tonight. I've been watching you dance with every girl out there," Brenda said grudgingly. "I hate having to pretend we're not together." She draped her arms about his neck, and her avid lips bridged hungrily to his.

"I'm sorry we have to keep our relationship a secret for now, but if it's any consolation, I *hated* dancing with every pretty girl in that party hall," he teased.

"*Sure* you did." Brenda rolled her eyes cynically. "I hate not having you with me," Clarke coaxed, bating the corners of her mouth in nuances, before ravishing every inch.

Arianna couldn't believe what she was witnessing. She wished for an alternate way out of the lab, so that she could escape the debauchery. From the outset, something about Emery Lloyd had rubbed her the wrong way. She'd never been on the bandwagon, no matter how many of the women around Portals were swooning over his *killer* good looks. She closed her eyes, and prayed that the couple would keep their clothes on. Yet and still, naked bodies, was only one thing she potentially had to contend with. It was Brenda and Emery's ensuing conversation that created a moral dilemma.

"I love my boss and this company. Still, I'll admit I was a little annoyed when he reminded me of Portals' policy regarding intra-office romances."

"When did he talk to you about that?" Clarke's heart jumped over Brenda's revelation.

"A few weeks ago. Apparently, 'it was brought to his attention' that I might be behaving 'inappropriately' with one or more coworkers. He was talking about *you*, you know?" Brenda stroked seductively on Emery's chest.

Bewildered, Clarke explored the matter. "We've been very discreet. How would they know something was going on?"

"I hate to be the one to tell you this, Emery. For one reason or another, I don't think *PM* and Sean trust you very much."

"*Me*...?" Clarke asked, feigning hurt feelings, but

utterly riveted. *Did Luke and Sean know his **true** identity?*

"I'm not sure why, but they've been suspicious." Brenda had a faraway expression.

"They're suspicious of *me*?" Clarke asked again, nonplused. "I've been the best employee around here."

"I know that," Brenda said. "Maybe, they think you're *too* perfect or something. But, it really doesn't matter, because *I* took care of *everything*."

Clarke pulled back, and stared into Brenda's face, perturbed. "What did you take care of, my love?" he asked through gritted teeth.

"Well, as you're well aware, one of the facets of **Dimension Four** is **Dimension** *Find Me.* The tracker has the capability of finding anyone in any given location. All that's required is the person's DNA. Well, *I* took the liberty to tweak the data you have on file with Portals-that is in the event you have a skeleton or two in your closet."

Clarke stared at Brenda in utter skepticism. She'd obviously had one too many drinks. Still, he couldn't say he wasn't pleased as punch to hear how she'd gone to bat for him. "My, you're something special! Do tell, love…"

"So, there's this thing that only a few of us are privy to about **Dimension Four**. Taking a microchip from the *Shield Me* accessory, can potentially render *Find Me* inept-at least for a while." Brenda inched up, and covered Emery's mouth in kisses. "I don't *know* whether or not you have a checkered past, but I really don't care. I love you, Emery!" she said brazenly.

Arianna was both horrified and grieved to hear Brenda spewing out top secret information to Emery Lloyd. Hadn't it occurred to Brenda that there was a reason why Emery wasn't in the loop? Tears looped over in her eyelids, because Brenda had betrayed them all. Arianna was heartbroken for Luke. Everyone hired to work through Portals had taken an oath to ensure confidentiality. Sadder still, was how enthralled

Brenda was with this man, while his feelings for her were lukewarm at best.

"You did all of that for *me*?" Clarke asked, eluding Brenda's admission of love. He hadn't intended for things to go this far. Nevertheless, everything seemed to be working in his favor. "What if I'm *not* the good guy everyone *thinks* I am? What if *our* bosses are right in suspecting that I indeed have a checkered past?" Clarke craftily presented a case in point.

"Well, then… That's a chance I'm willing to take, because you mean everything to me," Brenda reiterated. "Besides, I *know* you're really a good guy underneath it all." Brenda subtly began unbuttoning his shirt.

"*Do* you now?" Clarke teased, surrendering to her arms. "Thank you for your vote of confidence in me. I promise not to disappoint you."

"Just shut up and kiss me," Brendan ordered.

Arianna felt sick at heart. More than anything else, she wished she hadn't witnessed their salacious interactions. *If only she could find a way to escape from the lab…* She had to look away as Brenda and Emery took their little party to a whole other level. Arianna couldn't believe any of it. *What on earth was wrong with Brenda?* There wasn't a better boss, or a kinder human being than the one they had. She couldn't believe Brenda was putting it all out there for this *loser* of a man.

In light of all she'd seen, Arianna had to find Luke and Sean just as soon as possible. They *had* to know there was a defector onboard. Someone they'd trusted with such life-altering information was using it in the worst way. However, first and foremost, she had to wait it out until the couple ended their illicit exchanges. Arianna remained huddled to that corner, and tried to block out what was happening.

Clarke told Brenda he'd meet her over at her place in just a little while. She was too drunk to notice that he'd swiped her access key for the lab. The party was still going, but only a handful of employees remained out in the party hall. Clarke was grateful that Luke and Sean, along with their wives, had already left the building.

Brenda had shown him how to use the *Vortex to Vanish* feature of **Dimension Four**. So, Clarke had blinked out. He was completely undetectable, as he slunk down the hallway in order to return to the lab. There was quite a bit of exploring to do. At that hour, that area of Portals was entirely isolated, and the lights had dimmed down to a flicker here and there.

Since it was Christmas Eve, he hoped no one else had the *brilliant* idea to come out to the lab. Brenda had no clue her access key was missing. Clarke's plan was to slip it back into her pocketbook when he went by her place later. Even blinked out, Clarke prowled the area like a jewel thief.

Even if Brenda had disclosed that with *Shield Me's* technology implanted into his own access pass, not even *Find Me*, with its defining resolution of lenses, could detect him. Still, he had to be cautious. Clarke snaked around the corner, only a few feet away from the lab's set of doors. However, he pulled back when he heard noises. He picked up on noises coming from the lab. As he shrank back, someone guardedly issued from the lab's set of double doors.

Clarke gasped in shock to see Arianna Ward looking both ways before she began tiptoeing away from the area. All kinds of warning bells, and signals went off in Clarke's head. Hence, he too began creeping away from the area. He hadn't expected to see anyone in that perimeter of the building-least of all the pretty young blonde. Clarke was stunned for a number of reasons. It hadn't even been half an hour since he and Brenda had left the lab. Had Arianna Ward been there the entire time?

Clarke worried that Arianna had overheard his conversation with Brenda. It also wasn't outside the realm of possibility that she'd witnessed their inappropriate interactions within the classified lab. Clarke worried Arianna would go straight to Luke and Sean. That was something he couldn't risk. So, just then, he temporarily abandoned the idea of exploring the lab. Clarke rethought his plan.

He would follow Arianna Ward once she left the building. He had to ensure she kept her mouth shut. He'd been through hell in jail. Furthermore, Luke's downfall was something he'd planned for extensively. Not to mention having Melody back in his arms. So, failure just wasn't an option at this point.

"Has anyone seen Ari?" Peter asked the few partygoers remaining out in the hall. He hadn't seen Arianna since she'd rushed away from his office. From that time, Peter had searched everywhere for her. Arianna had alluded to going home. However, Peter knew she hadn't, because her car was still parked in its space out in the lot.

Everyone he'd asked had told him the same thing. They hadn't seen or heard from Arianna, since she'd made a brief appearance earlier on. Peter wandered out to a quiet spot out in the party hall, and tried calling her for the umpteenth time. "Ari, please call me. I'm really worried about you. I'm still over at Portals. You said you were going home, but I know you're still here, because your car's parked in the lot. Please, just call me to let me know you're all right. Please…," Peter shut down his phone, and sighed in frustration and uncertainty.

He wandered back out to the parking lot of the building. However, this time around, he was surprised to see that Ari's car was no longer parked out there. "I guess, she just left the building. I can't say I blame her for avoiding me all night." Peter shook his head in incredulity over the turn of events.

He wanted to go out to her condo. All things considered, he didn't want to be disrespectful, because it was after midnight. Still, he had to clear the air. Peter knew he wouldn't be able to sleep until things were right with Ari. So, against his better judgment, he hopped into his SUV, and decided to drive over to Arianna's condo out in Malibu Beach. He would be mentally and emotionally crippled unless he could tell her the truth. She was the one who held his heart, and that was never going to change.

***

"I hope she doesn't hate me for coming out here at this hour." Peter pulled into a parking space at Arianna's condo. Hopping out of his car, he rushed into the building. Impatiently pressing the up button for the elevator, he slid inside, and took it up to the second floor. Diffidently, he ambled down the hallway. His heart lashed with every step he took closer to Arianna's front door. For the obvious reason, he was hesitant to see her. No doubt, she probably didn't trust him anymore, because of what happened with Raya in his office. Not to mention the fact that it was very late.

Yet and still, Peter was terribly worried about her, so he refused to leave well enough alone. "Ari," Peter called out through the front door. He raised his right hand up in order to knock. Ringing the doorbell at that hour seemed intrusive. "Ari…" He knocked discreetly on the door. "It's me, Peter. I just came by to see if you're okay. You haven't answered any of my calls or texts. Ari…" Peter set his hand on the doorknob. Oddly enough, it turned in his hand.

Right then and there, Peter knew something was completely off. It was nervy of him to venture inside, but something was terribly wrong. So, Peter decidedly stepped into Ari's place, and shut the front door after himself.

"Arianna, it's *me*, Peter. I was worried about you. Are you here? Are you okay?" Peter spoke into the air, as he walked through the condo. It was odd that he'd seen her car parked in the condo lot, and yet there didn't seem to be any sign she was at home.

"Arianna, where are you?" Peter drifted into the living room, and then into the kitchen. His heart plunged, and a sense of foreboding dread hung over him like a black cloud. However, his greatest fear was confirmed when he turned a corner into Arianna's bedroom. Seeing her body stretched horizontally over the pristine cream-colored rug was a nightmare. "Ari...," Peter hollered, and dashed over to her side. "Ari, oh my god...!" Tears immediately flooded in his eyes, as he listened for a heartbeat, and checked for a pulse.

By the grace of God, Ari was still breathing, but her pulse was extremely faint. Peter collected her into his arms, while he called for an ambulance. *Why was she out cold? What on earth had happened?* It was annoying to be on the phone with a rescue dispatcher, when his thoughts were racing, and the woman he loved lay lifeless in his arms.

"No, I don't see any drugs around. She doesn't take drugs," Peter said irate. "Please, send someone right away. No, she was alone at her place," he said, frustrated. Tears dribbled down his cheeks, and fell like raindrops on Arianna's pretty forest-green party dress. She looked so beautiful that night. "I will gladly answer your questions, once the paramedics get here. Please...," he appealed.

"Oh, God, Ari," Peter moaned, grieved. "Who did this to you, and why won't you open up your eyes for me?" He rocked her body gently in his arms. There was no visible sign of an attack, or that she'd been in some way victimized. Maybe, she took pills, but there didn't seem to be any indication of that either.

Feeling like a lost child, Peter kept a firm grasp of her

in his arms. Seeing her so lifeless was the worst pain he'd ever experienced. Someone had impaled his *heart*, and he was holding the remains in his arms. "God, please don't let me lose her. Please, don't let her die. Please, God. Please, give me a chance to tell her how much I love her."

***

"Is it too early to say Merry Christmas to my amazing wife?" Luke kept his arms fastened around Melody's waist, while her arms were draped about his neck.

"It's never too early. Merry, Christmas, honey bear!" Melody whispered. Inching up on her tiptoes, she pressed her lips to his. "I'm so proud of you." She pulled back to look into his eyes. "I'm so proud of how successfully the party turned out tonight. It was beautiful! What I appreciated most was that we gave everyone a brief presentation on the *true* meaning of Christmas. 'A Savior is born this day in the city of David (Luke 2:11),'" Melody said sentimentally staring longingly into Luke's eyes.

"If *we* don't tell them, they'll think Christmas's all about getting bonuses at work, and getting wasted at parties all season. I've got to do my best to represent Christ. Jesus represented *me* when I had no representation," Luke said aimfully, with tears glistening in his teal eyes.

"The Lord has brought us both a very long way. I can't believe how different things were last year." Tears gleamed in Melody's eyes as well. "I wanted to be with you so badly last Christmas."

"Last year was the saddest Christmas *I've* ever spent-away from *you*, my family…" Tears looped over Luke's eyes, as he remembered drinking all through Christmas and New Year's. All that was before God had sent his saving grace.

Luke had been offered a programming position with Body Electric Era. He squeezed Melody in his arms all the more. "I was drinking all the time. I had to find a way to numb the pain of being without you," he admitted. "I honestly thought I was going to die. It actually felt like I had." He pressed kisses to Melody's face and temples. "I love you so much, Mel! There just aren't any words to define just how much of my heart belongs to you."

"I love you too, Luke, and I always will. *You're* my heart." She pulled away, and stared lovingly into his eyes.

"That's what makes this Christmas so special. It's our first one together-and as man and wife no less." Luke's face radiated, as he besieged Melody with kisses.

"Yes..." Melody laughed, because Luke had pelted her with kisses. "It's the first time we get to celebrate Christmas together, and I'm so happy!"

"I don't think you can be any happier than I am. I'm whistling in my dreams nowadays because of *you*, Mrs. Bryant."

"What are you whistling?" Melody teased.

"Oh, I'm whistling all kinds of love songs-all sappier and mushier than the next." He smiled into her eyes. Luke was about to demonstrate one of the songs, but Melody's mouth quickly covered his in order to silence the racket.

"Come here." Luke took Melody's hand in his, and led her out to their sizable family room. The expansive room with high ceilings was perfect for the gigantic Blue Spruce evergreen with white-themed sparkling décor. It looked like a diamond blazing in the sun. The angel at the top of the tree added just the perfect touch. There were decorative gift boxes of red, gold, white, winter-green, blue and silver stacked underneath the tree. The house smelled like apple cider and cinnamon, and there were huge Christmas stockings hung in every corner of the extensive room.

Later, they would be entertaining family. Luke's parents were already out in California. Sean and Nicole would be coming over. Serena and Dane were also expected in the late morning, and Melody was so excited she could burst. Luke knew how much Melody had missed her bestie. So, he wouldn't stop trying to find a way to get Dane and Serena to move out to Beverly Glen, or to one of the neighboring areas. Arianna and Peter were also invited over, and even Luke's baby sister Rachel would be there. She was currently staying over with their parents. Luke was excited for a number of reasons that Christmas Eve, but mostly because he had the best surprise for his wife.

The room was nice and toasty for a nippy night out in Beverly Glen. "I know you didn't bring me all the way in here to admire the beautiful tree, ornaments and presents." Melody gave Luke a knowing but curious wink.

Luke took both of her hands in his, and encouraged her to sit on the floor in front of the tree. "Well, it's all breathtaking, isn't it?" he teased.

"Luke…," Melody whined, staring nonsensically at him. "We said we'd only open one gift after midnight." Her face radiated the joy and excitement of a child's.

Mischief crinkled Luke's face. "I know. That's why I'm trying to stay true to my word." Luke reached underneath the tree, and pulled out a medium-sized gift box. The wrapping was ornate, and done in a forest-green and silver theme. His eyes were imbued with love, and sentimentality, as he explored hers. "Merry Christmas, honey baby?"

"Oh, Luke…" Melody's face warped in nostalgia. "What have you gone and done?" she playfully chided.

"Just go on and open it up," he heartened with an impish wink.

"Okay," Melody said quietly. "Thank you."

"You're welcome!" Luke's voice was gravelly. He was getting all choked up watching Melody open up one of his gifts. He gleefully observed his wife, as she opened up the present. Luke was on cloud nine.

Melody gingerly opened up the fancily wrapped

present. Her eyes connected expectantly to her husband's as she ventured in. "What's this?" She removed what appeared to be some kind of a portfolio from the gift box, and stared bewilderingly into Luke's face.

"Open it up, honey baby," Luke goaded.

"Okay…" Melody opened up the portfolio, and saw pictures of what appeared to be a renovated building. As she dug into the binder, she got a chance to look on the inside. It was a beautiful, spacious, newly remodeled storefront. The building was so contemporary, she couldn't help thinking how perfect the space would be for an art gallery. Examining the property got her creative juices flowing. "Are you asking me to design this place?" Her eyes connected to Luke's expectantly.
Luke smiled openly.

"You *could* say that. Why don't you lift the tissue paper, and dig into the bottom of the box?"

Melody gave him a nonsensical look. "Okay, if you say so, Mr. Bryant." Melody lifted the tissue paper out of the way, and at the bottom of the box were a set of keys. "Luke, what's this?" She held the set up inquiringly.

"Well, this building, formerly known as 'The House of Style' is free and newly remodeled. It's yours, Mel!" Luke beamed. "I thought you might want to use it as a hub for *Melody's Masterpieces*. You can start your own company."

Melody cupped her mouth in shock, and instantly began to tremble. Her face contorted emotionally, and she kept shaking her head in denial. "Luke…" Tears rolled down her cheeks. "You got me a *building* for Christmas?"

"Honey baby, you set aside your own goals and dreams just to support mine. I just wanted to do the same. I *know* how much designing means to you." Tears looped over in Luke's eyelids.

"Oh, Luke…." Melody threw her arms around him and cried. "How could you be so wonderful? But, I've *never* done anything like this before." She pulled away to look into his eyes. "Don't you want me at Portals?"

"Oh, *believe* me I do. But, I get that you have your own career to pursue. You're free to hire *anyone* who knows the ins and outs of the business. If you'd like, you can come out to Portals a couple of times a week to check in-"

"*Are* you trying to get rid of me?" Melody teased, covering his face in kisses.

"Not at all, my love. I just don't want to be selfish. I actually like it just a little bit too much that I can pop in and out of your office, whenever I have a free moment."

"You *do*?" Melody's voice was wispy, as she stared lovingly into his eyes.

"More than I can even explain. Having you working so closely to me is a dream." Luke cupped Melody's chin. "You've supported me so much on this entire Portals adventure, and I think it's high time that I returned the favor." His mouth bridged to hers. When he pulled away for a moment, he saw that Melody's eyes were flooded with tears. "What's the matter, honey baby?" he asked with a wavering voice.

"How can you be so wonderful?" Melody shook her head in skepticism. "I can't believe you've done this. Wow! You want me to lay the groundwork for *Melody's Masterpieces*. I *would* say I have no idea how to run a business, but I've been watching my savvy boss for months," she upheld.

"You can do anything to set your mind to, Mel. And, we can hire anyone you want to get started."

"I'm really excited, Luke. I mean, I want to get started right away, but I also love what I do over at Portals."

"You don't have to choose between the two. We just have to work out a schedule that'll allow you to manage the GDD, and oversee your own company." Luke smiled to see the sparkle of excitement in Melody's eyes.

"Okay, I think it might work," Melody acceded.

"I *know* it will, because my wife's super talented and a

business dynamo!" Luke tightened his grasp about her waist.

"And, my husband's totally perfect." Melody inched up, and pressed a kiss to Luke's mouth.

"You *know* just how imperfect I am, Mel. I sleep like a wild man-"

"And you hog up the sheets," Melody teased. "But, I can live with all of that, because I love you so much!" She draped her arms about Luke's neck, and held on lovingly.

"I love you too, honey baby!"

"Okay, so it's my turn," Melody said excitedly. She shimmied away from Luke's potent grasp, knelt down besides the Christmas tree, and retrieved a shiny red and gold wrapped gift box from the pile. "So, this is for you, Mr. Luke *Portal Master* Bryant." Sentimentality veiled her sweet face.

"Pour moi?" Luke razzed with his hands on his heart.

"Yes…totally *for you*. I wasn't sure what to get for the man who already has everything."

Luke set down in front of the tree, and gently nudged Melody to sit with him. "I *do* have everything. You're everything I need, honey baby," he said throatily, and wrapped his arms around her. "Thank you so much!"

"Open it, honey bear," she coaxed. "Merry Christmas," she said quietly, as she watched her husband cautiously undo the giftwrapping paper.

"What's this?" Luke pulled out the leather-bound album he was all too familiar with. It was the album labeled, "*Our Story So Far*," starring Melody and Luke. It was the gift Melody had given Luke on their one-month anniversary. At the time, he'd just returned to Sands Port, after an extended stay out on Rhode Island visiting with his sick father. Tears automatically glimmered in his eyes. "Melody Bryant, what have *you* done?" Luke shook his head in disbelief.

"Open it…," Melody whispered.

Luke ventured into the album that included every detail of their history, and saw the addendums Melody had made. Tears rolled down his cheeks, because she'd illustrated their year apart, and how miserable they'd both been. Moreover, just like the villain in a movie, their victory over Clarke Vale was also highlighted. Luke made a silent vow to add to that chapter, by eradicating anything having to do with Clarke from their lives.

Melody displayed their wedding and their honeymoon. She even depicted the moment they were now sharing, their first Christmas together. "I love it, Mel!" Luke's voice broke. Tenderly, he collected her into his arms. "I love you so much!" He lavished her with sweet kisses.

"I love you too, Luke! Now more than ever. I'm so glad you like it."

"Like it...? Thank God, our story just keeps getting better. Thank you for not making me wait until the sun comes up to open up such a special gift."

"You're welcome!" Melody said softly. "Do you miss Sands Port?" she asked suddenly. "It actually snows on Christmas sometimes."

"I do miss the East Coast at times. I miss having hot chocolate by the Christmas tree, and gingerbread cookies on a snowy Christmas morning, but I'm right at home out here."

Melody nodded. "So am I."

"Home to me is wherever *you* are, Mel," Luke said hoarsely. He gently took Melody in his arms, and began fondling her mouth in nuances.

Igniting a flame, Melody drank exigently from the stream of his mouth.

"Come here..." Luke took Melody's hand, and helped her up. Silently, he guided her back over to their bedroom. Scooping her up in his arms, he laid her gingerly on the bed. Caringly, he took her into his arms, and sheathed her in their private world of love.

However, before the love train left the station, Luke caught sight of several SOS messages texted to his phone. "Mel, something's wrong," Luke said, breaching a loving kiss.

"What's wrong?" Melody asked, startled and alarmed.

She and Luke sat up on the bed, while Luke accessed his phone messages.

Luke's face changed and warped in sadness. "Oh, no. Ari's in the hospital. She's unconscious. Pete found her a little while ago over at her place unresponsive." Luke's tear-filled eyes connected critically to his wife's.

Melody was already in tears. "What happened to her?" Her chest rose and fell dramatically, and she breathed spasmodically. "I saw her at the party, but I didn't get a chance to connect to her." Melody cradled her head in jeopardy.

"Peter says he thinks someone tried to hurt her over at her place. Mel, I'm sorry to have to cut our special Christmas Eve celebration short. I've got to get to the hospital."

"No need to apologize, Luke. I'm coming with you."

"Are you sure?" Luke tested.

Melody nodded. "Ari's going to need us all rallying around her right now." Fresh tears shone in her eyes.

"She sure will." Luke's thoughts raced. "What was going on? Why would *anyone* ever try to hurt Arianna?" His heart was broken over the news. Just then, his phone rang again. This time around it was Sean.

"You just got the news?" Luke said automatically.

"Yeah, I heard. Pete just texted me. I can't believe this. That poor kid," he commiserated. "Nicole and I are going out to the hospital."

"Mel and I will meet you there," Luke affirmed, shutting down his phone. His sad eyes bridged to his wife's.

"Oh, Luke…" Melody buried her head in his chest. "This is the worst thing that could happen-and on Christmas no less. I love Ari so much, and she doesn't deserve that."

Tears rolled down Luke's cheeks, as he held his wife potently. Arianna was family, and someone had just attack their family. So, he was willing to do whatever he had to ensure that the culprit was brought to justice.

Chapter Nine

"I'm so glad you're here, *PM*!" Peter was out of breath, as he rushed over to meet Luke and Melody in the ICU of Gloaming Oaks Hospital in Newport Beach.

"How is she, Pete?" Luke's face strained in concern. Melody stood by his side with a flagellating heart. Both were eager to hear the prognosis.

Peter shook his head in the negative. "She's in a coma." His face warped in misery. "They've drawn blood in order to determine if she was drugged. They've also checked for any indication of physical trauma."

"What happened?" Luke shook his head in mystification.

A winded and flustered Peter tried to explain what happened play by play. He even disclosed the part about Arianna finding Raya Hodges in his office kissing him underneath the mistletoe.

Luke's face creased in both sadness and regret. "So, *you* found her unconscious when you went out to her place from the party?"

Peter nodded. His eyes were red, and bloodshot from the emotional turmoil and fatigue. His face warped again, and he began to sob. "I keep thinking that if I'd gotten to her place a little earlier, her eyes would be opened right now."

"It's not your fault, buddy," Luke sympathized, throwing his arms around Peter in support. Melody also hugged Peter, and encouraged him.

"I don't know what to do right now, *PM*," Peter said thickly.

"That's all right. None of us have the answers right now, but we're going to walk each other through." Luke stared at Peter in commiseration. Peter was clearly heartbroken. If anyone knew how much Peter loved Arianna, it was Luke. So, Luke's heart went out to him.

"That's right. We're going to get through this together, and Ari's going to be alright," Melody heartened.

"That's right. We're one hundred percent here with you, Pete," Sean said. He and Nicole had just stepped into the ICU's waiting area.

"Sean, Nicole… Thank you for being here." New hope radiated on Peter's face.

"We all love Ari, and we're here to make sure she recovers from this." Nicole's face wrinkled in sympathy and compassion.

"Thanks for coming over so quickly, Sean." Luke patted Sean on the arm.

"We would have gotten here even sooner if we could," Sean told him.

Melody hugged Nicole, and they wept silently in each other's arms. This was a nightmare no one could have anticipated. Their buddy-one of the sweetest most selfless people they knew, was fighting for her life. Melody and Nicole prayed and cried together.

"So, you drove over to Ari's when you noticed her car was no longer in the Portals' lot? You have any idea what the timeframe was before you went over to her condo?" Luke verified, desperately trying to fill in the missing puzzle pieces of what had occurred.

Peter nodded. "It couldn't have been very long, because I spent about fifteen minutes in the party hall. I asked a few coworkers if they'd seen her, but they all said they hadn't. Then, I called Ari again, but it went straight to voicemail." Sadness shaded Peter's face.

"And, when you wandered back out to the lot, her car was gone?" Luke tested.

"Yes. I sensed something was very off. So, I went by her place to see if she was okay. I didn't even want to step foot inside her place at that hour, but something kept telling me to check in on her." Peter's eyes glazed over with fresh tears.

"There was no suspicious activity at the condo, and you didn't see anyone scurrying to leave the building?" Sean asked.

Peter shook his head contrarily. "It was late. As far as I could see, I was the only one on the second floor. I called her name through the door. I knocked a few times, but she didn't answer. So, I took a chance, and tried to let myself in. When the doorknob twisted in my hand, I knew something was very wrong.

"Ari would *never* leave her door unlocked at that late hour. So, I went in to look for her. I kept calling her name, but nothing... She didn't answer at all. I didn't even think she was home at that point. That was until..." Peter's face twisted in misery, and tears snaked down his cheeks. "Her bedroom door was opened, and I saw her lifeless body stretched across the floor," he said thickly.

Melody and Nicole listened with breaking hearts. Grieved over Peter's account of how he'd found Arianna, they tried to hold it together for his sake.

"Who would deliberately set out to hurt Ari?" Melody asked shakily, drifting back over to her husband. She was trembling, as she grasped his arm, and rested her head on his shoulder.

Nicole drifted back over to Sean's side.

"I'm not sure *what* to think at this point, honey." Luke secured Melody in his arms. She buried her face in his chest. "It makes no sense that Pete found Ari unconscious and alone over at her place. She wasn't sick," Luke argued, irritated.

"Why would *anyone* try to hurt Arianna? She's such a good girl. She doesn't deserve any of this." Melody blinked back tears.

"Don't worry, Mel." Luke rubbed Melody's back in comfort, with tears sparkling in his eyes. "I promise, we're going to get to the bottom of this. We're going to find out exactly what happened to Ari last night. It's all right, honey," he placated.

Luke's eyes found Peter's forlorn expression. "We're going to find out exactly what happened to Ari. Don't worry, Pete," his voice broke, as he clung to Melody.

"We're all in this together, Pete. Whoever tried to hurt her won't get away with it," Sean affirmed. "We *have* the resources to ensure whoever did this is dealt with."

"Sean's right. They *will* be dealt with, and you're going to be okay," Nicole told Peter. She set her arms supportively about Sean's waist, while they were waiting to have word with the doctor.

The group sat solemnly in the ICU waiting area. Luke had gone to the café to get coffee for everyone. Returning, he absently handed everyone a cup. For the first time in a while, he had no clue how to ameliorate the circumstances for the people he cared about. Peter was utterly traumatized, so Luke knew that if Arianna didn't recover, Peter wouldn't either.

"Thank you, sweetie," Melody said, taking the cup of coffee Luke offered. She rested the cup on a small table in the waiting area right next to her armchair. The table had magazines sprawled over it.

"You're welcome, baby." Luke issued a faint smile, and slipped into the chair next to hers. Pulling Melody gingerly into his arms, their heads propped in a sustaining manner.

Luke wanted to find the right words to eradicate the sadness. However, he realized that in this instance, it was probably best not to say anything at all. They would have to wait it out in to hear the doctor's prognosis of Arianna's sudden and mysterious illness.

Sometime later, a young Asian doctor stepped out into the waiting area, and made his way over to the group. Everyone stood to their feet, and automatically gravitated over to the man. In angst, they waited to hear what he had to say.

"Good morning! My name's Doctor Chen. You're all here about Arianna Ward?" he affirmed.

"Yes," they all said in unison.

"What's wrong with Arianna? What happened to her? Is she still unconscious?" Peter exacted.

Peter stood to Luke's left, while Melody stood to his right. Luke squeezed Peter's shoulder in support. "Easy, Pete…"

"I'm afraid, I don't have the best news," Dr. Chen said artlessly.

"What do you mean? *Is* she going to be all right?" Melody panicked.

Peter quivered like an evergreen tree in a blizzard. "Has she opened her eyes since she was brought in?" his voice wavered.

"Ms. Ward remains unconscious. At this point, it's rather difficult to predict how things are going to progress. It's still too soon to determine that." Grimness veiled Dr. Chen's face. "Ms. Ward was poisoned."

"*Poisoned*?" Luke face turned white as a sheet. Tears of shock immediately glimmered in his eyes.

"What kind of poison are we talking about here?" Sean asked, incensed.

Dr. Chen held his right hand out in a halting manner. "This was no ill-fated act. It's being considered an attempted homicide. There were two very small puncture wounds on her right arm. The perforations are so slight, they wouldn't be detected by the noticeable eye. The police are actually on their way, given that this *was* an attempt on Ms. Ward's life. She was given a lethal dose of Tetrodotoxin, and we also found and exorbitant amount of Morphine in her bloodstream. Tetrodotoxin is the poison found in Puffer Fish.

"We were able to detect traces in the blood right away. She's been intubated in order to prevent respiratory failure-as both the drug, and toxin have caused respiratory depression. Through her IV, we're administering fluids, Pressors and Antiarrhythmic in the hopes of restoring normal breathing patterns," Dr. Chen explicated. Seeing the stunned expressions on the faces of Arianna's friends and family, Dr. Chen momentarily held his peace.

"Someone tried to kill Ari?" Peter kept shaking his head in denial. "Someone *meant* to hurt her… This was a *deliberate* attempt. I can't understand or believe any of this. This is insane."

He moved in aggressively on Dr. Chen. Short of grabbing the man by the collar, he demanded, "You can't let her die. Do you understand? You've got to save her."

Both Luke and Sean held Peter back in pacification. Luke took his place discreetly between Peter and Dr. Chen. "This Tetrodotoxin, usually claims the lives of its victims in a matter of hours." Luke stared the man squarely in the eyes.

"That is correct." Dr. Chen's face crumpled in affect. Melody huddled close to Luke's side, and squeezed his hand in support.
"So, there's no guarantee that the toxin can successfully be flushed out of her system-that is without leaving some form of damage to her lungs and her heart?" Luke theorized.

"Yes, that's right. There is no known antidote for the poison, but we're doing all we can to flush it out of her system, and to eradicate it from her bloodstream. We're administering gastric lavage, and monitoring her vital quite aggressively."

"I both understand and appreciate all you're doing. She's got to be all right," Luke settled. "We can't lose Arianna." His heart thudded in angst, and tears brimmed over in his eyelids. *Attempted murder* was a whole other ballgame. Luke was shaken to the core.

Melody collected Luke in her arms, and rubbed his back in mitigation. She didn't know what to say at that point. She was still trying to process all she'd just heard. Her heart was broken, because of the uncertainty of the circumstances.

"Please, trust that we're doing everything in our power to counter the effects of the poison." Dr. Chen seemed tense and stressed at that juncture.

"Well, how are things looking for her right now?"

Sean asked straightforwardly.

"It's difficult to tell. The next few hours are critical. We're hoping that the measures we've taken to put her in the clear, will be enough to carry her through."

"So, what you're *really* saying, is that we're waiting to *see* if this poison claims her life?" Nicole's voice undulated, and a fresh sheet of tears coated her eyes.

Dr. Chen nodded. "Tetrodotoxin usually claims the lives of its victims in the span of six hours. Sadly, we don't know exactly when she was injected with the toxin. The most we can hope for is that she's strong enough to fight off the effect within the next few hours. I *am* sorry, but there's no other recourse at this time."

"So, we're sitting ducks waiting to see if she dies or not?" Peter's tone was irate, and tears of rage surfaced in his eyes. "So, there's a fifty/fifty chance she could die within the next few hours. This poison is slowly killing her, while you're out here *telling* us about it," he bellowed. "That's not good enough for me." His face reddened in indignation, as he got in Dr. Chen's face.

Luke pulled Peter back, and shielded Dr. Chen from Peter's wrath. Sean also kept a placating grasp on Peter's arm.

Melody and Nicole stood by watching the seen. They were frantic of an altercation. They rallied around the men, in spite of the direness of the circumstances.

"Is there anything else that can be done for Ms. Ward?" Luke tried to remain levelheaded. "Just tell us what we can do."

"Every possible measure is being taken to counter the effects of the poison in Ms. Ward's bloodstream. She may regain stability. However, if we can't normalize her heartrate, she could go into cardiac arrest." Dr. Chen felt compelled to say as little as possible. He was overwhelmed by the reaction of Arianna Ward's loved ones.

"So, I guess this is all one big waiting game. We have no guarantee that treatment administered won't *accelerate* the effects of the toxin," Melody rationalized.

Luke kept a firm hold on Melody, because she was virtually swooning.

Dr. Chen nodded in confirmation in response to Melody's supposition. "Ms. Ward will in all likeliness remain comatose for a while. However, we're monitoring, and doing all we can to counter the toxicity levels in her bloodstream, and control the abnormal heartrate." He gave them a reassuring nod.

"We're hoping for the best. It's a miracle she's even alive. However, she's quite young and seemingly strong. So, there's always a chance... Sadly, given the circumstances, there are no real guarantees."

"Can we go in to see her?" Peter was a bit more subdued at that point. He realized that he had to control his temper.

"I'm afraid Ms. Ward is still too fragile for visitors. We will keep you posted as to when it's all right for family and friends to see her." Dr. Chen gave them well-meaning looks.

"Is this *really* happening?" Melody's eyes connected direly to Luke's. There was a lost expression on her face. "Oh, Luke..." She sobbed into his chest.

Luke collected Melody into his arms, and crushed her to himself. Inwardly, he himself was faltering. However, he was too numb and shocked to react. Caressing Melody's face and hair, he pressed kisses to her forehead. "It's all right, honey. It's going to be okay," he told her, even if he felt as if his words were flat and ineffective.

"So, that's it? We're just *waiting*..." Peter felt totally adrift. His face turned scarlet, and angry tears burst from his eyes.

Sean set his hand on Peter's shoulders, and tried to extend comfort. "It's all right, Pete. It's going to be okay. You heard what Dr. Chen said. It's a miracle she's still alive. That means God's with her, and he's got her," Sean encouraged. "*You*, of all people, should know just how strong Ari is. She's one tough cookie, and her faith's even stronger."

"I *know* her faith in God is strong, Sean. So, I've got to believe God's looking out for her right now." Peter shook his head still dazed. "All the same, Sean, if she doesn't make it through this, I'll never be able to forgive myself. It's *my* fault she spent the entire night trying to avoid *me* at the party. Things weren't supposed to play out that way. We'd made plans to be together all night. If I'd kept Ari close, this wouldn't have happened. I wish we could go back, and start last night all over again." Peter's expression was strained.

"Let's just pray for the best, and surrender Arianna to God's care. There isn't anything too hard for God," Nicole uplifted.

"Honestly, Pete, the *worst* thing we can do right now is to panic," Sean relayed. Inwardly, his heart was broken. He had no idea how to make things okay for Peter, or for any of them.

Luke felt totally lost. Usually, he had an answer or a solution to the hard matters. However, this time around, he felt completely disconnected and inept. Things were falling apart. How on earth could this have happened? Someone had tried to murder his friend in her own home. Luke held Melody in his arms, and clung to her for dear life.

His attention suddenly shifted over to Dr. Chen, and Luke's eyes gunned into him. "Since this incident is now considered a homicide attempt, the police will undoubtedly be questioning *us*?"

"Yes, that's correct. I'm sure they'll be asking questions about your party last night." Dr. Chen's face was still taut in remorse.

"All right, once they get here, I have a few requests to make of my own. For starters, we're going to need round-the-clock security set up for Arianna's room. Furthermore, we're going to insist that no one who isn't standing in this room right now-with the exception of her immediate family, will be allowed in to see her," Luke delineated.

"Whoever tried to kill her, will undoubtedly be looking to finish the job. Hospital staff should handle this matter with extreme caution and delicacy. There's zero room for error. She *has* to recover from this," Luke said authoritatively.

"I understand your concern, Mr. Bryant!" It suddenly dawned on Dr. Chen who Luke was. He was standing in the presence of the *Portal Master*-for all intents and purposes, the richest man in the world! "Hospital security will *definitely* be notified. No doubt, Ms. Ward's room will be rigorously monitored by hospital security. In as far as police protection, that's something you've got to take up with the authorities." Dr. Chen wished he had more favorable news for the group.

"I appreciate your help in the matter," Luke's voice undulated.

"I will return in a while to discuss any tentative changes in Ms. Ward's condition."

The group agreed quickly. They were too flustered and drained to argue.

Dr. Chen turned, and ambled over to the set of doors leading back into the ICU.

Melody stared into Luke's forlorn face. She threw her arms around him, and squeezed him in support. "I'm so sorry."

"I'm sorry too, baby." Luke swallowed the chunk lodged in his throat.

The moment felt surreal. It was Christmas day, and here they were at the hospital, because someone had tried to murder Arianna. Luke felt totally responsible. He was the one who'd invited Arianna to move out to California, and work through Portals Unlimited. Arianna had left her family back out in Virginia. Now, she was laying comatose in the ICU, because an attempt was made on her life.

Luke felt as if he'd in some way failed her. The sting could not have felt any stronger, if it had occurred to a member of his own family. He loved and cared about Arianna a great deal. *How on earth was he going to tell David and Elizabeth Ward someone tried to kill their daughter?* And yet, Luke knew he had to find a way to tell her family. The very thought of putting in the call made him feel inwardly sick. Trembling in Melody's arms, he grumbled, "It's my fault, Mel. "I'm responsible."

"No, it's *not* your fault, Luke." Melody's heart broke for her husband. "It's not your fault. Please, don't say that. You're not responsible for what happened. How could any of us imagine something so heinous?" Melody's face twisted in compunction, as she tried to sustain her husband. It killed her to hear Luke blaming himself for what happened.

"I should have taken more precaution to ensure everyone's safety." Luke's thoughts whizzed, as he considered he could have used *Shield Me* to protect Arianna.

"No, Luke… Please, stop saying it's your fault. Please, don't break my heart that way." Melody cried.

"I'm sorry. I'm so sorry, baby. Please, forgive me. I'm so sorry. I won't say that anymore. It kills me that we couldn't protect her." Luke broke down, and clung to Melody as his lifeline.

"I know, honey, I know… It's killing me too. We've just got to hold on to faith right now. Ari has great faith. So, *we* can't let her down by doubting that God will give her a miracle."

Melody pulled away to look into Luke's eyes. "You're doing the right thing in taking security measures to keep her safe." She cradled Luke's face in her hands, then pressed kisses to his cheeks. "You are the most wonderful man in the world! And, you've been an amazing friend to Ari. She wouldn't want you blaming yourself, all right?"

Luke nodded absently. His mind was already going. He *had* to find out why anyone would want to hurt Arianna. She was an angel.

Sean's eyes connected furtively to Luke's at that moment. As always, they were in sync. He could undeniably read Luke's thoughts. He sensed Luke's misgivings about not using *Shield Me* technology to keep Arianna safe. The program would have undoubtedly kept her from being victimized. Sean also perceived how guilty Luke felt, because he'd invited Arianna to Los Angeles in order to work through Portals. Now, the girl was comatose and fighting for her life.

Emotionally spent, Sean sighed. He too felt helpless to mitigate the circumstances. Peter was falling apart, and Nicole was trying to keep him from a complete meltdown. The situation was messed up. Sean figured that there *had* to be a way to find out who was responsible for turning their lives upside down on Christmas day.

Luke and Melody sat quietly, and sustained each other in the waiting area of the ICU. They were all talked out and exhausted. The police had questioned the group extensively in respect to the chronological events of the night before. They all told the authorities everything they knew.

The police also informed the group that they would question other Portals employees in the days ahead. They assured the group that they'd find whoever had injected Arianna with the toxin. For Luke, the entire situation was bizarre. Hence, he'd have to share the bad news with the Ward family once the sun was up.

Whatever the outcome-as they were still waiting on Dr. Chen's update on Ari's condition, he would need to break it down to Arianna's family. Luke grasped that he wasn't the *only* one on edge. It was almost five in the morning. So, based on *their* calculations, the poison had been in Ari's system for a little over six hours. *Would Dr. Chen come out, and tell them she was gone?*

There was one bright spot to this tragedy. The authorities promised to honor their request in providing round-the-clock security, and surveillance of Arianna's ICU room. Only immediate family, and the five people present that morning, would be allowed to see her. Luke didn't care who they were, and how close they were to Arianna. *Everyone* was a suspect as far as he was concerned.

The authorities left the ICU at the top of the hour. They left viable phone contacts for the group, in the event they needed to reach out. The group was asked to call, if there were any new developments in the case. They all promised to do whatever they could to comply.

It was half past the hour, when Dr. Chen stepped back out into the waiting area.

Everyone instinctively rushed over to connect to him. Luke's heart raced in angst, and he could hear Melody's heart lashing, as they awaited news from the young doctor.

Peter's face was a mask of trepidation. His expression was that of a man awaiting sentencing from a judge. His eyes widened in nervousness, and his heart rose and fell dramatically, as he anticipated what Dr. Chen had to say.

Sean and Nicole held each other in support. Whatever the outcome, they were determined to remain brave. As new believers in Jesus Christ, they were learning how to pray, and how to call on the Lord in times of trouble.

"Ms. Ward's still holding her own, and she's stable. Her body's definitely fighting off the effects of the poison," Dr. Chen pronounced, smiling.

The group collectively released sighs of relief, and their faces unwound.

"Does that mean she's no longer in danger?" Luke asked, allowing himself to breathe again. He felt like jumping for joy, because Ari had made it past the six hours.

"She's not out of the woods yet. As I stated earlier on, she might be stable for now, but we're still monitoring the toxicity levels in her blood. There's also the Tachycardia. We're also doing everything we can to get that under control."

Dr. Chen smiled again. "However, if Ms. Ward's held her own for this long, that's a very good indication. It means, she's fighting the poison. There are no real guarantees in such a case, but we're hopeful. She's a very strong young lady, with an indomitable spirit."

"Thanks, Dr. Chen," Hopefulness resonated in Luke's tone.

"Thank you so much for all of your help," Melody echoed.

"You're welcome! I will be back tomorrow night. Just wanted to tell you the news before my shift ended." He smiled. "Merry Christmas!" he told them.

"Merry Christmas!" the group said in concert. They took turns hugging one another, as they celebrated the news. Once again, Dr. Chen disappeared through the set of doors into the ICU.

Luke pulled Melody graspingly into his arms. "Thank you, Lord! Thank you, Jesus for total healing for Arianna! Thank you for answered prayer." Tears rolled down his cheeks.

"That's the best news I've heard all morning!" Melody cheered.

Luke pulled away to look into Melody's eyes. She had tears of joy in her eyes this time around. "That is the best news, honey! Ari's made it through the past few hours. So, I *choose* to believe that God will carry her through this." Luke couldn't suppress his joy. Taking Melody in his arms again, he crushed her, and buried her in kisses.

"God is faithful, and he won't let us lose Ari," Melody uplifted. "I'm so grateful, Luke."

"So am I, baby, so am I..." They swayed together in a loving rhythm.

Still encircled in each other's arms, the couple caught sight of Sean and Nicole. They too were celebrating the great news.

Both couples pulled Peter into their hugs, and cheered. Peter was beside himself. He guffawed inanely over the turn of events, and seemed hopeful for the first time since they'd gotten there.

"She's strong, Pete." Luke cradled Peter's head in his hand. Luke loved Peter like a little brother. In fact, Peter *was* the younger brother Luke never had. Everything about Peter reminded Luke of *his* own younger more impetuous days. Luke also appreciated how in love, and totally committed Peter was to Arianna. Luke prayed God would give Arianna, and Peter a chance to explore their blossoming love for each other.

"Thanks, *PM*. It really means a lot to me that you're all here," Peter's voice broke, as his eyes connected endearingly to the group. "Thank you for being here with me this morning."

"Where else would we be, Pete? We love her as much as you do," Melody said.

"We sure do," Nicole upheld.

"Mel's right, Pete. We stick together as a family. Got that?" Luke affirmed.

Peter nodded, as stray tears rolled down his cheeks. He swallowed hard, and allowed himself to smile at Luke. "Thank you."

Luke winked, and squeezed Peter's shoulder. "It's like Sean said before, we're all in this together. And, I honestly believe Ari's going to beat this thing."

"She has to, *PM*. I honestly don't know how to live without her," Peter admitted unabashedly.

Luke smiled temperately at Peter. "I *know*," he said.

Luke turned, and found Melody and Nicole gushing. It was the first time they'd heard Peter profess his love for Arianna in such a forthcoming manner.

Sean shook his head, amused. "Now, there you go, Pete. You've got the girls all sappy and sentimental. So, we're never going to hear the end of it."

Peter laughed. "Sorry, guys…"

"Peter, don't you dare apologize. Luke and Sean don't appreciate the *sappy and sentimental* the way we do," Melody teased. She found Luke's eyes, and winked at him.

Luke shook his head humorously, and winked back at her. "Careful, Pete, before you know it, Mel and Nik will be planning your wedding. It might even be before the sun comes up."

"Don't listen to him, Peter. Come and talk to me and Nikki," Melody said lightheartedly. She and Nicole took Peter aside, and led him back over to the waiting area.

While the girls had word with Peter, Luke and Sean talked privately.

"Luke, don't get me wrong. I'm totally relieved that Ari's fighting this, but this is so messed up. Someone broke into her place, and injected her with Morphine and a lethal poison. What on earth? I can't believe any of this." Sean face flushed in irritation.

"I'm so ticked off right now, Sean. I doubt, there are any words to express the level of outrage I'm experiencing right now. This happened right under our noses. Why would *anyone* try to hurt Ari? Granted, I'm sure she deals with jealousy at Portals all the time.

"Some of her coworkers might be jealous of her status. I also suspect she gets a lot of hate because Pete loves her," Luke emphasized. "With all of that said, I still can't imagine anyone *truly* wanting to hurt her." Inwardly, Luke prayed for God's peace. Quite frankly, he was ready to find and destroy whoever had hurt Arianna.

"Pete says Ari left the party late. Although, he couldn't say for sure, because he was still inside the building looking for her. All he knows is that she left before midnight. From what he told us, it was roughly a quarter to when he noticed that her car was no longer parked out in the lot. So, Ari remained inside the Portals building long after Peter thought she'd left. What *I* want to know is where she was all along. Did she leave the building alone, or was she with someone?" Sean speculated.

"What *I'm* interested in knowing is who she came into contact with last night?" Luke had a faraway expression on his face. "I know that *fake*, Emery Lloyd, left the party before we did-at least I think he did. I sure hope Ari didn't come into contact with *him*." Luke frowned in jeopardy.

"What about Brenda? What time did *she* leave last night?" Sean asked warily.

"Not sure... Must have been shortly after Lloyd left. Why do you ask?"

"Just wondering… The two of them are trying so hard to convince everyone at Portals that they're not romantically linked. I wonder if they actually *left* the building, after they skipped out of the party. Maybe, they stuck around."

"What are you getting at, buddy?" Luke gave Sean a nonplused stare.

"Just thinking out loud," Sean said.

"You think Lloyd and Brenda are in some way tied into what happened to Ari?" Luke's eyed gunned critically into Sean's.

"It's a stretch. Still, nothing like this has *ever* happened to a Portals employee-at least not until this Lloyd guy showed up, Luke. If Lloyd's the reincarnation of Clarke Vale, Ari isn't the only one in danger. We all are. Though, we still haven't substantiated any real proof that he's our guy. All the same, we've established that Vale's out there, but there's still no way of exposing it." Sean sighed, frustrated.

"Oh *yes* there *is*, Sean," Luke settled. "For the next few days, I'll be working extensively on tweaking *Find Me*. It's high time we got to the bottom of why *Find Me* maintains Vale's dead."

"I'm not buying that he's dead either. Now more than ever, I think he's biding his time." Sean shook his head contrarily.

"Then so are we." Luke's eyes speared through Sean's. "We're going to figure this out, Sean. And, we're definitely going to stop him from hurting anyone else." Luke was incensed. "I'm also going to use *Shield Me* to protect Arianna while she's in here. The authorities will *supposedly* do their part in protecting her.

"All the same, whoever did this to Ari, will be looking to finish the job, once they're aware that she still has some fight left in her. That's not a chance any of us can afford to take. I'm still confused as to why anyone would want to hurt *her*. Unless…" A light switch went off in Luke's head. "Sean, is it possible that Ari stumbled upon something she shouldn't have?"

"Now, *that* makes sense. Maybe, we should start by utilizing *Find Me*'s *Contours* feature. *Contours* will help us to cover every square inch of the Portals building. So, we will have access to everything that took place during the party. We'll even be able to see what happened down to the building's foundation."

Luke nodded in agreement. "*Contours* will definitely be able to pin down where Ari wandered off to, when she fell off of the radar for those few hours. It's also the only way we can figure out if anyone followed her out to the parking lot. It shouldn't take too long for the program to generate exact images of every activity that took place inside Portals during the party."

"Can we access *Contours* on our phones right now?" Sean was anxious.

"We *should* be able to, but in order to do that, I would first have to deactivate *Shield Me*. Using *Shield Me* will definitely run interference with *Find Me Contours*. All the same, it'll probably take forever to load, but it isn't impossible." Luke pulled out his phone, and tried to load the program. However, he forgot to factor in their location. They were at a hospital. Medical equipment often created interference for some aspects of **Dimension Four**. "It isn't loading right now, Sean," Luke said, annoyed.

"The hospital's equipment and poor Wi-Fi barely supports **Dimension Four**. So, the intrusion makes it difficult for the programs to load. Once we leave here, we'll be able to access the program with very little interference. We can examine the images on *Contours* together later," Luke settled.

"Sounds like a plan." Sean nodded.

"But, I'm *not* leaving here this morning until I enable

Shield Me in and surrounding the perimeters of Arianna's hospital room."

"In light of all of this interference, can we enable Shield Me?" Sean's face strained in jeopardy.

Luke nodded. "I have my ways of getting around the clutter for *Shield Me*. However, I need to initiate the command now. It might take a while, because this isn't the most **Dimension Four** friendly environment." Luke frowned. "I will say this, Sean. If Emery Lloyd's behind this, he won't be able to find a hole in ground deep enough to hide out."

"You know I have your back whatever," Sean enlivened. "Ari sure doesn't deserve this."

"She's family. Honestly, if anyone ever did this to my baby sis, they wouldn't be around to talk about it." There was an icy quality to Luke's face and eyes.

"Are you okay?" Melody coasted over to join them, and wrapped her arms about Luke's waist from behind.

Luke veered, and gently pressed his lips to hers. "I'm all right, baby. How are *you* holding up?" He cradled Melody's head in his hands, and caringly brushed the sides of her face.

"I'm all right. I don't want to worry about Ari, because I have faith God will carry her through this."

Luke hunched down, and planted more kisses to Melody's lips. "I believe that too, baby." He crushed her in his arms. "Thank you for being here with me this morning."

"Where else would I be?" Melody stared lovingly into his eyes.

Nicole wandered over to the group, and rested her head on Sean's arm. "Sean, how are *you* holding up?" Nicole seemed a lot less stressed out at that juncture.

Sean gave her an amiable smile. "I'm fine, honey. I just want Ari to be okay." Sean took Nicole's hand in his, and pulled her into his arms. "Luke and I were just saying how messed up all of this is," he admitted to his wife.

"Tell me about it." Nicole sighed. "I'm just grateful

Ari's strong, and she's fighting off that poison. We've got to believe that she's going to pull through. I still can't believe someone tried to *murder* her..." Nicole blinked back tears. Sean gave her a comforting squeeze.

"Ari has the almighty on her side, and she's a fighter. So, she *will* make it through this," Luke maintained, pulling Melody a bit closer to his side.

"She's got to be all right, Luke. We *can't* lose her." Melody rested her head on her husband's shoulder.

Luke's eyes connected furtively to Sean's. Neither spoke a word, but their exchanges communicated volumes. Both knew what had to be done. Through *Contours*, they would be able to microscopically sweep over every square inch of Portals, and examine the activities which took place during the party.

"Hey, Pete." Luke gave him a heartening smile, when Peter sauntered over to join them. Peter seemed encapsulated in a world all his own. "Ari's fighting it out, and she's a lot stronger now. There isn't anything left to do but to wait it out. Why don't you come over to the house, and hang out with us for a few hours?" Luke suggested. "You shouldn't be alone right now."

"I don't want to leave her, *PM*," Peter argued. "What if something happens, and I'm not here."

"Nothing's going to happen. You heard Dr. Chen. Ari's stable *for now*, and she's going to come out of this," Sean reminded him. "More importantly, we're going to see to it that nothing, and no one gets anywhere near her."

"Ari isn't allowed any visitors. So, you should come home with us, and get a little rest," Melody heartened. "We're all coming back here in a few hours."

Melody turned towards Nicole and Sean. "In fact, Sean, Nik, you should come over to the house, and hang out with us as well." Her eyes shimmered in affect. "It would really mean a lot to us if you all stuck around for a bit."

"Mel, honey, it's all right. No one else is getting

hurt," Luke reassured. "Nothing's going to happen to any of us by the grace of God." He gave her a loving squeeze. "Everything's going to be all right. I promise."

Luke turned towards his friends. "Still…Sean, Nik, it *would* be nice if we all stuck together today. It's been a trying night, especially for Ari."

"We would love to hang out with you guys," Nicole settled. "In light of everything that's happened, I actually forgot that it's Christmas day. We were supposed to come over later anyway. So, we're just coming over a little earlier than planned." Nicole's heart whisked emotionally, because she perceived Melody's reluctance in letting any of them out of her sight.

"That sounds great! Thanks, Luke…Thanks, Mel." Sean smiled, and looked over at Peter. "What about you, Pete…?"

Peter surrendered to a slow nod. "Okay…" His eyes were red from all he'd endured that morning.

The group decided that they'd leave the hospital in a short while. Luke kept checking his phone to see if *Shield Me* had loaded.

Since he couldn't go into Arianna's hospital room, he used the program to pinpoint the location. Luke found the ICU Room CU17. He fiddled with the keypad on his phone, and commanded *Shield Me* to first cover Arianna. Issuing that command, meant she'd be covered at all times and anywhere she went. Also, Luke commanded the program to cover the perimeters in and surrounding her hospital room.

The indigo blue light app blinked a few times, then finally sustained a bright glow. The glow indicated that the area was totally secured and shielded. When he was done, he and Sean exchanged affirming nods. Sean ascertained that Luke had accomplished his mission. Luke and Sean read off *Shield Me's* potency in that area of the hospital. They concluded that it was at eighty percent. *Shield Me* was all squared away to protect Ari in the ICU. However, Luke and

Sean knew that in order to access *Find Me Contours*, they'd have to wait until they were a good distance away from the hospital.

Luke also accessed Arianna's DNA which was on file with Portals. He took a chance to see whether or not *Find Me* was in effect at the hospital. Luke issued a command to *Find Me* to generate an image of the young lady. *Find Me* was indeed in effect. It broke Luke's heart to see all of the wires, and the monitor connected to Arianna. She appeared so frail. He only shared the image with Sean.

Luke desisted in showing the image to Melody, or Nicole. As it was, they were both fragile, and had been traumatized by the turn of events. Furthermore, Luke didn't have the heart to show it to Peter, because he knew it would be a hatchet to Peter's heart to see Arianna looking so feeble. In spite of how terrible things appeared, Luke had faith in God's ultimate healing power. He also knew that God had Ari in the palm of His hand, and would snatch her from the jaws of this ordeal.

Before leaving the hospital that early Christmas morning, Melody and Luke suggested that they all come together in prayer. So, the group created a prayer circle, and prayed fervently for God's intervention.
Even if Peter hadn't yet confessed faith in Jesus Christ, he prayed in faith for God's help in the circumstances. He didn't care what he had to do. There was no way he would ever recover, if he lost the only woman he'd ever truly loved. Arianna meant the world to him, and the very thought of her slipping away was more than he could handle.

***

"I told you *not* to call me until you finished the job," Clarke hissed, while talking over the phone to one of his former lackeys.

"I *did* what you asked hours ago. I went over to that pretty little blonde's condo, and I put her lights out."

"I'm pleased, Dexter. Did you administer the dose I asked you to?" Clarke skimmed over Brenda's place suspiciously. Even if Brenda had passed out, after being *three sheets to the wind* during the party, one could never be too careful.

"*Yes*, I did everything as specified. I gave her the Morphine first before the poison. She collapsed immediately."

"Very good... If everything went accordingly, why are you calling me early this morning?"

"I wanted to wish you a Merry Christmas, Clarke," Dexter said caustically. "I'm calling, because the money isn't in my account like we talked about."

"It's the weekend, and it's also Christmas Day, *genius*. I can't transfer money from a foreign account-at least not for a couple of business days yet. I *always* pay my debts."

"Yeah, I'm counting on that."

"The funds will be reflected in your account by Tuesday morning."

"Okay. I'll be calling you again if nothing pans out."

"Of course, you will. Thank you, Dexter. Merry Christmas," Clarke said in a blasé manner.

"Thanks-"

Clarke abruptly hung up the phone. Worry creased his face. Hurting Arianna Ward wasn't a part of his plan, but she was a loose end he was forced to tie up. There was no way of knowing whether or not Arianna had witnessed or overheard his interactions with Brenda inside of the Portals lab. That was a chance Clarke couldn't afford to take. He was too close to getting Melody away from Luke, and from using one or more of Luke's **Dimension Four** features in order to destroy him. Unfortunately, Arianna Ward had gotten caught in the crossfire.

"Emery..., Emery...." Brenda staggered out to the

dining room hallway, and found him.

Like soft clay, Clarke's face stretched into an instant smile, as he walked stealthily over to connect to her. He instinctively threw his arms around her, and supported her flailing body. She was obviously still hung over from the Christmas party. "I'm right here, beautiful!" Clarke secured his hold around Brenda's waist.

"Come back to bed. I missed you." Brenda looked up into Emery's face, like someone looking up at a starry night sky.

"All right, my love. Let's go back to bed. Actually, let me help *you* back to bed." Clarke guided her back over to the bedroom.

"You're *not* staying? It's Christmas," Brenda argued. Her face soured in disappointment.

Clarke smiled artfully. "Remember, I said we *couldn't* spend Christmas day together. I have family coming over," he lied. Honestly, he just needed a break from Brenda. She was much too clingy for his taste. Even if his affiliation with her was helping him obtain everything he'd ever wanted, there were times when playing the role of her adoring boyfriend got to be a bit much.

"But you *did* say you'd come back over tonight?" Brenda reminded him, before she slipped back into bed.

"Yes. I *did* say that I'd come by *late* tonight." Clarke's smile had now cemented on his face. "But, I'm afraid I have to leave now." Clarke checked his phone. It was past 6 a.m. "There *are* just a few things I have to take care of before I entertain my guests."

Brenda inched up from off of the bed, and threw her arms around Clarke's neck. "Please, stay with me today?" She pressed her lips to his mouth, and nibbled on the corners.

Clarke laughed nervously, as he gently removed her arms from about his neck. He pressed a few kisses to her mouth. "I'm afraid I have to go, darling, but I promise to come back later." He kissed her once again on the cheek and smiled.

"All right. I guess, I'm just going to have to miss you until you come back tonight." She sighed. "Merry Christmas, Emery!"

"Merry Christmas, Brenda!" Clarke said plainly. He gave her one last affectionate squeeze before he grabbed his things, and left her place.

Once outside, he slid into his luxury car, and rolled away. All he needed was a little breathing room.

Brenda had been extremely helpful and useful in helping him to stay under the radar at Portals. Still, he needed some quiet time alone in order to figure out the next move. He had to find a way to execute *revenge* against Luke Bryant sooner than later. The young tycoon would pay dearly for destroying his former life, and setting it on its axis.

Chapter Ten

"Stop the footage for a moment," Luke told Sean. It was almost 8 a.m. on Christmas morning, and he and Sean had spent a couple of hours examining footage provided by *Find Me Contours*. Melody, Nicole and Peter were finally getting a little bit of rest. However, Luke couldn't rest until he found out what happened to Arianna. It was bad enough he had to contact her family later that day, and tell them she was in the hospital fighting for her life.

Sean's face strained in perplexity, as they studied the various pockets of activity taking place in the Portals building during the party. Sean's eyes squinted as he reviewed the feed. "Check it out, Luke. That's Ari headed over to the lab." He gasped in shock.

"Wow! All right. Zero in on Ari headed over to the lab."

Contours had a dozen different images and angles of the same event, but Luke was only interested in one. One angle displayed a clearer view of Arianna headed over to the Portals classified lab. "I guess, Ari was looking for a safe space after what happened in Pete's office with Raya."

"She probably figured that it was the one place Pete wouldn't think to look for her." Sean continued to monitor the feed, and saw Arianna using her access key to slip into the lab. Contours continued to show varying slants of what happened, but he and Luke got the picture.
Contours had the time stamps displayed on every screen for every bit of activity taking place during the party, whether it was in the lab, the ground floor or the parking lot.

"Sean, are you seeing this?" Luke's eyes narrowed, as he and Sean zeroed in on what happened next. "That's Brenda and Emery headed over to the lab? What on earth is Brenda doing?" Luke's heart dipped to the floor. He was stunned.

"That's definitely the two of them. Man, what's going

on there?" Sean shook his head absurdly. "What's wrong with that woman?"

"She's actually *leading* Lloyd over to the lab. Emery isn't a part of the Portals execs team. He has no business in that area of the building. Brenda's in direct violation of both Portals and governmental policies. She was obviously drunk, and made light of the matter." Luke felt as if he'd just been kicked in the gut. He was both disillusioned and grieved. Brenda was on a totally different page than the rest of the Portals family. It was a huge hit to Luke's heart, because Emery Lloyd had clearly found a way to mess with Brenda's head. For all intents and purposes, she was putty in his hands. Sadly, everyone else who worked through Portals, could no longer trust her. However, Luke didn't want to react before seeing how things played out that night.

"Man…" Sean was just as unsettled by this unexpected plot twist. "What are we going to do about Brenda and Lloyd, Luke? She's leaking top secret information about **Dimension Four** to this creep-and to Lord knows who else." His face reddened in irritation. "Doesn't she realize she could wind up in prison?"

Luke looked away from the monitor for a moment, and his eyes connected urgently to Sean's. "We don't do anything rash. We play dumb, while continuing to watch every move they make. It would be a mistake if we let them know that we're on to their game. Sean, now more than ever…," Luke's voice trailed, when he saw what happened next. His jaw dropped in utter dismay, when he watched Brenda use her access key to enter into the lab. Luke hadn't lost his temper yet, but he was getting there.

"There…" Sean pointed out, "Ari must have heard the sensor activation. So, she immediately hit under one of the lab tables. She didn't want anyone knowing she was in the lab. You see her hiding behind the lab equipment?" Sean was riveted. His heart whisked in angst for Arianna, and he hoped Brendan and Emery were none the wiser to her presence inside the lab.

"There they go," Luke said quietly, referring to Brenda and Emery. The couple walked into the lab. And, what ensued, nauseated Luke all the more over Brenda's breach of contract. Against all reason and common sense, Brenda and Emery consorted shamelessly inside the lab.

Luke also examined Arianna's freaked out expression. She obviously felt trapped, and desperately wanted to get away from the horrible movie unfolding right in front of her.

"So, Ari was stuck in the lab while these two...," Luke had to fast forward some of the images, because Brenda and Emery had taken their tryst to a whole other level.

"Brenda and Lloyd did a lot of talking in there, Luke. I wonder what they were talking about." Sean's expression was wary, as his eyes connected to Luke's.

"No doubt, Brenda probably told him everything she knows about *Dimension Four*. Now, we'll just have to see if there's a point where Lloyd's path intersected with Arianna's. I'm just guessing here, but something tells me Lloyd's going to try to return to the lab, after he says goodnight to Brenda. I think his end goal is to learn everything he can about *Dimension Four* and its accessories.

"Sean, *now* I'm really beginning to believe that Clarke Vale and Emery Lloyd are one and the same. If *I'm* right, at some point, we'll see him slithering his way back over to the lab," Luke theorized.

"This is more than a breach of Brenda's contract, Luke. This woman's deliberately trying to play us for a fool." Sean was livid. "Brenda and Lloyd *have* to go."

"I agree, Sean, but for now, we keep our enemies closer. We have to come up with a plan to snag them both. We should totally let them think they have the upper hand-at least for the time being. Then, when they least expect it, we'll pounce." Luke anxiously awaited to see what else *Contours* would reveal about that night.

"Luke, check it out, you were right." Sean marveled,

seeing Brenda and Emery leave the lab together after their scandalous connection.

"Wait for it," Luke said airily, even if he was honestly hurt and disillusioned by Brenda's betrayal. Luke couldn't fathom anyone jumping ship at Portals. Not to toot his own horn, but he was the most easygoing, and one of the kindest bosses on the planet.

Portals employees were treated like family. So, Brenda's treachery broke Luke's heart. Even so, he was trying not to take it too personally. "Wait for it," he said again. For the next half an hour or so, there was no activity in and surrounding the lab. However, moments later, Luke and Sean saw an orb-like light shimmering, and advancing in the direction of the lab.

"What...?" Sean's face strained in confusion. "What's that?"

"I believe that's Emery Lloyd returning to the lab. However, this time around, he's utilizing the *Vortex to Vanish* feature of **Dimension**. That's what that orb light is." Luke pointed at the monitor.

"How can you be so sure?"

"Because there are only two features of **Dimension** capable of displaying when someone has vanished through the vortex. They are *Shield Me* and *Find Me Contours*," Luke detailed. "Brenda must have shown him how to blink out using the vortex. Honestly, if we weren't using *Find Me Contours* right now, we wouldn't have been able to detect his presence there at all. You see there?" Luke pointed skeptically to the monitor again. "Ari was just about to come out of the lab." Luke's heart knotted up when he saw Ari come out of the lab.

"So, when *Emery* saw her, his plan to go in and explore was canceled," Sean presumed.

"Not only did Ari coming out of the lab alter his plan, but Lloyd probably felt threatened. He had no way of knowing if Ari had witnessed his and Brenda's little rendezvous. Sean, I think he was scared that Ari had overheard everything he and

Brenda had talked about."

"And, if *I'm* Clarke Vale, I can't afford to lose my job at Portals Unlimited. It's important to stay under the radar until I accomplish my goals-"

"That is to have Melody back in my arms, and to *destroy* the man responsible for bringing down my pharmaceutical drug/mafia empire," Luke theorized.

"Now, it's all coming together." Sean had a lightbulb moment. "There's that orb of light not too far away from Ari." Sean's eyes widened in shock. His eyes quickly skimmed over the feed of the building parking lot. "There's Ari. She made it out to the parking lot just fine."

Sean and Luke watched Arianna hiking over to the parking lot. She found her car, and drove away.

"If Lloyd follows, we'll know for sure he had something to do with what happened to Ari." Luke analyzed the images. "Look, there's Lloyd now. I *knew* he'd come out of the building, not even five minutes after Arianna had pulled away from the lot."

"He's visible again." Sean pointed out.

"He must have deactivated the vortex. There he is pulling out of the lot. Brenda had gotten a ride with another group, because she was wasted. But, Emery...*Clarke Vale* stayed behind. I get it now. He's trying to destroy *me* by learning everything he can about **Dimension Four**. Sadly, my glorified assistant, Brenda Fields, is helping him every step of the way."

"Why would she risk her job or even imprisonment? The nature of what we do at Portals is under extensive government scrutiny. She *would* risk it *all* for this loser?" Sean shook his head incredulous.

"He's in her head, and it's obvious she would do anything for him. Wait..." Luke's attention veered back over to *Contours*. Something had caught his eye, but he quickly dismissed it as anything of value. He went on to say, "Emery Lloyd's romancing Brenda, and filling her head with lies. She, in turn, is sharing highly classified secrets." Luke shrugged in resignation.

"Aw, man. Luke…" Sean shook his head apologetically. "I'm so sorry."

"I'm sorry too, Sean." Luke's forlorn expression connected critically to Sean's. "I'm sorry Brenda's letting this guy play her like a fiddle. She's probably taught him a whole lot in respect to utilizing **Dimension Four's** accessories. Even if she's only shown him a *few* things, anything's potentially dangerous in the hands of someone like that."

"You're not kidding. If *Clarke*-Emery-whatever he's calling himself nowadays, knows how to use the *Vortex to Vanish* feature of **Dimension**, there's no telling what he can accomplish."

"I'm not worried so much about the vortex, Sean. I can always use *Contours* or *Shield Me* to detect his presence, if he decides to blink out again. What I *am* worried about is him possibly accessing the *Power Portal*. If Brenda shows him how to use the portal, he could potentially pop up anywhere and at any time. Not to mention the fact that he could slip into **Dimension Four** itself."

"That might be a problem. Luke, I realize that they are aspects of **Dimension Four** you haven't shared with the group. So, let Brenda and Lloyd think they have it all figured out." Sean smiled artfully.

"*Exactly…* I plan on giving *Clarke* and Brenda just enough rope to hang themselves. Like I said before, we don't have to do anything right about now. All we need to do is to let them think they're gaining ground, and that they have the upper hand. Then, we'll be forced to show them that many of **Dimension Four's** components are still in the developmental stages. The program is *my* brainchild, and *I'm* still in the process of unraveling the mystery of what it can accomplish." Luke issued a sad smile. "It just sucks that Brenda has made such poor decisions."

"So, how do we handle this, Luke?" Sean seemed

resigned.

"We handle the matter cautiously and prayerfully. Now that we know for sure that Emery Lloyd and Brenda Fields did cross paths with Ari during the party, we can't go to the police with the evidence we've just viewed."

For the obvious reasons, they're going to need ironclad proof that Clarke Vale, who's parading around at Emery Lloyd was present. He *did* leave the building, and stepped out into the parking lot a few minutes *after* Arianna had driven away," Sean solidified.

"I *know*. But, theoretically, we're talking about Clarke Vale here, Sean. I'm sure he's still very much connected to his former life. No doubt, he still has lackeys willing to do his dirty work for a price."

"I figured as much. I doubt, he'd risk getting his own hands dirty. For all intents and purposes, he's supposed to be *dead*." Sean veered back towards the monitor for a moment.

"In any event, we definitely can't tell the authorities we used *Find Me Contours* in order to get a closer look at the activities that took place at Portals last night. Furthermore, we can't explain that Emery Lloyd's presence was detected by an *orb of light*, after he blinked out using the *Vortex to Vanish* feature of **Dimension**. Don't forget, that *orb of light*, followed Ari out of the lab," Luke created a case in point.

"No, we definitely can't tell them that. Still, I know we can come up with tangible evidence. We need to have that sleaze put away for good. Luke, we definitely need to tell Nikki and Mel everything."

"Absolutely, they should know it all. We should also explain how we've been utilizing *Shield Me* technology in order to keep them safe." Tears shone in Luke's eyes, because of what he and Sean had unveiled. The circumstances were critical. Arianna had been victimized, and it was all because of *their* affiliation with Clarke Vale. So, it was high time they cited their suspicions to everyone.

Their closest friends and loved ones had to know what

they presumed to be true. That was, Clarke Vale was alive and well, and working through Portals Unlimited. Everyone was a target at this point. Collectively, they had to come up with a plan in as far as how to take Clarke Vale, alias Emery Lloyd down.

"Serena and Dane should be here in a little while. Do we want to tell them?" Sean's brows arched in jeopardy, as his eyes linked to Luke's.

"Absolutely, Sean. If what we suspect is true, they're in just as much danger as the rest of us. Whether or not they're out in Sands Port or out here, is immaterial. What happened to Ari is proof that Vale doesn't discriminate.

"Once he gets wind that Ari's still alive, and fighting for her life in the ICU, he'll be looking to finish the job. So, for the next few days, you and I will be circumspectly watching every move that creep Lloyd makes. If it suddenly becomes imperative for him to visit Ari at the hospital, we'll know for sure he's trying to assist her in taking her last breath. And, that will only happen over *my* dead body," Luke said icily.

Sean sighed, bewildered and frustrated. He set his hand on Luke's shoulder in pacification. Honestly, he was at a loss for words. It felt as if they were about to start a new chapter in their ongoing battle against evil. The last time they'd gone to war, Sean had been Clarke's victim. However, this time around, he determined not to allow himself, or any of his loved ones to be in such a vulnerable position again.

***

Luke managed to get all of two hours of sleep on Christmas morning. He'd been up for a while bustling around his expansive kitchen making breakfast for everyone. There was Christmas music playing softly in the background, as he played the role of chef. Luke felt that a little holiday-themed music would lighten the sad tenor amongst them, as Arianna's condition still remained on the forefront of their minds.

Luke had made pancakes, waffles, eggs, bacon, sausage, fruit, muffins, and apple turnovers. He'd created a nice spread on the island counter. Prior to the incident with Ari, he'd planned an extensive breakfast for his guests on that very Christmas morning. So, in spite of the bitter twist which had negatively impacted them all, he still wanted to make good on his promise. Quite soon, Serena and Dane would be there. And, Luke wanted to paint a positive picture when the couple arrived.

He'd already checked in with the hospital. Arianna remained in stable condition. Her body was still fighting off the toxin she'd been injected with by a *murderer*. *Shield Me's* strength was at ninety-five percent in and surrounding the ICU room.

Using *Find Me*, Luke had also generated an image of Ari. In spite of the dire circumstances, she looked a lot better. Seeing her look better than she had before, encouraged Luke a great deal. All the same, he prayed for her to open up her eyes, and that there were no underlying complications in her condition.

Melody, Sean, Nicole and Peter were still asleep. They were all extremely tired. Luke took a moment to set plates, cups, coffee creamer, utensils and napkins on the counter. Everything had to be just right for his guests. He'd actually created a sort of serving station for the group. Sharing breakfast together on Christmas morning, was something they'd all anticipated. Shortly after, they'd made plans to rally around the Christmas tree, and open up presents.

However, Luke had no desire to move forward with the festivities, because Arianna wouldn't be with them. It was difficult to celebrate when she was still so frail in the ICU.

Even so, Luke didn't want to make that decision alone. He'd wait to see if there was a general consensus from the group, in as far as where they all stood on the matter.

Before Luke crossed back over to the bedroom to wake Melody up personally with breakfast in bed, there was something he had to do firsthand. No doubt, the aroma of bacon and maple syrup wafting in the air, would soon draw the rest of the group out into the kitchen. Neither of them had had anything to eat, only a coffee in the ICU hours ago. So, everyone was probably starving.

Luke took a linen napkin, and wiped his hands off after having washed them. Cradling the phone in his hand, he issued a sad sigh. He was about to put in the phone call he'd dreaded, since Peter had found Arianna unresponsive over at her place. "Mrs. Ward, hello," Luke tried to keep his voice from wavering.

"Luke, is that you? Merry Christmas!" Elizabeth Ward cheerily exclaimed. "So, I guess *you're* more committed to *this* family than my wayward daughter," she teased. "I haven't heard from Ari in a couple of days. It's totally unlike her *not* to reach out to me, her dad or her sisters on Christmas Eve-not to mention on Christmas day," she went on to say.

Luke guffawed ironically. "You're right. It's totally unlike her *not* to reach out... Mrs. Ward...," Luke hesitated.

"Luke, is there something wrong?"

Luke's face warped in melancholy, and tears immediately filled his eyes. "I'm afraid there is..." He bravely, yet delicately explained the circumstances to Mrs. Ward. At some point, David Ward got on the phone, and demanded to know what was wrong with his daughter.

Luke temperately clarified what had occurred. He was so remorseful he could barely speak. "I'm so sorry," he finally told them. He'd already booked flights for the entire family. Just as he'd figured, they wanted to fly out to Los Angeles right away.

Silence hummed over the line for a moment.

"It isn't your fault, Luke. I know you blame yourself. You've been so good and kind to my daughter. We're honestly grateful she's had you as family out there," Elizabeth Ward uplifted. "Thank you also for making accommodations for us. David and I will be coming out there as soon as possible."

"What about the girls?" Luke asked, referring to Arianna's sisters.

"Raina and Lexi will want to be there for Ari. So, of course, they'll be coming out there too."

"I didn't want you or your family to worry about anything. So, I also took the liberty to set up hotel accommodations. And, in the event you decide to stay a while longer, we can lease something out," Luke encouraged.

Elizabeth cried and sniffled over the phone, as she and her husband held each other in support. "That's very kind of you. Thank you for all you've done."

"It's the very least I can do, Mrs. Ward," Luke's voice broke. "Please, keep me posted about traveling plans."

"We will. And Luke...?"

"Yes...?" Luke said shakily.

"This isn't your fault. Ari definitely wouldn't want you blaming yourself."

Luke nodded absently. "Thank you for saying that. I appreciate it."

"Well, it's true. We'll be there as soon as we can."

Have a safe flight."

Thank you. Goodbye."

"Bye."

Luke shut down his phone and sobbed. He realized that the Wards had absolutely no idea that what happened to Ari *was* completely his fault. Ari was a casualty of his ongoing war with Clarke Vale. She'd just gotten caught in the crossfire, and had stumbled upon the monster, who'd made their lives a living hell last year. Now, Vale had resurrected, and he'd returned to continue his reign of terror.

"Lord, please help us through this. Help us to disable Clarke Vale once and for all. He's hurt too many people. Please, Lord, let Arianna come out of this situation without any complications." Luke wiped the tears from off his face. "You are the healer, and we depend on *you*. Also, help me to utilize the secrets you've revealed to me through **Dimension Four.** Let me figure out aspects of this mystery to gain ground over my enemy. Your word says you always give us the victory in Jesus. So, I'm depending on that now.

"Father, how can I thank you enough for the gift you've given to the world, in sending the light of your Son Jesus Christ? In spite of our circumstances, we celebrate your precious gift to us on this Christmas day…," Luke prayed. He lifted up his hands in praise to God.

Shortly after, he fixed a plate for Melody and set it on a tray. Luke included fresh fruit, freshly squeezed orange juice and coffee. He also set a colorful arrangement of flowers set in a light green-colored vase. He smiled contemplatively, because he loved surprising Melody. Hearing the doorbell ring, he set the tray on the counter for a moment.

Excited, he immediately rushed over to the front door. His smile brightened when he saw Serena and Dane through the door window. Luke instantly opened up the door. "Wow! I guess, you guys are nothing if not punctual," he celebrated.

"Luke!" Serena threw her arms around him in celebration. "Oh, my goodness! It's so good to see you!" Sentimental tears shone in Serena's eyes.

"It's so good to see *you*, Serena!" Luke crushed her to himself, stirred by the accolade. Tears shimmered in his eyes, because he'd truly missed Serena and Dane. Luke was also heartened, because Serena's presence would undoubtedly lift Melody's spirits. "Merry Christmas!" Luke told her. Gently pulling away, he pressed a warm kiss to Serena's cheek. "You look beautiful!" he uplifted.

"Doesn't she?" Dane's baritone reverberated. 'She's always perfect!" Dane stared devotedly over at his wife.

"Dane! What's up, buddy?" Luke pulled Dane in for a robust hug. "I've missed you guys so much!"

"Dane crushed Luke affectionately. "We've missed you too! I can't believe we haven't seen each other since the wedding."

"I *know*. It's been too long. But, Mel and Serena talk every minute of the day," Luke teased.

"I can't help it if I miss my bestie. We *are* living on two different coasts now," Serena defended.

Luke and Dane exchanged knowing looks.
"It's *totally* normal to call someone *ten* times a day," Dane razzed.
"No comment, Dane." Luke tried to hold back laughter.
"You're looking good, Luke!" Dane acknowledged.

"He *does* look good. I'm glad to see you've put on a little weight, Luke," Serena appraised.

"Well, it's nice to actually be *eating* again," Luke humored. "Being married to Mel has actually brought my appetite back. Come on in, guys." Luke gestured.

"We still have a few bags out in the car I have to bring in," Dane said.

"Need my help?" Luke asked Dane.

"Sure. That would be nice." Dane hauled his and Serena's luggage into the house, while Luke showed Serena into the house.
Serena was already way ahead of him. In fact, she followed the aroma of maple syrup and bacon. "What smells so good?" She veered towards Luke.

"Well, there's like an entire breakfast spread out in the kitchen." Luke smiled.

"You cooked?" Excitement sprinkled over Serena's pretty face.

"As a matter of fact I did. Help yourself."

"Where's Mel?" Serena first had to know.

"She's still asleep. I was just about to surprise her with breakfast in bed before you guys got here. So, stand by.

I might need your help in surprising her." Mischief danced on Luke's face.

"I'm totally up for surprising Mel. But, first, I think I'll help myself to a little breakfast. It's after eleven a.m. out here. I'm surprised Mel's still asleep."

Luke's face changed temporarily, but he worked past the sadness. "We kinda had a late night."

"I heard about the Christmas party. Did you guys stay up to the wee hours of the morning?" Serena presumed, turning back to give Luke a befuddled look.

"*Something* like that," Luke said quietly. He wouldn't go into the details of what had occurred until they were all together. Then, he'd break down the disturbing news. He didn't want Serena and Dane to be weighed down the moment they'd stepped through the door. That part would come soon enough.

"I'm gonna help Dane with the rest of your bags." Luke abruptly turned away.

"Okay," Serena said. "Thanks, Luke."

"Of course," Luke called back out to her.

Serena watched Luke stride away in the opposite direction. She sensed something wrong, because Luke was always upbeat and easygoing. Maybe, he *was* tired, as he'd said earlier on. Thus, Serena imagined running a multibillion-dollar empire, and attending the Christmas bash of the year, had probably taken a toll on him.

Serena was both delighted, and surprised by the presentation of Luke's breakfast spread. For all intents and purposes, a professional caterer had created such a mouth-watering work of art. Luke was an awesome cook and organizer. So, Serena was excited to dig in. Serena was all the more excited about visiting with her bestie. It had been way too long since they'd spent time together.

The breakfast alarm went off for Sean, Nicole and Peter. It didn't take very long for the group to pull back their covers. They were up, and followed the enticing smell of amazing breakfast foods through the Bryant's kitchen on Christmas day. They all dug into the delectable fixings, elaborately displayed in the kitchen. They were honestly grateful for such a thoughtful and talented host and chef.

Sometime later, Luke had Dane and Serena stand to the side of his and Melody's bedroom door. Luke wanted to give them the cue, as when it was okay to charge into the bedroom in order to surprise Melody.

Luke used the food tray to push open the bedroom door. He drifted over to Melody's bedside, and set the tray on the end table.

Sitting on the edge of the bed, Luke scrutinized his slumbering spouse. Melody looked so beautiful and peaceful. Luke *almost* hated waking her up. However, he knew Melody wouldn't be happy, if he didn't, especially in light of everything which had recently occurred.

Hunching down, he rested his head on Melody's face. "Wake up, Mel. Baby, please wake up…" He covered her face with tender kisses. "Wake up, my love. Merry Christmas!" Luke pressed his lips repeatedly to hers.

"Merry Christmas, honey bear," Melody muttered groggily. She draped her arms acquisitively about his neck. "Honey bear…" Melody pelted Luke with kisses. "What a wonderful surprise! I can't think of a greater blessing than being awakened by my handsome husband on Christmas day." She fondly reciprocated his embraces.

"There's only *one* greater blessing," Luke said throatily.

"What's that, honey bear?"

"It's being able to wake up *my* beautiful with breakfast in bed on Christmas morning. I have all of your favorites,' he coaxed, as they nestled.

"You brought me breakfast in bed?" Melody sat up suddenly, with Luke's head still cradled lovingly in her hands.

Luke laughed over her reaction, and tried to readjust himself on the bed. "Merry Christmas, baby!" He gently broke free from her loving grasp. Picking up the tray from the end table, he set it in her lap.

"Merry Christmas, honey bear!" Melody's face warped in sentimentality. She reached over, and pressed her lips to Luke's yet again. "I love you so much!"

"I love you more, honey baby! Merry Christmas," Luke said falteringly.

"This looks so amazing!" Melody perused everything on her plate.

"Thank you. Thank you so much for everything! I can't believe all you've done. You *actually* want me to start my own company?" Melody's eyes misted, as she recounted their special Christmas Eve celebration, prior to everything falling apart.

Luke nodded. "I honestly believe in you, baby! I *know* how talented and capable you are. So, I'm confident you're going to rock out this new venture." He winked.

"I want you to know how much everything you've done means to me." Melody's face warped emotionally.

"*You* mean *everything* to me, and you've made me the happiest man in the world." Luke smiled into her eyes. "I'm also the *luckiest* man alive!" He pressed a kiss to her forehead. "Mel, I want you to know that I'm *not* the only one who's dying to wish you a Merry Christmas this morning."

"You're not?" Melody stared cagily all about the room.

"No. There are a couple of individuals quite eager to wish you a Merry Christmas," Luke teased.

"Well, I already wished Sean, Nicole and Peter a Merry Christmas…," she speculated.
Luke shook his head contrarily to indicate that he wasn't referring to Sean, Nicole or Peter. "Try again." He gave her a playful wink.
"Okay…" Melody stared warily at him.
Luke stood to his feet, and ambled over to the door. Opening it up, he gave Serena and Dane the cue to come on in. He was ecstatic when Serena and Dane popped into the bedroom and

heralded, "Surprise!"

Melody's face turned from suspicion to shock. Tears immediately flooded her eyes. "Reena!" she shouted, setting her breakfast aside, and jumping out of the bed. Melody rushed over to her BFF, and threw her arms around Serena in celebration.

"Oh, Mel, I'm so happy to see you!" Serena was in tears as well. The two held on for a moment, and trembled in each other's arms.

Luke and Dane watched the scene, completely stirred to see their wives reunited after months of being apart.

"Dane," Melody rejoiced. "So glad you're here. Merry Christmas! I've missed you!"

Dane laughed, because Melody's hug had knocked the wind out of him. "I've missed you too, Mel! I don't think I've gone one day without hearing, 'I miss Mel. I want to go out to California, Dane,'" Dane did his best Serena impersonation, causing laughter to erupt in the room.

"Luke, we should go back out to Sands Port. I can't live without Serena,' Luke parroted his wife. He found Melody's eyes from across the room, and shrugged inanely.

"That's very funny, Luke." Melody set her hands cheekily on her hips. "You and I are going to talk about this later," she razzed.

"Uh-oh," Luke said with a farcical impression on his face. "I love you, Mel!" he backpedaled wisely.

"Uh-huh." Melody nodded. "*Sure* you do." She tried to keep a straight face.

"You're right, Luke. Uh-oh. Sorry, Mel," Dane said.

"That's all right. I forgive you." Melody pressed a kiss to Dane's cheek.

Her eyes fastened to Luke's, and they exchanged a special smile. However, Melody didn't hesitate to grab Serena by the arm, and drag her over to the bed. Serena hopped onto the bed, and the two began to chat it up, as if they were picking up exactly where they'd left off.

"Now, *we're* invisible," Dane told Luke.

"That's all right. Come on out to the kitchen, Dane. I'll fix you a plate. We'll join Sean and Peter. They're invisible too. Once Nicole finds out Serena's here, we're going to lose her as well." Luke shook his head humorously, as he watched Melody engage in conversation with her bestie. It was only a matter of time before Melody broke the news to Serena about Arianna's condition. As soon as *he* had a moment, he too would fill Dane in as to what was going on.

"I think I'll take you up on that offer, Luke. It's obvious Serena and Mel don't even know we exist right now." He frowned facetiously.

"I got your back, buddy. We knew it was going to be this way the moment they got together again. Don't take it personally." Luke patted Dane on the back, as they drifted out into the kitchen. There, the two caught up with Sean, Nicole and Peter. Just as Luke had predicted, the moment they made their way out to the kitchen, Nicole saw Dane. She gave him a warm, but quick greeting, then rushed away to the bedroom in order to join the ladies.

It was a late Christmas morning full of warmth, sentiment and love. For Melody and Luke, it felt good to be surrounded by their closest friends. However, the tenor was grim, because of the attempt made on Arianna's life. Peter was eager to go out to the hospital. However, Luke reassured him that Arianna's condition was pretty much stable, and she was still holding her own.

Luke asked that Peter hang out for just a little bit longer, because they all wanted to go over to the hospital together. However, before they went to visit Ari, the group had to have a much needed conversation. So, after breakfast, everyone gathered in the family room. They all agreed to put off opening up presents until later. Solemnness hung over them, because of what Arianna was going through.

Luke hated the idea of weighing Serena and Dane down upon their arrival. However, he assented to the fact that the couple had to be brought up to speed in respect to recent developments. Serena was glum. Her eyes were red and puffy, because she'd shed so many tears after hearing about Arianna. Dane's expression mirrored his wife's, and he grew eerily silent.

Luke wanted to give the group the head's up regarding all he and Sean had discovered.

"Is everything all right, honey bear?" Melody propped closely to him on the couch. She took his hand in hers, and squeezed it comfortingly.

Luke nodded. "Everything's fine, babe. There *are* a few things Sean and I have to tell you." Luke delved urgently into Melody's eyes.

"Okay...," Melody said, frowning in uncertainty. Her heart lashed, as she sized up the critical expression on Luke's face, and how nervous Sean looked. Sean sulked, while agitatedly wringing his hands together.

Nicole seemed befuddled by Sean's odd behavior. "Sean...? Luke...?" she questioned, staring from one to the other. "What's going on here?"

Sean gave Luke a knowing look, indicating that Luke initiate the conversation.

Both Luke and Sean had dreaded this moment. However, it was high time they all learned the truth. "Dane, Serena, I apologize for dragging the two of you into this mess. You just got here." Luke's face strained in remorse.

"Luke, don't apologize. We're all family here. If one of us is down and out, then we all are," Dane said thickly.

"That poor girl." Serena kept shaking her head in denial. "Arianna doesn't deserve what happened. Dane and I want to help in any way we can." Serena's face puckered in sorrow.

"I'm glad you said that, Serena. We're going to need everyone's help. We're dealing with something totally unexpected." Luke turned towards Melody. "Mel, remember that morning a while back when I came down to your office, and you were all shaken up...?"

Melody nodded. "I was freaked out, because it was Emery Lloyd's last day in my department. He was acting strange. *Everything* he said and did reminded me of Clarke Vale," Melody recounted, as her eyes connected critically to Luke's. "I was *really* upset that morning. Why would you bring that up, sweetie?"

"Mel, there's a reason why everything about him reminded you of Clarke Vale..." Luke took his time, because he just didn't want to spring the news on his wife.

"Luke, what do you mean? Clarke hung himself in his jail cell months ago..." Melody face twisted in angst, and her heart drubbed.

"Mel, Sean and I aren't too sure of that." Luke kept his arms protectively around Melody, because he feared she'd pass out, once he finished citing his suspicions.

Melody was trembling, and tears filled her eyes. "I don't understand. Clarke *is* dead, Luke. We saw it in the papers. It was all over the news. He can't terrorize our lives anymore," Melody argued, terrified.

Luke crushed her in his arms in pacification. "It's all right, honey. It's okay. You're right. He *can't* terrorize us anymore. We're not going to let him," he stated emphatically. "I promise, I won't let him get close enough to cause trouble for us again." Luke blinked back tears.

"But he *is* dead, isn't he?" Melody pulled away, revealing a tear-streaked face.

Luke shook his head contrarily, and his eyes connected warily to hers. "We have reason to believe he's still alive." Luke took Melody's hands in his. "Mel, I need for you to hear me out right now."

Melody seemed dazed, as if what Luke had just revealed had gone over her head. "I'm listening."

"Sean, is this true?" Nicole was horrified. "How long

have you and Luke known Clarke Vale is still alive? We all saw the footage on the news channels. He committed suicide. Sean, I won't go through that again. I almost lost you." Nicole trembled, and tears snaked down her cheeks. "I won't go through that again," she kept saying, distraught.

Sean pulled her into his arms, and silenced her. "I promise you won't have to, babe. Nothing's going to happen to me." Tears sparkled in his eyes over Nicole's reaction. "Please, just hear us out." Sean stared all about the room, and remarked the lost expressions on everyone's faces.

"There are a few things you all need to know." Luke kept his arms securely around Melody, as he addressed the group. Everyone seemed stunned and mystified. And yet, Luke knew he had to tell them everything he presumed to be true. Luke and Sean took turns detailing why they suspected Clarke Vale was parading around as Emery Lloyd.

They also disclosed all they'd learned on their recent excursion to the Sands Port Jail. They told everyone about Phillip Lombard's confession of helping Clarke fake his own death. Moreover, they divulged the specifics of their bizarre trip out to Croatia using the *Power Portal*. Luke and Sean even detailed their brief discussion with Dr. Anselm's housekeeper Velda.

They emphasized how Velda had confirmed Clarke's presence on the island and in the mansion. Then, Luke and Sean brought up the most bizarre aspect of their findings. They told everyone how Clarke paid Dr. Felix an obscene amount of money to alter his physical appearance, so that he would look like a totally different person.

Melody was emotional and couldn't stop trembling. "So, all this time… All this time, he's been around us every day." She kept shaking her head in denial. "From the moment I laid eyes on that man, I felt uneasy. The way he stared at me, almost as if he knew me. I was uncomfortable around him from the start. Regardless, you and I wanted to be fair, Luke. We wanted to give him a chance, and *hired* him." Melody had a crazed and overwrought expression.

"I know, baby. He had us all fooled for a little while. However, at this point, there's no doubt in my mind that Vale and Lloyd are the same person. Sean and I believe he came out here to get a job through Portals, so that he can finish what he started. Mel, he's trying to get you back, and he wants to use **Dimension Four** to destroy us all."

"Nicole and I talked about why I always feel so ill-at-ease around Emery. We concluded that it was because of his eyes. His eyes are like Clarke's. We couldn't have fathomed." Melody seemed a million miles away.

"I *did* tell Melody that Emery Lloyd's eyes were just like Clarke's. I had no idea that he *is* Clarke Vale," Nicole verbalized, dumbfounded.

"So, what are we going to do about this?" Dane folded his hands in introspection.

"That's what we're here to figure out today," Sean told him.

"We need to confront him, and let him know that we're on to his game." Peter's face flushed red in outrage.

"It isn't that easy, Pete. What Sean and I *haven't* explained is that there's someone helping him. In fact, that someone is supposed to be one of our top and most trusted employees." Luke's face grimaced in sadness.

"Someone from Portals is scheming with Vale?" Serena baulked. "Does this person *know* who they're dealing with?"

"I doubt she knows that Emery's dangerous. Who would *ever* believe that Clarke Vale submitted to facial and physical reconstruction, and is parading around as someone else? Besides, he's obviously swept her off her feet. So, she's powerless to deny him anything he asks," Sean explicated.

"He's filled her head with so many lies, and she's buying into it," Luke added.

"You're talking about Brenda, aren't you, *PM*?" Peter asked sardonically. "I've seen her and that *Emery* guy flirting

when they think no one's watching. I can't believe Brenda
would infringe the law, and risk imprisonment for this guy."
Peter was reflective.

"In one way or another, Brenda thinks *we're* the
enemy, because we're trying to keep her away from the man
she loves." Luke shook his head inanely over the matter.

"But, someone's got to warn her about him. Clarke's
dangerous. He wouldn't hesitate to hurt Brenda, if she made
the slightest mistake." Melody's face strained in appeal.

"Absolutely, baby. We'll keep close tabs on Brenda,
and do whatever we can to keep her safe. However, we can't
trust her. We can't tell her the man she's fallen for is a
notorious and dangerous criminal. She'll call us bold-faced
liars to our faces. Then, she'd go straight to him, and tell him
everything." Luke gave Melody a comforting squeeze.

"So, what's the plan here, *PM*? This is insane. I
seriously doubt Brenda's going to stop helping Lloyd/Vale-
whatever his name. She'll probably keep dropping classified
information. I'm so ticked off right now," Peter huffed.

"Brenda's sharing Portals' top secrets with a known
criminal. Not to mention the fact that their twisted liaison hurt
Ari. I believe you're right. This monster had someone hurt
Ari, because she saw him with Brenda in the lab. I'm sorry,
PM. I think both Lloyd and Brenda should be arrested," Peter
said bluntly.

"Pete, Sean and I are sharing all these details with you
to get you prepared. We have to play it cool. We can't afford
to let Emery Lloyd know that we're on to him. In order to set
the proper trap, we have to play coy. It would be unwise to let
him know we're on to his game. He's got to keep thinking we
have absolutely no idea who he is and what he's after," Luke
formulated.

"In the meantime, Brenda's teaching him how to
utilize certain aspects of **Dimension Four,** and *that's*
dangerous." Nicole caught her husband's and Luke's eyes
upon saying those words.

"Nik's right. Can you imagine the kind of destruction Clarke could bring about with *your* technology?" Serena addressed Luke.

"Based on what we've discovered so far, Clarke knows how to use the *Vortex to Vanish* feature through **Dimension**. We don't know for sure what else Brenda's taught him, but it really doesn't matter." Luke issued a clever smile. "Brenda has a very limited knowledge of **Dimension Four** and its components."

"She might *not* know all there is to the technology, but whatever she's showing him how to utilize, could potentially cause a lot of trouble for all of us," Dane said.

"Honestly, my only concern is that Brenda will teach him how to use the *Power Portal*," Luke told them.

"Luckily, the *Power Portal* can't be used without your consent, and your unique biometric identification, *PM*." Peter looked over at Luke.

Luke set his index finger on his temple, and grinned waggishly. "That's right." He looked over at Sean and winked. Both knew the depths of the mystery of **Dimension Four**, and there were certain aspects of the technology they had yet to share with the general public.

And yet, Luke was prepared to utilize these esoteric features if the circumstances called for it. Luke respected Peter a great deal, and trusted him. However, none of his employees knew *everything* about **Dimension Four**. And, in light of Brenda's lack of loyalty to Portals, Luke thought it best to keep it that way.

"Luke, I don't even know if I can return to Portals. Clarke's there on a regular basis." Melody's thoughts raced. I'm *really* scared," she admitted.

Luke pulled her into his arms, and held her meaningfully. "You've got nothing to be afraid of, Mel. He *can't* hurt you." Luke brushed comfortingly on her back.

"Mel, Luke and I have been utilizing *Shield Me's* technology to keep you and Nik safe for a while. With the shield set in place, no one can come close enough to cause any harm. What you might not know about *Shield Me* is that the shield locks in for protection, once harm is detected. It creates this impenetrable cask, and locks out any predator." Sean gave Melody a reassuring smile.

"That's right, my love." Luke gave Melody a loving squeeze. Sean and I set *Shield Me* in place when we first suspected Clarke had found a way to evade jail time. So, you see…?" Luke explored Melody's eyes. "He can't touch you."

Melody nodded and acquiesced. "I trust your technology, and I trust *you*." She rested her head on Luke's shoulder.

"You can trust *Shield Me* to keep us safe." Luke kissed Melody's forehead.

"In fact, Luke, everyone here should be covered by *Shield Me* technology. We also need to protect Brenda-that is, in the event things go south with Clarke," Sean told Luke.

"You're absolutely right, Sean. Everyone here *will* be covered by *Shield Me*. And, you're right about Brenda. *Shield Me's* the *only* way to keep her safe, until she comes to her senses, and decides to pull away from that creep."

Luke still marveled over Brenda's lack of wisdom. "So, we do what we can to keep *her* protected from Vale. However, we can't let Brenda know we're on to her game with Lloyd. No one's to bring up what happened between her and Emery over at the lab during the party. Furthermore, Lloyd can't even suspect that we're aware that he stole Brenda's access pass, and used the *Vortex to Vanish* feature of **Dimension** *Find Me*."

"I only wish that I'd stayed close to Ari the whole time just like we'd planned. If she hadn't gone into the lab, she wouldn't have seen or heard anything incriminating. If *Lloyd* or *Vale* hadn't seen her leaving the lab, he wouldn't have had her followed." Peter brooded.

"I wish we'd *all* kept an eye on Ari that night, Pete. We're not sure if Lloyd followed Ari home, or if he had someone else go out there, and hurt her." Sean speculated.

"I hate this, Luke. It feels like part two of the nightmare we had to deal with last year. I wish I'd never met Clarke Vale or Darien Stiles." Feeling completely overwhelmed, tears brimmed over in Melody's eyes.

"Honey, no one's going to put us through what we endured with Vale." Luke crushed Melody in his arms. "I will *never* let you go through that again."

"Luke, he's been in our faces for months, plotting and scheming. I thought we were finally free of this monster. I guess, we *were* safe for a while, but this man refuses to go away."

"You *are* safe, Mel, and that's the way it's going to stay." Luke's heart splintered to see his wife so distraught. "I will *see* to it that he leaves us alone for good."

"He'd better leave us alone. We're not going to live out that nightmare again. But, are we really safe? If *Emery Lloyd* hurt Arianna, we're probably all a target." Serena's face twisted in sadness. "I feel as if he can strike anywhere and at any time."

"Trust me, Serena, we're all going to stay safe because of *Shield Me*. Vale's pattern is to stay close to Melody and Luke. I think he hurt Ari, because he was worried that she'd expose what happened between him and Brenda in the lab," Nicole told Serena. "Since Portals is his hub, and ***Dimension Four*** is what he plans to use to destroy us, we have to find a way to use it against *him*." Nicole shrugged, as she stared from one face to another.

"Nicole's right. Even if Brenda taught him the basics, there are so many facets to ***Dimension Four*** she has yet to learn for herself." Peter stared over at Nicole. "It takes a lot more than knowing the basics to maximize the use of its potential. It's complicated."

"Still, what Dane said earlier on is on point. We don't want any aspect of ***Dimension Four*** to fall into the wrong hands. The repercussions can be deadly if the technology is misappropriated," Luke substantiated.

"What do you mean by that, Luke?" Melody asked critically.

"Well, for instance, you and I discussed the *Vortex to Vanish* feature of *Find Me* when we first used it together in that underground complex."

Melody nodded. "You said, someone could possibly get lost within the vortex field. You told me that they could probably find their way back, but it would take a while."

Luke pressed a kiss to Melody's cheek. "You were *actually* listening. But, that may not always be the case. If the vortex isn't used in the correct way, the unsuspecting user could vanish for good."

"You mean into another dimension?" Nicole's eyes were wide with shock.

"Absolutely. Hence, ***Dimension Four***," Sean told his wife.

"Is that even possible?" Dane asked, surprised.

"I assure you that it is. Only my biometric qualifications can authorize a safe passage through the portal. And, only my specific DNA, and those authorized to utilize the vortex, can safely step in and out of ***Dimension***. If Vale decides to utilize the Power Portal, and pulls someone else in, that individual could also potentially slip into another realm."

"PM's one hundred percent right," Peter assented. "We take it for granted that we're authorized users of the portal, and can safely utilize the vortex. All the same, consent to travel safely through the portal, and slip in and out of the vortex, is facilitated by *your* biometric passport. I still can't believe Brenda was careless enough to let Lloyd swipe her access key, and that idiot actually used the *Vortex to Vanish*."

"Yes, he was lucky this time, because Brenda's key was the biometric passport. However, a person can potentially access the portal or the vortex without authorization. They would only need to access the gateway," Luke informed.

"You're saying if Vale tries to access the portal or the

vortex on his own, he could possibly be absorbed through either?" Peter's expression brightened. "Brenda will probably teach him how to access the gateway. It would solve all of our problems if Vale slipped into the vortex, or was absorbed by the portal," Peter said scathingly.

"No, Pete. That's a fate we wouldn't wish on our worst enemy," Luke argued. Skimming over the room, he remarked that everyone was eerily quiet. Luke perceived they were all mulling over what Peter had just said. "What's going on here? Are you all thinking the same thing?" Luke asked, disconcerted.

No one spoke. So, Luke grasped they were all in agreement. They were all thinking of ways to lure Clarke into the gateway. Ensnaring Clarke Vale through the *Power Portal*, or getting him to use the vortex without prior authorization through the gateway, was the best possible case scenario. Luke realized where this was all going. "There *are* other ways we can trap him through **Dimension's** technology, without having him absorbed, or hurled into another dimension."

Melody's eyes connected to Luke's, and she squeezed his hand in support. "You're right, sweetie. Even a horrible person like Clarke doesn't deserve that. As gratifying as it is to think about making him disappear through the portal or the field, we're *not* those kinds of people. We profess to love Jesus Christ, and the word of God teaches us not to reward evil for evil." (Romans 12:17).

Melody pressed a kiss to Luke's cheek. "I honestly believe we'll figure out the right way to eradicate Clarke Vale from our lives. However, luring him to use the gateway in order to access the portal or the vortex field, is rewarding Clarke for all of the evil he's put out there." Tears shone in her eyes.

"I'm with Mel. We're smart enough to set a viable trap for Clarke Vale. And, we will figure it out as a team." Sean's eyes connected to Luke's.

Luke gave him a knowing look. "We just need to come up with the right plan. But, make no mistake about it. *We're* setting a trap, and Clarke will take the bait."

Everyone brainstormed as to how to get Clarke to play into their hands. In the days ahead, the group would strategize ways to beat the man at his own game. Working together, they would finally expose and eliminate Clarke Vale from their lives for good. He'd caused a heap of trouble and heartache for everyone involved. So, it was time to break free from his reign of terror.

Chapter Eleven

"I'm afraid visiting hours are over," one of the nurses told Peter. It was almost eleven p.m., and everyone else, including Arianna's family, had already left the hospital. Luke and Melody, along with Sean and Nicole and Serena and Dane, had left about an hour ago. However, Peter couldn't bring himself to leave her side. His aim was to remain as close to Arianna as possible. She was still fighting off the effects of the toxins in her bloodstream, but she was a lot stronger. And yet, she remained unconscious.

"I realize what time it is, but I'd really like to stay," Peter's voice undulated. "I don't want to leave my girlfriend alone tonight." He took a bold stance by referring to Arianna as his *girlfriend*. Ari wasn't yet his girlfriend, but Peter hoped to rectify that issue, once she was out of the woods.

The nurse's face warped in commiseration. "I'm not supposed to let anyone stay in her room, but I will make an exception. Things get really quiet around here around this time of night anyway. So, you *didn't* see me, and I *certainly* didn't tell you it was all right to stay here." She pointed an accusatory finger in Peter's direction.

Peter guffawed, and laughed lightly. "No, I certainly *didn't* see you. So, you couldn't have *possibly* told me that it was all right to be here tonight."

"Just so long as we're clear," the young lady told Peter.

"We're crystal clear. Thank you." Peter gave her an affable smile.

"*I'm* not here, so I didn't hear a word you said." She winked. "I'll get you a warm blanket, but don't touch anything." She smiled.

Peter nodded, and gave her a pleasant look. The nurse left the room for a moment. So, Peter veered towards Arianna's lifeless body. "I miss you so much! I'm so sorry we didn't get to talk at the party. I'm sure you weren't aware of it, when you stopped in by my office, and saw Raya… Well, I had planned on telling you that *I love you*." Tears rolled down Peter's cheeks.

"I love you so much! I loved you even when I didn't think I had a chance. I loved you when you decided you weren't going to *like* me, because *I'm* such a player." Peter laughed ironically. "I guess, you have no idea." He shook his head nonsensically. "The moment I laid eyes on you, when I started working through Portals back in the spring, everyone else ceased to exist for me." Peter took Arianna's limp hand delicately in his. Bringing it up to his lips, he pressed kisses to it. "Please, come back to me. Give me a chance to show you how much you mean to me. I can't live without you, Ari. Please, don't leave me."

Peter pulled the green upholstered hospital armchair close to the edge of the hospital bed. Setting down, he lowered his head in prostration in order to say a word of prayer. Luke and Sean were never ashamed to pray, and ask God for help. And, Peter considered both the coolest guys on the planet. So, he knew that there was definitely *something* to prayer.

Maybe, the Creator of the universe was accessible, if a person opened up their hearts, and took time to acknowledge Him. That night, Peter took a moment to seek out His Creator and God. He pleaded, cried and *prayed* for a miracle for the woman he loved. No doubt, everyone's prayers for Ari, were keeping her from succumbing to the poison. So, Peter was hopeful of a miracle for Arianna's complete recovery. Without that hope, there seemed to be very little to live for.

The sun speared through the hospital room curtains the next morning. Peter opened up his eyes, and examined his surroundings. Rubbing his achy neck from having spent the night on an armchair, he instinctively glanced over at Arianna. Springing from the armchair, he bounded to his feet, and examined her face. She looked beautifully serene laying there.

Her face had regained life and color. *If only she'd open up her eyes…* Peter hovered over her with a face wrinkled in sadness, because she was still comatose. He took her lifeless hand in his, and kissed it repeatedly. "I love you, Ari! Please, come back to me…"

"I'm afraid Ms. Ward isn't allowed any visitors. Immediate family only," Peter overheard outside of the hospital room. Alerted, he immediately opened up the hospital room door to see who the visitor could possibly be.

His face reddened with outrage, and indignation whisked on the inside like turbulent ocean breakers in a perilous storm. Peter couldn't wrap his head around it, but there *he* was. Emery Lloyd stood at the nurse's station requesting permission to go in and visit Arianna. Incensed, Peter charged over to the nurse's station. "What are *you* doing here? Except for immediate family, and a few close friends, Arianna isn't allowed any visitors." Peter stared dauntingly at the man.

Clarke felt totally out of his element, as he stood at the nurse's station holding a bouquet of flowers. He'd anticipated seeing Arianna Ward, because he'd heard she was still alive. So, he *had* to pay her a visit to ensure that the error was rectified.

He smiled artfully at Peter. "I was just concerned for Arianna. I came by to be supportive to one of my colleagues." Clarke's face warped in feigned commiseration. "What a horrible thing to happen. It could have easily been any one of us."

Peter breathed in deeply, so that he wouldn't tear into the man. Remembering some of his past blowups, Peter knew he couldn't risk wearing his emotions on his sleeve around Emery Lloyd, especially if he was the infamous Clarke Vale, a career criminal.

Peter offered a cunning smile, and tucked in the angry feelings. "It was *very* thoughtful of you to come here, and to bring flowers for Arianna." His handsome face stretched out into a temperate smile. "However, as per her parent's instructions, she is *not* to have any visitors. I'm not sure you're aware that this has turned into a potential homicide attempt, and the incident is currently under police investigation."

Peter's eyes delved astutely into Emery's. "The authorities are concerned that whoever hurt Arianna, might be looking to finish the job. Hence, the security guard posted by her door." Peter pointed out, and looked over at the officer posted to the side of the ICU room door.

"Oh, I wasn't aware she couldn't have visitors," Clarke lied. "Neither was I aware that her room was under surveillance. My apologies," he said tactfully.

"It's an honest mistake." Peter crossed his arms over his chest in an intimidating manner.

"I assure you I will respect, and abide by her family's wishes. I was just concerned, and I wanted to extend my support."

"Well, that's very *nice* of you," Peter said, hinting at sarcasm.

"Am I allowed to leave this arrangement of flowers?" Clarke tested. One way or another, he was going to have to find a way to silence Arianna Ward. Undoubtedly, she'd witnessed his exchanges with Brenda in the lab on the night of the Christmas party. Worse yet, Arianna had in all likeliness overheard their conversation. So, he had to keep her quiet.

"Sure." Peter nodded, and issued a cunning smile. "You can leave the flowers with me. I'll let her family know that you were gracious enough to bring them."

"Of course..," Clarke said, and handed the arrangement to Peter. Inwardly, he seethed, because he couldn't help thinking that he'd failed in some way. Failure was *never* an option. The fact that Arianna Ward was still breathing was a personal threat. He'd worked too hard to get close to Melody, and to destroy Luke, to run into any interference.

Peter's plastic smile matched Emery's, as he took the flowers. "I'll be sure to tell her family that her coworkers are all so *very* concerned," Peter added adeptly.

"Thank you, Peter," Clarke said cordially. He lingered there a moment staring at Peter. It seemed the young man had taken it upon himself to oversee Arianna Ward's security.

With his arms crossed defiantly over his chest, Peter undauntedly stared into Emery's fake expression.

"Take care now," Clarke said, turning away.

"You too," Peter said. He didn't budge from his post. In fact, he followed Emery's gait until the man disappeared out of the ICU.

"What was *that* all about?" one of the nurses asked, perturbed by Peter's interactions with Emery.

"Oh, nothing," Peter said. He then looked at the arrangement of flowers in his hand, and instantly dumped them into the trash bin. "No one's permitted anywhere near Miss Ward's room. They are not even to come through those doors." Peter pointed to the set of double doors leading outside of the unit.

"If their names aren't on the list, they have no business being here," he censured. He was miffed, and couldn't believe Emery Lloyd had the nerve to come by the hospital to see Ari. *How dare he make an attempt to see her, especially since he was the one responsible for hurting her?* Peter had to get a hold of *PM* and Sean. Determined to keep Arianna safe, he would do his part, even if it meant guarding the room himself.

***

Luke sat at his desk in his office waiting on Brenda. Another day was winding down over at Portals Unlimited, but he *had* to have word with her. There were a number of matters they needed to discuss. Luke had already made up his mind *not* to bring up her indiscretion with Clarke Vale alias Emery Lloyd at the Christmas party. In light of everything he and the group had discussed on Christmas Day, taking a different approach with Brenda Fields, seemed the viable solution. The old adage was true. It was easier to catch flies with honey than with vinegar.

Honestly, Luke was still reeling from the sting of her betrayal. However, he avowed to kill Brenda with kindness, while systematically trying to protect her, if perchance he could undo some of the damage already done. Luke busied himself with work until Brenda got there. Inwardly, he prayed for God's wisdom to handle the matter delicately.

Brenda hesitated at the set of double doors. Her heart hammered in angst, because her boss had asked to see her. Her thoughts were all over the place. Only days shy of the New Year, she couldn't figure out why *PM* had requested a special meeting that afternoon.

Feasibly, her boss knew she'd had one too many drinks, and had snuck Emery Lloyd into the lab during the Christmas party. Notwithstanding, she and Emery had behaved inappropriately. Maybe, *PM* would request she give him her access key, and demand that she tender her resignation. Brenda was aware of the penalties of bringing an unauthorized member of the Portals team into a top secret area. She was looking at least a decade of prison time.

Regardless of her obvious dread and fear, she *had* to act naturally and play it cool. Even if she wasn't sure why *PM* had asked to see her, she was prepared to play coy if an accusation was made. So, after a moment of deliberation, she found the courage to knock on her boss's office door.

"Come on in, Brenda," Luke called out from his desk, keeping a pleasant smile painted on his face. He watched as Brenda cautiously open up one of the doors. She slunk into the room, and had a timid smile on her pretty face, as their eyes fastened. "Hey, Brenda, how are you?" Luke said amiably.

"I'm fine, *PM*. How are you doing today?" Brenda consciously took steps towards Luke's desk. However, she stood a good distance away. "You *wanted* to see me?"

As a matter of fact, I did. Have a seat." Luke gestured. Folding his hands together primly, he watched Brenda amble awkwardly over to his desk. In a circumspect manner, she sat down in the armchair across from his. "Everything all right?" Luke asked, exploring her eyes.

"Everything's fine. Why do you ask?" Brenda asked warily.

"You just seem a little nervous." Luke smiled. "There's no need for any of that around here. We're family, so you should definitely breathe," he joked.

Brenda laughed nervously. "Yes, I know that, *PM*. I tell everyone I know how lucky we are that we have *you* as our boss." She smiled uneasily, and her eyes temporarily wandered away from Luke's probing stare.

"Is there anything *you* want to tell me?" Luke's face wrinkled in introspection.

"No. Everything's great! There are hundreds of investors interested in *Shield Me* technology. We're already making billions, even if the program hasn't official hit the market."

"So I've *heard*. That's fantastic! Keep up the good work getting the word out there."

"Well, there isn't very much to sell, *PM*. Government officials, homeland security, the military, the FBI and the authorities, all want to trademark *Shield Me* as their defense of choice. You should be *really* proud." She uneasily looked away again.

"Well, **Dimension Four's** still a mystery to me. I always thank God for giving me the wisdom to tap into the perplexities of using chronological phases, molecular manipulation, enhanced space and the elements, to bring about such an enigmatic breakthrough."

Brenda's laugh was exaggerated. "But, the technology

was entrusted to *you*. So, if you don't mind my saying, I think you're quite humble."

"Thank you for saying that." Luke smiled, but his face instantly changed, and he brooded. "You've been a little withdrawn lately," he brought up. "Are you *sure* everything's all right? I've been concerned." Luke's probing eyes delved critically into hers.

Brenda's head slumped, and she nervously played with her fingers. Forcing herself to reconnect to Luke's intent stare, she said, "I guess, I have been a little stressed lately. Don't get me wrong, it's got nothing to do with my work here," she quickly added.

Luke sighed, and tried to come from another angle. "I hope you weren't offended I brought up the importance of safeguarding boundaries, in as far as intra-office romances. Honestly, our employees are free to see whomever they like outside of this setting. But while here, we like to keep it strictly professional," Luke emphasized yet again. It was his way of issuing yet another warning that she stay as far away from Emery Lloyd as possible.

Embarrassment shaded Brenda's face. *Why had PM brought the matter up again?* He'd made it clear the first time. It was all she could do to keep from trembling. Her heart drilled in her chest. The most she hoped for at that moment, was that the floor would open up, and swallow her whole.

Maybe, *PM* knew what happened in the lab during the party. Was he giving her just enough rope to hang herself? Whatever the case, Brenda resolved to maintain aplomb. "I totally understand your viewpoint, and I am *not* the least bit offended. You're absolutely right and totally fair." She set her hand on her heart. "Have *I* done something wrong, *PM?*" Her heart plunged to the floor in angst.

Luke smiled disarmingly. "No, not at all. You've been amazing! I'm proud of each and every one of you. You guys come in here every single day, and make this venture worth fighting for. Two things," Luke said evenly. "As you've probably heard, there was an attempt on Arianna Ward's life-"

"I *know*, *PM*. That entire situation breaks my heart. I can't believe something so awful happened to her. She's the sweetest person."

Luke gave Brenda a surprised but wary look. "Well, it's only by the grace of God she's still alive. Just to give you the head's up, the authorities will be questioning Portals employees-primarily those who attended the Christmas party. Did you see, or speak to Arianna that night?" Luke tried to erase the ominous expression on his face again.

Distress and sorrow veiled Brenda's face. "No. I didn't see her at all. I thought it odd that we didn't see her all that night. I honestly thought she and I would have bumped into each other... In any event, the entire situation is very sad."

"It *is* quite unfortunate that a member of the Portals family has suffered such a horrific ordeal. Just to warn you, the authorities will be questioning staff. I didn't want anyone to be alarmed, or on the defensive. The police are treating what happened as an *attempted homicide* investigation." Luke's eyes searched Brenda's again.

Brenda's eyes shied away from her boss's penetrating stare. "Of course... I'm sure everyone will do whatever they can to comply." Her wavering eyes finally found his. "We all want to see this monster brought to justice," she stated emphatically.

Luke wondered if Brenda realized that her boyfriend was most likely the monster behind the attack made on Arianna's life. He honestly couldn't see Brenda being a party to an attempted murder. Brenda was confused, misguided, and probably in love with the wrong man. However, Luke was certain Clarke was only using her as a means to an end.

Brenda had no clue about his *extracurricular* activities. Clarke probably kept her in the dark about everything. Just then, the texting notification on Luke's phone went off. However, he ignored it for the moment. "That's what we all want, Brenda. I'm sure whoever did this to Arianna *will* be brought to justice." Luke glanced at his phone.

Sean had finally texted him. Luke had been waiting on that text for a while. Sean confirmed that he'd just accessed Brenda's phone in *her* office, and had successfully linked it to *Shield Me*. Regardless of Brenda's betrayal, she still needed protection from the likes of Clarke Vale. Part one of their mission was accomplished.

Now, Luke had to get Brenda to buy into part two. They'd all decided that Peter would *train* her extensively on **Dimension Four**. This training program would include revealing a few more of the inscrutable facets of the knowledge Brenda might not be too familiar with. Of course, Peter would only train her on the features they *wanted* her to know. There were limitations, and Brenda would be kept in the dark in respect to *other* aspects of **Dimension Four**.

It was their way of testing Brenda to see what she'd do with the newfound knowledge. They were hoping she'd share her pearls of wisdom with Emery Lloyd. If she did, it would be buying straight into their plan. Peter would train Brenda on the intricacies she probably thought she'd been kept out of the loop about. However, Peter would deliberately hold back critical information. If everything worked according to their plan, Brenda in turn, would train Emery in the very same way.

"I sure hope so, because that's just a despicable thing to do." Brenda seemed to be all fired up. "I pray for Ari and her family. Has her family flown in from Virginia?" Brenda asked.

"Yes. They flew out here as soon as they heard the news."

"It's nice to have family." Brenda's nervous smile returned. "Was there anything else you wanted to discuss this afternoon, *PM?*" she asked politely.

"As a matter of fact, there is," Luke announced. His

smile was brighter than a silver coin blazing in the sunlight.

Brenda crossed her legs and sighed restlessly. "All right, I'm all ears," she tried to sound unaffected.

"Well, we're having Peter conduct additional training for *some* of our execs. There are aspects of ***Dimension Four*** which have been kept classified by the government for a while. However, since ***Dimension Four*** has been in circulation for months, it's time to bring some of our execs up to speed in the knowledge of this breakout mystery."

"Oh...?" Brenda's eyebrows arched, and she perked up. "That sounds fascinating. When will Peter start conducting this additional training?"

"Well, that's what I wanted to tell you. Since you're one of our very top execs, he'll be working with *you* first. Sean will initiate the training program, because Peter has requested a few days off."

Brenda nodded in agreement and smiled.

"Sean will get you started. Then, once Peter gets back, he'll finish up the training. Is that all right?" Luke tested.

"That's fine. Will my work schedule change at all?" she inquired.

"No. The training will take place during regular work hours. Each session will be about forty minutes, right before your lunch break," Luke detailed.

"Will it be every day?"

"Three times a week," Luke clarified. "Will that work for you?"

"It's fine. I'm actually excited to learn as much as I can about ***Dimension Four***," Brenda said earnestly.

Luke smiled. "It's settled then. We want all of our execs to be *in the know* about ***Dimension Four***, and the functions of its multifaceted accessories. I'm equally excited. Thank you for taking time to meet with me this afternoon, Brenda." Luke's pleasant smile only widened. "I want you to know how much we appreciate your hard work, and your *loyalty* to Portals," he emphasized.

"It's my pleasure, *PM*! Was there anything else?" Brenda's expression was strained, even if she'd pasted an artificial smile to her face.

"Nope, we're done. Keep up the good work!" Luke stood to his feet, as Brenda pulled back from her chair, and stood to hers.

Luke graciously walked Brenda over to the set of double doors. "The authorities should be here shortly." His eyes connected sincerely to hers. "So, don't be alarmed if they single you out to ask a few questions. Getting to the bottom of what happened at the party, is paramount in bringing the lowlife who hurt Arianna to justice."

"I'm sure they're just doing their jobs, so no worries."

"Thank you." Luke watched Brenda turn away, and saunter down the hall. He shut the set of doors, then veered with his back pressed up to them. Luke sighed. "Lord, help us figure this out. We're depending on you to keep us safe, while Clarke Vale's walking up and down these halls."

Just then, Luke's cellphone rang. Seeing Sean's name on the screen, he answered instantly. "She just left my office," he told Sean. "She's *excited* about the new training. No, but you should have seen her. She was so nervous and jumpy. I guess, she has a guilty conscious. Thanks for linking *Shield Me* to her phone.

"Of course, we're the ones controlling it on our end. Linking it to her phone, only magnifies *Shield Me's* potency. The truth is that all of our employee's DNAs are already locked into the technology's databank. Yep, that's all we need. So, if Clarke Vale rears his ugly head, and the other shoe drops, at least Brenda won't be another one of his victims.

"What we do *now* is offer **Dimension Four** training to Mr. Emery Lloyd himself. We *have* to emphasize just what a fantastic job he's been doing in software developing, and that he's totally due for another promotion." Luke chuckled. "Of course, buddy. We're going to teach him everything he's *ever* wanted to know about the technology, and some additional things he shouldn't. In the near future, we'll see what he does with the knowledge. Yeah, well, that remains to be seen. Thanks a lot, buddy." Luke shut down his cell and exhaled.

So far, things seemed to be going according to plan. They were all taking the necessary steps to blow Clarke Vale right out of the water. Hopefully, Clarke and Brenda would readily take the bait. When it was all said and done, Emery Lloyd alias Clarke Vale, would be apprehended, and dragged back to jail where he belonged.

Luke and Sean hung back, as they watched Portals' employees file in and out of Luke's office. They were being called in for questioning by police and detectives, concerning their activities on the night of the Christmas party. The authorities also looked into their whereabouts after they left Portals. For most, the authorities had to check out their given alibis. As Co-CEO's of Portals, Luke and Sean were allowed to sit in during the interrogations. So, they listened cagily to everyone's account, in as far as their own perspectives. Before long, the moment Luke and Sean had anticipated finally arrived.

Emery Lloyd was ushered into the office. By his inert stride, Luke could tell he was uncomfortable. Luke and Sean exchanged knowing looks when Emery sat down in the armchair across from Luke's desk. There was a peculiar smile on his face.

Detective Strong sat in Luke's office chair, while Officer McGill stood to his right-hand side. Luke and Sean were standing opposite from where Officer McGill was positioned, as they inspected Emery Lloyd's every move.

"Mr. Lloyd, based on what we know, you've only been with the company for a short while?" Detective Strong presented, as his sharp eyes delved critically into Emery's

"Yes, that is correct," Clarke said plainly, with a cement smile. "I worked through the Graphics and Designs department at the beginning, but my fine bosses here..." His eyes skimmed over Luke and Sean. "Well, they were generous enough to offer a promotion as a software developer."

"That's very nice," Officer McGill said flatly. "As you're probably aware, there was an attempt made on the life of one of your coworkers. She was attacked in her condo early Christmas morning, after she got home from the Christmas party. She was injected with a toxin, and Morphine for sedation."

"Yes." Clarke's face warped in commiseration. "I *have* heard of the incident. It is *quite* unfortunate. My heart goes out to the young lady and her family," Clarke did his best sympathy impression.

"I'm sure you're concerned for the young lady and her family. Still, we're interested in knowing if you saw her at all that night. Did you interact with her at all?" Detective Strong asked plainly.

Luke crossed his arms over his chest, as he critically analyzed Lloyd. No doubt, Lloyd's answer would be telling. Lloyd was indeed a fine actor. In fact, his performance warranted an Oscar nod. Luke's brows furrowed, and he zeroed in on what *Clarke* was about to say. Luke held his breath, and braced himself to hear how creative his lies would be.

Sean's eyes remained transfixed to Emery, as he tried to pick up on any inconsistencies. Sean wanted to see if Lloyd would tense up, loosened his collar, or if there were other inflections attesting to his guilt, while he remained in the hot seat with the authorities. Sean deemed that Emery, AKA Clarke Vale, was totally out of his element. Anyone would have concluded that he'd break out in hives, because he was clearly allergic to the police. Perhaps, Sean considered, *Emery* was terrified that the more time he sat in that armchair squirming, the more likely it was that he'd be recognized.

Sean smiled artfully, as he waited for Emery to say something to trip himself up.

"I *did* see the young lady for a short while in the party hall that night," Clarke said evenly with a strange smile.

"Did you speak to her at all that night?" Officer McGill asked.

"No not at all. I'm afraid, Arianna Ward and I don't have much of a relationship. We're cordial around the office, but that is the extent of our connection," Clarke delineated.

"You said you only saw her in the party hall? So, you *didn't* see Ms. Ward beyond the party hall, or quite possibly out in the parking lot?" Detective Strong cross-examined.

Clarke's face twisted in uneasiness. "That is correct. I left the party after eleven p.m. Some of my fellow coworkers left around the same time. However, I didn't notice Ms. Ward," he explained.

"Mr. Lloyd, did you go straight home from the party?" Officer McGill prodded.

"Well, no actually. I believe I stopped in at a local gas station. I was running low. Shortly after, I went over to a friend's." Clarke's face was a mask of skepticism and mistrust.

"Could we possibly give your *friend* a call? We're just trying to establish where everyone was on the night in question."

"Of course," Clarke said breezily. He reached for a post-it off of Luke's desk, jotted down a phone number on it, and handed it over to Detective Strong.

"We really appreciate your cooperation in this ongoing investigation. There are no further questions we want to ask at this time. Mr. Bryant...?" The detective addressed Luke.

Luke was still engaged in watching Emery Lloyd *breathe*, and trying hard *not* to glare. All the same, he realized that his glower could have burned a hole through the man.

"Mr. Bryant...?" Detective Strong addressed Luke once again.

"Oh, I'm sorry. I guess, I just have a lot on my mind. You were saying...?" Luke redirected.

"We're pretty much done here-at least for now. Officer McGill and I will weigh in on all we've heard today. If for one reason or another we should need to ask a few more questions, or if someone should be determined a person of interest, we will reach out to you."

"Absolutely," Luke said. "Whatever it take to ensure Ms. Ward is vindicated of her attacker."

"Thank you for coming out here this afternoon, gentlemen." Sean shook hands with Detective Strong and Officer McGill.

"Am I free to leave now?" Clarke asked, seemingly impatient to distance himself from Luke's office. He didn't appreciate being dissected like a bug under a microscope. He was convinced no one knew who he really was, but he still felt malaise around the authorities.

"Yes, you're free to leave, Mr. Lloyd. Thank you for your cooperation," Officer McGill told him.

"Thank you." Clarke stood to his feet, and pushed away from the desk. He started to walk away, but he needed to add just a little more syrup to his pancake performance. "What happened to Ms. Ward is *very* unfortunate. I sure hope you find the person who did it." Clarke issued an astute smile, as he coasted over to the set of doors.

Luke stared over at Emery in utter disbelief before the man left his office.

Sean caught his eye, and shook his head inanely. "Unbelievable," he susurrated.

"Well, *he's* certainly a strange one," Detective Strong commented after Emery Lloyd left.

"He *is* a little strange, isn't he?" Luke's face rumpled in contemplation. There was very little else he could say to the authorities. How could he possibly explain their suspicion that the man they'd just questioned was the ill-famed Clarke Vale? It was too outlandish and totally bizarre. Exposing Emery

Lloyd as a fake, and bringing him to justice, were tasks he and Sean had to handle on their own. "I honestly don't care how *weird* someone is. I'm only concerned if they're doing their job," Luke jested.

"That's right. That's what's important." Officer McGill chortled.

Soon after, Luke and Sean saw the men out of the office. They assured the authorities of their complete cooperation. Thus, they agreed to reach out to the police, if there were any new developments having to do with the case. Officer McGill and Detective Strong promised to work aggressively on the case. They were determined to find the culprit responsible for hurting Arianna Ward on Christmas day.

Luke and Sean considered the irony of it all. The powers that be had no idea they'd *just* questioned the person responsible for the crime. However, Luke and Sean realized it was going to take a lot more than a police investigation to bring Clarke Vale out of hiding. They both agreed that it required **Dimension Four** technology, and its multifaceted tools. It was the only way they'd be able to trap him.

"Did you see his face when he walked in here?" Sean asked Luke, once they were alone in Luke's office. Sean sat across from Luke's desk.

"Yeah, I know. He looked like a man who just peed in his pants, and realized he wasn't wearing an adult diaper." Luke chortled. "He was horrified."

"I can only imagine. Like water and oil, police and Vale don't mix. They caused trouble for him in his *past* life. I guess, old habits die hard." Sean was incredulous. "The nerve of that guy! He *hopes* they catch the person who hurt Ari."

"His MO is to deceive, but he's not fooling anyone around here. I know *exactly* who and *what* he is. He doesn't need to hope. *He* will be apprehended for hurting Ari, and won't know what hit him. When we get through with Vale, he'll wish he'd stayed in that jail, and hadn't made any waves."

Melody had paperwork to drop off on the main floor of the Portals Building. Ensuing, she'd take a walk over to Luke's office, and they'd go home from there. Setting the paperwork in a folder, she left a note for Terri Morgan on her desk. Melody shut the office door behind her. However, her heart dipped down to her feet when she veered, and found Emery Lloyd standing right behind her. He was so close she could feel his breath on her neck.

Horrified, Melody clutched her chest, as her heart flagellated. "Emery…," she said, winded.

"*Mrs. Bryant*, how are you?" Clarke's entire face lit up.

Melody inconspicuously pulled back. Knowing exactly who he was, she didn't want to make any sudden moves, and she couldn't take to running. Her heart flogged in angst, and yet she forced a sympathetic smile. "Emery, you *really* scared me." Melody cautiously inched away from him, because he'd violated spatial boundaries

Clarke shook his head apologetically. "I'm truly sorry. I didn't mean to startle you. It's just been quite a while since I've seen you. I mean, I *did* see you at the Christmas party, but..."

"I know. We didn't even get a chance to speak. We hardly see each other anymore." Melody tried to maintain eye contact, and to keep her voice from wavering. The truth was that she was absolutely terrified. Memories of her horrible experiences with Clarke, washed over her like a torrential downpour. Rehashing what occurred at his underground complex at gunpoint, made her flinch in dread. "It's *really* nice to see you! Merry Christmas!" Melody crossed her arms nervously over her chest.

"Merry Christmas!" Clarke reciprocated. "How are you?"

"I'm great!" Melody smiled yet again. However, her body tensed up, and her heart refused to stop lashing. "My husband says you're doing really well with software development. Congratulations!"

"Thank you." Clarke's eyes burned into hers. "As much as I like it up here, there *are* certain things I miss about the GDD."

"Is that so?" Melody gulped.

"It *is*." Clarke took her hand in his, and pressed a kiss to it. "I miss my amazing boss!" His eyes explored hers in an objectifying manner.

Melody quickly, yet unobtrusively reclaimed her hand. "We miss you too, Emery, but we're not selfish. We knew you were destined for bigger and better things," her voice undulated.

Melody now reconsidered her decision to keep working through Portals, until things came to a head with Clarke. She and Luke had concluded it was best that she remained close by, until Clarke was no longer a factor. Hence, she'd be free to pour into her own business. They figured that working off site, was an invitation for Clarke to pounce. Regardless, Melody couldn't say she had a handle on the matter. Knowing Clarke Vale was lurking in their midst, was beginning to unravel her.

"Software Development has *nothing* on the GDD, because they don't have *you*," Clarke said throatily, as his eyes sedulously skimmed over every square inch of Melody.

"Oh, you're much too kind," Melody said skittishly. "It's so nice bumping into you today. In case we don't see each other again, just wanted to wish you a Happy New Year!" Melody quavered. Her eyes desperately flashed over the hallway, in the hopes that someone would materialize. It really didn't matter who. Instead, that area seemed completely isolated. It was just her luck, because Portals was usually humming with bustle and activity.

"Happy New Year!" Clarke extended. "It's such a

pleasure seeing you today. You've really made my day!" he admitted.

"Actually, I have an appointment in just a little while. So, I actually need to get going." Melody's eyes kept shifting down the hallway.

"I *also* have to be getting back to my office," Clarke announced, virtually X-raying Melody, and undressing her with his eyes. He had *trained* himself to behave more discreetly, but at that juncture, he couldn't seem to help himself. She was more beautiful than ever! Now more than ever before, he had to have her. "Have a great rest of your day," he crooned.

"Thank you. I hope yours is great as well." Melody lingered out in the hallway for a moment, waiting for him to leave first. Luckily, he offered a friendly smile, and sauntered away. She followed his spirited stride until he turned a corner. The moment he was gone, she buried her face in her hands, and surrendered to tears.

However, it only took seconds before she felt gentle yet strong hands, prying hers away from her tear-streaked face. "Luke...," she cried, and threw her arms around her husband. She buried her face in his chest and bawled.

"It's all right, honey. You're all right. I wasn't too far away. I *saw* you with him. I was with you the entire time, Mel." He pulled away, and cradled her face in his hands. "I promised that I wouldn't be too far away. He can't hurt you... *We're* on top of every move he makes."

Luke stared devotedly into her eyes. "Don't cry, baby. Please..." He crushed her in his arms, and they swayed in a loving rhythm. "I love you! No one's going to hurt you. I promise... It's all right, honey. I would never leave you alone with him," Luke reassured.

It was at that moment, Luke realized it was time to wrap things up with *Emery Lloyd*. He couldn't see Melody crippled by fear every time they came out to Portals. It wasn't fair to her. Luke prayed for an efficient, and speedy technique to rid themselves of Clarke Vale once and for all.

***

"I love this shade. The entire front lobby of the building should be painted in this color," Serena assessed. She admired a particular shade of soft coral, as she and Melody poured over paint swatches, and picture magazines, containing office designs and furniture trends. Melody had asked Serena's help in figuring things out for her impending business, Melody's Masterpieces.

Having Serena there kept her sane, even if Melody had a lot on her mind. Focusing on her new venture should have kept her from obsessing about Clarke Vale, but the potential danger worried her. "Did you say something, Reena?" Melody had the color samples in her hand, but seemed utterly disconnected from the task at hand.

"I *said* I like this color, and I think it would be a great storefront color for the business." Serena's face warped in concern, and she automatically set the material aside. "I doubt we're going to get much work done, because you're obviously somewhere else."

Serena sighed, and took Melody's hands in hers. "You don't have to worry, sweetheart. It's all under control. Clarke Vale would be stupid to make any sudden moves. No doubt, he's plotting and scheming on the sneak, but so are we. Luke, Sean and Peter, will find a way to stop him before he gets anywhere near you." Serena's face wrinkled in commiseration.

"I *know*. Clarke needs to be at Portals, so that he can execute whatever plan he has for me, for Luke-or any of us for that matter. Any wrong move could cost him his job. And, I doubt that's something he's willing to risk." Melody shook her head contrarily. "Honestly, Reena, I feel very uncomfortable going into work knowing he's there. It's a total nightmare-"

"It *is* a nightmare, but the nightmare's quickly coming to an end. We're not supposed to live in fear (2 Tim 2:7). Fear is from the enemy, so we have to live by faith. The enemy wants us to live in fear of this man, but we have authority over all of Satan's schemes. Clarke Vale's going down, and he's *not* coming back this time," Serena declared. "Leave Clarke Vale in the hands of God. God is the one who avenges his children. Mel, you have so much to be happy about right now." Serena smiled.

Melody guffawed ironically. "Yeah, I'm blessed beyond my wildest dreams. I love Luke more than I ever thought possible. Oh, Reena, he's such a great husband!"

"Uh-huh," Serena reproached, '*Luke and I are just friends…*' That's what *someone* told me when they invited Luke to Descending Dove Church out in Sands Port." Serena laughed. "'He's *not* my boyfriend…," she razzed on Melody.

Melody chortled. "Okay. So, you *have* to keep reminding me how clueless I was when Luke and I first met? How was I supposed to know he would be the greatest blessing in my life?"

"Hate to say Dane and I told you so…but we did," Serena teased, trying to take Melody's mind off of Clarke Vale.

"Yes…absolutely. You and Dane *did* tell me Luke was playing for keeps." Melody shook her head nonsensically. "I can't believe he went and got me a building, so that I can start this business."

Sadness suddenly shaded Melody's face. "I'm so overwhelmed, Reena. I *am* excited about starting the company, but there's so much that's got to get done. For starters, I have to conduct interviews, so that I can hire the right people. It also doesn't help that I'm in a totally different headspace." She propped her head in her palm.

"Well, how would you like some help?" Serena gave Melody an impish smile.

"What do you mean, Reena? You and Dane are going back to Sands Port on Monday right?"

"Well, Dane and I didn't want to say anything yet..." Mischief sprinkled over Serena's face, and she seemed antsy. In fact, Serena felt as if she would burst from excitement.

"Reena, what are you saying?" Melody's face and eyes lit up in anticipation. "You and Dane didn't want to say anything about what?" She was smiling from ear to ear at that point.

"Well, Dane and I are actually in process of closing on a house about a block away from you."

Melody leapt gleefully onto Serena and screamed. "No way...?" she doubted.

"*Way*," Serena argued, striving to catch her breath. Melody's bear hug was sapping the life out of her. Serena bobbed up and down in Melody's arms, as they celebrated. "If everything goes according to plan, the deal will probably be finalized in March." Serena laughed, because Melody refused to let her go, and she could hardly breathe.

"Oh my goodness! Reena, I can't believe this." Melody's had tears of joy in her eyes, when they finally pulled away. "Luke and I have hoped and prayed that you guys would move out here. Why didn't you tell me?" She punched Serena lightly on the arm.

"We wanted it to be a surprise." Serena's eyes glistened in affect. "We've hoped and prayed too. I don't think Dane has the heart to see me in tears every time I say, 'I wish Mel were here.'"

"But we *have* to wait until March?" Melody frowned.

"Actually, Dane and I will be flying out here on and off, until we close on the house. So, it's likely that I'll come out here at the end of February, and hang out with you and Luke for a while. Dane has a very important investment conference in Atlanta that week. So, you'll have *me* all to yourself. So, we can tentatively make plans for Melody's Masterpieces," Serena encouraged.

Melody kept shaking her head in denial, as she brushed tears away from her eyes. "Serena Michelle Hennessey, you've just made my day!" Melody was so excited she could burst. At that moment, she felt prompted to ask Serena a very important question. "Can I ask you something, Reena?"

"Of course, you can. You've never needed my permission before," Serena razzed.

"I know it might not be something you anticipated, but would you like to be my business partner?"
Serena flinched in shock. "What...? You want me to be your partner for the design firm?" She shook her head in incredulity.

"I can't think of *anyone* better to work with. I'm going to need all of the help in the world. And, honestly, I don't know anyone more business savvy than my BFF. We can call it Melody and Serena's Masterpieces," Melody devised.

"Mel, are you sure?" Serena tested, taken aback by Melody's offer.
"I've never been surer of anything. We can talk, text and email ideas back and forth. Also, you can help me look over resumes for our potential applicants. It'll be so much fun putting it all together." Melody took both of Serena's hands in her own. "Mostly, we'll be together again. Being apart these past few months has been super weird.

Serena was the one who felt overwhelmed at that point. "Mel, I can't believe this offer. It's absolutely perfect! It's been such a long time since I've been excited about a project. So, I think you really got me. By the way, I agree. It *has* been super weird not having you out in Sands Port. It's almost like a part of me has been missing."

"Thank you so much for agreeing to partner with me, Reena. It means so much." Tears formed in Melody's eyes again. "I can't wait to tell Luke that we're all going to be neighbors soon. He'll probably be even more excited than I am," she cheered.

"Dane and I are pretty pumped about the move too. It took a lot of doing. It also took a lot to convince Dane. You *know* his family wasn't going down without a fight." Serena chuckled.

Melody laughed heartily, and threw her arms around Serena. "No one said it'd be easy, but I'm so glad you pulled it off. I can't wait to bake you a pie, neighbor!"

"Oh, Mel, you're so crazy, but I love you!" Serena was grateful to have temporarily taken Melody's mind off of the situation with Clarke Vale.

In the months ahead, she and Dane would move out to Beverly Glen. Even so, she was worried about leaving Melody even for a day. However, Serena knew that she had to stand on the word of God.

They would not live in fear, because God had control over all things. God had given them the victory in a battle with Clarke Vale months ago. For that reason, Serena was confident, and would stand on Isaiah 54:9 "No weapon formed against them would prosper…"

Chapter Twelve

It was a few minutes past nine p.m. on New Year's Eve. Luke was sat at Arianna's bedside at the hospital. Arianna's parents and her sisters had just said goodnight. Sean and Nicole had driven Melody, Dane and Serena back home. However, Luke had decided to hang back. He wanted to give Peter a break. The poor guy had been spending every waking moment at Arianna's bedside since Christmas. That night, Luke had finally convinced Peter to go home, and get a few hours of rest.

Portals Unlimited would have been hosting a New Year's Eve fundraiser banquet that night. The party to help the poor, would have included dancing, then watching the ball drop in order to ring in the New Year. However, Luke and Sean decided to call off the festivities. Instead, they'd made substantial donations to their favorite charities. With Arianna in such a fragile state, and with Clarke Vale on the prowl, a party would have only brought about even more confusion.

Luke felt the weight of guilt as he sat at Ari's bedside. Tears glimmered in his eyes, as he internalized how she'd been targeted, because of her affiliation to him. It broke his heart, because she meant a great deal to him. A contemplative smile colored his face, when he remembered meeting Arianna back at BEE out in Virginia. From the outset, she was friendly and welcoming. Even if *he was* the hired exec, Arianna had shown him the ropes in as far as how everything worked at the company.

"I knew you and I were going to be friends from the moment we met. You gave me one of those killer smiles, and said, 'Wow! Mrs. Sanderson and his team *finally* hired someone cool for a change!'" Luke chuckled. "You *always* made time for me, even when you had so much on your plate."

Luke took Arianna's limp hand in his. "Ari, we miss you so much! You're like this little pocket of sunshine, and we haven't seen the sun in a while." He swallowed the lump in his throat, and brushed tears away from his eyes. "Please, open up those eyes.

Everyone's just holding their breath, until you open those pretty eyes of yours, *especially* Peter."

He sighed, and his head slumped, as he whispered a prayer for his friend. Suddenly, Luke felt a light squeeze to his hand. Startled, he looked up, and realized Arianna had compressed his hand. Her eyelids fluttered, and it seemed she was ready to open her eyes. "Ari…?" Luke questioned, stunned. However, he didn't want to hinder her progress in any way. "Arianna, can you hear me? It's Luke."

Arianna's eyes opened up deliberately. "Luke…?" she said faintly.

A ripple of laughter issued from the hollow of Luke's throat, and he immediately bounded to his feet. Setting his hand tenderly to the side of her face, he marveled. "It's me, Ari." He stared down at her pertained.

Arianna's eyes were now open. She set her left hand over the one Luke had to the side of her face. "Luke, where am I?" her voice was feeble.

"Listen, sweetheart, please don't try to talk right now. Let me alert medical staff that you're conscious. Luke picked up the cord, and pressed on the button indicator. Medical personnel *had* to know there'd been a change to Arianna's condition. "You are such a sight for sore eyes right now." Luke brushed her hair back, and pressed a kiss to her forehead.

"What happened to me?" Arianna tried to move, but realized she was connected to a number of wires. Her face warped in misery.

"You're all right, Ari. What's important is that you're going to be okay. I don't want you thinking about anything else right now."

"Luke, I remember. I remember what happened when I got home from the Christmas party."

Luke's face twisted in sadness, and tears flooded his eyes. "Ari, we don't have to talk about anything right now. What matters is that you're safe, and you're going to stay that way…," his words trailed.

"There was a stranger inside my place and...," she muttered. "I can't remember what happened next, but there was a stranger at the condo, Luke."

"Ari, I don't want you upsetting yourself right now. Please... You've got to get stronger," Luke's voice broke. He was surprised to see how vividly Arianna remembered the events. All the same, he didn't want her upsetting herself. So, he placated, "You have to get stronger, Ari."

Suddenly, a team of hospital personnel filtered into the room, and Luke was asked to step aside.
"Luke, please don't go," Arianna's voice sounded strained, as the staff began checking her vitals.

"I'm not going anywhere. I'm here, Ari," he reassured. Luke watched on in jeopardy, as the medical staff assessed Arianna's condition. Luke was nervous, and feared too much activity would cause Arianna a setback.

"Luke...," Arianna cried out, amidst the confusion.

"I'm still here, Ari. I'm not going anywhere."

One of the nurses turned to Luke with a displeased expression. "You *really* shouldn't be in here right now. Please, wait outside until we're done. I assure you she's in good hands. We're going to make sure she's okay," the woman said, adding a spoonful of honey to her acerbic rant.

Luke felt conflicted. He didn't want to leave Arianna's side-not even for a second. His greatest fear was that she'd slip back into unconsciousness. Still, he knew that he had to comply with the medical staff's request. "All right," he acquiesced. "I'll be right outside, Ari. I'm not leaving," he raised his voice just before stepping out of the room.

Luke immediately caught sight of the police officer posted just outside the room door. There were a myriad of emotions at play just then. He hated having to wait outside. Nevertheless, he was overjoyed that God had answered their prayers. Arianna's eyes were opened. Moreover, she was lucid. In fact, she seemed a little bit too lucid. Arianna distinctly recalled the details of the morning she was attacked.

Luke coasted a few feet away from the hospital room. He had to put in a few phone calls. First, he had to call Ari's family, and tell them the good news. Then, there was Peter... Luke knew for sure Peter would never forgive him, if he didn't call to say Arianna was now conscious.

However, first and foremost, he had to tell Melody the good news. Luke quickly autodialed his wife to tell her the good news. Melody was ecstatic to hear it. Luke promised to call her back, after he spoke to the Wards and to Peter.

"Hello," Elizabeth Ward's voice was weak.
Luke could tell he'd probably awakened her. "Mrs. Ward, I'm so sorry. I didn't mean to wake you."

"Luke, is everything all right?" Panic now resonated in her tone.

Luke laughed lightly. "Everything's wonderful! Ari opened her eyes about five minutes ago. I'm over at the hospital right now. No. She isn't alone. The medical team is in with her. They're checking her vitals, and making sure she's going to be okay." Luke's eyes glistened in affect.

"Luke, you have no idea what this means to me...to her dad and her sisters. You've made my New Year's!" Elizabeth cheered with a wavering voice. "Thank you so much for being there for her. Thank God for all her friends. I feel as if she's found a second family out here with all of you," she uplifted.

"She *has* found a second family with us. We all love her a great deal. No, it isn't necessary for you to come out now-that is unless you want to. But, she's fine. I'll hang out here for a while, until Peter gets back," Luke told her. "She won't be left alone for a moment," he reassured.

"I don't think I've *ever* seen anyone more devoted to my daughter," Elizabeth heartened.

"I can personally attest to the fact that Peter Lawton is head over-heels in love with your daughter," Luke disclosed.

"I *know* how much Peter loves Ari, but I was talking about *you*. You are such a wonderful friend and big brother to her."

Tears brimmed over Luke's eyelids. "She means a great

deal to me. I feel responsible for her in so many ways."

"Her father and I love and respect you a great deal. We truly believe God sent you into Ari's life as an angel."

"I don't know about all of that." Luke guffawed. "But, I thank you. Don't worry. She's in good hands."

Soon after, Luke called Peter to give him the news. He didn't even get the chance to go over the details, when Peter said he was already outside in his SUV, headed over to the hospital. "All right, Pete. Drive safe..." Luke shook his head comically.

Luke called Melody again. She was overjoyed, and wanted to come out to the hospital to see Ari. Luke had to talk her out of making the trip. "Stay right where you are, honey baby. Ari knows how much we all love her. Of course, I'll tell her how much you've missed her. Baby, I promise to come home just as soon as I can. I love you!" Luke reluctantly got off of the phone with his wife.

Moments later, Luke gingerly pushed the hospital room door open. He lingered in the doorway and smiled, because Arianna was staring back at him. Luke smiled. "Hello, there, stranger." He strolled over to her bedside.

Arianna smiled back at him, and took his hand in hers. "Fancy bumping into you here," she said, still sounding a bit frail. Tugging on Luke's hand, Arianna indicated he come closer. "Luke, what *really* happened to me?" Her expression was sullen.

Luke frowned in remorse, and he shook his head in the negative. "Ari, I don't think we should talk-"

"Please...," she entreated, looking conflicted. "I was at the Christmas party. Peter and I were supposed to meet there. I looked for him out in the party hall, but he wasn't around. So, I decided to pop into his office." Arianna grimaced.

"Ari, you *don't* have to go over the details of what happened that night," Luke mitigated.

"Yes, I *really* need to, Luke. I need to piece it all together for myself." Her inert eyes connected to his. "I found Peter in his office kissing Raya Hodges. I left his office feeling disappointed and upset. I just wanted to put some distance between us. So, I wandered around the building that night feeling totally lost." Tears rolled down her cheeks.

Luke squeezed her hand. "You don't have to say anything else," he said throatily.

"Please... Let me finish."

"All right," he granted.

"I just wanted to be someplace where Peter couldn't find me. I knew if I went home, he would have followed and driven over to the condo. I wanted to be alone for a while. So, I used my access key to hide out in the lab," Arianna explicated. She also divulged what happened shortly after. Arianna openly told Luke that Brenda and Emery Lloyd were in the lab. Arianna even recounted their conversation. Arianna had to stop midway, because Luke didn't seem the least bit surprised. "Did you hear *anything* I just said?"

Luke nodded. "I *know*. I know Brenda brought Lloyd into the lab, and that they behaved inappropriately. She breached her confidentiality agreement by sharing classified information with him." Luke stared at Arianna in concern.

"I was so hurt for you, Luke. It felt like a total betrayal. It made me sad mostly, because of how great you are. You're like the best friend and boss to all of us." Arianna grimaced, and surrendered to tears. "I can't believe Brenda would jeopardize her position at Portals, and hurt *you* that way. It made me so angry," she emphasized.

Luke silenced her, and stroked her hand in comfort. Ari had just confirmed everything he, Sean and Peter had theorized. Luke also now understood why *Find Me* kept maintaining that Clarke Vale's DNA no longer existed. Brenda had tampered with his file, removed critical information, and had replaced it with doctored material. Moreover, she'd used a microchip from *Shield Me* to temporarily disable *Find Me*. Using a microchip from *Shield Me*, was the only way of rendering *Find Me* temporarily inert. Brenda had used their technology to protect Clarke Vale.

Luke tried to mollify, as Arianna went into the details of how a stranger had gotten into her condo. The intruder had waited until she got home from the party. "Someone grabbed me…a *man*, the moment I stepped into my bedroom."

"Did you see his face, Ari?" Luke prodded.

"No. I know it was a man, because he was wearing black jeans, black hoodie and lumberjack boots. He was very strong. Because of the hood, I couldn't see his face very well, or the color of his hair," she clarified. "All I know is that he grabbed me, muffled me, and stuck a needle in my arm."

Hearing the account brought tears to Luke's eyes. He tried to keep Arianna from upsetting herself even further, but she wanted to go on. And yet, there was something Luke had to make clear first and foremost. "Ari, I *can't* go into the details of what we *suspect* happened that night, but you've got to trust me. You're safe now, and you're going to be just fine." He swallowed hard. "We almost lost you."

"Why would someone try to hurt me, Luke?" Arianna constrained.

Luke kept shaking his head in the negative. "Ari, please…," he implored. "We just got you back. Please, stop upsetting yourself, sweetheart. Give yourself a chance to get stronger. You're no longer in danger. That's all I can say. Do you trust me?" His eyes connected urgently to hers.

Arianna nodded. "Yes…with my life."

"Then, please trust that you're safe, and you're going to stay that way. I promise to explain everything when you're better, all right?"

Arianna nodded, and squeezed Luke's hand.

"Your parents and your sisters are here. They're staying at a hotel in Corona Del Mar. They took a flight out here the morning after the incident. You've got me, Mel, Sean, Nicole. Even Serena and Dane have dropped in a few times, but they're going back to Sands Port in the morning."

Arianna smiled hopefully. "I've missed everyone so much." Her face warped in sentimentality.

"We've all missed *you*," Luke emphasized. "Not to mention the fact that *everyone* over at Portals is rooting for you."

Luke gave her a winning smile.

Heartened, Arianna smiled back. "I've got *all* those people, huh?" She winked at him.

"Not to mention the fact that you've got someone truly special who loves you-"

Arianna looked away in indifference, because she knew Luke was referring to Peter. "Luke, don't-"

"Ari, listen to me. What happened in Pete's office that night was a huge misunderstanding. Raya dropped in to see *him*. She wanted to surprise him with a kiss underneath the mistletoe. *He* didn't plan it that way. He spent that entire night looking for you after you disappeared. He was so worried about you, Ari. Pete felt as if needed to clear the air. So, the poor guy went out to your condo to make sure you were okay, because you weren't returning any of his calls or texts. If it wasn't for Pete's quick thinking…," Luke's words trailed.

Arianna gasped, and tears glimmered in her eyes. "Peter found me?"

Luke nodded. "*Peter* found you, called an ambulance, and rode along. Ari, he's been by your side every single moment of the day since this happened. He's spent every night in here with you in tears, holding your hand. He loves you so much!" Luke said plainly.

Arianna's face warped in compassion and surprise. "He's spent the nights in here with me?" she asked, floored.

"Holding your hand and even *praying*. I honestly believe that almost losing *you*, brought Peter closer to God. He's watched us pray for, and over you during this crisis. So, it's definitely bolstered his faith."

Arianna laughed faintly. "I would give anything to see Peter praying. He's such a mess, *always* putting his foot in his mouth." She smiled.

"Well, that's what happens when you're head-over-heels in love. I'm sure he'll be less inclined to put his foot in his mouth, if you give him a chance. You *know* how protective *I* am of you. If I'm *endorsing* Peter, that means I heartily approve." Luke smiled into her eyes.

Arianna took his hand and stroked it fondly. "Thank you for your blessing, big brother," she whispered.

"Is *that* what I am?" Luke cocked his head back playfully, and gave her a curious look.

"You're the best friend and brother I've ever had, and I will always love you!"

"I love you too, Ari. Welcome back!" Luke hunched down, and gingerly pressed a kiss to her cheek.

***

Luke managed to make it home about a half an hour before ringing in the New Year. His smile was irrepressible, and he was quite surprised to see Melody in the family room sitting on the sofa. She was watching the New Year's Eve celebration on TV. Quite soon, there would be a countdown until the ball dropped. Luke tried not to startle her, as he made his way over.

However, Melody veered, and saw him. She instantly leapt off the sofa, and literally jumped into his arms. "Luke, you're home!" She draped her arms around his neck, and pelted him with affectionate kisses. "I'm so glad you're home! It's the best news about Ari! I can't wait to see her!" Melody celebrated.

Still winded from Melody's loving pounce, Luke laughed. He pulled back a bit to look into her eyes. "It *is* the most wonderful news! She's going to be all right. She said she can't wait to see you either. Pete's with her now."

"He must be floating on a cloud, because she's going to be okay."

"I don't think I've ever seen Peter smile so much since I've known him." Luke shook his head humorously.

"I'm glad he's smiling. He's been so sad lately." Melody's face puckered in commiseration.

"I'm glad too, baby. Now, we can all breathe again," Luke admitted.

Luke embraced Melody meaningfully. Pulling back, he cradled her face in his hands. "Did you wait up, so that we could ring in the New Year together?" He was overjoyed.

"Uh-huh," Melody confessed. "I stayed up, even if I lost Serena and Dane at about nine. They have an early morning flight. So, they didn't feel the least bit guilty for not staying up to watch the ball drop with me. *I* forced myself to stay awake." Melody's face puckered emotionally.

Luke's shifted over to the side of the end table, and saw the two glasses of champagne. Melody also had a plate of sugar cookies on a tray. "Champagne and cookies." He smiled. "Am I not the luckiest man in the world?" He pressed a kiss to her cheek. "You're my sweet honey baby." Luke's eyes glimmered in affect.

Melody wrapped her arms securely around Luke's waist. "This is a milestone for us. It's our first New Year's Eve together."

"Yeah, it's our very *first* one. I'm so glad to be ringing in the New Year with you, Mrs. Bryant!" Luke declared. Hunching down, he fondled Melody's lips with his. "I fall more madly in love with you every single day, did you know that?" he asked between fluttery kisses.

Melody stared dreamily into his eyes. "Thank you for telling me. I seem to have the same issue." Her face radiated. "*I* fall more madly in love with you! I can't wait to see what the future holds for us, Mr. Bryant."

"Neither can I, but I'm honestly excited about the future, because I know that my precious wife will be by my side every step of the way." Luke searched her face and eyes endearingly. "I promise to protect what we have with my life, Mel. I won't let anything or anyone get in the way." He gave an affirming nod. "Nothing and no one's going to hurt you again, okay?" Luke's face bridged to hers.

"Okay, honey bear. I *know* that I'm safe with you. I knew that the day we met on the beach out in Sands Port," Melody reminded him.

"Is that so?" Luke teased, and baited her mouth with sugar kisses.

"It *is*," Melody said breathless, as she reciprocated Luke's gumdrop kisses.

Before long, the television host announced the countdown before the ball was dropped.

"They're almost ready to drop the ball!" Melody cheered, securely wrapped in Luke's arms.

Luke laughed, but kept a firm grasp about her waist. "Here we go Mel." His face propped affectionately to hers, as they counted down… "10…9…8…7…6…"

"Happy New Year, honey baby!" Luke said hoarsely with tears in his eyes. Immense gratitude filled his heart, because God had kept them, and their families in one piece for an entire year.

"Happy New Year, honey bear!" Melody planted a kiss to Luke's nose. Luke found her lips, and overtook them with exigent kisses. They held each other potently, and their bodies swayed to the traditional strain of *Auld Lang Sine.*

Luke and Melody shared a tender dance on their first New Year's celebration together. Luke didn't want to ruin the serenity of the moment by sharing his New Year's resolution. It was the *one* resolution he vowed to keep. He would ensure that it was Clarke Vale's final chapter in their lives.

***

Clarke felt out of sorts, as he headed over to Luke's office. It was the first Wednesday of the New Year. However, Luke had sent an email for him to report to the main office ASAP. As much as he hated to admit it, Clarke was worried about this little impromptu meeting. He wondered what Luke wanted. It wasn't outside the realm of possibility that Luke and Sean were aware of his indiscretion with Brenda Fields in the lab at the Christmas party. From what Clarke gathered, Arianna Ward was expected to recover.

She was also under police protection, and it was all because his lackey had failed to silence her forever. Clarke was incensed, because he'd paid Dexter Gambit a hefty sum to do the job right. However, that wasn't something Clarke could focus on. Perhaps, he considered, Luke and Sean were on to him. Whatever the case, he resolved to maintain his composure. His policy was to play it cool even under extreme pressure.

If Luke and Sean wanted to address his and Brenda's indiscretion at the lab, Clarke was more than ready to finagle his way out that dilemma. Even if they decided to let him go, Clarke knew that he'd be walking away with invaluable secrets about **Dimension Four**. Brenda had taught him a great deal. She'd taught him how to use the *Vortex to Vanish* feature of **Dimension Find Me**. She'd also shown him a shortcut to the gateway.

Learning how to use the vortex was instrumental, because quite soon, he'd need to use the feature again in order to get Melody alone. Once Clarke *did* get her alone, he would take her away from Luke for good. At that juncture, Clarke felt as if he'd paraded around as the model employee for far too long. It was high time Luke and Melody *felt* his presence. It was also high time that he stopped playing games, and put his plan in motion. The time to take Luke and his followers down had finally arrived.

Clarke knocked discreetly on the set of doors of Luke's office. He waited for a moment for Luke's cue, announcing it was all right to come in.

"He's here, Sean." Luke's smile was cunning. Sean sat in Luke's armchair at the desk, but Luke stood to the side of it.

"Yeah, I know…and just in time." Sean feigned a tipped hat at Luke. "All right, let's do this, buddy," he said quietly.

Luke moved away from the desk, walked stealthily over to the set of doors. With a curious smile on his face, he opened them up. "Ah, Emery!" he announced. "Step into my office," Luke said pleasantly, gesturing with his hand.

"You wanted to see me?" Clarke followed Luke inside the luxury office. "Is everything all right?" he added quickly with an awkward smile.

"Everything's just fine," Luke assured. "Have a seat." He motioned.

"Mr. Winters," Clarke acknowledged. It felt strange to be sitting across from Sean Winters. Clarke remembered how close Sean had come to dying last year. One of his henchmen had put a bullet through his chest. So, it was quite unnerving to see Sean still breathing, healthy and as handsome as ever!

"Mr. Lloyd," Sean said perfunctorily, with a rehearsed smile.

"Well, we're just going to get right down to it." Luke's eyes gunned into Emery's.

"All right," Clarke said compliantly.

"It has been brought to our attention that..."

"I apologize if I've done anything out of turn," Clarke filled in. His heart whipped in his chest. *What had been brought to their attention? Was it the encounter with Brenda over at the lab?*

"Oh, no, *Emery*, you've done everything *right*," Sean refuted. "In fact, Luke and I can't stop raving about how talented you are at your job." Sean gave Emery an expectant smile.

"*Have* you now?" Clarke asked, bewildered. This wasn't the inquisition he'd expected, but it was difficult to tell what they wanted. *Why had they requested a meeting that afternoon?* "You're much too kind. It's *always* been my motto to do things right the first time. So, I take my work here at Portals very seriously," Clarke stated emphatically.

Luke nodded in agreement. "Absolutely. We've noticed all your hard work. That's why we wanted to offer you a position as one of our own execs," Luke proudly announced. Luke hoped that the smile on his face wasn't coming off as artificial. Playing this role successfully was paramount, if he wanted to convince Clarke Vale alias Emery Lloyd.

Clarke issued an inward sigh of relief. All the same, he was stunned over Luke and Sean's offer. "What are you saying?"

His face furrowed in confusion.

"Well, only a handful of us here at Portals, are privy to the esoteric nature of **Dimension Four**. Only our top people have a broad knowledge of the telecommunication," Luke explained.

"Luke and I are in total agreement that *you*, Mr. Lloyd, would be an asset to our execs team. You've been the model employee since the day you walked through our doors," Sean inspired.

Clarke couldn't contain his joy. Sunbeams radiated on his face and in his eyes. He was so relieved that the other shoe had not *yet* dropped. *These idiots were buying into his act, and wanted to make him one of Portals very on execs.*

This was the break he'd waited for. If he got in with the *big wigs*, he'd know everything there was to know about **Dimension Four**. That would bring him several steps closer to destroying Luke, and getting Melody back. "I'm truly honored you think so highly of me." Clarke's face radiated with new life.

"We've been keeping an eye on you for a while now. We've noticed what a conscientious worker you are, and how often you've worked overtime over the weekends. Someone as tenacious as you are should definitely be an exec." Luke's face rumpled in urgency. He couldn't help noticing the smile melded to Clarke's face. "So, what do you say, Emery? Will you do us the honor of joining our team?"

Clarke's blue eyes emitted a special glow. Nodding affirmatively, he reassured, "It would be an *honor* to be a part of your team. I am *truly* humbled by your offer." Clarke tried to switch out his arrogant demeanor for one of humility and self-effacement.

Luke gave the man a curious look. "Does that mean yes?"

Clarke nodded in agreement. "That is an absolute yes." He reached across the desk, and extended his hand to Sean.

Sean shook his hand firmly, and gave Emery a pleasant smile. He was over-the-moon that Emery had jumped at the opportunity.

Luke extended his hand out to Emery as well, and they

shook on the agreement. "I'm glad you've chosen to join our team! You will be training with Sean-that is until you broaden your knowledge of the technology," Luke told Emery.

Unable to tuck in his joy, Clarke quickly agreed to everything. *Was it even possible for Luke and Sean to be playing into his hands in this way?* How he'd racked his brain trying to figure out a way to master ***Dimension Four*** and it components! He couldn't have imagined Luke and Sean handing the technology over to him on a silver platter. Things were falling into place quickly and efficiently. "Of course…," he told Luke and Sean. "I look forward to learning everything I can. I can only hope that I'm as proficient as the two of you, once I'm done with the training."

Luke gave Sean a knowing look, and they exchanged quiet smiles. Clarke Vale was exactly where they wanted him. "You're much too kind," Luke addressed him. "I'm sure you're the perfect addition to our team! We're looking forward to working with you!"

"Absolutely… I also look forward to working with the both of you! Thank you so much! I truly appreciate this opportunity. I promise not to let you down."

"You haven't let us down so far…" Sean gave him a reassuring smile. He then pushed the rolling armchair away from the desk. It was his was of indicating that their little powwow had come to an end.

Luke walked from around his desk, and extended his hand out to Emery again. Their eyes fastened peculiarly, as they shook hands.

Sean began walking Emery out of the office. However, he waited on Luke's cue. He and Luke decided to play a little game. So, Sean took his time walking across the spacious office, while Luke hung back, and stayed close to his desk. The office phone rang at that moment.

Luke had asked Peter to call him, then to hang up once he answered. So, Luke put on a performance for Clarke's sake, and kept talking on the phone long after Peter hung up. In fact, Luke acted as if he were conducting business with a client. "Yes, we talked about it," Luke went on to say. "I've heard that it was *Clarke*...," he paused.

Sean watched as Emery immediately tense up. The man froze in his steps, the moment Luke said the name *Clarke*. His eyes were wide in angst, as he reflexively turned to look at Luke.

"*Clarke Montero* wants to invest...," Luke finished his train of thought. He *had* to try hard not to laugh. Emery Lloyd had taken the bait. He'd reacted to hearing his *real* name. Responding to hearing ones primary name was innate, even if an individual had changed it to something else.

"Something wrong, Emery?" Sean noticed how the man's eyes were fastened to Luke, while Luke remained on the phone. If Sean hadn't known any better, he would have guessed Emery had just seen a ghost.

"I'm fine, Mr. Winters," Emery said temperately. The malleable smile was painted back on, as his eyes gunned into Sean's.

Sean held one of the doors open for Emery. He had to keep a straight face until Emery left the office. "Again, allow me to welcome you to our execs team!"

"Thank you very much, Mr. Winters." Clarke stepped out of Luke's office feeling conflicted. He felt tremendously gratified to finally be getting everything he wanted. Quite soon, Melody would be in his arms again. The taste of her cherry lips was still palatable. And, the feel of her body pressed against his, literally made him insane. If everything worked accordingly, he'd soon be able to indulge in the most decadent confection of all.

However, Clarke censured himself for losing his aplomb a minute ago. He'd stepped out of character, overhearing Luke refer to someone else named *Clarke* on the phone. It dawned on him that he'd not trained himself extensively enough *not* to respond to his real name. Clarke Vale had been his name for thirty-seven years. So, responding to that name was indeed inherent. He hoped his reaction hadn't weirded out his bosses. Nevertheless, Clarke refused to dwell on such a minor blunder. There was so much he had to do. Notwithstanding, after all he'd endured, his sacrifices were about to pay off in a huge way.

***

A week later, Luke, Sean and Peter met in Sean's office. They were there to discuss how training was coming along with Brenda and Emery Lloyd. Luke was particularly interested in how much progress Brenda and Emery were making in respect to *Dimension Four's* latest feature. It was the latest addendum to *Shield Me*. The technology was called *Dimension Snare Me*. Whereas *Shield Me* was designed to protect the masses from impending danger, *Snare Me* worked in the opposite way.

Snare Me not only shielded the innocent from being victimized by a perpetrator, it stopped the culprit in his or her tracks by automatic encapsulation. Thereby, keeping the offender imprisoned. Only a given command from the user had the capability to deactivate it. It was a virtual prison cell. It kept the perpetrator frozen and trapped until law enforcement could step in. Luke had perfected the technology as a request from a law official.

Luke sat at the edge of Sean's desk to his right-hand side, and Peter sat across from them in a comfortable leather armchair.

"So, how's the training coming along?" Luke stared from Sean to Peter.

"Very well…" Sean nodded, smiling. "Everything's going according to plan."

"We've got both Lloyd and Brenda believing that *Snare Me* doesn't only encapsulate an offender, but incapacitates them. They also think the technology can cause temporary paralysis, and render its victim totally powerless-if that were ever to be the protocol." Peter shook his head absurdly.

"Clarke's eyes lit up like fireworks when we told him about *Snare Me*. He's probably chomping at the bit to use it on us." Sean chortled.

Luke smiled, and nodded in agreement. "What he doesn't realize is that if he ever fiddles with this add-on to the *Shield Me* technology, he'll actually be immobilizing himself. He *might* very well want to use it on us. I doubt that he's figured out that with *Dimension*, unless all your ducks are lined up in a row, you're playing at your own risk, and more than likely to lose the game."

"So far, he's buying right into our hands. He's desperate to use *any* of *Dimensions* components against us. He's just biding his time, and waiting for the right moment. It's sad that the man thinks he knows *so* much, when he's *just* a beginner. And yet, there's no doubt in *my* mind he's planning some form of an attack. He wouldn't be Clarke Vale if he didn't try." Sean sighed. "If he wasn't so evil, I would actually feel sorry for him. Everything we need to stop him is contained within *Dimension* technology."

Peter nodded. "I *have* to say, of all of the latest advancements Sean and I discussed with Lloyd/Vale, *Snare Me* appealed to him the most. It's at the very top of his list." Peter laughed. "Like a mouse drawn to a piece of cheese on a trap, he's dying to try it out."

"And, we're *just* as eager to have him try it out," Luke said satirically. "Once he does take the bait, he'll realize he's been barking up the wrong tree all along. What about Brenda?" Luke frowned in concern. "Are you training *her* on the various ways to use the *Power Portal*?"

"Yes… Brenda and I went over that drill in depth. I've even authorized *your* unique biometric key in the event *she* should need to utilize it. I *did* warn her of the danger of accessing the portal without prior authorization via the gateway. In spite of it all, something tells me she's already shared the details with Lloyd." Sean felt sorry for Brenda.

"Of course, she has. She's probably explained the basics in as far as how to use the portal. Unfortunately, if Emery risks stepping into the portal without authorization, I've commanded the technology to lock him in. Like moving a chess piece on a board, there's more than one strategy set in place to freeze him out. It's only a matter of time." Luke set his hand on his chin introspectively. "I'm actually curious to see which of *Dimension Four's* facets Vale *chooses* as a weapon against *us*." He shook his head inanely.

Sean laughed. "Sad, but we've had to rig all of *Dimensions* tools against him. We have Ari to thank for that. She helped us solve the mystery of why Vale was coming up dead. Thank God we were able to override that feature, and *Find Me* finally verified Clarke's DNA. Now that we know for sure that Emery Lloyd and Clarke Vale are the same person, using any of *Dimension's* features, will either snare, lock or expose him."

"That just about sums it up," Luke said, smiling.

"So, what's the protocol of the day, *PM?*" Peter asked warily.

"We continue training him on the programs. At some point, we *know* he's going to try to use the technology against us. When *that* happens it's bye-bye, Clarke." There was that *crazy like a fox* expression on Luke's face and in his eyes. "Also, as delicately as we can, we drop hints that we know who he is."

"I have to agree with you there, buddy. If Clarke feels cornered, he'll be more inclined to do something desperate," Sean estimated. "Now more than ever, we have to keep a close eye on everyone-especially Mel, because she's his obsession."

Luke's face tensed in dread. "He isn't getting anywhere near Mel, or anyone else for that matter. I'm just hoping this little charade comes to an end painlessly. Then, we can deliver a criminal to back to the authorities, and explain this bizarre story. Still, we need ironclad proof Clarke faked his suicide with the help of hire ups within the Sands Port jail. He traveled to Croatia, and submitted to facial and physical reconstruction, etc..."

Sean sighed. "That's one hard pill for anyone to swallow, but we *know* it's true. Clarke's been lurking around here for a while now." Sean shifted in his chair.

"He won't be for very much longer. Let's see how much time it takes for him to bite. I honestly don't think it's going to take very long." Luke hopped off the desk, and stood to his feet as he brainstormed.

"You said we should drop hints around Vale. What kinds of hints are we talking about, *PM?*" Peter's face crinkled in uncertainty.

"I've got a few ideas," Luke said cryptically.

"I may have a few of my own." Sean brooded. "We can't drop the ball too hard, Luke. We've got to leave just enough rope for Lloyd/Vale to hang himself."

A clever smile spread across Luke's face. "I think I know just the person to reach out to."

Sean and Peter's faces were full of intrigue, as they watched Luke pull out his cell phone. Luke actually took a moment to punch in a long number on the phone's keypad. He paced around the room with the phone cradled to his ear and chin.

Luke was totally encouraged when he heard the phone ringing. "Dr. Felix, please," he requested over the line.

Sean and Peter shared perplexed looks as they listened.

"Yes... Hello, Velda. How are you?" Luke's smile was genuine. "Dr. Felix? No. I'm actually calling to speak to *you*. I hope you remember who this is..." Luke reminded her of his and Sean's visit out to Croatia months earlier. The older woman was ecstatic to be hearing from him. Luke genuinely liked Velda. He was also very appreciative of her cooperation when he and Sean had visited the island. She had literally stuck her neck out to help them.

"It's so nice to hear from you, Luke. I'm glad to finally know your name," she delighted. "Happy New Year to *you*!" she offered graciously. "You know, ever since you and your friend popped up at the mansion a few months ago, I'd hoped you would return. It was the most excitement we'd had in that lonely place for years."

"I never got a chance to properly thank you for what you did for us that evening. I *did* say you should give us a call sometime," Luke reminded her. "Well, Velda, I'm not sure quite how to put this."

Luke tucked his left hand into the pocket of his slacks, as he deliberately paced the plush carpeting. "When was the last time you got away from it all, and took a vacation...?" he propositioned. Catching Sean's eye from across the desk, Luke winked.

Sean smiled quietly, and shook his head humorously, because he grasped what Luke was up to. Luke was trying to get Velda to come out to California. If he understood Luke's train of thought, he wanted Emery Lloyd to see Velda. When Emery *did* see her, he'd probably be freaked out. It was more than likely that Velda in turn would recognize *him*. Clarke/Emery would have a total meltdown, and probably come out of hiding.

Sean had to give *props* to Luke for coming up with the plan. Luke plans seemed work, because by the end of his conversation with Velda, he was talking travel arrangements.

Sean had an idea of his own, but decided to share it with Luke later. Yet and still, he had to admit that contacting Velda out in Croatia as another measure to *ensnare* Clarke Vale, was ingenious.

Peter sat there feeling totally lost. Luke and Sean seemed to be *in the know*, but *he* felt totally out of the loop. However, Peter couldn't say that he wasn't riveted. He actually couldn't wait to hear their plan. For Peter, it was indeed an *education* hanging out with Luke and Sean. The two were totally in sync. They seem to be able to read each other's minds. Peter decided to just watch and learn. Under the tutelage of his employers and good friends, he too would be able to fly high above the radar.

***

"Can I open my eyes now?" Arianna asked, smiling ear to ear. Peter had accompanied her to her follow-up appointment with the doctor. After undergoing a battery of tests, by the grace of God everything turned out okay. Her labs were perfect.

"Almost...," Peter teased. Standing behind Arianna, he had

one hand covering her eyes, and the other set about her waist, as he guided her over to his place. He'd promised to bring her home from the appointment, but he'd taken a slight detour.

"Pete, this is driving me crazy. What are you up to?" Arianna's beautiful face radiated new light, energy and joy. "Why are we stopping?" She realized they were now standing still. Peter's right hand had dropped from about her waist, and she heard the clinking of keys.

"Hang on a moment. Please, keep those beautiful eyes closed for just a minute longer." Peter found the house key, and opened up the front door. With his hand still veiling her eyes, he guided her inside, and cautiously shut the front door after them. Peter was bursting at the seams to surprise her.

It was the middle of January, but he'd kept his Christmas tree up. Furthermore, he had his entire place decked out like a virtual winter wonderland for Arianna. He'd created a forest of blue spruce trees, and had enhanced the décor with movie-prop snow. For all intents and purposes, they were venturing inside a snow globe.

Although it was the middle of the afternoon, Peter had shut down the blinds, and had dimmed the lights around the house in order to highlight the festive Christmas paraphernalia. He guided Arianna over to the living room at the center of the display. The myriad of gifts Arianna had received on Christmas were propped underneath the tree. Peter's smile was infectious, because Arianna was almost where he wanted her.

"Peter Jared Lawton, you've got to stop torturing me this way," she complained.

"All right, I will stop torturing you just about…now," Peter said mischievously, gently unveiling her eyes.

Arianna gasped, and cupped her mouth in shock. Tears gleamed in her eyes, and her face warped in sentimentality. "Peter, what's this?" her voice wavered. "What have you gone and done?"

Peter smiled, and pushed back tears of his own, as he tenderly took her hands in his. "Merry Christmas, Ari!" he said hoarsely, as his eyes delved urgently to hers. "I'd like a chance to relive what should have been our date at the Christmas party?" He swallowed the chunk lodged in throat.

"Oh, Pete…" Arianna found herself at a loss for words. She kept shaking her head in skepticism. "This is beautiful and amazing! But, I don't have on my wintergreen dress. I wore that dress especially for you on Christmas Eve," she admitted, and smiled nostalgically into his eyes.

"Thank you for wearing that beautiful dress just for me, but you're just as stunning in your jeans and ice blue sweater!" he uplifted. "Arianna…" Peter searched her eyes. "There's so much I wanted to tell you that night, but I never got the chance to."

Arianna stared at Peter in awe and wonder, as one would admire a shooting star darting from the sky. She now realized just how truly amazing he was. "I'm here…I'm listening," she said softly.

"First off, allow me to apologize for what happened with Raya-"

"You don't have to explain about Raya-" Arianna tried to counter.

"Ari, you need to know why I was in my office to begin with." Peter gently released her hands. Hunching down, he gathered up a small, red and silver horizontal-shaped gift box, and also the card and letter he'd written out in his office that night. "Well, maybe, this will explain things a little bit better." Peter smiled sappily at her.

Arianna brushed back tears from her eyes and smiled. "Are those for me?" she asked wispily.

Peter nodded. "And, also all of these…" He displayed the myriad of presents under the tree.

"Well, I guess I'd better get busy opening them up." She laughed.

Peter stood in close proximity to Arianna-intimate enough to hear her heartbeat. He wondered if she could hear *his* flagellating inside his chest. With bated breath, he watched her open up the first present. It was a locket in the shape of a portal, with a clear square stone in the center, and a blood-red garnet heart.

The square and garnet created a prism-like effect. It read: *You own the key to the **portal** of my heart.*

"Peter, this is breathtaking!" Arianna's face warped emotionally. "It's perfect." She threw her arms about his neck, and hugged him meaningfully.

"I *thought* it was rather unique, and quite special just like *you*." He crushed her in his arms. The moment felt surreal. It was the first time he'd been this close to Arianna. Having her in his arms was indeed problematic, because he just didn't want to let go. "Do you like it?" He buried his face in her hair.

"I love it!" Arianna pulled away to look into his eyes. "Will you help me put it on?" she asked excitedly.

"Of course, I will." Peter unclasped the necklace. Arianna turned in the opposite direction, and lifted her hair out of the way. Peter gingerly clasped the necklace about her neck. Unable to resist, he arched down, and pressed a kiss to her shoulder.

Arianna got butterflies in her stomach, because of Peter's tender kiss. Her heart dipped like a roller coaster when she turned and saw his perfect face again. "How does it look?" she asked delicately.

"Incredible!" Peter took a moment to admire her. "Ari, please open up the card," he prodded. "That night, in my office, I was trying to find the right words."

Arianna nodded in concurrence. "All right," she acceded. First, she opened up the envelope and read the card. "I love it, Pete!" she announced. However, it was the letter creased inside that left her totally stunned and speechless.

Peter stared at her with a sense of expectation. "Ari, say something… That's what I wanted to tell you that night," he admitted.

Arianna was trembling and in tears, as her eyes connected to his. She couldn't stop crying.

Peter eliminated the small gap between them. Cradling her face in his hands, he gently brushed her tears away. "I wanted you to know that I love you!" Peter hunched down, and softly pressed his lips to hers. His embrace was delicate at first. However, as he explored the regions of her mouth, like a man parched in the wilderness, he drank thirstily and savored the honey stream of her mouth.

Arianna caressed every inch of Peter's mouth with avidness and desire. "I love you too, Peter!" she told him in between kisses.

Peter was so shocked to hear the words, he jerked back instantly to see if he'd heard right. "What did you just say?" Tears glimmered in his eyes.

Arianna laughed, and shook her head humorously. She clasped his head in her hands, then reached up and kissed every corner of his mouth. "I love you so much, Peter Jared Lawton!"

Overwhelmed, Peter just held her acquisitively. "I love *you* so much, baby!"

"I'm so sorry for all the times I misunderstood." Arianna grimaced in remorse, as she raked her fingers through hit perfect sable hair.

"I'm sorry for the times I made you doubt me." Peter pulled away, but his arms still encircled her waist. "Didn't you know? I loved you from the first moment I laid eyes on you that afternoon at your desk," he admitted. "I haven't *looked* at anyone since. You love me?" he questioned again.

"More than I thought I could love anyone," Arianna admitted.

All of a sudden, the entire world had melted away. What Arianna felt for Peter, and processing *his* love for her was indeed a gift from God. She couldn't even remember ever loving anyone else. For that very reason, Arianna recognized the hand of God at work. There'd been a time not too long ago where she could not have imagined loving anyone in the way she'd loved Luke. However, Peter had found a way to redefine all of her expectations.

Chapter Thirteen

The setting was rustic. Hunting and fishing trappings, and sports memorabilia ornamented the perimeters of the Big Game Bar and Grill. On a Friday night in the middle of January, Luke and Sean invited Emery for a beer after work. It was the last day whereby he'd received training on *Dimension Four*. Luke and Sean were confident that Emery had been properly briefed in the technology-at least in the way they'd hoped. Emery had learned many of the facets of *Dimension Four* he'd aspired to from the outset.

Luke was actually surprised that Emery had agreed to have a beer with them. The idea of having drinks after work was Sean's, so Luke was anxious to see what Sean had up his sleeve.

"Congratulations, Emery!" Sean told him. The three were seated at a table towards the back end of the spacious bistro.

Clarke smiled widely. He was still baffled by the fact that his enemies had invested in training him on the components of *Dimension Four*. Now, the possibilities were endless. "Why thank you. I truly owe it all to you and to Peter. I have to say you truly know your material." Clarke gestured towards Luke and Sean.

"It was an absolute pleasure to show you the ropes! After all, a model employee like you should be *in the know*. You've earned the right to have access to *Dimension*. Welcome to the future, Emery!" Luke raised his beer mug.

"Here, here!" Sean echoed and raised his.

"Well, in that case... Here, here to the future!" Clarke raised his glass in celebration. A cunning and irrepressible smile decorated his sharp features. Everything was falling right into place. Life was good! He had access to hidden, classified knowledge. He was alive, good-looking, out of prison, and he had a simpleton of a woman at his beckon call.

"What I find the most intriguing, I must say, is the power of the portal. That's indeed one tool we couldn't have envisioned having access to in the twenty-first century," Clarke delineated.

His eyes explored Luke's curiously. "What you've done is amazing, *PM*!"

Luke took a long swig from his beer glass, but his eyes never wavered from Emery. "I can't take credit for any of it. Just like with many inventions, I kinda stumbled upon **Dimension Four**. I was never good at chemistry. I was just a computer geek, but somehow, the mystery incorporates a variety of sciences."

"You're absolutely right about that." Clarke nodded, smiling.

"Don't listen to Luke here," Sean said. "He's much too modest. I've always known he was a genius, and he's proven to be just that." Sean gave Luke an impish wink.

"That's hardly true," Luke argued, critically searching Emery's eyes.

Clarke was beginning to feel out of sorts. It seemed his employers were scrutinizing him. What he knew of Luke and Sean was that they were both intense. However, while sitting there, he somehow felt as if he was under a microscope.

"So, *Emery*, how do you feel about California so far?" Sean asked. "I have it on good authority that you actually uprooted in order to come out here and work through Portals. Where exactly did you live before all of this?" Sean's face crinkled in introspection.

Clarke laughed nervously, but thought fast on his feet. He *was* originally from Chicago, so that seemed as good an answer as any. "Actually, there wasn't very much uprooting to do. I just took a flight out from Chicago, when I heard Portals Unlimited was hiring." His eyes shifted from Luke to Sean.

"Ah, Chicago-the windy city," Luke examined. "Do you miss being out there?"

"Hardly at all. The winters are brutal," Clarke said naturally. "I love the weather out here, the sunny skies, the beaches…"

"I can't believe Luke had to *talk* me into coming out here. I had finally gotten used to living out in Sands Port, Maryland. That's where we're both coming from," Sean detailed.

Clarke flinched upon hearing Sean mention the town of Sands Port. However, he played it off and feigned nonchalance. "Sounds quaint," he commented, with a keen smile.

"It *is* a very quaint little town. That's why it's so hard to believe such a scandal took place there last year." Sean shook his head inanely, as he stared squarely at Emery.

Luke smiled cleverly, and realized exactly what Sean was doing. *He* was now *ready* to play along.

"Scandal...?" Clarke questioned, with a quizzical expression on his face.

"Yes... One of the biggest scandals of our time. You *have* heard of Clarke Vale? He was the CEO, founder and owner of Vale Pharmaceuticals."

"Oh yes, I *think* I might have heard something about that story," Clarke said uneasily. His face soured, and beads of perspiration issued from his flustered pores.

"Well, in case you're *not* familiar with the story, let me bring you up to speed."

Sean began to elucidate how Clarke Vale had moved out to Sands Port for the advancement of his pharmaceutical business. However, his business was a covert operation for his illicit drugs, and black market dealings out in the Caribbean and Central America. Sean explained how Vale bargained with Luke after Luke's dad had succumbed to stroke, and their home was pending foreclosure. "Vale told Luke he would take care of all of those expenses, if Luke ended his relationship with Melody."

Shock and dismay wrinkled Clarke's face. He remained speechless, as he listened to *their* account.

Luke picked up exactly where Sean had left off. He went on to say how Clarke Vale abducted Melody, and brought her down to a subterranean complex. However, Clarke and his henchmen were discovered and defeated. Luke highlighted the account of Clarke's arrest, and how Darien Stiles' stood to stand trial in April.

As Luke and Sean took turns rehashing the fate of *this Clarke Vale*, it was difficult to escape the inflections and nuances on Emery Lloyd's face. The man was clearly flustered, and beads of perspiration were on his forehead. Emery kept loosening his tie, and smiling nervously.

Clarke swallowed hard, but tried to retain aplomb. A rubber smile stretched across his face. "Sounds like a very *bad* man. From what *I* understand, he was found hung in his jail cell late last year."

"So, you *do* know a little bit about the story?" Sean gave a knowing nod.

"They *say* he hung himself in his own jail cell, but *I* never bought it," Luke said cunningly.

"CNN and other major news channels kept showing the footage," Clarke argued. At that point he was irked. *What was this about? Why had Luke and Sean chosen to discuss the fate of Clarke Vale?*

Clarke wondered if they were on to him. And yet, in spite of it all, he knew it was best to continue playing it cool. He had to maintain his composure. Undoubtedly, Luke and Sean were just sharing a very poignant and recent interpretation of what they'd endured.

"Yeah, all the major news channels showed the images of Vale's *alleged* suicide," Luke emphasized again. "Something about that whole thing never sat well with me."

"I never bought it either, Luke," Sean said. "A man like Vale had too much money, and too many connections to end up hanged in some jail cell. I didn't know him as well as Luke here. But, from what I understand, he was a narcissist. People like that commit murder all the time, but suicide...not so much." Sean's expression was cagy, as his eyes speared through Emery's.

"If *I* had that kind of money, and *I* was facing multiple counts of murder, extortion, fraud, drug dealing and blackmail, and looking at consecutive life sentences in prison, I would definitely *fake* my suicide.

"I would go far away to some obscure country in Europe, have plastic surgery and change my identity." Luke stared squarely into Emery's nervous eyes. The man's face was as maroon as sugar beets by then. "What do *you* think, Emery? Does that sound like something a man as powerful and connected as Clarke Vale would do?"

Clarke felt the weight, and the fire of their gapes as they awaited an answer. *What on earth was this about? Was it possible that they'd discovered his true identity?* Hearing Luke cite the details of what a man *like* Clarke Vale *would do*, sounded totally bizarre-almost like something from a Sci-fi movie.

A nervous, but exaggerated laugh issued from the hollow of Clarke's throat. "Oh, that's really good," he played off. Clarke pointed a liable, yet playful finger at both men. "You really had me going there for a minute." He shook his head humorously and laughed. "Go to some obscure country out in Europe, and change my identity...sounds like Sci-fi stuff." He was still perspiring. His eyes were jumpy, and his face could be mistaken for a blood orange.

Sean cocked his head back, and a ripple of laughter roared through him as well.

Luke followed suit and chortled. "You're absolutely right, Emery. I'm sure Vale's dead. Sean and I are still a little paranoid, because of what we went through."

"Yeah, Luke's right. CNN and other major news sources verified his suicide. And, that's got to be good enough for us," Sean said generically. He laughed again. "Plastic surgery out in Europe..." He shook his head comically.

"Soon, we'll be saying he was abducted by aliens, right Emery?" Luke razzed and laughed again.

"Right...," Clarke's laughter was unnaturally exaggerated. Clarke was convinced Luke and Sean weren't serious about their theories. All the same, he couldn't get out of the restaurant fast enough. "My goodness, look at the time!"

"Come on, Emery, hang out with us. We haven't even ordered anything yet," Sean coaxed. His hands clasped together as if he were about to say his prayers.

"Actually, I am meeting someone later. I'm honestly grateful you asked me to come out here this evening. It makes me feel as if I'm *finally* a part of the Portals' family," Clarke brownnosed.

"The pleasure was all ours." Luke stared affably at him. "Believe me when I say you're one of Portals' key players." Luke held up his half-empty beer mug, and heralded again, "To one of Portals' latest and greatest finds!"

Sean and Emery held their beer mugs up, and cheered in concurrence.

"I'm afraid I have to leave now," Clarke said, agitated. He had to get away from them. He needed a moment to process what was happening. *Were they on to him?* It didn't seem possible, but he had to be prepared for any eventuality. The uncertainty of the matter was a sobering reminder of how shrewd Luke and Sean were. Clarke had to get away in order to plan out his next move. He had to move fast, because his house of cards was beginning to topple over. "Now, if you will excuse me... Gentlemen, it's been a pleasure. Goodnight."

"Goodnight, *Emery*," Both Luke and Sean said in concert, as they exchanged knowing looks. It took tremendous restraint not to laugh, as they watched Clarke scurry out of the restaurant like a frightened rabbit.

"Sean, that was brilliant!" Luke held his hand up, and high-fived his buddy. He burst into laughter. "Great plan."

Sean smiled cannily. "Thanks. You see his face when you started that whole, *what I would do if I were Clarke Vale rant*?" Sean snickered.

"Yeah, if he had a kidney stone, he would have passed it right then and there," Luke razzed. "I love it. He's coming apart at the seams, and it won't be long before he's snared."

"Tell me about it. I can't wait to see his face when Velda comes into town."

"'*I can't take it anymore. I've got to find a way to make Luke and Sean disappear for good*,'" Luke did his best Clarke impersonation. "'So, I plan on using **Dimension Four** to incapacitate and paralyze them.'"

"'*Even if I have absolutely no idea what I'm doing*.'" Sean shook his head humorously, and laughed.

Luke was stoked, because Clarke seemed to be playing right into their hands. In fact, the man was unraveling before their very eyes. No doubt, seeing Velda again would bring Emery Lloyd totally over the edge. And, when that happened, he and Clarke would engage in battle again. However, it was Luke's vow to make this *mortal* combat their last. At the end of the day, *Clarke Vale and Emery Lloyd* would never rear their ugly heads to make trouble for them again.

***

"Are you sure that's the man you saw out on the colonnade at Dr. Felix's mansion?" Luke asked Velda.

She was now out in California. In fact, she was currently staying with him and Melody over at their home in Beverly Glen. That evening, Luke and Melody also invited Sean and Nicole over for dinner. Luke was in process of working out the details of Velda's *indefinite* stay out in California. Velda had said she no longer wanted to continue working for Dr. Felix out in Croatia.

The older woman nodded in confirmation. "I'm sure of it. I came out that morning to offer the man you call *Clarke Vale* breakfast, but he was gone. However, the man you introduced me to in your office this afternoon, was out on the colonnade that morning."

"Did you have word with him at all?" Sean queried.

"I asked about breakfast choices. I'd come out to ask if he wanted anything aside from what was already out on the breakfast table," Velda explained. "Why did that Emery Lloyd stare at me in such a bizarre way earlier?" Her face furrowed in alarm. "He turned white as a sheet."

Luke and Sean laughed, because they'd issued a final blow earlier on. Velda was in Luke's office, when they'd invited Emery in to sign off on paperwork. He and Sean had introduced Velda as a member of Sean's family visiting from Europe. The look on Emery's face was priceless. His expression was that of a man inches away from a beehive, and allergic to bees.

"Velda, I don't think you were aware of it at the time, but the man you saw that morning was *Clarke Vale*. Dr. Felix's biogenetic work on him was *that* good," Sean told her.

Velda gasped in shock. "Oh my goodness, I had absolutely no idea! It was all so strange. At the time, I was under the impression that Dr. Felix had brought a new houseguest into the mansion. This was a totally different man." She kept shaking her head in incredulity.

"Well, that's why he paid Dr. Felix so much money. He *wanted* to be unrecognizable," Luke pointed out. "I'll bet anything, if he *didn't* know we were on to him, seeing *you* today confirmed it."

"Are you in some kind of danger?" the older woman asked in angst.

"*You're* fine, Velda. That's why Luke and I want you to stay here with *us* for a few days. No one can touch you while you're here.' Melody gave Velda's hand a supportive squeeze.

"I highly doubt Clarke Vale would *try* to hurt you in any way now, Velda. So, you're pretty much safe. If anything, he regrets not reaching out to you before you showed up here," Nicole humored.

"Won't he suspect we're trying to flush him out of hiding, and turn him over to the authorities?" Velda's voice was shaky, and her eyes shifted fearfully.

"That's *exactly* what we want. We *want* him to react now, because we're positioned to take him down once and for all," Sean explained.

"Now, we figure that his next move will be to ask for a few days off from work, or he'll hand in his resignation." Luke's smile was calculating.

"Good riddance!" Melody shuddered. "I still can't believe Clarke submitted to facial and physical reconstruction with Dr. Felix. That's more than just a little creepy."

"Dr. Felix is excellent at what he does. I guess, he's better than I thought. When it was all said and done, Clarke Vale had literally vanished." Velda reflected.

"Except for his eyes," Nicole commented. "Believe me, it isn't your fault, Velda. Clarke paid Doctor Felix an obscene amount of money to *make* him disappear. And, that's exactly what he did."

"I can no longer work for a man who would help a known criminal mask his identity." Tears shone in Velda's eyes.

Luke reached across the table, and gave her hand a sympathetic squeeze. "Don't worry, Velda. You won't have to. You can stay out here for as long as you like. And, we can figure out a position for you-that is if you *have* to work." Luke winked at her. "Thank you so much for agreeing to come out here. At least, now we've solved the mystery of the man you saw sitting out on the patio that morning."

"What does it all mean?" Velda was still anxious.

"It means, now that Clarke Vale knows that we're on to him, he'll be looking to strike," Sean said plainly. "In fact, that's what we were hoping would happen after he saw you."

"And *boy* are we ready for him!" Melody had a determined expression. "I can't wait for all of this to be over. Clarke has been a thorn in our sides far too long." Her eyes fastened to Luke's.

Luke pressed a kiss to her cheek. "Don't worry, Mel. Like Sean said, Clarke's ready to issue a first strike, but we'll have all kinds of surprises coming his way." Luke glanced quickly about the room. His demeanor was tense, as he contemplated bringing the charade to an end. However, like sunlight filtering through overcast skies, the clouds passed, and he smiled. "Anyone want more dessert? I'd sure love another piece of pie."

***

Clarke made a dash for his apartment condo out in Newport Beach. What happened at work earlier on had left him completely rattled. He'd just seen Dr. Anselm Felix's housekeeper and cook sitting in Luke Bryant's office. From what they'd told him, the woman was a distant relative of Sean Winters.' However, Clarke wasn't buying it at all. Now he knew for sure that Luke and Sean knew his true identity.

At that point, the curious powwow at the bar and grill days ago made sense. Clarke wasn't sure how they'd learned his secret, but he was certain they had. In no uncertain terms, they'd put it out there that they knew the entire story. He'd faked his suicide, submitted to facial and physical reconstruction, and he was working for them. "Distant relative of Sean Winters', my eye! They know exactly who I am, and they're plotting against me."

Clarke walked into his spacious closet, and pulled out a suitcase. He packed up his things just as quickly as he could. Then, after making a few bank transfers, he put in a few very important calls. There had to be a way to make good on his plans before he went away. One thing was certain. When he *did* go away, Melody was coming with him. He was now skeptical of the training he'd undergone with Sean and Peter Lawton on *Dimension Four.*

However, Brenda *had* taught him a thing or two. So, he figured, even with bits and pieces of the knowledge, he could still find a way to take Luke Bryant down. Clarke was determined to sever Luke's heart in half. After all, that's exactly what Luke had done to him last year. He wanted to make the young tycoon pay for interfering in his life, and with his business.

As Clarke made tentative plans on how to flee, and take Melody with him, his cellphone went off. The number was unknown, so he automatically answered-thinking it was one of his contacts. "Hello," he said generically.

"Emery...?" Brenda's tone was uncertain.

"Brenda?" Clarke questioned, irritated. "Hello, darling," he automatically slipped into acting mode. "I didn't recognize the number."

"I'm using my landline, because you wouldn't answer any of my calls. I've also texted you a dozen times. Is everything all right?" Brenda's voice resonated in hurt and disillusionment.

"Everything's just fine, muffin. I've had somewhat of a hectic day. There's a lot going on that I didn't want to trouble you with," Clarke said shrewdly. "I apologize. There's a family related crisis, so I'm afraid I have to leave town for a few days."

"You're going away?" Brenda gasped, surprised. "Have you told *PM* and Sean?"

"I was actually hoping that *you* would relay the message. But, I will definitely give them a call in the morning," Clarke lied.

His intention was to distance himself from Portals Unlimited. Going back there would only mean trouble. Perhaps, Luke and Sean were lying in wait to have him apprehended by the authorities on any given workday. Now that Velda had seen him, and could positively link him to Dr. Felix, he had to make himself scarce.

"Is there anything *I* can do to help?" Brenda felt totally disconnected from the man she loved.

"That's very kind of you to offer, but no. It's something I've got to handle on my own. I've got to go now, Brenda."

"But Emery-" Brenda cradled the phone in her hand, as tears looped over in her eyelids.

It didn't seem to matter how arduously she'd tried to get close to Emery. Every time they took one step forward, it seemed they took a dozen backward. She felt totally used and unappreciated. She'd risked it all for him, and had put her heart on the line. And for what? He didn't even have the decency to say goodbye, neither did he promise to contact her once things settled down. She buried her grimaced face in the palms of her hands, and wept in abandon.

Clarke had gotten all of his affairs in order. He was all packed up to disappear for a while. He'd secured a remote location in the event he had to go into hiding again. Unlike his subterranean refuge, which had been raided by police and the FBI, he had a rustic lodge in the Redwoods in Arcata. It was a virtual ghost town with very few tourists and visitors. It was beautiful, historic, and overlooked the Pacific. Clarke decided to use the lodge as a temporary asylum.

If everything went according to plan, he'd have Melody by his side by the time he made the three-and-a-half-hour trip to that remote area. First, he had to check in on his benefactor, Dr. Daniel Sands. Dr. Sands was in the process of creating technology which could possibly rival a few of *Dimension Four's* modules. He was paying Dr. Sands millions for a scientific breakthrough that could potentially exceed the effectiveness of *Dimension Four.* Clarke hoped Dr. Sands would have good news, when they convened in his office later.

***

"I'm so glad you've taken time to meet with me, Dr. Sands," Clarke said politely. It was pretty late, but Clarke had requested the meeting with Dr. Daniel Sands. Dr. Sands was a physicist and expert in Quantum Mechanics, Biochemistry, Meteorology and Alchemy. A friend of a friend's had told Clarke about Dr. Sands shortly after Clarke had moved out to California.

Dr. Sands was working exhaustively to supersede Luke's discovery and enhancement of *Dimension Four*. For that very reason, Clarke had partnered up with-and subsidized his research. Dr. Sands was currently working on advancements in Biometric Engineering, space and time travel, molecular, and element manipulation.

Clarke had kept Dr. Sands in the loop regarding everything *he* knew about *Dimension Four* technology. All the same, Clarke realized they were running out of time. So, he needed answers in respect to how to override *Dimension's* components, and safely take Melody away. Now that Luke and Sean were on to him, he didn't have a moment to waste.

There were things Luke and Sean *weren't* aware of. For starters, Clarke had been working with Dr. Sands for a while to create an applied science capable of *weakening* **Dimension Four**, and its multidimensional tools. Clarke figured Luke and Sean were probably using some aspect of the program to keep their loved ones safe. So, Clarke presumed, the only way he could find Melody in a vulnerable state, was to compromise the hedge of protection around her. That was probably the case for Luke *and* his entourage.

"I'm glad you're here, Emery," Dr. Sands addressed him properly. The man had an artful smile on his face, as he traipsed over to his private office. The lights inside the research center were dim, as he used a set of keys to open up the door.

"I *hope* you have good news for me," Clarke said, following behind him.

Daniel Sands entered the office, and turned on the lights. He then sauntered over to his desk, and sat down in the armchair. Clarke took his place across from the man.

Dr. Sands smiled cannily once more. "I think you're going to be pleased by what I have to tell you tonight, Emery." He clasped his hands together simulating an arch.

"Now, *that's* the kind of news I want to hear. Have you found a way to override the effectiveness of *Dimension Four's Shield Me* technology?" Clarke cut straight to the chase.

"Before I proceed, do you have what we agreed on?" Dr. Sands' eyes lowered critically, and his brows raised in wariness.

Clarke removed an envelope from the inner pocket of his suit jacket. Setting it over the glossy dark wood desk, he slid the envelope over to the man. "A twenty-million-dollar Cashier's Check-like we agreed on," Clarke said discreetly.

Dr. Sands picked up the envelope without hesitation, and perused the check. "I haven't come up with a telecommunication to rival or supersede *Dimension Four*- at least not yet."

Clarke scowled in irritation. "Then, why on earth are you wasting my time?" he asked coarsely.

"You didn't let me finish," Dr. Sands placated. "What I *have* discovered is a way to get exactly what you want. You *are* interested in technology capable of temporarily rendering *Dimension Four's* accessories inept, as a means to an end?"

Clarke set his right hand on his chin introspectively. "You know that's *exactly* what I'm looking to do."

"You wouldn't have to tear *Dimension Four* apart per se. Believe me, this *kid* has made it virtually indestructible. What you would need to do is to disable it long enough to accomplish your goal. Am I right?"

"What are you getting at, Doctor?" Clarke said impatiently.

"Well, I honestly believe I've come up with just the device you need. It is called the *Mediator*. The Electromagnetic waves create a makeshift barrier that will indisputably interfere with

Dimension Four's frequencies. It will warp its effectiveness by thwarting contact to areal satellites."

"English please, Doctor Sands?" Clarke's face wrinkled in exasperation.

"The *Mediator* makes it difficult for *Dimension Four*, and its mechanisms to connect to surrounding waves and satellite. The stall can last anywhere from twenty minutes to half an hour. Once the interference stops however, all *Dimension Four* modules will need resetting in order to regain effectiveness. You can think of *Mediator* as a winter coat. It buffers from the cold. However, if you stay outside too long, you can potentially freeze to death. *Mediator* stands in between the electromagnetic waves which empower *Dimension Four.*"

Clarke nodded with a satisfied expression on his face. "So, this *Mediator* will allot a little window of time to undermine *Dimension Four* accessories, while simultaneously enacting revenge on Luke Bryant, and taking what's rightfully mine…" He had a villainous expression. For all intents and purposes, he had on a virtual reality cap, and engaged in living out his fantasies.

Dr. Sands nodded. "The *Mediator* will allot you a little time-that is once, *Dimension Four* is temporarily immobilized. Besides, I'm confident that you will share *Mediator* technology with the world. That will make *us* multibillionaires a few times over." Dr. Sands' expression was wistful.

"Yes. I do believe that sounds like a plan. Are you sure this *Mediator's* failsafe?" Clarke face wrinkled in uncertainty.

Dr. Sands nodded again. "I *know* it is. I've tested it on similar technology such as this groundbreaking *Shield* Bryant has set in place. We will go over to the lab, so that I can show you the device. However, there is just one more thing I should tell you," He said cryptically.

Clarke flinched, and he shuffled nervously towards the edge of his chair. "Is there a problem?"

"No, not at all. Everything's just fine, but I need to explain how the *Mediator* works.

"I thought you explained how it works a moment ago."

Clarke rolled his eyes, irate.

"I did…for the most part. You should know… Once the *Mediator* loses its effectiveness after disabling *Dimension*, once reset, all of *Dimension's* components will magnify in strength. Then, it will be the *Mediator* that will require a hard reset. And, that could take a few minutes.

"For example, if Bryant's using *Shield Me* to protect someone, if you're unable to override it the first time, Shield Me's effectiveness will be augmented. Then, it will take a few minutes to reboot the *Mediator*. So, you must act quickly, or risk having to start the process all over again-"

"Are you ready to show me the device or not?" Clarke asked, clearly annoyed.

"I *am*." Dr. Sands pushed out of his armchair, and headed for the office door. Clarke followed behind him through the dimmed corridors.

Dr. Sands took a moment to open up his expansive lab. He walked in, and the lights automatically flickered on.

Clarke shadowed the doctor, as he undid the lock for a private safe stored within the lab. Clarke warily skimmed over the place, as Dr. Sands lingered near the safe.

Dr. Sands managed to remove what appeared to be a small glass encased *watch* from the safe. "You're the first person to see the *Mediator*." Dr. Sands' expression was that of a mad scientist's.

Clarke sneered in skepticism, and gestured dismissively. "It's a watch."

"Yes, it *looks* exactly like a watch, but…" Dr. Sands removed the device from out of the clear glass case. He then asked Clarke to extend his hand. Clarke was grudgingly compliant, as Dr. Sands adjusted the watch on his wrist. Dr. Sands went on to show Clarke the features on the watch, and instructed him on how to use them. He also explained that the *Mediator* was programmed by minutes. So, just like a stopwatch, when time ran out, he would instantly need to reset the program.

Clarke studied the watch on his wrist, and all of the features it contained. "So, you're telling me that by pressing this little button to the side of the device, ***Dimension Four's*** effectiveness will temporarily stall?"

"Absolutely. So, use that little window of time wisely."

"How long does it take for the ***Mediator*** to reset after its initial use?" Clarke was curious.

"There are ten-minute lapses for every use of the device."

"Why ten minutes?"

"Because the barrier has to encompass all satellite fields in order to thwart the power of ***Dimension Four***." Dr. Sands smiled artfully. "If used wisely, you will fulfill your goal, and keep your enemies at bay."

Clarke's face stretched out into a discerning smile as well. "Well, Doctor, I'm beginning to think you're right." He extended his hand. "It's been a total pleasure doing business with you."

Dr. Sands laughed lightly. "The sentiment is mutual, Mr. Lloyd!"

***

Lightning flashed through the window curtains. The overcast skies were somber, and the downpour assaulted the ground. Los Angeles was under one of its rare cool spells. The chill in the air empowered the storm. Melody had just finished dressing for a business meeting. In her mint-green colored skirt suit, matching heels and accessories, she felt ready to face the world. On that morning, she'd be meeting with a contractor to discuss floor and ground plans for *Melody's and Serena's Masterpieces.*

While brushing her hair, and securing her crystal loop earrings, Luke drifted into their bedroom, carrying a tray with scrambled eggs, bacon and orange juice. "You're not leaving here without breakfast." He set the tray on their dresser.

"Luke, I'm already running late. I don't have time."

Luke took a piece of toast from off of the plate, walked

across the room, and popped it into her mouth. "At least, have a piece of toast and some bacon..." He insisted. "You *sure* you don't want me to come *with*?" He frowned, as he watched Melody bustle about to get ready. She took a couple of bites of toast, and rested the piece of bread on the plate again.

Melody shifted and sighed, as she draped her arms around Luke's neck. "I'll be fine. *Shield Me's* in effect, and Trevor's driving me downtown." She inched up on her tiptoes, and pressed her lips to his.

Luke folded Melody in his arms. "I guess, I'm a little put out that you're not driving into work with me this morning," he admitted, and propped his head against hers.

"But, you, my love, also have an investment meeting in Pasadena in about an hour. So, we would have *had* to part ways for a little while."

Melody's face warped in sentimentality. "I'm going to be fine. God's got me. Besides, just like we suspected, Clarke hasn't returned to Portals since he saw Velda sitting in your office."

"He had some kind of a 'family crisis,'" Luke derided. "I'm not even worried about him. I just don't like being away from you right now. Promise, you'll call and text me the moment Trevor drops you off. I've already made him promise not to move until you come out of that office building." Luke covered Melody's face in tender kisses. "I love you!"

"Melody pressed her lips repeatedly to his. "I love you too, honey bear, and I'm going to be just fine." The two nestled. Just then, thunder crashed, and lightning flashed through the bedroom curtains. "This isn't a very pretty morning," Melody pointed out, as yet another crash of thunder boomed throughout the locale.

"I know, baby. Hopefully, the sun will come out soon. We can spend a little time out on the beach, and bring sleepy Cupid with us. I'll only be around Portals till about three this afternoon." Luke's expression was laced in mischief, as he tried to entice his wife.

Melody smiled. "That actually sounds nice. But for now, it's off to the rain I go," she sang.

"Before you go…" Luke led her back over to the dresser. He picked up the fork, and created a sizable bite of scrambled eggs and bacon, then coaxed Melody into opening up her mouth. With his free hand he cupped her chin.

"Luke…," Melody whined, but her mouth was too full. So, she grudgingly chewed on the bite he'd fed her.

Luke then took the small glass of orange juice, and encouraged her to take a few sips.

"You are *such* a breakfast police," Melody teased, as Luke followed her out to the front door.

"And *you* are under arrest," Luke badgered, slipping a granola bar into her pocketbook. "I love you, Mel!" Luke reached down, and pressed his lips to hers. "You've got everything you need right?" he double-checked. For one reason or another, he was having a difficult time letting her leave the house. "You have your phone, right?" he tested.

"Yes. I have everything." Melody secured her pocketbook closer to her right flank. Her face wrinkled in sappiness. "You don't have to worry about me. I'm going to be okay," she heartened.

Luke nodded quiescently. "Okay. Ah, Trevor's here." Luke saw the limo pulled up through the glass window. Hunching down, he brushed his lips over Melody's again. "I love you! Call me, text me."

Melody draped her arms about his neck, and squeezed lovingly. "I love you more, and I will definitely call and text you."

Just then, Trevor rang the doorbell. Luke opened up the front door. "Morning, Trev!"

"Morning, *PM*," Trevor reciprocated affably. His smile seemed to transpose the melancholic backdrop. "Are you all set?" he asked Melody.

"I'm all set," Melody affirmed. She took Luke's hand in hers, and pressed a kiss to it. "Bye, honey."

"Bye." Luke smiled sadly.

He watched Trevor lead Melody outside to the limo, while holding a sizable black umbrella over their heads. Luke stood in the doorway, and watched Trevor secure Melody inside the car.

For reasons unknown, Luke felt a sense of malaise and disquietude letting Melody go off to her business meeting. He smiled, and waved through the window, as they pulled away from the house. He and Melody had discussed the matter extensively. There was no way Clarke Vale was getting anywhere near them. So, they refused to live in fear.

***

There was still a chill in the air in the late morning, and the torrential downpour showed no signs of stopping. Thunder rumbled and lightning danced in the horizon. "How was your meeting, Mrs. Bryant?" Trevor asked timorously, as he opened up the building door for Melody, while simultaneously holding the umbrella over their heads. His facial expression was strained, and his eyes shifted in fear.

Melody was all smiles, totally excited about putting hers and Serena's new project in motion. "It was great… Trevor, are you all right?" Melody frowned in concern, when she remarked the horror-stricken expression on Trevor's face.

Trevor forced a smile. "I'm okay. I'm glad your meeting went so well." He led Melody over to the limousine.

"Thank you, Trevor. I'm so excited about making solid plans for our new business venture." An excited smile ornamented Melody's face, as Trevor opened up the car door. Melody slipped into the automobile absently, and waited for Trevor to take his place behind the wheel. However, Trevor lingered to the side of the car.

Melody rolled down the window. "Trevor, are you all right?" Her face veiled in apprehension and dread.

Trevor wasn't given the chance to respond, because he suddenly collapsed to the side of the limousine.

It was then Melody saw the blood seeping through the back of his black suit jacket. "Trevor!" Melody cupped her mouth in shock after letting out a bloodcurdling scream. She tried to get out of the limo, but her door was locked, and then someone slid into the driver's seat.

"Sorry, Melody, Trevor's indisposed at the moment. But, never fear, sweet girl, *I* will take you anywhere you want to go," Clarke made a dramatic turn to look at Melody.

Melody trembled in shock and fear, as the man they'd come to know as Emery Lloyd, began rolling away from that area. "What is this?" she asked tremulously, as tears looped over in her eyelids.

"Don't play games with me, Melody," Clarke hissed. "You know *exactly* what this is."

"I don't know what you're talking about." Melody reached for the phone in her pocketbook, but her hand froze, when Clarke veered towards her again.

"Your phone will be disabled for a while." Clarke checked the ***Mediator*** watch on his wrist. "So, you can just forget about trying to contact your loving husband."

Clarke drove quickly taking every yellow light. He had to get out onto the interstate just as soon as he could. "And, if by chance he *was* using *Shield Me* technology to keep you safe, it's been disabled," he said smugly.

"Why are you doing this?" Melody asked, terrified. She couldn't believe what was happening. They'd planned so cautiously to ensnare Clarke, but he'd still found a way to get to her. Now, all of the details seemed shaky. Clarke Vale had finally managed to have her in his grasp again. Melody's greatest fear was that she wouldn't be able to escape this time.

"You know *who* I am, and you know *exactly* why I'm doing this. What's the matter, Melody, don't you like the new me?" Clarke asked acerbically. "You lied to me for months-all the while plotting with *him* to destroy me."

"Clarke…?" Melody's voice was faint.

"Don't act so surprised. You knew it was only a matter of time before I resurfaced. I vowed to marry you, and to make you mine. But, you and Bryant made a fool of me in that underground complex last year. You never loved me at all did you?" Hurt resonated in his tone.

Horrified, Melody couldn't stop shaking. "Clarke, please. Don't do this. There's no need to rehearse the past. You have a chance at a brand new life as Emery Lloyd. Why would you want to jeopardize that? You can go away, and get a fresh start. You would be free-not like Darien who stands to face trial soon."

"I *can't* just be free. I have loose ends to tie, and I have this pesky little problem." He tried to keep a steady eye on the road, as he slipped into the highway.

"Whatever the problem, we can work it out," Melody appealed, shaking her head in denial and incredulity. She kept thinking how devastated Luke would be if anything happened to her.

"That pesky little problem is that I love you. I can't believe I *still* love you after everything that's happened. You set me up for a fall, and made a total fool out of me, but I still love you. I lost my empire, my dignity and my freedom because of *you*." He turned back to look at Melody upon saying those words.

"Clarke, please, let me go. I never meant to hurt you, you *know* that. I tried to be a good girlfriend and fiancée. However, learning of your criminal involvements, made it impossible not to waver."

"So, you decided to set me up, and marry another man? You have any idea how it felt to watch your grandiose wedding televised? Do you know what it was like to watch *him* grow to the status he now has in the world? Luke Bryant gloated over my defeat and downfall. Now, I'm taking away the most precious thing he has…you.

"I'm not only taking you away, because I know it will destroy him. I'm taking you away, because you should have been mine. I will never stop loving you, Melody."

Melody took deep breaths, so that she wouldn't lose it. She couldn't give in to despair. Her only recourse was to pray to her heavenly father. She could not have foreseen being Clarke Vale's victim that morning. However, the worst possible case scenario had occurred.

Yet and still, Melody was resolved to hold on to God's word and his promises. The same God who'd brought her out of the lion's den before, would do it again. Psalms 34:19 "Many are the afflictions of the righteous, but the Lord delivers him out of them all..." Even if Melody tried to remain calm, her heart dipped lower to the ground with every mile Clarke covered behind the wheel of the limo.

***

Luke had worried about Melody since she'd left the house earlier on with Trevor. Unable to keep her off his mind, he'd canceled his investment meeting out in Pasadena. Instead, he decided to take a drive over to the House of Style. It was the hub for Melody and Serena's new business. Luke got a sick feeling in the pit of his stomach when he heard sirens blaring, a sea of police cars, and yellow tape a good distance away. In fact, the spectacle kept everyone stalled in traffic.

Luke's heart twisted in knots, as he jumped out of the car. He pulled out his phone, and checked the *Dimension Four* apps. The app had blinked off. He tried to power it up again, but to no avail. So, he autodialed Sean's number. "Sean... I'm on the corner of Havana running towards Melody's new workplace."

"Luke, I can barely make you out. You're breaking up."

"Sean, I'm not sure yet, but I think something's going on over at the House of Style. Phone reception's tenuous, and *Dimension's* deactivated."

"Luke, what's going on? Where's Melody?" Sean asked, concerned.

"I'm headed over to the building now to get her. I need to

pick her up, and get her away from the mayhem," Luke told him. "Sean, try to keep everyone close by today. Go home, and pick up Nicole. Get my parents and Rachel. Find Ari, Peter and even Brenda. Keep everyone over at Portals. We need to keep them safe. It's hard to know where Vale's going to strike next."

"I'll take care of it," Sean reassured. "Luke, is Mel close by?" Sean felt conflicted.

"I'm almost there. I hope Trevor found a way to get her away from the confusion." Luke's eyes squinted in order to get a better look at what was happening ahead. "Something's going on up the road. There's a mob out in the street, police cars everywhere, and yellow tape. I'll have to call you back."

"Sure, buddy. Be safe."

You too. Bye."

Gushes of rainwater accosted Luke, as he raced in the direction of the turmoil. His heart flagellated, as he cut through the throng of spectators. Tears flooded in his eyes, when he realized that the pandemonium was happening right in front of the House of Style Building.

"Melody," Luke shouted in jeopardy. "Oh, God! Where's my wife?" He stared frenziedly about. In the downpour, Luke pushed through the mob. And, now he had a clear view of what was happening. Trevor was being placed on an ambulance gurney. "Trevor," Luke hollered, and tried to get over to him. However, the authorities held him back.

"It's all right. He's my friend and employee." Luke tried to shove away. "He works for me." The police finally released their grip on Luke, and allowed him to get close enough to Trevor.

"I'm so sorry, *PM*," Trevor's voice was faint, and his eyes were fluttery. He was obviously struggling to remain conscious and lucid. "*I'm* sorry, Trev. I'm so sorry you're hurt. Please, tell me what happened to Mel," Luke prodded discreetly.

"The guy who shot me took her away," Trevor's voice faltered. "It's that weird guy who works for *you, PM*." Rainwater splattered all over, and around the stretcher.

"*Emery*…," Luke verbalized, suddenly overshadowed by

despair.

Trevor nodded feebly.

"You don't need to say anything else, Trevor. Please, don't die on me." Luke swallowed the chunk lodged in his throat, as he watched the rescue workers lift the gurney up into the back of the ambulance. Luke cradled his head in his hands in complete jeopardy. The authorities began ushering everyone out of the way.

Luke took hold of his phone again. However, the signal strength for the phone itself was compromised. Notwithstanding, *Dimension's* app was inept. So, not only was *Shield Me's* protection virtually nonexistent, but he couldn't even issue an order to *Find Me* to track Clarke. It then dawned on Luke that Clarke probably had *everything* to do with why **Dimension** technology's strength was only at seven percent.

Luke perceived Clarke had found a tool capable of running interference with **Dimension Four**. Regardless, Luke still had a few tricks up *his* own sleeve. There were still levels of **Dimension** to explore. And, he himself had just begun to get a handle on the mystery. The truth was, some of the facets in the discovery were still too scary to entertain. However, desperate times called for desperate measures.

Luke was in tears, as he cried out to God for an answer and a solution. Losing Melody just wasn't an option. He would undeniably lose the battle if anything ever happened to her. As from the very beginning, long before God had revealed the groundbreaking enigma of **Dimension Four**, Luke relied on God's wisdom, his infinite knowledge and strength. He'd worked too hard to get Melody away from Clarke Vale the first time.

So, Luke prayed for God's intervention in order to make their enemy a fading nightmare. Trying not to allow his emotions to get the better of him, he had to think fast on his feet. Assenting to defeat in this case just wasn't feasible.

Luke autodialed Sean's number again. He vowed not to fall apart, as both his heart and thoughts raced. "Sean, Mel's gone. Clarke took her away. He shot Trevor in the chest," Luke's voice broke. "The worst part is that he's found a way to temporarily disable ***Dimension.*** *Shield Me* must have been deactivated by the time she got into the limo."

Sean's heart dipped down to his chest. "Luke... I'm so sorry. What can I do to help?"

"As soon as you're certain everyone's safe, meet me over at the Command Center. Powering up our backup system will get ***Dimension*** back on track," Luke spoke like a programmed robot. There was no time for emotion. He had to take quick action.

"All right. I'll get started right away. I'll ask Peter and Ari to get all of our tech support people together. Luke, you okay?" Sean vicariously felt Luke's pain and conflict.

"Yeah, I'm fine. I hate the fact that *he* has her right now." Tears pushed through Luke's eyes. "As much as I hate it, I know how obsessed Clarke is with Mel. So, he won't hurt her."

"Yeah, we know that much. He would never hurt Melody," Sean reassured.

"I'll get the authorities on this, so that they can GPS track Vale's location. Before the ambulance took Trevor away, he told me Vale was in the limo. The limo should be easy enough to track. However, all too familiar with Vale's MO, he'll probably ditch it."

"I'll figure things out with tech support, and meet you over at the Command Center."

"Yeah...," Luke said absently.

His thoughts were whizzing. Knowing Clarke Vale had Melody was driving him completely insane, but he couldn't afford to lose it. He couldn't afford to lose *her*. Melody was his entire life.

"Mr. Bryant, don't worry. We're going to find the man who abducted your wife. I've already notified the authorities in this county, and in all neighboring counties. He could not have gotten very far, even if he decides to switch up from driving the limo. We will find her." Detective Bannon gave Luke a reassuring pat on the arm.

Luke had just spent the past forty minutes talking to the

police. He told them that Emery Lloyd wasn't only responsible for the shooting, but that he'd also abducted Melody. Luke chose not to tell them that Emery Lloyd was Clarke Vale. The story was just too fantastic.

And, until the matter was resolved, and Melody was back in his arms, Luke refused to waste their time trying to convince them Clarke Vale's suicide in the Sands Port jail was a complete farce. Instead, Luke handled the necessary protocol of getting the authorities onboard. Now that he'd put in the police report, Luke knew what had to be done. He would bring out the big guns. The ultimate aspect of *Dimension Four* was still esoteric. The only person Luke had shared the secret of *Dimension Destiny* with was Sean. Luke himself only a vague understanding of how it worked.

At that juncture, Luke realized he would probably need to employ this arcane technology, if he wanted to get Melody back. He would shut Clarke down in every possible way. First things first. He had to override and/or abort whatever Clarke had used to compromise *Dimension Four* and its tools. As soon as Luke got done talking to the authorities, he tried to power up *Dimension Four* on his phone again.

Luke was heartened when he saw the flickering lights on the app. The program seemed to want to power up. However, just as quickly as the mesh of lights had sparked, they ebbed and shorted. Luke had hoped to issue a command to the *Power Portal*, so that he'd be transported over to Portals. However, things being what they were, that wasn't going to happen. So, he ran the two blocks down the road where he'd left his car parked. Hopping in, he revved up the engine, and burned rubber rushing away from the area.

Chapter Fourteen

"Please, eat something, my love," Clarke coaxed. "I've made this special just for you with extra butter on the vegetables." His face twisted in jeopardy, as he pleaded with Melody.

Melody stared all about her surroundings feeling totally disconnected. After Clarke had taken her away from the city at gunpoint, he'd ditched the limo. Hence, they'd driven for a little over two hours in one of his cars. Ensuing, Clarke had brought them over to a beautiful remote cottage overlooking the ocean. At Clarke's request, Melody sat at the kitchen table. He'd just fixed her dinner.

"I'm not hungry, Emery or should I call you *Clarke*?" Fresh tears gleamed in Melody's eyes, as they speared into his. It was bizarre to stare into the face of Emery Lloyd, knowing he was *really* Clarke Vale. The only recognizable feature were his eyes. The longer Melody stared into them, the more familiar they seemed. The horrible experiences she'd had with Clarke came rushing back.

Clarke hovered silently over Melody. Then, hunching down, he gently took her hands in his. Helping Melody to her feet, he slipped his arms around her waist, and crushed her to himself. "I would actually like for you to *call me* the man you love." He breathed into her hair. "Oh, darling I've missed you so much!"

Melody squirmed in Clarke's arms, and her face warped in misery. She couldn't believe what was happening. *How had Clarke Vale wheedled his way back into their lives?* If felt as if her heart would pop right out of her chest. It killed her to imagine what Luke and her family were going through. Melody was perplexed as to why Luke hadn't found her yet, and why *Shield Me* had failed them.

For that reason, she honestly believed Clarke had done something to interfere with **Dimension Four**. Melody couldn't help thinking that the complex digital watch Clarke kept fiddling with was responsible. Her phone didn't seem to be working at all, and Clarke hadn't even bothered taking it away.

"I love you, pretty lady!" Clarke crushed Melody to himself, and pelted her with kisses.

"Clarke…" Melody tried to break free from his arresting grasp. "Please…, I'm a married woman now. Things are different. I'm no longer free to be your girlfriend…" She set both fists up to Clarke's chest, and tried to yank away. However, Clarke's grip only tautened.

His head jerked back instinctively to connect to her eyes. "You *are* free, Melody, and you *will* be mine. You were *supposed* to be mine. *We* were supposed to be married, remember?" His lips explored the edges and rims of her face, her ears and nose.

Melody flinched in dread. "Clarke, we were only going to be married, because you were keeping me hostage in that underground bunker a few months ago. You can't hold someone at gunpoint, and *force* them to love you," she complained. All the while, Melody kept her eye on the contraption on Clarke's wrist, which mimicked a watch. Now that he was closer up, she realized it wasn't a watch at all. It was an intricate device, which was quickly becoming her new fascination. She *had* to know what it was, and how it worked. Even if she wasn't one hundred percent sure, Melody perceived the device was a hindrance to Luke finding her.

"I would like to think that you love me too. You *did* love me, Melody-at least you were beginning to. Were it not for Bryant's interference, we would be together. We would have had a good life." Clarke pressed his mouth forcefully on hers.

Melody wanted the earth to swallow her up at that point. The last thing she wanted was to overtly reject Clarke, because she would undoubtedly set him off. Nevertheless, she was repelled by his touch, and even more nauseated by his lips on hers.

"Clarke, please…" Melody pried away. "You've got to accept the fact that I'm married now. Things did *not* work out for us. So, you need to let me go. Luke and I never meant to hurt you…" Melody regretted saying those words no sooner than they issued out of her mouth.

Clarke's face fused red with blood. *"Luke*... Luke has been a thorn in my side for the longest. You have any idea how much I despise him? He humiliated me, stripped me of everything near and dear, had me captured and thrown in jail," he bellowed. "Oh, don't worry, Melody, I plan on making your *ex-husband* pay dearly for his mistakes."

"Ex-husband...?" Melody questioned shakily.

"Of course, darling. We're only staying here until tomorrow night. A very discreet gentleman will be coming by in the morning in order to facilitate your divorce," Clarke informed.

"What...?" Melody's face wrinkled in horror and confusion. "Divorce...?"

"Yes. Yes, you and I are going to take a little trip out of the country." Clarke's eyes gunned into Melody's. "And, this time around, we *will* be *married*, Melody. Make no mistake about that. I love you, and I'm no longer playing nice."

"Clarke, please...," Melody entreated, as Clarke continued to force his brand of love on her. He refused to let go, and overpowered her. "Let me go, please..."

Clarke began ushering her over to the bedroom. "Oh, God, no..." She sent prayers heavenward, and asked God to come to her defense. The word of God invited believers to call upon Him for deliverance in trouble (Psalms 50:15). She couldn't stand Clarke's slithering hands on her. No doubt, she'd come apart at the seams, if he tried to initiate any other form of intimacy.

"I've wanted to be with you for so long, darling. Do you know what it's been like to see over at Portals, be close enough to touch you, but having to pull back? You have any idea how difficult it's been to resist?" Clarke encouraged Melody to lay down on the bed.

Melody grudgingly complied, and rested her weary body tautly on the bed. Cagily, she watched Clarke slip his shoes off, take off his suit jacket, and yank off his tie. He then got on the bed next to her, and folded her possessively in his arms. Melody couldn't stop the flow of tears on her cheeks. She was terrified not knowing what would happen next.

Clarke prompted her to turn around, and face him. He took her hands, and set them about his own waist. "I *know* I've been angry and somewhat harsh, but I never want to be that way with you," he said earnestly. Smiling, he shook his head in irony. "You don't have to be afraid, because I would never hurt you. You *do* believe that, don't you, darling?" He pressed a kiss to Melody's forehead.

Melody nodded, still quavering like a leaf in a thunderstorm. "Please, let me go." Her face warped in misery. "You say you love me, Clarke. When you love someone, you don't force them to do anything against their will." She kept shaking her head in denial.

As if he hadn't heard a word she'd said, Clarke planted another kiss to her forehead. "I love you so much, darling! All I want is to make you mine forever. There was a time you were happy with me-a time when you felt secure and protected. Don't worry, pretty lady, everything's going to be all right once we're married and living abroad. You rest now. It's been quite a long day for both of us. You rest, and let me take care of you. I can't wait for our wedding night..." Clarke had a faraway and dreamy expression on his face, as he cuddled Melody closer to his chest.

Melody wanted to stop shuddering, but couldn't. She also wanted the flow of tears to stop, but they didn't. For all intents and purposes, she was trapped in a tarantula's web. She kept praying that God would lead Luke to find her. Then, there was the elephant in the room. She had to figure out a way to separate Clarke from the simulated watch on his wrist.

However, for the time being, all she could do was to lay there. She was enfolded in the arms of a man, who committed murder as easily as he shaved. This was a man who'd compromised and endangered the lives of many. Thus, he conveniently justified his horrible actions by blaming others. Melody thought of Trevor, and wondered if he was still alive. She closed her eyes, and blinked back even more tears, as she awaited deliverance in one form or another.

***

"We've tried a dozen combinations now, Sean. I don't know if we'll be able to get *Dimension* and its components up and working fast enough. Even if we do, it's going to be a while," Luke said frustrated, as he fiddled with his laptop keypad, while the technical support team worked on the issue over at the command center.

"I'm working on my end here too, Luke. Trust me, we're going to get the right combination to abort whatever Vale did to disable *Dimension*." Sean stopped for a moment, and stared into Luke's face. Luke was obviously desperate and overwhelmed. "We're going to figure this out." Sean gave him an encouraging look.

"We have to," Luke said generically, as he examined the intricacies on how to enable *Dimension Destiny*.

"Are you sure we can utilize *Dimension Destiny* as a final resort?" Sean's eyes delved urgently into Luke's.

"It might be the *only* way, Sean. To even consider using it scares me. It's *that* powerful. But, I don't think I have a choice. In one way or another, Vale tapped into something that's interfering with *Dimension Four's* main functions.

"However, *Dimension Destiny* doesn't heavily rely on Satellite signals. It's empowered by the elements, and utilizes concentrations of electromagnetic waves. *Destiny* will take us all back to this morning when Mel was abducted. It will enable us to redo the events in a time warp, without altering the memories of what's already happened," Luke explained.

"So, *everyone* will relive everything that happened this morning, without altering the events, all the while fully aware that it's something they've done before?" Sean decoded.

"Yes," Luke said, still working on the technology.

"So, it'll be vague sort of a déjà vu experience?" Sean clarified.

"It's something to that effect. We'll redo this morning, knowing exactly how things played out, and set a trap for Vale.

Trevor will sense something off just before he picks Melody up. It'll be like he's having a premonition of sorts. So, he will avert getting shot.

"*We* already know what happens. Clarke goes down to the House of Style and abducts Mel. So, this time around, I will tag along with her to the meeting. More importantly, Clarke will be apprehended by the authorities before he can execute his plan. *Everything* worked out for Clarke this morning. So, I seriously there's anything he would do differently. What he *won't* know is that we plan on changing the outcome. It's like take two of a movie. Only, *one* of the main characters, have a few surprises coming."

"Everyone will be fully aware that it's something they've done before, but it'll be so vague, they won't be able to pinpoint what's happening? Sean verified the facts.

"You got it, buddy! My only concern is that storm we had this morning." Luke's face tensed critically.

"What about it?" Sean asked.

"Its strength could potentially be magnified. We're messing around with time, and the elements here. I wouldn't want a hurricane or a tornado on our hands." Luke's face rumpled in jeopardy.

"We trust God, Luke. If this technology will take you back in time, before Vale shot Trevor Remsen and abducted Mel, we've got to try. We'll pray for the best possible outcome," Sean supported.

Luke forced a smile, but his eyes were flooded with tears. "I can't fail Mel this way. I promised to keep her safe," his voice broke. "I hate that she isn't near me right now."

"We're fixing it, Luke. We're going to rectify it as soon as possible. When can *Destiny* be set up?"

"We would need to set it up before midnight. That's when the elements will begin to shift things back in time. Then, we can relive the morning of January 21st."

"So, let's do this. Let's pray for a favorable outcome. Hopefully, the weather patterns won't be too greatly affected by the shift." Sean nodded affirmatively.

"I don't want anyone getting hurt. This is a huge risk. *Dimension Destiny* isn't even tested yet." Luke shook his head in conflict.

"Well, there's a first time for everything. It seems as if we're about to give *Dimension Destiny* a trial run," Sean heartened. "Luke, we *are* doing the right thing. It'll be all right. God entrusted the mystery of *Dimension Four* to you some time ago. He gave you the tool, because he trusts *you*. God knows you would never abuse such power." Sean offered a hopeful smile.

Luke smiled faintly through the tears. "I believe you're right. I've been on the fence about using *Dimension Destiny* since this happened. I just hope we're not turning the entire world upside down for everyone else."

"You can look at it this way, man. Anyone who got hurt this morning in any way, shape or form, will most likely avert the danger. In fact, they just might know how to set a trap for their enemy.

"Case in point, if someone got into a car crash, they'll know exactly what to do to prevent it. If a doctor lost a patient, they'll get a redo, and maybe take another course of action. And, if someone committed a crime, or even committed suicide, they'll possible get a second chance to rethink their decision," Sean theorized. "*Dimension Destiny*'s like the do over we all wish we had after making some of the biggest mistakes."

Luke nodded and smiled through the tears. "I guess, I've never looked at it that way. Unfortunately, there'll always be that select group of people, who'll probably squander away their second chance."

"But, it's *always* that way. It's *their* destiny to repeat their mistakes," Sean said insightfully.

Luke pondered the impact of using this life-altering tool. "Yeah, I guess you're right. So, let's do this. Let's fulfill the world's destiny by utilizing *Dimension Destiny*! So, you and I will meet at the command center's tower at around eleven tonight.

"The tower has the greatest concentration of strength for

our technology. In spite of the interference we've encountered, we can utilize electromagnetic and radar waves to shift things back," Luke strategized.

"There will undoubtedly be *some* weather pattern changes, as the elements and the electricity manipulates the time, and sucks us all into its warp." Sean kept checking his phone.

"That's a chance we're going to have to take," Luke said.

"Then, it's settled. Have you explained thing to Peter?" Sean asked.

"Yeah, he knows. As soon as everyone's settled in for the night, he'll meet us over at the tower too. Pete has a key role to play in making sure Clarke falls right into our net. So, we go back in time and redo this morning. Only, this time around, I'll insist on going to the meeting with Mel. I'll have the cops buzzing all about that part of Downtown Burbank like bees. I'll give Trevor the head's up not to hang out in the city. I'll probably send him home," Luke finalized the plan. Sean shared a few suggestions of his own to ensure that their new plan and do over would be failsafe.

***

"Are you *sure* you're okay, baby?" Luke's mom, Ruth, threw her arms around him.

Luke crushed her to himself, and pulled away to look into her eyes. Cradling her face in his hands, he reassured, "We're all going to be just fine, mom. I promise. I just need for you, dad and Rachel to hang out here for just a little while longer."

Luke's immediate family, and close friends were secure inside the Portals building. Luckily, it was a very lavish and upscale place to be stuck in. Luke and Sean had seen to it that everyone *stuck* there had everything they needed.

"I trust you, son. I know that you're asking us to stay here is for a good reason." Luke's dad, William Bryant, gave him a loving squeeze.

"Thanks, dad." Luke smiled, stirred by his father's words.

Just about the same time last year, his dad could barely speak after succumbing to a major stroke. So, Luke was grateful for a number of things. He hadn't yet told his family, or Melody's that she'd been abducted. No doubt if he did, the panic factor would have been too great.

"How much longer do we have to stay here?" Luke's baby sister, Rachel complained. She seemed lost in the shuffle.

"Rae, just trust me, okay," Luke addressed her. His eyes explored her baby blue ones. "I promise, it won't be for too much longer." He pressed a kiss to her cheek.

"I trust you, big brother, but this really sucks." She sighed.

"I think the café's open. Let's go downstairs. I don't know about you, but I could sure use a cup of coffee," Arianna suggested. She tried to take Rachel's mind off of being on temporary lockdown.

"Sure," Rachel acquiesced, and gave Arianna an amiable smile. Before Rachel sauntered out of Luke's office, her eyes caught his, and she shrugged nonplused.

Luke gave her a quiescent smile, and nodded in order to convey everything was going to be all right.

"Just spoke to the guys over at the command center. There's still interference with **Dimension Four** from an outside source. They haven't gotten around it yet," Peter told Luke.

"Yeah, I would imagine Clarke's working around the clock to keep it that way." Luke seemed unaffected. He ushered Peter to the side. "So, when we do a trial run of *Destiny* after midnight, I need you to utilize **Dimension Find Me**, and track Vale's every move. *You're* going to find out where he was this morning. That way, we can determine what he did to interfere with the effectiveness of **Dimension Four**.

"I'll forfeit my morning workout routine just to find out." Peter patted Luke's arm in reassurance. "Anything else I can do for you, *PM?*" He frowned in concern.

"You're doing plenty, Pete. I honestly appreciate it." Luke smiled.

"Anything for you, *PM*. If you need anything at all, I'll be around."

"Thanks, Pete."

Later that night, Luke, Sean and Peter ensured the safety of their loved ones before going over to the command center tower. Their family and friends were for the most part secure, and asleep in different areas of the building. Sean checked in with Nicole to make sure she was okay for the night, and Peter took a few minutes to connect to Arianna before *he* had to leave.

Luke, on the other hand, hung out in his office taking care of a few last-minute details. However, the last person he'd expected to knock on his door was Brenda. Shame and sadness veiled her pretty face. In fact, Brenda had had that forlorn expression since Pete had escorted her into the building. Brenda lingered in the doorway and knocked diffidently.

"Hey, Brenda, come on in." Luke temporarily set his laptop aside, and watched her traipse hesitantly over to his desk. "Have a seat." He gestured.

Brenda was so ashamed she found it difficult to establish eye contact with Luke.

"You needed to see me?" Luke stared warily at her.

Brenda finally stared into Luke's sad eyes. "I just wanted to apologize for everything."

"Bren-"

"Look…," she abruptly halted him. "I know you're aware of everything that's happened. I've breached my contract, behaved inappropriately… You probably know it all, even the part where I kept you all in the dark about *Emery* while he worked here." Tears rolled down Brenda's cheeks. "I'm sorry, *PM.* I had no idea who he was, and what he was after. I trusted him, and allowed myself to get totally swept away," she confessed. "I can't even imagine the pain I've caused for you…for all of you." Her face warped in penitence.

Luke stood to his feet, came from around the desk, and walked over to Brenda. Holding his hand out to her, she diffidently took the hand he'd extended. He then helped her to her feet.

Brenda buried her face in his chest, as he held her comfortingly. "I know. I know…," he silenced her. "He's really good at laying on the charm. It's all right…"

"I'm so sorry. It's my fault that… It's my fault. If anything happens to Melody, I will never forgive myself." She cried with abandon. "I know that I no longer deserve to be here. I don't deserve to work through Portals…"

"We'll work it out, Brenda. And, by the grace of God, nothing's going to happen to Melody," Luke avowed.

"I'm so sorry, *PM.* Please, forgive me. I didn't know, and I didn't understand…" Brenda was overwhelmed by guilt.

"I know, Brenda. It's all right. We're going to work it out. It's okay…" Luke hushed her.

***

Later, Luke and Sean, along with Peter employed optimal concentrations of electromagnetic and electric waves in order to manipulate the elements. After a while, the weather patterns showed signs of variation. As they looked out through the windows of the command center tower, they saw thick, sable clouds huddling in the horizon like a team of ominous horses. They themselves remained secure within the tower, as a menacing twister snaked all about the area. Strong gusts of wind shrieked violently like a magnified tea kettle, and the gales moved objects about as if they were feather light.

"It's working, guys," Luke told them. "In a few minutes, we'll no longer be here together. We'll have a hard reset of yesterday morning, January 21st," Luke explained. He checked the time indicator, and it read two minutes to midnight. "As I recall it, we were home asleep at this time. So, once **Dimension** *Destiny* has culminated, we're going to revert back to everything we did yesterday morning."

"Luckily, we were all asleep at home." Sean shook his head in irony. "So, we'll wake up with the awareness that we're reliving that day?" Sean verified.

"Absolutely... You'll wake up with the knowledge that we're in *Destiny's* time warp."

"Meaning... **Dimension Four**, and all of its components will be in effect, just like they were yesterday morning before things went south?" Peter questioned.

"Yes. That's why *you're* going to skip your routine workout at the gym, and use **Dimension** *Find Me* to access Vale's locations. Then, you're going to use the *Vortex to Vanish* feature to pop into his hiding place. We need to find out what he did to pull interference on **Dimension**," Luke strategized.

Peter nodded in agreement. "Got it, *PM*. And, I won't let you down."

"This *will* work, Luke," Sean gave him an affirming nod.

"It *has* to," Luke's voice broke.

Luke was becoming emotionally overwrought over the thought of seeing Melody again, and holding her in his arms. "Gentlemen, we're about to warp in just about ten seconds," Luke announced. There was a brief countdown. However, before they got a chance to say the number one, they were sucked into the warp, which automatically shut down all activity inside of the command center. And, off they went to relive yesterday morning.

***

Luke awakened in the early morning to the sounds of torrential rain. Thunder crashed and lightning flashed like fireworks through the windows. Instinctively, he looked over to the other side of the bed. And just like yesterday morning, Melody wasn't in bed next to him. Luke jumped out of the bed in angst. However, his heart settled, when he heard the shower going in their adjourning bathroom. "Mel...," he said with tears in eyes. "Of course… *You* were in the shower, while I was in the kitchen making breakfast," he said quietly, and sighed in relief.

Luke wandered out of their bedroom, and drifted into the kitchen. This time around, he rushed through the process of making breakfast, and snagged a couple of granola bars from the kitchen pantry. His goal was to spend a little more time with Melody before *they* left for the House of Style.

Melody felt as if she'd awakened from a nightmare. Had it been a nightmare after all? Had she dreamed that Emery Lloyd had abducted her, and that he was keeping her hostage in some faraway cottage by the ocean? In the dream, Emery/Clarke had forced her to lay down with him, and had refused to let her go. Furthermore, as a result of his coercion, she'd been on the cusp of signing divorce papers to dissolve her marriage to Luke.

Melody took a few deep breaths, as she processed that it was all just one big nightmare. She still found herself trembling and in tears. However, she had to pull it together, because she had a very important business meeting over at her new work hub in Downtown Burbank. Melody tried to stifle the debilitating feelings of dread and fear through prayer.

Stepping out into her cool, dry bedroom, she picked out a mint-green colored skirt suit. After drying up and applying moisturizer, she slipped on her outfit. Letting her hair down, she flat ironed the bangs until they cascaded over her shoulders and back. She'd just secured her crystal loop earrings, when Luke returned to the bedroom holding a breakfast tray. Seeing her handsome husband automatically brought a smile to her face.

Luke's eyes were inundated with tears of joy, when he saw Melody standing in their bedroom. Smiling wistfully, he eliminated the space between them, took her into his arms, and crushed her meaningfully. Luke trembled to have her in his arms. "You are *such* a sight for sore eyes, do you know that?" He pulled back, and cradled her face in his hand. "I love you so much!" his voice broke.

"I love you too, honey bear," Melody said sweetly. She

was confused as to why Luke refused to let her go, but she held on to *him* just as potently. "I love *you* so much! Are you okay?" She inched up on her tiptoes, and pressed her lips to his.

Luke nodded, unable to stop gawking at her. Luke stared intently at her. It was like watching a miracle unfold before his very eyes. "Would you like me to tag along?" He delved deeply into her eyes.

"I should be just fine," Melody said bravely. Truth be told, she was still a little shaken by the nightmare. It seemed all too real. However, she didn't want to tell Luke about it. The last thing she wanted was to give him a reason to worry.

"Mel, I'd *really* like to come with you-if that's alright," Luke asserted.

"I would love that, baby. I thought you had that investment meeting out in Pasadena?" she questioned.

"I've already called and canceled." Luke clasped her face in his hands, and covered it in kisses. He kept squeezing her in his arms. "I just want to hang out with my beautiful wife this morning." He pressed kisses to her temples. "Oh, Mel, I love you!"

Melody was a bit nonplused, but she held, and squeezed Luke with as much intensity. It felt good to be cradled in his arms, especially after the horrible nightmare she'd just had. "I would love nothing more than to hang out with my gorgeous husband!" Melody collected Luke's face in her hands, and held it caringly. "I love you too, honey bear! You are my whole world!"

Luke was finally able to let go. Just like the first time, he encouraged her to have a bit of breakfast. Before long, Trevor swung by to pick them up. Trevor came up the walkway, and didn't even have to ring the doorbell, because Luke already had the door opened. "Morning, Trev," he greeted affably. Luke was happy to see Trevor in one piece, not bleeding to death on an ambulance stretcher.

"Morning, *PM*!" Trevor said cheerfully. "Are you all set, Melody?" He smiled at her.

"I am, but *PM's* coming with us." Melody pressed into

Luke's chest in celebration.

"I'm glad to hear it," Trevor affirmed. He looked curiously over at Luke. "May I have a word with you, *PM?*" Trevor asked discreetly.

"I'll be right back, honey. I forgot my planner," Melody told Luke.

"I'm not going anywhere, baby."

Luke watched Melody drift back into the house. Moments later, he invited Trevor inside. "Everything okay, Trev?" Luke asked warily.

Trevor shook his head in uncertainty. "I'm not sure. This entire morning has been strange. I feel as if I'm living in déjà vu mode. It feels as if I'm playing a role in a movie I've already watched. I don't know. It's weird. It's like the Twilight Zone. I have a bad feeling about going downtown this morning." He had a gloomy expression on his face.

Luke gave Trevor a reassuring smile. At that point, he knew for sure that **Dimension** *Destiny* was doing its work. "It's going to be all right, Trev. We're all going to be all right." Luke stared out into the tenebrous overcast skies, and heard an ominous crash of thunder. Lightening also flitted across the horizon. "Trust me." Luke's eyes delved into Trevor's.

Trevor laughed lightly, and shook off feelings of foreboding dread. "Yeah, somehow I honestly believe we're going to be okay."

Luke set his hand on Trevor's left shoulder in reassurance.

Soon after, Melody rushed back out to them. Luke threw his arm around her, as Trevor guided them over to the limo under a blanket of pouring rain. Trevor opened up the car door. Luke secured Melody inside of the automobile, and kept her pressed close to his side.

He sighed in relief, as Trevor pulled away from the house. Luke couldn't stop celebrating the fact that Melody was back in his arms. He determined to do everything in his power to ensure she remained there. And, it didn't really matter what it cost him personally, he'd *never* let her go again.

***

"Sean, why are you up so early? You don't have to leave for another hour or so?" Nicole complained. She was still exhausted from running errands the day before.

Sean was already up, showered and dressed by six a.m. There were a few things he needed to handle to ensure the morning went exactly as he, Luke and Peter had planned. So, far things were playing out exactly the same way as they had yesterday morning. Nicole was tired and sleepy. "I'm sorry, baby. I have a few early morning responsibilities." Sean reached down, and coated kisses to Nicole's face.

"Umm...," Nicole murmured, as she lovingly draped her arms about Sean's neck. "Please, stay home today? Stay with me?" she cajoled.

Sean smiled pleasantly, and allowed himself to drift into paradise for one moment. His face propped to Nicole's, and they nestled. "I promise to take you out tonight." He planted a kiss on her nose.

"You smell so good." Nicole held him close for a moment. "All right," she acquiesced. "I'll give you up this morning, but you're all mine tonight."

"You, Mrs. Winters have got yourself a deal." Sean pressed a quick kiss to her lips. "I love you!"

"Love you too!" Nicole said, still a bit groggy, as she watched Sean dash out of their bedroom.

Sean was headed over to the precinct. His job was to alert the authorities of what would take place over at the House of Style in Downtown Burbank later that morning. First, he would swing by Luke's and pick Velda up. Velda had agreed to issue an official statement that Clarke Vale was still alive. Furthermore, Velda had to verify that Clarke had indeed submitted to facial and physical reconstructive surgery with Dr. Felix out in Croatia.

Sean was now ready to extend proof that Phillip Lombard, and other prison officials were paid handsomely to help Clarke fake his suicide out in Sands Port, Maryland. So, by the time Emery Lloyd found his way downtown later that morning, he would unavoidably be apprehended.

***

Clarke was up by six a.m. on the morning of January 21st. The downpour, flashes of lightning and crashes of thunder had left him feeling unsettled. He rubbed his head, as he sat up on the bed. His face furrowed in confusion, as he considered how it had rained yesterday.

He'd just had the most vivid dream. The dream had seemed all too real. He'd executed his plan, and had taken Melody away to a remote location overlooking the Pacific. Clarke could still feel Melody in his arms, and how good it felt to have her close. He took a moment to contemplate the glory of having her all to himself after months of being apart.

As in his reverie, he'd held Melody in his arms all through the night. Hence, also according to his plan, a legal representative had come out to the cottage with divorce papers, all drawn out for her to sign. Melody was on the brink of signing divorce papers when he'd awakened.

Clarke was frustrated, because he realized that it'd been a fantasy. However, *today*, that very morning, he would solidify all of his plans. It was bizarre how the dream had-to the letter, played out sequentially just as he'd planned. Now, he had to execute the design play by play. When it was all said and done, Melody would be in his arms, and he would *never* let her go.

However, for the time being, he had the ***Mediator***. The device would temporarily deactivate ***Dimension Four's*** functions. That was paramount, especially in the event *Shield Me* was set in

place to protect Melody. Clarke pushed back the covers, and
sprang out of bed. He wanted to get an early start.

His bags were all packed to make the trip up to the cottage
in Redwoods Arcata. After he showered and dressed, he'd utilize
the *Mediator* to interfere with **Dimension Four**, before he went
over to the House of Style to snag Melody. Supposedly, she had a
business meeting at that location this morning. Clarke would go
down to Downtown Burbank and surprise her. His face radiated in
exhilaration, and he whistled as he tentatively planned out his day.

***

Peter used the *Power Portal* in the early morning of
January 21st. Based on recent information, Clarke was still staying
in a condo out in Newport Beach. Peter issued a command to the
portal to transport him outside of Clarke's condo. He was grateful
to have found a temporary solace from the storm through the portal.
His plan was to utilize the *Vortex to Vanish* to determine how
Clarke had interfered with **Dimension Four**. It felt strange to be
reliving yesterday morning- totally conscious of the fact, but also
having the ability to tweak things here and there. So far, everything
happened just as Luke had said. **Dimension** *Destiny* had offered
them all a do over of the day before.

Odder still, only Luke, Sean and himself, were completely
aware they were reliving the events. In as far as the general public,
the day would play out as a vague déjà vu experience. Yet and still,
those individuals would perceive what to embrace and what to
avoid. If they'd encountered negative events yesterday, there
would undoubtedly be some form of internal alarm to avert the
negative. They would also sense the people, the places and or
situations to evade. In that regard, Peter hoped and prayed the
whole world would use this second chance to make better choices.

Peter issued a command to the portal to be transported into
Clarke's condo. It was still quite early in the morning, and Peter
had ditched his routine. Instead of going to the gym, he was about
to shake Clarke Vale down. Peter blinked out of sight using the

Vortex to Vanish feature. He had to be completely undetectable. Hearing voices, Peter knew Clarke was already up and about. In fact, the man was bellowing over the phone.

Clarke's booming voice led Peter over to the bedroom. Peter noticed the man's luggage set to a corner of the room. Vale shut down the phone, but sat on the edge of his bed fiddling with a watch-like device. Peter found it unnerving hearing him think out loud.

"Dr. Sands said the green button to the right of the *Mediator* would temporarily disable the ordinary functions of *Dimension Four*. The orange button next to it runs interference with areal satellite systems.

Peter smiled cunningly, as he scrutinized every dial Clarke fiddled with on his very *fancy watch*. Peter hovered to the side of the bed, only inches away from Clarke. Clarke took his time to program the device, while Peter took notes on how the *Mediator* worked. The device wasn't on Clarke's wrist, and Peter prayed for him to momentarily abandon the apparatus. It would give him time to undo the programming. If Clarke put the device on his wrist, Peter knew his plan would go up in smoke.

Suddenly, it dawned on him what needed to be done. Peter slunk back out of Clarke's condo, and rang the doorbell. He had to distract Clarke long enough to make him abandon the *Mediator*. Peter rang the bell a first time, to no avail. Clarke didn't seem interested in coming out to the front door. However, he rang the bell again, then heard Clarke making his way over. Peter waited for Clarke to open up the door. The moment he did, Peter cautiously brushed past him, and drifted back over to the bedroom. Seeing the *Mediator* on Clarke's bed, Peter issued a sigh of relief.

He immediately picked up the object and studied it. Peter wasn't sure how the device worked. However, he'd watched Clarke programming it. So, Peter used the head of a pin to fiddle with the dials and gadgets. He had to create the illusion that the object was still perfectly intact. So, he left the blinking green light undamaged, and didn't fiddle with the time indicator.

Moments ago, Peter had heard Clarke say the orange button

on the device interfered with areal satellites. So, using the pin, Peter dismantled the feature. After rendering the mechanism totally useless, he gingerly set the orange button back in its place. Luckily, he didn't have to glue it back on. Peter wasn't totally sure how the *Mediator* worked. However, he knew the device had been compromised, because he'd removed certain key modules.

Peter circumspectly set the useless thingamajig back where Clarke had left it. He then searched the room for Clarke's gun. Peter wanted to take the bullets out. He figured that by doing so, Clarke wouldn't be able to hurt Trevor Remsen, or anyone else later that day. Peter searched extensively for the gun, but came up empty. Moments later, he heard Clarke's footsteps drawing closer to the bedroom. Before long, Clarke charged back into the bedroom wearing a robe. Apparently, he'd just showered.

Peter quickly tested *Dimension* to see if they were in business. He was all smiles when *Dimension* powered up without incident. After which, he used the *Vortex to Vanish* feature to blink out of Clarke's condo. He still had a few loose ends to tie before the showdown at the House of Style in Downtown Burbank later that morning. Peter was all in. His duty was to make sure that *Clarke Emery Vale Lloyd* was put away for good. However, for the moment, Peter was glad that he'd successfully deactivated the *Mediator*. That horrible device had caused so much trouble yesterday morning.

***

Melody was nonplused as to why Luke was virtually glued to her side during her meeting with Thomas Hobbs. The entire morning felt like a scene from a movie. She loved having Luke close, as she and Thomas discussed building designs and floor plans for the business. However, she didn't know why he was so fidgety. Not only was he staring cagily about the place, but he kept checking his phone. "You okay, sweetie?" Melody set her hand to the side of his face, and got his attention, when Thomas momentarily stepped out of the room.

Luke smiled, and pressed a kiss to the hand she had up to his face. "I'm fine, honey. I'm just a little preoccupied. There *are* a few things I might have overlooked at the office."

"Sweetie, you should go in. I wouldn't want to keep you from your work." Melody frowned.

"Honey baby, you *are* my business, my work, my life." Luke hunched down, and gave her a kiss. When he glanced at the phone again, Luke realized that it was nearing the time he'd left home to find Melody yesterday morning. Clarke wouldn't step inside the House of Style, so he knew it was best if Melody remained there. "Honey baby, will you excuse me for a moment?" He stood to his feet. "Mel, can you please stay in here? I'll be back in a little while." He caressed her face.

"All right," Melody agreed, still puzzled. "Is something wrong, Luke?" Her face wrinkled in angst.

"Uh-uh." Luke gave her a reassuring smile. "Everything's fine." Hunching down, he planted another kiss to her cheek. "Will you wait in here for me?" His eyes delved urgently into hers.

"Sure, honey. I've got to wait for Mr. Hobbs anyway."

"Please, apologize to him for me. I hate to be rude."

"I will," Melody said feeling adrift, as she watched Luke stride out of the conference room. Because the door was open, she saw him slip into the elevator. Melody had no idea what to think at that point. However, she prayed that everything was on the level. Trusting God meant not giving in to worry or fear. Melody also trusted Luke. She knew her husband seldom took action without premeditation.

Out in the pouring rain, as thunder roared and lightning glimmered in the horizon, Luke found a safe spot outside of the building. Just then, he called the authorities. They confirmed their presence in the area, and were waiting for his cue. Furthermore,

Luke was reassured that they were monitoring activities taking place in and surrounding the locale. Sean had taken Velda over to the police precinct. She'd issued a statement that Clarke Vale had been one of Dr. Felix's patients in Croatia, circa the same time he was presumably found hung in his jail cell in America.

Sean promised to help them locate Phillip Lombard, Seth Nugent, and others who'd worked through the Sands Port Jail. They'd unleashed Clarke Vale out into the world, and had to be dealt with. As a precautionary measure, Luke had sent Trevor Remsen home. This time around, when Clarke issued the strike, Luke would be the one in the limo. With all of **Dimension Four's** features amplified in strength, Luke was ready for mortal combat with Clarke.

Luke checked the *Find Me* feature on the phone. The tracker indicated that Clarke was about ten minutes away. The fact that Dimension's strength had been amplified, attested to the fact that Peter had successfully disable the **Mediator**. Peter had taken a picture of the device, and texted it to him. After studying the device, Luke was certain that they would be able to render it completely useless. No doubt, the creator would be looking to duplicate the contraption. Compared to the mystery of **Dimension Four**, the technology truly had no leg to stand on.

"I'm here, Sean-right outside of the House of Style. Where are you?" Luke talked to Sean on the phone.

"I'm just a few doors down from you. I'll be there to step in if you need me."

"It should be a piece of cake this time," Luke said confidently.

"How's Mel?"

"She's okay. She's still upstairs discussing plans with the contractor. Vale's about eight minutes away. You all set?"

"I'm ready. I also have a statement from Phillip Lombard. Taking a trip back out to the Cayman Islands using the *Power Portal* earlier was so much fun. I decided to bring Mr. Lombard back with me, seeing that he'll no longer have any use for his luxurious trappings out on the island. I thought I might help him get acclimated to his new home in a jail cell."

"I agree, buddy. Great job," Luke advocated. "Sean, thank you."

"What are you thanking *me* for, buddy?"

"I'm thanking you for being the best friend and brother on the planet. I couldn't do anything without your support. I just thought you should know that."

"Luke, we've done everything together since we were ten. I doubt that's ever going to change. We're family forever! I'm honestly glad and relieved this day is finally here!" Sean sighed in relief.

"I second that. It's the day we say goodbye to Clarke Vale, and start living our lives without having to look over our shoulders... Sean, hold on a minute, Peter's on the other line."

"Yeah, sure," Sean told him.

"Pete, what's up? Everything all right over there at Portals?" Luke asked warily.

"*Your* family, Ari and Nicole are fine. Mel's mom, her brother and stepdad are good. I even called your brother Branden. He, his wife and kids are safe. Brenda, on the other hand, is still tussling with a guilty conscience, but at least she's safe. How are you and Sean fairing down there?"

"Well, the countdown's on until event time. Vale's about five minutes away. Thanks for immobilizing that stupid gadget the *Mediator*. You did a great job."

"My pleasure, *PM*! Be careful. You and Sean stay safe."

"We will, Pete. Thanks again."

Luke ended the phone call to Peter, and got on the other line with Sean. "Let's do this, buddy." Luke affirmed.

"Whatever happens, I've got your back, buddy."

"I know, Sean. You know that I've got yours too." Luke shut down the phone.

***

Clarke had the Lyft pull up to the curb on Havana Street, about a block and a half away from the House of Style. From a distance, he saw Melody's limo driver pull up in front of the building. In spite of the torrential downpour, he'd decided to keep a bit of distance for the time being. Clarke shook his head nonsensically, because everything was playing out exactly as they had in his dream. It was an odd premonition. He was convinced that when it was all said and done, he'd have Melody, and they'd be driving up to Redwoods together.

Clarke patted the inner pocket of his suit to make sure his silenced gun was in place. At that juncture, he had to be ready. He walked both deliberately and stealthily down the block. There were a few people sprinkled here and there. However, the streets were for the most part isolated, because of the thunderstorm. Before long, Clarke found himself only feet away from the limo. The lashing showers were forceful on his head, and bounced over the shiny chrome of the automobile.

The windows were tinted, and also hazed over by mist and rainwater, as he used the gun handle to tap cogently on the driver's side window. However, Clarke was ill-prepared for what happened next. The driver didn't roll down the window as expected. Rather, the person behind the wheel forcefully pushed the car door open. The impact of the heavy door thrust into Clarke's chest, and propelled him backward. However, Clarke rebounded instantly, and brandished the gun on Luke.

Wanting to give Clarke the illusion that he had the upper hand, Luke stepped out of the limo with his hands held up in mock surrender.

"You...," Clarke hissed with a face twisted in animosity and disdain.

"It's nice to see you too, *Emery*-or should I say *Clarke*?" Luke's face and eyes flitted in mischief.

"I'm so glad we no longer have to put on airs. It's been such a drain having to pretend to be someone else," Clarke finally admitted, gesturing aggressively with his gun. He began ushering

Luke over to the House of Style's set of doors. "Well, I must say how lovely it is to see you again, *PM*, or should I call you *Janitor Boy*?" Clarke denigrated.

"You can call me anything you like, *Emery*," Luke said derisively. "I will *gladly* hold the title of the world's most affluent and influential janitor." Luke laughed, and shook his head facetiously.

"It doesn't matter what your status is now. To me, you're still that kid who walked away from the woman you love, because you didn't have enough to keep her." Clarke sneered, as he dredged up the past.

"Well, I'm glad to hear that in *your* head I'm still that kid. Everyone else would totally disagree. And, I'm almost certain that *my wife* would feel differently. Sad the lengths you've gone to. Submitting to facial and physical reconstruction. That's just sad, because I was *just* beginning to get used to your old face," Luke mocked.

"There's no need for you to pity *me*, Luke." Clarke indicated for Luke to keep moving towards the front of the building. "What's sad is that you're going to be leaving that beautiful wife of yours. In the event you weren't aware, this is your last day on earth. 'Pity,' they'll say, 'he was so young, and had everything going for him.'"

"I guess, you have it *all* figured out, Clarke." Luke's hands were up, as they neared the building's entryway doors. "I've got to admit. You got me. Boy, do you have me. Everything's going according to *your* plan."

"What...? You honestly didn't think you'd seen the last of me down in that bunker last year, now did you? Didn't you know I'd find a way to come back? Didn't you know that I would make you pay for ruining my life, and taking away the most precious thing to me?"

Luke shook his head contrarily. "No. I honestly never thought we'd see you again, Clarke. I never thought you'd come here and work for *me*." Luke had a canny expression on his face. It felt as if the temperature had just dipped.

"You were supposed to *stay away* from Melody. I helped your family, had their home restored, and paid outstanding hospital bills for your father. I even saw to it that your brother found an excellent job out in Oregon. All I asked was that you stay away from Melody, but you couldn't do that." Clarke scowled. Against the dreary backdrop, he looked quite intimidating.

"I honored our agreement-that was until *you* endangered Melody's life by exposing her to your criminal lifestyle, and your questionable associates. I don't regret taking Melody away from you," Luke argued, buying time. He perceived that Clarke was on the cusp of doing something drastic.

"Well, I'm *sorry* you feel that way. You're about to *regret* all of it." Clarke pointed the gun directly at Luke, and pulled the trigger.

"Did you miss?" Luke derided. He was totally unharmed and secure within the confines of *Shield Me.*

Clarke's face was a mask of confusion and vexation, as he checked the *Mediator* on his wrist. "What's going on here?" He took a moment to fiddle with the dials. "This is supposed to work." He stared Luke straight in the eyes, and pulled the trigger again. Outraged, he kept repeating the process.

Luke stood undaunted with his arms crossed firmly over his chest. His smile was irrepressible, because Sean was standing close by, and the authorities had Clarke surrounded.

"Clarke Vale, Emery Lloyd, lay down your weapon," the warning was issued.

Clarke looked up from tinkering with the *Mediator*, and found himself completely surrounded. His face soured, and he baulked. "No." He stared all around at the myriad of police and unmarked FBI vehicles standing by. "No, you won't take me in again. I won't let you." He refused to be taken in, but Clarke was smart enough to drop the gun. The object fell forcefully to the ground, and created ripples, and a splash of rainwater.

"Luke, are you okay?" Sean rushed over to Luke.

"I'm fine, buddy," Luke assured.

The two stood back, and watched on as Clarke unraveled.

"No way. You're not going to take me back to some dreary prison cage like some hamster. Melody *will* be mine at last. We will be married, and go away together." A crazed and twisted expression veiled his face.

"Please, put your hands up. We don't want to have to shoot," the authorities admonished.

Just then, Melody made her way outside of the building. Seeing the mayhem through the glass door, she immediately rushed out to her husband. "Luke...," she cried out horrorstricken. "Are you all right?" Throwing her arms instinctively around him, she held on for dear life.

"I'm fine, babe." Luke crushed her in his arms. "We're fine. It's all right, we're all safe now."

Sean stood to Luke and Melody's side, and watched guardedly over them, while keeping a keen eye on every move Clarke made.

"Luke, why won't he surrender to the authorities?" Melody was horrified to see how Clarke continued to defy the law.

"Clarke, this isn't the smartest move on your part. They're going to kill you, and you'll fall to your death in this freezing rain. Is that the way you want to die?" Luke asked.

"You're a shrewd man, Vale. Clever men usually know when they've been outsmarted," Sean told Clarke, trying to jar him back to his senses. It was the first time in their history where he *actually* felt sorry for the man.

Clarke grimaced and scoffed in insolence. "I will never be defeated. I am invincible. Don't you know they call me *invalable*?" Realizing that the **Mediator** had failed, and that **Dimension Four** was still viable, Clarke cautiously slipped his phone out of his pocket. "You're not the only ones who can use the *Power Portal*."

"No, Clarke, don't...," Luke pleaded with a horrified expression.

"You and I will meet again, Bryant. I will always love you, Melody."

"Clarke, don't use the gateway. It isn't safe," Luke warned

again.

However, Clarke ignored their admonition. The lights of the portal field began to snake around him.

Luke was incredulous, and his heart lashed, as he, Melody and Sean watched the portal field encase and consume Clarke.

"Shut it down, Clarke. It isn't too late," Sean advised.

The authorities began shooting, but they were only pumping bullets into the air.

"They'll never take me back to that cage…," Clarke's voice echoed throughout the chamber, as the vivid purple and smoke gray lights overcame him.

Luke knew what the deep violet and gray lights meant. Clarke hadn't been absorbed by the portal. He'd used the gateway to access the *Power Portal* without prior authorization. So, they stood there, and watched Clarke virtually slip into another realm. Luke knew Clarke Vale alias Emery Lloyd, would probably *never* be seen or heard from again.

Melody looked up into Luke's eyes with a face warped in sadness and regret. "He's...?" Tears brimmed over in her eyes, and she trembled.

"He's gone, Mel," Luke's voice broke. His eyes also sparkled in affect, because this wasn't the outcome he'd foreseen or expected. No matter how much they'd wanted Clarke Vale out of their lives, having him commit virtual suicide through unauthorized use of the *Power Portal*, held no true satisfaction.

Melody turned away from the scene, and buried her face in Luke's chest. Luke crushed her protectively in his arms. Both Luke and Sean remained stunned, as they stood there deluged by rainwater. They couldn't believe what they'd just witnessed.

The authorities were stumped, because Clarke had vanished. All the same, some continued to scour the area looking for him. Luke and Melody, along with Sean stayed camped out in front of the House of Style. In the deluge, they were shocked and overwrought by what had just taken place.

It wasn't the ending they'd expected, but God had answered their prayers. Melody cried in Luke's arms over the tragedy. As Luke comforted her, he was suddenly gripped by a healthy fear of ***Dimension Four***, and the *Power Portal*. The mystery was something he'd never take for granted, as it continued to unfold with time.

Chapter Fifteen

"Are you *sure* there isn't anything *I* can do to help?"
Luke's face strained in concern, as he addressed Brenda. She'd just
packed up the last of her things from her office. She was moving
on from her job through Portals Unlimited.

"Luke..." Brenda stared sympathetically at him. "You've
already gone to bat for me. Because of *you*, I'm not facing prison
time." Her head slumped despondently. It was difficult to stare
Luke in the eyes. He was the best person, and the best boss in the
world. Sadly, she'd betrayed him in the worst way for a lowlife
criminal.

Luke propped Brenda's head, and made her look up into his
eyes. "We have so many satellite offices out in New York, Atlanta
and Seattle... I could have you transferred," he offered. "This
doesn't need to be a *thing*. We've all made mistake, Brenda."

"Oh, but it *is* a thing. I messed up in the worst way. It
wouldn't be fair to everyone else who did the right thing, if I stay
on at Portals." Brenda smiled sadly, as she explored Luke's eyes.
"Maybe, in a year or two," she shrugged, "I'll knock on your doors
again. Once a person has worked for *you*, nothing compares." Her
smile brightened.

"That means a lot. Thank you. All right then..." Luke
began walking Brenda over to the set of doors. "Don't be a
stranger, and if you ever need anything..."

"You're so kind. I can't believe you're *still* being kind..."
She shook her head incredulous.

Luke smiled warmly at Brenda. "Our doors are always
open. I will say this. If you hadn't taught Clarke Vale how to use
the *Power Portal*... Well, in my estimation, you, Brenda Fields,
are a hero."

Brenda guffawed ironically. "You *would* think so. Thanks,
Luke."

"Sure." Luke nodded. Hunching down, he pressed a kiss
to her cheek. "Take care."

"Bye."

Brenda turned, walked through the set of doors, and drifted out into the hallway.

Luke stood in the doorway, and watched until she disappeared at a corner. He sighed and shut the office doors. He was grateful things hadn't turned out worse for Brenda. She could have wound up in jail. Worse yet, Clarke could have killed her. However, God had spared her life. Luke would pray for Brenda. In spite of it all, he actually anticipated her reaching out to them in the future. What she'd said was more than true. Once a person worked through Portals Unlimited, it was difficult to work anywhere else.

***

The ladies agreed to have lunch together on Valentine's Day. Melody and Serena, along with Nicole and Arianna, met at an upscale restaurant out in Beverly Hills.

Serena was in town again finalizing the deal on hers and Dane's new home out in Beverly Glen. "I *really* like the girl we interviewed with this afternoon," Serena told Melody. She and Melody were tentatively moving forward with their design firm.

"I like her too, Reena. I'm glad you connected with *Fran*. She'll be such an asset to the company," Melody upheld.

"Things are *really* coming together for you guy." Nicole cheered. "Must be so exciting!"

"It is, Nikki. You're always welcome to join us." Melody gave her a beguiling look.

Nicole smiled sheepishly. "I'm working on a few personal projects right now, but maybe in the future." She shrugged. "Who knows?"

"Well, whenever you decide, don't hesitate to jump right on board." Serena gave Nicole an optimistic smile.
Appetizers had just been brought over to their table, along with a refreshed pitcher of water and lemon.

For the most part, Arianna had remained quiet, as the ladies discussed the ins and outs of spearheading a business venture. She found herself unable to stop smiling, as she buried her face in the menu. Her friends had commented on the goofy expression on her face since she'd joined them for lunch.

"Ari, what's going on over there?" Melody stared keenly over at her. "You haven't been able to stop smiling. Is there something you care to tell us?" Melody propped her chin in introspection.

"Leave her alone, Mel. Ari's in the *love zone*. Have you seen her and Peter together? They're constantly staring into each other's eyes, and saying *I love you*!" Nicole caught Arianna's eye, and winked.

"Well, whatever *is* going on with Ari, she looks radiant and happy," Serena uplifted. "I'm so happy to see you…all strong and alive…"

Arianna nodded in agreement. "*I'm* happy to be all strong and alive." She chuckled. "I'm so glad we all got a chance to hang out for lunch today!" she said, pumped. "To me, Valentine's Day has never been just about *romantic* love. It's a day we set aside to show appreciation to those whom we love most. And, I love everyone at this table!" She stared empathetically at her closest friends.

"Aww… We love you too, Ari," was the general sentiment. The ladies all held up their wine glasses and cheered.

Arianna's eyes twinkled, and she just kept on smiling sappily. Tears of joy shimmered in her eyes, as she stared at her best friends. "There *is* something else," her voice undulated for a moment. She held up her left hand, and revealed a diamond solitaire so stately it literally looked like a rock.

Melody, Serena and Nicole all gasped in shock.

Arianna released a delightful scream. "Peter asked this morning when we went out to breakfast!" she announced. "We're getting married!"

Melody's eyes flooded with tears. Reaching across the table, she took Arianna's hand in hers, and examined the breathtaking ring on her finger. "I'm *so* happy for you!"

"Oh, Sweetheart, that's the best news!" Nicole cautiously wiped tears from underneath her eyelids, as she scrutinized the sizable diamond ring on Arianna's finger. "Peter did a good job!"

"Not too shabby, right?" Tears of affect sparkled in Arianna's eyes.

Serena's face warped in sentimentality. "Congratulations, we're so happy for you!"

Melody stared at Arianna in awe and wonder, as she listened to her gush about how Peter had surprised her that morning. Apparently, he'd propped the ring into a cranberry orange muffin. Melody smiled nostalgically. She remembered how hurt Ari had been after she and Luke got married.

Melody surmised Ari had honestly believed God had forgotten all about her. And now, seeing how deeply in love she and Peter were, overwhelmed Melody with hope and faith. Not only had God healed Arianna's body *and* her broken heart, he'd exceeded her expectations, and had blessed her with someone as wonderful as Peter.

Arianna wanted Melody to be her Matron of Honor. Moreover, Peter wanted Luke to be his best man. Sean and Dane were on the list to be groomsmen. And, Serena and Nicole would definitely be her bridesmaids. Arianna and Peter wanted to hold their wedding in June.

Melody was stoked about the upcoming wedding. In fact, she couldn't wait to start working on the project with Ari. Melody also encouraged Ari to reach out to Luke's baby sister Rachel. Rachel was an actual wedding and event planner.

Finally, things were at a good and stable place in Melody's life. She was deliriously happy and blessed! Notwithstanding, fearing Clarke would emerge from the shadows to cause trouble, was no longer a factor.

Clarke Vale was gone for good. His disappearance had come about in the worst way, but it no longer broke her heart. Melody could only humbly thank God for having *his* way in the circumstances. No matter how sad the outcome, she acquiesced to the fact that God's ways were not like hers. They were considerably higher. (Isaiah 55-8)

***

    Trevor pulled up in front of the Bryants' home out in Beverly Glen on Valentine's Day night. Luke stepped out of the limo in order to help Melody. They'd just had the most wonderful night out of dinner and dancing. Luke was still mesmerized by how beautiful Melody looked in her stylish red dress. In fact, he was so spellbound, it felt like a first date.

    Melody was as bashful and shy as a little girl, as Luke took her hand in his, and conveyed them up the house walkway. She was more in love with her husband than ever! Luke had left her virtually breathless in his dark blue dress suit. Melody couldn't remember *ever* seeing him look so dashing-and that was saying a lot. She imagined how silly she looked, gawking unabashedly at her princely husband.

    "I'll be right back, Mel," Luke said throatily.

    "Okay." Melody gave him a quiet, yet soulful smile.

    Luke walked back over to the limo, and handed Trevor an *envelope*. "Happy Valentine's Day, Trev! Please, don't take this the wrong way." Luke smiled, and gave Trevor an impish wink.

    Trevor laughed. "I promise not to take it the wrong way. Thanks, *PM*. I truly appreciate it! You need me to stick around tonight?" Trevor double-checked.

    "Nah, you're free to take off. Go and do something nice for Victoria." Victoria was Trevor's wife.

    "I definitely will. Thanks. Nite, *PM*."

    "Night, Trevor."

    Trevor walked around to the driver's side, and slipped back into the limo. Luke watched the vehicle slowly pull away from the house. He then turned, and headed up the walkway. He was all smiles to see Melody standing outside waiting for him. Once again, he was winded. "Did you have a good time tonight, honey baby?" Luke wrapped his arms acquisitively around Melody's waist, and his head bridged to hers.

"I had the best time with you, honey bear. Thank you so much, and Happy Valentine's Day!" Melody pressed her lips to his. "I love you so much! You have any idea how happy you've made me?" She showered him with tender kisses.

"I have *some* idea," Luke said thickly, then pelted her face, her nose, and lips with a hailstorm of kisses. Soon after, he opened up the front door. He had the lights dimmed, and there were lit candles and flower petals outlining a path over to their bedroom. The moment would have been sublimely romantic, if Cupid hadn't jumped them right outside the bedroom.

"Leave it to *you* to ruin my romantic plans, Cupid," Luke said facetiously, delightfully rubbing Cupid's collar. "When a man tries to surprise his wife on Valentine's Day, his dog shouldn't interfere." Luke frowned playfully.

"Here we go again. Are we *fighting* Cupid on Valentine's Day?" Melody razzed. She was blown away, as she continued to follow the path of rose petals. She cupped her mouth in shock to see what Luke had going on in the bedroom. Melody was amazed to see the flickering lights of votive candles everywhere. The tapers emitted a fragrance more aromatic than a rose garden.

Luke had also taken the time to overlay their comforter with blood red rose petals. Furthermore, he had Valentine's Day balloons in every corner. On the bed was the biggest Valentine's box of chocolates Melody had ever seen, and there were ornate holiday-themed gift boxes spread over the heart-designed comforter.

Tears were in Melody's eyes. "When did you have time to do all of this?" her voice wavered.

Luke drew her into his arms, and squeezed her potently. "I *did* have a little help." His head propped lovingly to hers. "Happy Valentine's Day, honey baby!" he said croakily.

"Oh, Luke, this is amazing!" Melody took in the décor. "Happy Valentine's Day!"

Luke led her over to their bed, and encouraged her to sit down. He cautiously found a spot on the bed close to Melody. The chocolates and presents were wedged between them. "Do you want to open your presents now?" he coaxed, lovingly delving in her eyes.

"I'm excited about my gifts-and the *chocolates*." Melody smiled back. "I have a few things for you too, honey bear," she said reticently.

Luke set his right hand over his heart in awe. "You've just made my night." He reached for her hand, and pressed loving kisses to it.

"As excited as I am about my gifts and the decadent candy, there's only one thing I want right now." Melody gingerly set the Valentine's Day paraphernalia aside. She inched in closer to Luke, draped her arms about his neck, and began coaxing his mouth with gumdrop kisses. "This is what I've wanted since the moment I saw you in this suit earlier on."

"So, you like the suit, huh?" Luke's mouth tenderly flowed over hers. "Can I tell you something?" he asked in between sugar-dipped kisses.

"Anything…," Melody said breathily, as she snuggled affectionately with her husband.

"*You* take my breath away every single day, and I'm absolutely crazy in love with you!" Luke took Melody up in his arms, and rested her quiescently on the bed. In a gentle way, he took the time to become reacquainted with his wife. Like a man parched in the desert in search of an oasis, he'd found a source of water, and just couldn't get enough to drink. "I have a surprise for you," he whispered, as he held Melody protectively in his arms, and demonstrated a whole new level of passion.

"I love surprises." Melody held on to Luke for dear life. She felt safe, secure and completely loved. "I'm ready." She closed her eyes like a little child in wonder.

Luke issued an order to **Dimension Four** on his phone. He commanded that he and Melody be encapsulated within the *Power Portal*. Before long, they were embraced by the portal field, and floating in a world of virtual clouds. The couple hovered over the material realm, and drifted in a bubble of love, passion and fire. "I will *never* let you go," Luke said huskily. Fire blazed, as he consumed every inch of the woman he loved.

"Promise you never will. I am so in love with you!" Melody breathed, transported.

***

Melody's eyes flashed open, and she stared warily all about. The sun filtered through the frilly curtains in her bedroom, and affronted her eyes. Closing her eyes again, she rested her head on her pillow, and contemplated the dream she'd just had. She wasn't fully ready to awaken from the most beatific fantasy she'd ever had. In a tactual way, she could still feel *Luke's* arms around her, and his kisses still burned on her lips. She lingered on bed for a while, trying to recreate every touch, kiss and caress she'd shared with Luke.

Feeling frustrated, Melody finally sat up on the bed. She was unable to grasp the wind in her hand. The reverie was intangible. Furthermore, she couldn't conjure up any of the experiences she'd had. It was morning, and she was suddenly hit by the cold reality of her life. It crushed her spirit not to be able to return to the safe and happy world she'd just left.

In the dream, she'd met the most wonderful man named Luke Bryant. She and Luke had shared many great adventures. Furthermore, Luke had invented a revolutionary means of travel, and telecommunication called ***Dimension Four***. Hence, his gifts and talents had made him the richest man in the world. She'd face great dangers with Luke, but in the end, Melody knew he was her soulmate.

Never had she imagined such a powerful and unadulterated love! Tears were in her eyes, as she internalized the reality of it all. It was *only* a dream. Her history with men so far had been atrocious. Finding someone who loved her as completely as Luke had in the dream, seemed an impossibility.

It was early Saturday morning, and time to get up for her

morning run out on Mooney Beach. It wasn't easy, but Melody managed to drag herself out of bed. She sighed, and sulked, as she put on her running gear and sneakers. Darien Stiles was no longer a part of her life. She'd kicked him to the curb after finding out that he was a married man, only interested in dogging her around.

Not only was Darien married, but he was waist-deep in illegal activities. Darien had come by the Radical Interiors Designs office that week just to perpetuate his lies. His intention was to keep her hanging on a string, but Melody was grateful that God had given her the strength to resist him. In no uncertain terms, she'd told him she *never* wanted to see him again. And now, she was on her own again, no boyfriend or dates.

***

Melody sat cross-legged on the warm sand at Mooney Beach. She enjoyed the golden rays of the sun, the silver waters crashing into, then rolling away from the pockets of the sand. The gentle May breezes felt good against her flustered face. A light layer of perspiration shone on her skin as she rested for a moment.

All that morning, she'd rehearsed the special dream, and meeting Luke. Melody closed her eyes, and tried to revisit that world. She yearned for the kind of love she'd found with this man in another place and time. Melody tried to pull it together. After all, God was in control of her life.

It wasn't always necessary to have a boyfriend. In fact, she didn't need a boyfriend. She needed someone to share her life with. Right then and there, she made up her mind to focus on all the things she *did* have, rather than the one thing she wanted. She assented to the fact that it was *okay* to be alone at times, even if she hoped, and prayed that it wouldn't be for too long.

She lifted up her hands in praise to God for all her blessings. Mulling over how well things were going over at work, brought a fleeting smile to her face. Melody was also happy that her best friend Serena had finally married the great love of her life,

Dane Hennessey. She imagined how happy they were on their honeymoon. Melody silently prayed for God would bless her with someone as wonderful as Dane. Her best friend Serena had indeed been blessed beyond measure!

Unwinding her achy limbs, Melody stood deliberately to her feet. She started heading away from Mooney Beach. Slowly, she sprinted, and tried to build up to jogging again. She was only a few feet away from the boardwalk, when she heard the blaring of a dog. Melody turned instantly, and saw the large, Golden Retriever running in her direction. From a distance, she could see its owner tailing. The young man was frustrated that the dog had gotten away, and he kept censuring the animal for being disobedient.

Melody stood there with her hands held out, and pleaded for the man to call off his dog. She didn't want to run, because she'd heard dogs usually attacked whenever they *smelled* fear.

"Don't worry, he won't hurt you," the young man called out to reassure Melody, as the dog drew closer.

Melody suddenly gasped in shock and bewilderment, because it hit her. This was what had occurred at the beginning of her dream. Suddenly, she was no longer afraid. She laughed heartily when the *Cupid* knocked her off her feet.

When his owner came to adjust *Cupid's* leash, and to help Melody up out of the sand, she stared into his eyes, and immediately got the feeling she was coming home after a long trip.

It was *Luke*-the guy from her dream. He was just as perfect as he'd been in her dream. His features were well-defined, and he had just the right amount of upper brawn. His teal blue eyes were like the blue of the ocean, and his light brown curly hair flitted in the wind. His smile was so welcoming, it had the power to set the entire planet on its axis.

"Have we met?" Luke's brows crinkled in introspection, before he introduced himself.

Melody couldn't help smiling. In a reticent manner, she explored his beautiful face and eyes. "I don't think so. I'm Melody Bryant!"

Luke's smile was captivating, as he explored the honey

brown eyes of the most beautiful woman he'd ever laid eyes on! "I'm so sorry for *Cupid's* bad behavior. Are you all right?" His face strained in concern. "I'm Luke Bryant, by the way," he said with reddened cheeks.

"I *know*...," Melody stopped short from saying those words. She knew *exactly* who he was. However, she desisted from telling him so. "I'm fine. It's really nice to meet you, Luke!" Melody smiled into his eyes.

That morning, she and Luke talked for a little while. Sequential to her dream, when Melody began floating away, Luke and Cupid followed her up to the boardwalk. When Luke asked Melody if she wanted to meet for breakfast on the following Saturday, Melody wasn't the least bit surprised, and agreed quickly. Tears were in her eyes, as she drifted away from Mooney Beach. It killed her to have to separate from Luke and Cupid. She didn't want to let this *dream man* out of her sight. However, Melody perceived that she and Luke would be seeing a lot more of each other from that point on.

Melody smiled all the way home that Saturday morning, as she contemplated the beginning of her journey with Luke Bryant, and his adorable dog Cupid. She had to pace herself, and not give too much away, because there were a lot of great adventures coming their way. Some of their experiences would be pleasant, while some others would be hurtful and scary. Even so, none of their escapades would ever be devoid of love. She had undeniably found her soulmate. He was her forever love, the man who'd remain by her side until the end. Their destiny had been *revealed* through her prophetic dream. It would be tested and *challenged*. Then, by God's faithfulness, their destiny would be *fulfilled*.

Other titles from Higher Ground Books & Media:

Destiny Revealed by Marjorie Joseph

Destiny Challenged by Marjorie Joseph

Of Love and Witches by Marjorie Joseph

Erin & Oliver by Marjorie Joseph

Max by Marjorie Joseph

Raven Transcending Fear by Terri Kozlowski

The Power of Knowing by Jean Walters

God's Whispers by Christine Nekas-Thoma

Oasis or Mirage by Terra Kern

In the Wash: The Rona Shively Stories by Rebecca Benston

Losing the Sound of Your Own Stride by Stephen Shepherd

The Real Prison Diaries by Judy Frisby

The Words of My Father by Mark Nemetz

The Bottom of This by Tramaine Hannah

Add these titles to your collection today!

http://www.highergroundbooksandmedia.com

HIGHER GROUND BOOKS & MEDIA IS
AN INDEPENDENT PUBLISHER

Do you have a story to tell?

Higher Ground Books & Media is an independent Christian-based publisher specializing in stories of triumph! Our purpose is to empower, inspire, and educate through the sharing of personal experiences. We are always looking for great, new stories to add to our collection. If you're looking for a publisher, get in touch with us today!

Please be sure to visit our website for our submission guidelines.

http://www.highergroundbooksandmedia.com/submission-guidelines

HGBM SERVICES IS OUR CONSULTING FIRM

AUTHOR SERVICES

HGBM Services offers a variety of writing and coaching services for aspiring authors! We can help with editing, manuscript critiques, self-publishing, and much more! Get in touch today to see how we can help you make your dream of becoming an author a reality!

*****

We also offer social media marketing services for authors, small businesses, and non-profit organizations. Let us help you get the word out about your book, your projects, and your mission. We offer great rates, quality promos, consistent communication, and a personal touch!

http://www.highergroundbooksandmedia.com/editing-writing-services

Need Bulk Copies?

If you would like to order bulk copies of this book or any other title at Higher Ground Books & Media, please contact us at highergroundbooksandmedia@gmail.com.

We offer discounts for purchases of 20 or more copies. Excellent for small groups, book clubs, classrooms, etc.

Get in touch today and get a set of great stories for your students or group members.

www.ingramcontent.com/pod-product-compliance
Lightning Source LLC
Chambersburg PA
CBHW051434260626
47162CB00001B/84